I0601759

Pay to the order of: _____ $ _____

_____

Mastermind

BLANK CHECKS

MMXXV / II

by
Genevieve Marshall

ISBN: 979-8-9937972-0-5

Imprint: Independently published.

Cover design by: Genevieve Marshall

10 9 8 7 6 5 4 3 2 1

ALSO BY GENEVIEVE MARSHALL

Non-Fiction
Unexpected Adventures
MORE Unexpected Adventures

Lined Journals
No Regrets Journal
All Thoughts I Want to Remember
My Beliefs & Opinions
Boredom Led Me to These Great Ideas
My Gardening Journal
My Daydreams
Memory Aid
Imagine the Impossible
Deep Reflective Thoughts
You don't have to be Perfect to be Amazing.
Inspirational Quotes & Verses
God will Answer my Prayers for I Believe

****

All can be found on Amazon

Genevieve Marshall

Blank Checks

ACKNOWLEDGEMENTS

Writing this, my very first novel, has been nothing short of a soul stirring adventure, one that filled me with joy, surprise, and a sense of purpose I never anticipated. It turned out to be more rewarding than I ever dared to dream.

But this story would never have come to life without the unwavering support, wise guidance, and loving persistence of my family and friends. They believed in me, challenged me, and, when I needed it most, gave me the gentle (and sometimes not-so-gentle) push to keep writing boldly, and to express myself more truthfully and deeply.

A special thanks to those whose real lives inspired some of these stories and allowed me endless artistic liberty: Mike, Sherry, Andrea, Debbie, Minda, Mona, Tobie & Joel, Sam & Brenda, Ed & Mary Ann.

To my Beta Readers: Becky, Debbie, Daq, Mike, Mona, Sarah, and Sharon. Your insightful feedback, keen eyes, and unwavering support helped shape this book into what it is today. I am forever in your debt.

I want to give extra special thanks to the following people:

To my husband, MFB, who patiently listened to my ideas, gave me sound advice and supported my countless hours of writing. Thank you for being there day after day. YIG xxxxxxx

To my daughter, although an ocean away, provided much needed suggestions to improve my writing technique and allowed me to bend her ear from time to time. Thank you for your wisdom and for choosing *me* to be your mother.

To my dear friend, Mike, who never gave up on me, keeping me on the straight and narrow by gently correcting and editing my work along the way. Thank you for the dinners, the laughs and for continuing to edit me, even when I speak!

Finally, to my dearest Debbie. My friend who first heard of this literary idea that was in my head, who was there day after day, reading the story as it unfolded. Thank you for the endless hours, pouring over each character, each story and every chapter, allowing them to unfold in ways we never could have imagined.

—AND SO, THE STORY BEGINS—

1

September 2023
Undisclosed Location

In a sophisticated circular room of dark tones and smooth textures, an elegant man sat in his Scandinavian, black-leather chair, staring at the image before him. It was a cosmic display of pure magic and intelligence.

Spanning half of the heavily padded walls around him were several floor-to-ceiling screens that offered an unobstructed view into a sea of twinkling stars scattered across the velvety black fabric, creating the illusion of floating in outer space. Far in the distance was a small, bright blue speck.

Crossing his legs, he took a deep breath and eased back into the chair. He smiled. All those years of planning and dreaming were finally coming to fruition. As he quietly contemplated what was about to unfold, his heart began to race. It was time.

With one swipe of his hand through the air, a gentle hum broke the silence. The stars began their steady movement, gradually drawing closer in view towards the room. The blue speck moved forward as stars occasionally began to flash along the edge of the screens and out of sight. The movement was delightfully realistic and soothing, making him reflect on the mysteries and marvels of the universe. It was a reminder of Earth's smallness and all those worlds beyond its existence.

Within a few minutes, the suspended blue speck of Earth rapidly drew closer, revealing the green and brown patchwork of land and the deep blue oceans beneath the swirling white clouds. Her fragility was heightened against the infinite cosmic backdrop. As the vulnerability of life intensified within his soul, a tear rolled down his cheek as a deep sense of cosmic connection tugged at his heart.

When the Earth filled the screen and stopped, it measured nine feet across. The cosmic background remained suspended in time.

It was time to forever change the lives of a few fortunate souls and observe the world being pulled into the gripping social media frenzy that was about to begin.

Sitting up in his seat, he swiped his white gloved hand over the sleek moon shaped desk. The Earth slowly began to spin.

December 2023
Anthony

A heavy, ghostly fog clung to San Francisco like an old secret, whispered low and slow, muffling the city's usual hum beneath its silvery shroud. Streetlights shimmered like distant stars, halos blooming in the mist as Anthony's Bentley glided to a smooth stop at the airport's departure terminal, quiet, effortless, like a sigh against the sleeping city.

The door swung open, and there stood Marcus, his ever, steady presence wrapped in warmth and quiet dignity. His nod was both professional and personal, the kind of gesture that said more than words ever could. In Anthony's whirlwind of travel, meetings, and time zones, Marcus was a rare, grounding constant.

The late-night flight to Singapore was delayed, just slightly, held in limbo by the moody fog. Anthony hoped the skies would clear. He handed Marcus a plain white envelope, the gesture understated, yet sincere.

"You didn't have to, Mr. Anderson," Marcus said, eyes crinkling at the corners. "You already pay me more than fair to look after your car. Thank you, really. You're too kind, sir. My family appreciates it."

"You're a good man, Marcus," Anthony replied, his voice tinged with something wistful. "Enjoy the holidays with your family. You're lucky to have that time."

A glance at his watch. A deep sigh.

"Well, I'd better not tempt fate. Don't want to miss this flight. Happy New Year, Marcus. I'll see you in two weeks."

"Till then, Mr. Anderson. Safe travels, and Happy New Year to you."

Marcus's voice carried after him, rich with sincerity, as Anthony disappeared into the luminous halls of the terminal.

Inside, the air buzzed with motion, suitcases rolling, voices rising, flight numbers crackling over the loudspeaker. But Anthony's mind was already drifting… homeward. He tapped at his phone, and in an instant, his son's face blinked onto the screen. Philip. Nine years old, eyes already etched with that familiar sorrow of a father departing… again.

The boy sat curled on the couch, bathed in the gentle light of their living room lamp. His small fingers traced invisible shapes into the cushions, the way kids do when their thoughts are too heavy to speak aloud. It crushed Anthony, that look, that quiet, resigned ache.

He swallowed hard. Tried a smile. It came out thin and tired.

Then she appeared, his wife, her face softly lit, steady as ever. She was his anchor. Her gaze locked with his, and in that pause, that brief breathless space, everything he couldn't say passed silently between them.

The final boarding call sliced through the moment. Cold. Final.

He tightened his grip on the phone for just a second before he exhaled, surrendering to what he couldn't control.

One last glance. One final tether to home.

The screen went dark.

Anthony squared his shoulders, straightened his coat, and stepped onto the jet bridge, his heart a little heavier with every footfall. The distance settled in again, a quiet companion he knew all too well.

For decades now, Anthony had lived a life among clouds, jet engines, glass towers, strange currencies, champagne at 35,000 feet. He had spent thirty years in motion, chasing contracts across continents, polishing pitches in plush boardrooms, and waking in unfamiliar hotel beds more often than his own. The perks were there, sure, but so was the cost.

He was ready, or almost. Six more years. That's what it would take to vest fully. Then he'd be sixty-five. His boy would be fifteen.

Time, that relentless thief, had already made off with too much.

He didn't want to dwell, not tonight, not on another holiday departure. As the cabin lights dimmed, Anthony eased into his first-class suite: leather reclined, champagne chilled, a cocoon of quiet opulence wrapped around him.

Dinner. A film. A few emails. Sleep.

Routine. Numb and necessary.

And yet, fifteen hours and fifty-five minutes later, as the plane began its descent into the soft pink haze of a Singaporean sunrise, a familiar ache stirred in his chest. The skyline glittered like a promise, but he felt only the weight of absence.

Another city. Another deal. Another stretch of time stolen from the people who mattered most.

For the first time, the company had granted him a rare indulgence, a free morning, a fleeting breath of freedom before the grand spectacle of the New Year's Eve corporate gala. Tonight, the glittering elite of Sentosa Online Ltd. would gather under dazzling chandeliers, clinking glasses of vintage champagne, their conversations a careful dance of power and pretense. But for now, Anthony had the morning to himself.

Despite the illusion of autonomy that came with his monthly trips to Singapore, the company's grip remained unyielding. Anthony and his wife Carol were expected to embody a life of privilege, pristine, curated, and dripping in luxury. A country club existence wasn't merely a perk; it was an unspoken mandate. At Sentosa Online Ltd., opulence was the uniform, and deviation was not an option.

Anthony had married late, at thirty-seven, to the radiant Carol, ten years his junior, with a charm that could light up a room. Their first eight years together had been blissfully simple, nestled in the quiet, sun-drenched town of Santa Venetia, California, just beyond the hum of San

Francisco. Life had been unhurried, unpretentious, almost magical in its simplicity.

Then came the fateful business trip to Singapore. A chance encounter with his childhood friend, Asher, set off a domino effect Anthony never saw coming. A friend of theirs was launching a gaming startup, and thanks to Asher's recommendation, Anthony was offered a seat at the table, a key role as the company's marketing strategist. Within months, he signed a seven-figure contract, and life as they knew it shifted overnight.

Pacific Heights became their new home, a sleek company car sat in the driveway, and exclusive memberships to San Francisco's most prestigious clubs filled their social calendar. Almost instantly, their once, intimate life was devoured by gala invitations, high-stakes networking events, and endless rounds of small talk over gourmet dinners. The company's soaring success was, in no small part, due to Anthony's relentless efforts. But Carol played a role too. Though never officially on payroll, her impeccable social graces turned investors into allies, clients into friends. She was the unseen force behind their meteoric rise.

For five years, it was exhilarating, glamorous, even. The whirlwind of country club living, jet-setting between California and Singapore, and basking in the prestige of Anthony's high-powered career. Carol had been fascinated by the glimpses of Anthony's past, the echoes of his childhood as the son of a British naval officer. But Singapore had changed. Gone were the modest landscapes of his youth, replaced by towering skyscrapers and a level of wealth no one could have ever imagined.

On the surface, they had it all. People envied them, admired them. But beneath the polished veneer, cracks were forming. The relentless social engagements drained Carol. She grew weary of the forced smiles, the hollow conversations about everything and nothing. Worst of all, she and Anthony rarely had a moment alone. Their life, once deeply intertwined, had become a carefully orchestrated performance.

And then there were the expenses. The staggering paycheck came with equally staggering bills. The company's vision of their life left little room for financial independence, let alone savings. More than once, Anthony had floated the idea of moving somewhere more manageable, perhaps just outside Pacific Heights. Each time, the answer was the same: a polite but firm no. The lifestyle was non-negotiable.

Then, thirteen years into their marriage, fate delivered an unexpected gift. Carol became pregnant.

Little Philip arrived like a beam of light, illuminating their grand but empty home with his laughter, his tiny fingers wrapping around their hearts. For the first time in years, Carol found a way to step back from the social whirlwind. She poured herself into motherhood, cherishing every milestone, every sleepy cuddle. But Anthony? His world remained unchanged, still governed by meetings, flights, and obligations that left him a mere visitor in their son's life.

They spoke often of leaving, of reclaiming their quiet life. But talk was all it ever was. Every plan collapsed under the weight of "just a little longer" and "maybe next year." Desperate to hold on to some semblance of normalcy, Carol hired a nanny. The decision felt like a betrayal; she had never wanted someone else raising her child. But what choice did she have?

Over time, she learned to delegate. The younger, eager housewives were all too willing to take on some of her social responsibilities. No one seemed to notice her gradual retreat. Increasingly, she stole back precious hours to spend with Philip. Yet even with her newfound freedom, something vital was missing. She longed for Anthony to be present, to see their son's firsts, to share in the quiet joys of their little family.

She knew walking away wouldn't be easy. This was Anthony's dream job, the pinnacle of his career. But was it worth the cost?

Each night, as she lay in bed staring at the ceiling, she whispered the same silent vow:

"I'll find a way out. One day. I must."

During the drive towards his hotel, Anthony seized the moment to call home, his heart warming at the thought of hearing Carol's voice. She told him about her day, mentioning how Brenda had taken full charge of the evening diners and cocktail parties with remarkable confidence. With a small team of friends assisting her, the transition had been seamless, allowing Carol more time with Philip and a much, needed sense of calm.

Anthony shared that his flight had been smooth and uneventful, giving him ample time to finalize preparations for the New Year's Eve presentation. He was excited about the generous bonuses and gifts for his team, acknowledging the efforts of Nathan and Asher in making employees feel valued.

As their conversation drifted to his plans for the day, he admitted that he was finally fulfilling a long-held dream of spending the day at Universal Studios. The thought of immersing himself in the whimsical world of Far Far Away, surrounded by castles, talking donkeys, and green ogres, filled him with a childlike thrill.

Past conversations about bringing their son to Singapore together lingered in his mind, a bittersweet reminder of dreams yet to be shared. Carol's laughter reassured him, and she spoke of their future visit as a family.

Philip's bright, and excited voice came through the phone, eager to hear about his father's adventure. He playfully requested one of the magic potions his father had always joked about, imagining the mischief he could cause if he turned invisible. Anthony promised to find something special for him, chuckling at his son's boundless imagination.

Philip was thriving, Carol noted, having found close friendships within his soccer team, some of whom lived nearby. It warmed Anthony's heart to know his son was happy and settling in well.

As their conversation ended, Carol reminded him to take plenty of pictures, selfies included. With lingering words of love exchanged, Anthony ended the call, his heart full yet aching with longing.

As the chauffeur drove through the lush, green canopy toward his hotel, Anthony could see the Equarius Ocean Suites in the distance. His pulse quickened. Even after ten years, stepping into this place still filled him with childlike wonder. It wasn't just a suite, it was a sanctuary, a place that felt inexplicably like home. The company had ensured the same two-story suite for his monthly visits, a perk he never grew tired of.

As he stepped into the ground floor of the suite, at the far end of the room, there it was, the breathtaking, floor-to-ceiling glass panel that opened into the mesmerizing underwater world of marine life. Schools of fish shimmered like liquid jewels, while stingrays glided past with an almost knowing grace, as if greeting an old friend. The view extended into the ensuite bathroom, making the entire lower lever a window into the underwater aquarium.

Taking a deep breath, he set his bag down and let the tranquil sight settle his soul. But time was short. After a quick shower, he was off, stepping into the whimsical world of Far Far Away. The hours flew by in a blur of wonder, laughter, and the quiet ache of missing Carol and Philip. *One day, we'll come here together.*

Returning to his suite, he rested for an hour before preparing for the grand evening at the Ocean Restaurant. The annual New Year's Awards event wasn't exactly his scene, but he understood its importance. Nathan and Asher took immense pride in recognizing their employees, and the joy on their faces made it all worthwhile.

As he stepped into the underwater dining hall, the scene before him was nothing short of magical. Manta rays soared like celestial beings, reef sharks prowled the depths, and vibrant fish darted through the water like scattered stars. The eight-course meal was an indulgence of flavors, but for Anthony, the highlight was the laughter, the camaraderie, and the unshakable feeling that something was missing.

His mind wandered to Carol, to Philip, to the life waiting for him beyond these glittering waters.

One day soon, he promised himself. One day, they'd share all this together.

January 2024
Carol

The New Year's Eve party, hosted by Carol and her friends Sarah and Brenda, in San Francisco, was a resounding success. The private evening exuded extravagance. With two hundred guests in attendance, all connected to Sentosa Online Ltd., it was an evening filled with awards, accolades, fine dining, and music. To end the year and begin the new, a fireworks display that Sarah and Brenda had arranged was nothing short of spectacular. The two amigas had attended the Macau Fireworks Competition just a few months prior and secured additional funds to put on an unforgettable New Year show. It paid off. The flawless and captivating performance was enhanced by a nonstop display of vibrant colors and intricate designs, all choreographed and synchronized to a mix of musical tracks.

The show began two minutes before midnight. Graceful twirls, sparkles, and flower bursts started the show. "Goodbye 2023" illuminated the sky, followed by a ten-second countdown of numbers. What would normally be considered a Grand Finale was just the beginning of the show. With an illuminated burst of "2024", the dazzling ballet dance of fireworks twirled around, glowing down on the water with "Auld Lang Syne" drifting through the air.

Anthony, relaxing after *his* big New Year's event, watched from across the ocean on the big-screen TV in his suite. His angel had a true knack for hosting events.

Hours after all the guests had left, Carol was back at home, catching up on her rest. The first day of the year was always quiet – a day for relaxation. With Anthony in Singapore and Philip at a slumber party, Carol was able to unwind for the entire day. Thrilled with how the evening had turned out, she was glad it was behind her. By the time the clock struck noon, she decided she would catch up on personal messages and browse online for ideas for her next shindig.

Just a few hours into her research, the file on her desk was full of notes and photos Carol had printed out, complete with table décor and festive food displays for a buffet luncheon. Carol had not been able to adhere to just notes and photos in a computer file. She had to be old school and have tactile imagery and notes in front of her.

The creative food displays she had picked out were insane, and she loved that creative people would post the pictures so she could pass on the image to her catering staff to recreate in their own way. While scrolling and printing off ideas, a reel caught her eye.

Carol,

How much would you write on this blank check?

 On the screen was a blank check with her name on it.

Pay to the order of <u>Carol Penelope Anderson</u>. Beside it was a pen. A hand appeared, picked up the pen, and hovered over the check.

She stared at the screen. *How do they know my middle name?* Confused, she carefully read the message.

The image changed to a simple white background with black lettering displaying the following message.

All your Dreams can come True

If you have the Courage to Pursue them.

The screen changed once again.

To apply, enter your Name and Cell Phone Number.

Intrigued, Carol entered the information. Another message appeared.

You are now entered for our monthly selection. Beginning this month, January 2024, ONE fortunate person from around the world will be chosen to fill out their amount on a blank check.

Carol was curious and excited. Her heart was racing. This could be the solution she had been looking for. The screen changed again.

The Blank Checks app has been downloaded to your phone. You may follow along each month to see the amount collected and deposited TAX-FREE to that individual's account. Dream BIG.

Sure enough, the Blank Checks app appeared on her phone.

The clutter-free app took very little time to navigate. Seconds later, Carol sat back and began to dream. *It did say to Dream BIG. So, let's dream BIG.*

Having thought about an exit plan for over a year, Carol began to put pen to paper and imagine what it would take for her family to break away from Sentosa Online Ltd. Her mind started going into overdrive, her excitement making her heart race. *This is such a silly game. What am I doing here and what are the chances of us getting this opportunity? Should I be wasting my time?*

Carol stared off into space. *Oh, what the heck. I'll play with this for a bit then get back to my planning board. At least I don't have any engagements tonight.*

After an hour of pushing numbers around and deciding what it would take, her final number came out to a staggering ten million. *Well, that's crazy. Who would give away that much money? We would need twenty million if we didn't go back to work.*

Carol ran her fingers through her hair as she looked up at the vaulted ceiling. *What am I thinking? I just wasted precious time on nothing. Besides, Anthony will be retiring in six years. Then we can talk about downsizing and Philip will be halfway through high school. We can wait unless we come up with another plan before then.*

January 2024

Sean

The seductive blue waters of the Bahamas improved Sean's well-being day after day. After six months of island living, he began to experience what a life, without pain, could be like. It was a true miracle.

Just eleven months prior, he had followed his doctor's orders and had taken a much-needed getaway to convalesce. He had chosen a small island in the Bahamas with very few tourists, where he found the peace and quiet he needed. A few weeks into his stay, Sean realized he himself was the problem. Not the job. He had put too much pressure on himself which was showing up in physical ailments, causing him much discomfort every day.

He had made plans early in his career and had stuck to them, never imagining his dream would materialize in half the time. It cost him dearly in the end, nearly taking his life, but he was given a second chance, and he knew it.

During his time convalescing, he spent his days swimming in the alluring blue waters and enjoying life in the Bahamas. It didn't take long for him to decide that chasing work every day to get by was a thing of the past. While relaxing at the Cottage of Serene Happiness, he had stumbled upon a house for sale in the local paper, just a few blocks up the road. Intrigued, he investigated, and within one month, he became a homeowner on Staniel Cay. Within days, he resigned from Tillman Investigations in Boston, MA, and went home for a week to pack, sell his belongings, and move permanently to paradise. No more private investigation cases, and no more hiding behind bushes, nor engaging in Oscar-worthy performances to obtain information. Those days were over.

The clear blue water soothed his body as he swam back towards his bungalow. He was enjoying his new lease on life and was thankful for a second chance to live.

Sean climbed up the wooden ladder onto the floating platform and strolled along the dock to the beach, where the winding stone-walled path led to his bungalow on the hill.

As he drank his coffee, he knew the allure of living in paradise would eventually wear off and he would soon have to find something to keep his mind occupied. He didn't believe in retirement. That word alone gave him the heebie-jeebies.

He picked up his phone to check on messages and his Instagram account, specifically reels of the swimming piglets and larger pigs on Pig Beach, just a fifteen-minute boat ride away. He loved sitting back and catching all the action online from the comfort of his new home. As he scrolled through the reels, he felt more relaxed and happier. "This is where I want to be," he thought out loud. "No need to ever leave paradise."

The next scroll stopped him in his tracks, almost making him choke.

"What in the world? This can't be," he uttered to himself.

January 11, 2024
Undisclosed Location

The circular room contained several floor-to-ceiling screen panels that covered half the room. On this particular night, the mastermind was getting excited over the beginning of the game that would begin shortly.

During the last three months of 2023, over one percent of the earth's population had signed up on the Blank Checks App. Eighty million people loved the idea and seemed to be hooked. It would only be a matter of time before most of the world would find out that this was not just a game.

The fun was about to begin.

A gloved hand reached out and touched a few imaginary points in midair. The screens illuminated, showing the earth floating and rotating amidst millions of specks of light in the complete darkness of the universe.

Watching the Earth slowly rotate, it was time to begin the show.

The gloved hand picked up an imaginary object from the slick black table. As if holding a dart in midair, the hand moved, releasing it towards the rotating Earth. The floating Earth stopped spinning, and the small dart image appeared on the western part of the United States. With an outward swipe of the hands, the image zoomed in, allowing the viewer to see the imaginary dart in San Francisco. Immediately, a panel of rectangles appeared on the bottom of the screen, all with fast spinning numbers. Another touch into midair, and the numbers on the first rectangular panel stopped. This sequence continued until a grouping of numbers were set. The phone number was now complete.

"So, who is our lucky number one contestant of the Blank Checks?" whispered the male voice.

Another touch into midair and the panels revealed an array of photos, newspaper articles and more.

"Hello there Carol Penelope Anderson. Let the fun begin."

January 11, 2024
Carol

Carol spent the morning preparing for her day ahead. She jumped when her phone chirped and started talking to her. A male voice read the message before she had time to touch her smartwatch.

"Carol Penelope Anderson. You have been our first selected participant of Blank Checks. Please meet us at four this afternoon at The Richmond restaurant on Balboa St. to fill out your blank check. You can bring a few family members and friends along if you wish. Best of luck to you. And remember, DREAM BIG."

Carol's heart was racing. *"Why am I getting so excited?"* she said to herself as she touched her smartwatch and read the message multiple times. *"I can't believe this is happening. Is this real?"* She took a deep breath and tried to focus.

"Four o'clock. That's only six hours from now. I need to call Brenda and Sarah. They're not going to believe this," she said to herself as she picked up her phone.

On the three-way call, Sarah was the first to answer. "Hello there Goldilocks. Time for another get-together? Happy hour would be great today."

"Sarah, I want to wait for Brenda to answer. I have something you both need to hear."

"Wait a minute. You're going to make me wait in suspense until Brenda picks up?" replied Sarah, just as Brenda's voice chimed in.

"Hello there, girlfriends. It's been a while since we had a three-way call. What's going on?" asked Brenda in her usual cheerful voice.

"Carol won't say. We were waiting for you to pick up," replied Sarah in a huffy voice. There was silence on the line.

"Carol. Are you there?" asked Brenda.

"Yeah, I'm here. I need to run a few things by you, so don't start asking me questions until I finish, OK?"

"Well, you know we are now super curious. What's going on?" asked Sarah.

"On New Year's Day while I was relaxing and brainstorming ideas together for our next big bash, I saw this reel on Instagram about a Blank Checks App. I got curious and submitted my name into the drawing."

"You did what?" cried out Brenda.

"I submitted my name and phone number for the drawing."

"Yeah, yeah, I heard you. Are you crazy? Did you have too much to drink that night?"

"No, I was just curious."

"So why are you calling us now? That was a week and half ago?"

"Well, I just got a text saying that I am the first person chosen to fill out the blank check. They want me to meet them at four this afternoon at The Richmond Restaurant. I can bring family and friends."

"Tell me you are not thinking of going. This could be a scam, you know," said Brenda.

"Well, I think she should go," said Sarah. "I sent in my information as well."

"Have you both gone crazy? Am I the only one being reasonable here?" said a very frustrated Brenda. "What does Anthony have to say about all this? Oh wait, I bet you haven't told him. Have you?"

"No, he doesn't know," sighed Carol as she started to question herself.

"I think we should all go together. I'll call our friend Max, the owner, and see what he knows. I'll get back to you in a minute," chimed in Sarah, quickly hanging up.

Within minutes, Sarah was back on the call with her friends. "This is crazy. Max says that arrangements were just made to close the restaurant for an hour starting at four. He asked why, and they explained the whole Blank Checks App and even paid him twenty grand for the inconvenience. The money was in his bank account instantly. He wanted to know what I knew, so I gave him a quick overview of the events. He asked if we could get there a bit early. He's going to call in one of his cop friends to see if he can be there as a waiter, just to make sure nothing goes sideways. He says we should be at the restaurant at 3:30. This is getting exciting. What do you think, Brenda?"

"I still think it is crazy. How real can this whole thing be? I guess I am not as worried since Max has been contacted. Gotta run and get some errands done before then. I'll see you both there in a while."

Carol's heart was pounding with excitement. She could not remember when she last felt so intoxicated with joy. She was dying to call Anthony, but she knew his routine when he flew. He would be asleep and catching up on his rest. Plus, what if this *was* all a scam as Brenda thought?

Carol began talking out loud to herself. "Better wait to let him know what transpired. Heaven only knows what is about to happen."

January 2024
Sean

Sean was more perplexed than ever, and he could feel the discomfort creeping in. He could not take his eyes off the words and images.

Stewart,

How much would you write on this blank check?

 On the screen was a blank check.

Pay to the order of <u>Stewart O'Cleary</u>. Beside it was a pen. A hand appeared, picked up the pen, and hovered over the check.

His mind was racing. *How can this be possible,* he thought. *How did they find my birth name? That was supposed to be buried forever.*

January 2024
Dee

Dee was doubled over in laughter, her eyes glistening with delight as the tiny, grooving babies on her Instagram feed wiggled to the rhythms like they were born to dance. For a few precious minutes, time dissolved. This, this absurd little joy, was her daily medicine, her breath of light in a world that too often felt steeped in shadow. Each day seemed a little less heavy, especially since Claire had walked into her life like sunlight cracking through a storm cloud, reminding her, gently but insistently, that happiness wasn't a relic of the past. That she could still feel it. Still live it.

It hadn't come easily. It took effort. Tears. Therapy. Silence. But somewhere along the way, Dee had begun to choose joy, to reach for it, to claim it as hers. And that was no small victory.

But happiness is fickle, and grief is patient.

Later, as she settled into the creaky chair on her back porch, coffee warming her hands, a familiar chill curled around her chest. That old, unwelcome whisper of despair. It crept in slowly, like mist through an open window. She squeezed her eyes shut, willing it away. Why couldn't she shake this feeling? Why did it still hold her in its grip, even after all this time?

She wanted to vanish. To fold into herself, to disappear into some deep, dark place where the pain would simply unravel into silence. No more bills. No more pretending. No more waking up alone to face a house that echoed with absence.

It had been months since her husband's sudden death, and still the questions circled her like vultures. He had always been the planner, the one who obsessed over savings and spreadsheets, always talking about 'their future'. But now that future felt like a cruel joke. She was in her mid-fifties, broke, and bewildered trying to rebuild her life on top of ashes she hadn't asked for.

And yet, somewhere in her, a quiet ember still flickered.

But tonight, in this fragile moment, she wasn't sure if it would be enough.

Dee stared out over her backyard, her mind numb and blank. When she tried to form a single thought, she was met with a pile of random, useless images that made no sense. Her mind was in a fog, and she was bored to tears.

Life had left a gaping hole in her heart years ago that never seemed to heal. The tragic loss of her only two children seemed to toy with her emotions at every opportunity. The memory and sadness tugged at her, holding her forever in a painful vice.

Her only joys were her three grandchildren and the adorable dancing babies on Instagram that made her laugh uncontrollably.

The more she laughed, the better she felt, but her mind and body had other ideas. They did not want to be happy. They yearned for the pain and agony. They began to plead for another dose of depressive poison in her system, which she had become accustomed to.

"What the hell," she said out loud. "Guess I'll just waste another day away." Slumping into her chair, she put her phone down and quickly began to feel the depression take over.

It didn't take long for her will to wake up. "No, no, no…I want to live. I want to be happy," she heard herself say out loud. "I want to be happy. Please, please, please. I want to be happy," she begged the heavens above as a tear rolled down her face.

A small breeze drifted over the porch. Dee took a deep breath and smiled. *I can do this. Remember what Claire told you. Just focus.*

She grabbed her phone and started flipping through the Instagram posts. She clicked on the reels of dancing babies, grooving to amazing tunes from around the world. She smiled as she watched the little human bodies in their large diapers move and shake to the music. To be so innocent and carefree, that is what she wished for.

As she scrolled through each video, she felt more relaxed and happier. "This is where I want to be," she thought aloud. Suddenly, the next scroll stopped her in her tracks. She was confused.

"What in the world? This can't be." Before she could process the image on the screen, her phone went dead. The battery was gone.

She scurried into her bedroom, picked up the charging cord, and plugged it into her dead phone. She had enough time to make a bathroom break and get a glass of water before her phone would get the minuscule amount of power it needed to turn on again. The wait was killing her. *Come on, come on,* she silently thought as she bounced up and down in confusion.

The excruciating minutes slowly passed. Finally, her phone pulsed back to life. Just as she had left it, the image on the screen still left her in bewilderment.

Debbie,

How much would you write on this blank check?

On the screen was a blank check with her name on it.

Pay to the order of <u>Debbie Patricia Reynolds</u>. Beside it was a pen. A hand appeared, picked up the pen, and hovered over the check.

Her mind was racing. *"How* can this be possible," she thought? "I just changed my name yesterday."

January 2024
Sean

Sean's mind was spinning out of control. As he continued to gaze at the screen on his phone, he could not imagine how the system was able to get access to his birth name.

The image suddenly changed to black lettering against a simple white background with the following message.

All your Dreams can come True

If you have the Courage to Pursue them.

A few seconds later the screen changed again.

To *apply,* enter your Name and Cell Phone Number.

Sean pondered over the instructions. Not one for these types of games, he would normally keep scrolling, but the fact that this intelligent, invisible system could access his birth name made it intriguing. He had to continue. He entered the information. Immediately, another message appeared.

You are now entered for our monthly selection. Beginning in January 2024, ONE fortunate person from around the world will be chosen to fill out their amount on a blank check.

Sean scratched the side of his head. The screen changed again.

The Blank Checks app has been downloaded to your phone. You may follow along each month to see the amount collected and deposited TAX-FREE to that individual's account. Dream BIG.

Sean's curiosity deepened with every passing moment. "I'll have to investigate this later this afternoon," he thought as the Blank Checks app popped up on his phone, its logo a simple design that resembled a crossroads; sharp and sleek. Sean's intrigue had only intensified, leaving him eager to understand how this system functioned.

January 2024
Dee

Flabbergasted and confused, Dee was hypnotized by the screen. The image suddenly changed. A simple white background with black lettering showed the following message.

All your Dreams can come True

if you have the Courage to Pursue them.

The screen changed once again.

To apply, simply enter your Name and Cell Phone Number.

Intrigued and more than curious, Dee entered the information. Another message appeared after she hit enter.

You are now entered to be selected in our monthly selection, beginning in January 2024, where ONE fortunate person from around the world will be chosen to fill out their amount on a blank check.

Dee's heart was racing. What was it about these games and giveaways that made people so curious and excited? The screen changed again.

The Blank Checks app has been downloaded to your phone. You may follow along each month to see the amount collected and deposited TAX-FREE to that individual's account. Dream BIG.

Sure enough, the Blank Checks app appeared on her phone. Simple and clutter-free. She liked that.

January 11, 2024
Carol

Brenda, Sarah, and Carol parked in unison in the restaurant parking lot at 3:30 a.m. Max was at the front door waiting for them.

"Hello darlings," cried out Max as he ran out to greet his lady friends. "You three continue to surprise and amuse me daily, but this one takes the cake. Let's go inside. Please, this way," he said in his sultry, British accent as he gracefully gestured with his arm towards the building. The three ladies walked past him and towards the front door.

"I am sure Sarah has already told you about the arrangements that have been made. I cannot explain it, but I am so excited," said Max as Brenda quietly shook her head. "Come, let's go into the back room where we will have complete privacy."

At four o'clock on the dot, two men and a woman, elegantly dressed in black and white, entered the front door. Sam, the undercover cop, disguised as a waiter, silently locked the door and showed the trio to the back room. Max, Brenda, Sarah, and Carol just stared at the tall, beautiful people as they entered the dining room.

"Greetings to you all," said the first man, his voice very calm and soothing. "We are delighted to begin this worldwide adventure here in San Francisco with you Carol Penelope Anderson. In a few moments, you will write in your desired amount on this blank check." The second man pulled out a rolled-up device and extended it flat onto the table. Displayed on the sleek device was the image of a check with Carol's name. All that appeared at the upper-left corner was a modern lined logo. It matched the lapel pins worn by the three people. The signature at the bottom of the check was illegible.

"Now, Mrs. Anderson, before we proceed, you can choose to be filmed as you fill out your amount, or we can block out your name and just film your hand. For further protection, your handwriting will be instantly converted into a basic font on the screen. Which method do you prefer?"

Without hesitation, Brenda chimed in. "Hand-fill the check. Just saying." Turning, she looked straight into the ladies piercing blue eyes and continued. "Why are you filming this anyway?"

"Because it is a social media adventure."

"Well, that was simple and to the point," whispered Sarah into Brenda's ear.

"So, Mrs. Anderson, have you decided?"

"Yes, I am opting for the hand and check only." Instantly, with a graceful swipe of the hand over the device, Carol's name became a blurry translucent rectangle. All eyes watched in awe.

"It is time. With your finger, simply hover over the device and write your amount on the line. The device will automatically transpose that amount into numerals in the rectangular box. When you are ready, you may begin. Remember, Dream Big."

The tall woman zoomed in on the check and began to film with a device, the likes of which Brenda and Max had never seen before.

"I'm ready," said Carol as her trembling hand hovered over the blank check. Standing behind the woman, Sam could see none of Carol's jewelry. The curiosity was starting to make his head spin. *Concentrate,* he told himself. *You are here to protect and keep an eye on the situation.*

Carol's vision started to blur. She blinked a few times getting her contacts to center and focus. She had gone through the numbers so many times, but now her mind was blank. *Focus.* Staring at the device, she began.

Twenty Million

Within a few seconds, her phone chirped.

"Congratulations Mrs. Anderson. You are our first big winner. An additional app has just been installed on your phone. This app is a private bank account where the twenty million has been placed in your name, tax free. On the app, you can access and transfer however much money you would like to any account in the world. Simply follow the instructions, and voila. Also, here are two debit cards for this account for your convenience."

The room was silent. No one seemed to believe what had just happened.

The tall woman walked over and stood beside Carol. "Here is the video that will be placed on social media. To maintain your anonymity, your name has been blocked out, and your jewelry is not visible." Everyone in the room crowded around the woman and watched the short clip. It ended with a bright white burst of light, and the words "Congratulations to our first winner in San Francisco, CA. Twenty Million."

"Wow," said Max, "There is no way they will be able to tell it is your hand. That's better than the beautify setting on our phones."

"Before we leave, Mrs. Anderson, we would like for you to transfer an amount of your choosing to your bank account. We want to make sure you are comfortable with how the system works."

Minutes later, Carol received a message from her bank of the transaction for four thousand dollars.

"May I purchase something now with the debit card? Just to make sure it works as well," asked Carol.

"Of course you may. Order some food from your friend here. You will see how simple it is."

Moments later, with the transaction complete, Max had the kitchen staff start the meal order. As everyone chatted amongst themselves, the three tall people quietly left, unnoticed.

"What is Anthony going to say about all this? He's not going to believe it," said Brenda.

"I don't know, my head is still spinning. I guess we will see how it all plays out," responded Carol, still dazed. "He lands in a few hours. I know he will have so many questions."

January 2024
Dee

Dee had stared at her phone for far too long when she first saw the Blank Checks message and app. She smiled as she fantasized about what she would do with the money. First, how much would she write down? *A few hundred thousand would get me out of the mess Mark left me in. Add a bit more for some fun in life. Maybe half a million. Would that be too much? What the heck. At least I can dream.*

It didn't take long for the dark cloud to appear and start smothering her thoughts. The events that had shaken her world began to linger and dominate her mind. How could her life have spiraled out of control so quickly? She despised the force that continued to creep into her world. She could hear Claire in her head. *"Take a deep breath. Clear your mind and focus on something that makes you happy. When you see those bad memories appear, just watch them float by. Tell them you are busy now focusing on something positive and enjoyable. Concentrate."*

It was easier said than done. Claire had insisted that she practice every day for thirty minutes. To Dee's surprise, after three months, she noticed how much easier it was to control her thoughts. She could relax more easily and became more positive throughout her day. She didn't need to remain in despair or fear for the rest of her life.

"Time to relax and let my mind wander." Dee closed her eyes, took a deep breath, and imagined those adorable, chubby, babies moving and jiggling about to the music. A smile appeared on her face as her body relaxed into the joy of the moment. Inside her brain, the chemical factory continued to undergo a massive overhaul. Those old addictions to negativity, sorrow and despair were disappearing more.

January 11, 2024
Anthony and Carol

Carol had contacted Marcus who had rushed over to pick her up at the restaurant. Along the way, Carol briefed him on what had just transpired, leaving Marcus both bewildered and excited.

At the airport, Anthony saw the Bentley pull up. Instead of Marcus stepping out, Carol jumped from the car and ran to him, embracing him tightly and holding on longer than usual. Her excitement was palpable.

She urged him to quickly take a seat in the car, her enthusiasm making it clear that something significant had happened. Marcus, standing by, confirmed that she would explain everything on the way home. Anthony agreed, watching as Marcus placed the bags in the trunk.

As they settled into the car, Carol revealed the astonishing news; she had participated in a social media game that had launched that month and had just won twenty million dollars, tax-free. Anthony initially dismissed it as a joke, but Carol assured him it was real.

The timing was uncanny. On the plane, Anthony had overheard passengers discussing a viral video about something called "Blank Checks." The commotion had even delayed deboarding. He hadn't paid much attention at the time, but now, Carol showed him the very video that had caused the stir. In it, she had chosen to remain anonymous, with her name blurred out and her jewelry digitally removed to conceal her identity.

As they drove home, Carol filled him in on the details, answering his many questions. As they neared the Anderson residence, she shifted the conversation, casually mentioning that Brenda, Sarah, Sam, and Max were at the house. She extended an invitation to Marcus, welcoming him to join them.

"Thank you, but I really should get back home. Our first grandson was born this morning, and I'd like to stop by and visit with him again."

As the couple watched Marcus drive away, they stood in silence. It would not be long before they would start making changes for a life they had both dreamt of.

2

February 2024
Sean

Not a single day passed without Sean thinking about the app that seemed to be taking the internet by storm. The first video had gone viral within hours, amassing an overwhelming number of views. Two days after the release of the first winner, Sean began investigating the app's origins and its IP address. Despite his focused efforts, using his specialized access to information far beyond the reach of the public, he came up empty-handed. Where there should be detailed data, there were scrambled text and unfamiliar symbols.

Sean reached out to a few former contacts, pulling strings to see if they could uncover any details about the elusive app. Every lead hit a dead end.

"Whoever's behind this is a genius," Sean muttered aloud, scratching his head. "It takes a brilliant mind to hide and encrypt this much information. I still can't figure out how they've managed to cloak their location." Sean did not like the unknown, and this was starting to fester deep inside his soul.

February 2024
Paolo & Vittoria

Thursdays were more than just a tradition between Paolo and his mother; they were a cherished ritual of connection, beauty, and the simple joys in life. Since their arrival on the Island of Mallorca twenty years ago, mother and son had enjoyed their weekly Thursday "get out of town" routine to explore the charming mountain villages and picturesque harbor towns on the coast of the island. Every Wednesday night brought a surge of anticipation, as Vittoria never knew what her son Paolo had in mind for the next day's adventure.

In recent years, however, Vittoria had started to feel her nearly eighty years of age. The hour-long drives and hilly walks were more challenging and troublesome to her weak, tired body.

Having diligently worked most of her life as a house cleaner, the bone and joint pain was a reminder of all the hard work she had experienced. Although her face beamed with the contentment of someone who had experienced much of life, and still found wonder in the present moment, deep down she yearned for a little less movement. She found the courage to tell her son that she was no longer enjoying the long drives and suggested a calmer, easier trip for their excursion day. It didn't take long before Villa della Speranza, a twenty-minute drive from the city, became their weekly outing.

The charming Spanish inspired villa featured one main plaza with several colorful courtyards. Each outdoor area housed many tall trees, providing shade to seating areas, benches, tables and chairs. Several fountains provided a soothing ambience with the water continuously cascading, offering the residents a peaceful, yet picturesque area to walk, relax, and eat. On occasion, the scent of freshly baked bread and roasted coffee would fill the air, creating a very inviting atmosphere.

Streetlamps lined the sides of the plaza, providing a warm glow for the evening enjoyment. Once a week, live music would take center stage where residents and guests could enjoy the sound of the music from their balconies overlooking the plaza, or amidst the tall trees, twinkling with intricately woven lights throughout the branches.

The enchanting aura of Villa della Speranza was born from the imagination of Italian artist Antonio Salucci, a visionary with a heart full of devotion to his aging parents. Antonio had dreamed of crafting an architectural haven, a place of beauty and serenity where they could savor their twilight years. What began as a humble finca flourished over decades into a verdant, ten-building estate, now home to two hundred spirited senior citizens. Antonio's dream had not only come to life but exceeded even his boldest aspirations.

The Villa radiated a timeless charm; its tranquil grounds open to the public throughout the year. Yet, its secluded nature lent it an air of mystery, a secret oasis known only to the fortunate few. This exclusivity made it even more alluring for Paolo and Vittoria, who found solace in its quiet corners and joy in its lively plaza. The couple cherished their visits, savoring not just the camaraderie but the culinary treasures scattered throughout this vibrant "village." For them, Villa della Speranza was more than a retreat. It was a sanctuary brimming with life, flavor, and soul.

A decade ago, over a leisurely lunch at the enchanting Barbaflorida Café in Valldemossa, fate brought Paolo and his mother, face-to-face with the captivating Francesca. Seated at a nearby table, Francesca's ears perked up at the sound of Italian, an accent she hadn't heard often during her time on Mallorca. Intrigued, she wasted no time introducing herself. What began as a chance encounter blossomed into hours of lively conversation, during which they marveled at the coincidence that their hometowns were just a stone's throw apart. For Francesca, who had met so few compatriots on the island, the meeting felt serendipitous. Warm and welcoming, she extended an invitation to visit the stunning Villa della Speranza, where she worked. And with that, a remarkable friendship was set in motion, woven together by shared roots and an unforgettable afternoon.

Paolo and his mother had moved to Valencia, Spain shortly after his father had left the family. Paolo was only five years of age. There were no family photos nor memories of his earlier years. The absence and secrecy behind the sudden change in his life had left Paolo with a distant, but constant nagging in his heart. His mother refused to talk about the circumstances behind his father's departure.

Moving to Valencia had given Vittoria a fresh new start. With little to no education, Vittoria had few choices in life. She quickly found work as a house cleaner, for several Italian families, enabling her to provide for her and her son. With her past behind her, the days and months became years, and before long, Paolo was out of school and working at a local museum.

Paolo, fueled by his passion for art and history, advanced from gallery assistant to curator within a few years. Impressing his supervisors with his dedication and fresh ideas, the museum arranged a temporary transfer to Mallorca to assist with a new exhibit at the Contemporary Art Museum in Palma. Mother and son quickly developed a deep affection for Mallorca. When the project came to an end, Paolo requested for a permanent position, which the museum happily approved.

When Francesca had first met Paolo and Vittoria, she had instantly fallen in love with them. They often spent Thursday's together whenever she could take time off work. Francesca often found herself driving into town to pick up Vittoria and taking her to enjoy leisurely lunches along the coast. Despite the eighteen-year age difference, the two women found plenty to talk about, especially during moments when Paolo wasn't around.

Their bond grew stronger over the passing seasons. Each week, Francesca and Vittoria would stroll through the bustling markets, admiring colorful displays of fruits and flowers. They often stopped at their favorite café, where the scent of fresh pastries filled the air. Over their favorite carajillo (black coffee mixed with brandy or rum), they shared stories, dreams, and laughter.

Over time, Francesca discovered that Vittoria wished to relieve Paolo of his responsibility to care for her. However, their limited financial resources made it challenging for her to avoid placing additional burdens on her beloved son.

Now in her later years, Vittoria looked back at her life and felt the deep sadness creeping up more often. It pained her so much to think back to those earlier days. Over a few glasses of wine one day, she broke down and shared her story with Francesca.

For his mother's eightieth birthday Paolo surprised her with a dinner for three at her favorite Italian restaurant, La Bottega di Michele. Following their delicious meal, it was time for Paolo to surprise his mother, once again.

"Mama, I have a special gift for you. I do hope you like it," said Paolo, as he handed his mother a beautifully wrapped box. He had given the gift much thought and decided on a thoughtful and modern present: a genetic DNA testing kit. He imagined she would be thrilled by the opportunity to learn more about her ancestry and heritage. However, when she opened the box, her reaction was nothing like he anticipated. Her face grew somber, and she quickly pushed the gift away. With trembling hands, she buried her face in them, as if overwhelmed by a flood of emotions she couldn't contain.

"Mama, what's wrong? I was so sure that you wanted to know more about your Italian heritage." Paolo said.

"Oh, my son, if I do this, it will reveal so much that I would prefer to leave in the past. Maybe Francesca would like to have it," she said as she handed the box to Francesca.

"What could be so bad about the past that would change our lives?" said Paolo as Francesca looked at Vittoria. There was something they were not telling him.

"Vittoria, I think it is time to tell Paolo about his past. He deserves to know," said Francesca.

"You're right," she replied, turning to look at Paolo with deep sadness in her eyes. "But first, there is something I must tell you both that will come as quite a shock. I must tell you because it will be revealed in this test, I am sure."

"Please, please mama, what in the world are you saying?"

"What I want to say is that I am not your mother. You are not my son even though I have raised you as if you were my son." As tears flowed down her face, Francesca and Paolo stared at each other in disbelief.

"Vittoria, I had no idea," said Francesca, very lovingly.

"There's more?" asked Paolo. "What does Francesca know that I need to know?"

"Just give me a minute. I will explain. It's been such a long time. Please." The pain in Vittoria's eyes saddened Paolo. "I'm sorry mama. It's just all so confusing. Please, forgive me. I'm listening."

"In 1958, when I was sixteen, I gave birth to a son, Vincenzo. Many years later, he married a girl from Greece named Renata while he was with the Italian navy. Renata gave birth to you while he was away at sea," she explained, wiping a few tears from her cheek. "They are your parents. You, my dearest Paolo, are my grandson." Her voice was trembling. "I do hope you can forgive me for having kept this from you." Tears were flowing down her face as Paolo held her in a deep embrace. "You will always be my mama. I love you even more now," whispered Paolo into her ear. Francesca was wiping away her many tears as she knew there were more revelations to come.

"Please let me continue. Your father was a rebel and caused many problems daily. When you were five years old, your mother and father, along with two other friends, made a grave mistake that forced them to be banished from our village for the rest of their lives. Let me give you a little background. On that fateful day in 1984, Mario Andreoli had just retired from his days as a railway worker and was dedicating his time to creating additional figures for the hillside nativity scene. Mario had started the nativity scene with just one cross in 1961 after his dying father asked him to restore an ancient pilgrim's cross that stood on the hilltop of the family vineyard in Manarola. He decided to illuminate it, using a car battery which created a beautiful spectacle. Year after year, Mario crafted new figures and characters out of iron and recycled, salvaged materials, scattering them over the terraced hill overlooking Manarola. On the eve of December 8th, 1984, thirty life size figures were to be illuminated with hundreds of lights." Vittoria began to weep as the overwhelming grief of reliving that moment got to her.

"You don't have to continue if you don't want to. I can't imagine how difficult that must have been for you," said Paolo, a sense of anger growing inside of him.

"No, I must tell you the story. It has been buried in my heart for far too long." She took a deep breath, wiping away the tears. "Your father was born reckless and mischievous. He continuously acted without thinking of the consequences. After he and your mother brought you into the world, they did not change their ways. In fact, they abandoned you at my doorstep saying they had to get away for a few days. I prayed that they would never return, and for a while, I thought my prayers had been answered. Five years later, they came back to the village. No one missed them nor their antics, but the cruel reminder of their practical jokes was an unwelcome return. It was hard to hide their presence as even today, only three hundred and fifty people live in the village." Vittoria took a sip of water and asked Francesca to bring her a glass of red wine.

"Late on the night of December 7th, your mother and father along with their two unknown friends, intentionally damaged and destroyed over half of the figures, and all the lights, totally disregarding the significance of the site. When the Andreoli family awoke the next morning to the destruction, it caused an unimaginable outrage in the village. All fingers pointed to your parents and their friends. The elders chased the four out of the village with sticks, brooms and metal bars all the way up the hill to the main road. When the elders returned to the village an hour later, they were fuming. I was told that they would never be allowed to return. If they did, there would be consequences. I was forty-two years old and raising you as my own. The burden of guilt was heavy on my heart, and it shamed me to venture out of the house. A month later, with the assistance of my dearest friend and her husband, they helped me relocate to Spain, where friends of theirs were willing to extend much needed support for our new beginning."

Paolo hugged his mother/grandmother and whispered into her ear. "You are the most amazing person in my entire life. I owe you the world and I love you more than you will ever know."

"I love you that much as well. That is why I decided it would be best for us to leave Manarola. I did not want you to grow up with a dark shadow cast over you for the rest of your life. I hope you will forgive me for keeping all this from you for so long."

"There is nothing to forgive. You did what was best at the time during a circumstance that you had no control over."

"Do you remember the long train ride we took when you were five?"

"I do. Well, maybe bits and pieces. What I remember was changing trains many times and the uncomfortable hard seats. I also remember you crying every now and then when you didn't think I was looking. I just thought you were sad to be leaving our cat behind for our vacation. It was a vacation that you said we were on, wasn't it?"

"Yes, I didn't know how else to tell you what was happening, so that was the easiest way for me to explain it to you. By the time we arrived in Valencia, Spain, and settled into our home, and you in school, I erased the past from my mind and focused on my house cleaning business. Before I knew it, you were finishing up school and working at the Museum."

Francesca glanced over at Vittoria; glad she had revealed the dark hidden truth to Paolo. "I too, remember that day as if it happened yesterday," she began, her voice steady but soft. Paolo, stunned, looked at her in confusion. "I was twenty-four, caught amid preparing for my dreaded wedding. I didn't love the man I barely knew, yet my family insisted on pushing me into that next chapter in my life. On the morning of December 8th, I recall the anger and chaos that gripped our village. Rumors spread quickly within the villages, and we were warned to beware of the hoodlums from Manarola. If they came into town, we were ordered to chase them away."

Francesca gently reached out, taking Vittoria's trembling hand in her own. "I'm so sorry. It must have been incredibly hard for you, but I understand why you had to leave." A shared sadness clouded both women's faces, the weight of the past heavy in the air.

"I, too, had to leave as I couldn't follow through with my marriage. I ran away to Corsica for a few years, and after a visit to Mallorca, I realized I preferred that island. It was around the time that I met Antonio, the visionary behind Villa della Speranza. We were together for a year but discovered that we were better as business partners than as a couple. Together, we brought his artistic vision to life. It was a labor of love and has brought so much joy to so many families. I am happy that you get to enjoy it every week."

At the beginning of the year, under the shimmering lights of Mallorca's lively promenade, Francesca and her four girlfriends laughed and clinked their glasses, reveling in the New Year's magic. The air buzzed with music and joy as fireworks illuminated the night, casting a golden glow on their faces. Between spontaneous selfies, and bursts of laughter, they toasted to friendship and new beginnings, promising that 2024 was going to be an unforgettable year.

Weeks later, while enjoying their afternoon hot chocolate and churros at a local café, the five decided to simultaneously join the Blank Checks social media game which had gone viral during the first week of the year. They each felt a thrill as they completed the process on the app.

"So, Francesca. How much would you write on the blank check?" asked her closest friend Miranda. "Remember. It suggests you DREAM BIG."

"That's a great question. Let me see…."

"Stop thinking so much. Just spit out the first number that comes to mind," blurted out Miranda.

"Ok, ok. Five million. I would share it with each of you" replied Francesca.

"Five million split between us? Are you serious?" Liliana leaned forward, her hot chocolate and churro half-forgotten on the table. "Francesca, you're not just talking crazy, are you?"

"I'm serious," Francesca said, her lips curving into a sly smile. "I do have some other ideas so why not go crazy. I'd write in ten million."

"Ten million?" Emilia scoffed, shaking her head. "Be realistic."

"I am being realistic. Why not aim big?" replied Francesca. "What about you Isabel? You are being mighty quiet. What do you think?"

The table went silent. All eyes were on Isabel, who leaned back in her chair, as she tapped her fingers on the table, her expression unreadable. "I have a few ideas, but right now I say we focus on what you'd do with it. Hypothetically, of course."

Francesca smiled. "Let's just say the money's real, and it is mine to give. I would still share one million with each of you. I'd give one million to my parents, half a million to Vittoria and half a million to Paolo. That would leave me with three million. I think I can have some fun with that, don't you think?" The table erupted into uncontrollable laughter.

February 9, 2024
Undisclosed Location

The tall man stood confidently, dressed entirely in black, giving him a polished and professional look. His hands were in form-fitting gloves, which added a touch of mystery to his appearance. His posture exuded focus and authority. As he looked out into the vastness of the Universe on the screen before him, he swiped his left hand in an arch over his head. A small translucent window appeared on the large screen. The information brought a smile to his face. "Now that is good work," he said to himself, beaming with pride. "Forty percent of the population have now joined the game."

Easing gently into his sleek chair, his heart began to race.

"Time to change another life."

With a few swipes in the air over the slick black table, the little blue speck rapidly grew till it filled the screen and began to rotate. The twinkling of stars shimmered against the inky blackness. The man, for a moment, lost himself in the infinite beauty of the universe.

The gloved hand hovered over the slick black table, miming the act of picking up an invisible object. It released the imaginary dart, towards the rotating globe. The rotating Earth halted its spin, the dart symbol appearing in the Mediterranean Sea. With a sweeping gesture of his hands, the screen zoomed in, revealing the dart's location: Mallorca. Instantly, a row of rectangle panels appeared at the bottom of the screen, each flickering with rapidly changing numbers. Another precise motion in the air stopped the numbers on the first panel. The process repeated until all the panels displayed fixed numbers. The sequence was complete.

"So, who is our lucky number two contestant of the Blank Check?" the man's voice uttered softly.

A whisper of touch in the air, and the panels unveiled a large collection of photos, newspaper articles and other items.

"Oh, how interesting. I see there are secrets to be revealed. This will be a fun adventure to follow. Good luck, Francesca Gómez. Let the fun begin and remember to Dream Big."

February 9, 2024
Francesca

It had been two days since Francesca had called in sick. She rolled over and looked at her clock, the sun piercing through the opening in the curtain. "Ten o'clock," she said as she rolled over and sat up slowly. "I do feel better. A shower and some coffee sound fabulous." In the kitchen she started her coffee, sitting down at the table by the window that overlooked the park. Minutes later, she savored the warmth of her coffee before stepping into the shower.

Sensing her strength coming back to her, she picked up her phone to call into work to say that she would make an appearance later in the day. She didn't want to jump right back into work and find herself in bed again for a few more days. Slowly, she would be back to full throttle.

With a few hours to spare, she checked her messages, replied to a few inquiries and decided to head down to the market for some groceries.

She was startled as she walked to her door. Her phone chirped and began speaking to her. **"Francesca. You are our second selected participant of Blank Checks. Please meet us at five this afternoon at the Antigua Palma Hotel to fill out your blank check. When you arrive, the front desk will escort you to the Superior Suite. You can bring a few family members and friends along if you wish. Best of luck to you. And remember, DREAM BIG.**

Francesca's heart was pounding in her chest. *Why am I so nervous and excited?* she wondered, as she read the message several times. She took a deep breath, attempting to steady herself. "I must call the girls. They will help me to get things under control. Oh dear, they are going to freak out."

After several phone calls and a quick visit to the Villa della Speranza, Francesca and her four friends arrived at the hotel and were escorted up to the Superior Suite. Inside, two men and a woman, dressed elegantly in black and white, were waiting inside.

"Good evening, ladies," said the first man, his voice calm and reassuring. "It is our pleasure to begin this global journey with *you*, Francesca Gómez, here in Mallorca. In just a moment, you'll be able to write the amount you wish on this blank check." The second produced a sleek, rolled-up device and unrolled it across the table. On the device's smooth surface appeared an image of a check bearing Francesca's name. The upper-left corner displayed a modern logo, matching the lapel pins worn by the three individuals. The signature at the bottom was unreadable.

"Now, Señora. Gómez," the first man continued, "before we proceed, you have the option to be filmed while you write the amount, or we can block out your name and simply capture your hand. For added security, your handwriting will be instantly transformed into a basic font on the screen. How would you prefer to proceed?"

"I'm not sure. What if I'm not happy with being filmed?" asked Francesca.

"We can film you from behind, looking down at your hand, if that makes you more comfortable.

"That sounds good," as she looked for confirmation from her four friends that all nodded in agreement.

"Then it is time. Simply hover your finger over the device and write your amount on the line. The device will automatically convert it into numerals in the rectangular box. Once you are ready, you can begin. Remember, Dream Big."

The tall woman was positioned and ready behind Francesca.

Francesca paused, her mind swirling with so many questions as her finger twitched, suspended above the Blank Check. Her friends stood in silence, waiting. The air in the room grew heavy as the seconds ticked away.

"Remember. Dream big," mumbled Isabel. "Ten million."

Her finger wrote out ten million.

Her phone chirped.

"Congratulations Señora. Gómez. You are our second big winner. A new app has been installed on your phone, where a private bank account has been created in your name with ten million placed, tax free. Through the app, you can easily access and transfer any amount of money to any account worldwide. Just follow the simple instructions, and you are all set. Additionally, here are two debit cards linked to your account for your convenience."

The four friends were crying and hugging each other. "Can you believe this?" cried out Miranda. "It's so hard to believe."

The tall woman motioned for the four friends to stand by Francesca. "Here is the video that will be shared on social media." They watched the video featuring a grand fireworks display accompanied by the message: "Congratulations to our Second winner in Mallorca. Sra. Gómez. Ten Million."

"Does this meet with your approval?" asked the second tall man.

"Yes, that looks fine," said Francesca, still in a state of shock.

"Before we leave, Sra. Gómez, we would like for you to transfer an amount of your choosing to your bank account. We want to make sure you are comfortable with how the system works."

"I can send money to anyone right now?"

"Yes, just type in their name and city. When you can confirm that they are the correct contact, a bank account will be created for them as well within the system. They will be notified once you have sent the money." Tears began to run down Francesca's cheeks.

"Can I send money to several different people?" she asked.

"As many as you would like. There's no rush."

One by one, Francesca sent money to her four friends. She then proceeded to share additional funds with Vittoria, Paolo and then her parents as she had planned. The phones in the room beeped as each transaction was completed.

Like a magician performing a trick, the tall lady handed a debit card to each of the four women. She then gave Francesca four more cards; two for parents, one for Vittoria and one for Paolo.

As they celebrated, the five friends never noticed the tall ones leave.

After an hour of celebrations in the suite, the girls stepped out to leave only to find the doorman standing just outside. He informed them that the room was theirs for the night. "This year is turning out to be a dream come true," said Francesca as the five entered back into the suite and ordered room service.

While they waited, Francesca called her parents, to share the exciting news about the evening's events and explain the bank accounts that were in their names. They were shocked by the news but eternally grateful for the generous gift.

Francesca had a few surprises up her sleeve when Paolo and Vittoria arrived six days later at the Villa for their weekly outing. After finishing their meal in the garden, Francesca asked for them to take a walk with her. As they approached the building at the end of the plaza, housing four of the largest suites, she opened the door and welcomed them in. Vittoria, confused, asked why they were there.

"My dearest friends. So much has happened in the last week and I know you have plans of your own with the money I gifted to you. However, I have another surprise for you today." Tenderly looking over to Vittoria, she continued. "Vittoria, you have been so dear to me. I know how much you have longed to be a resident of the Villa. You don't have to wait any longer. This suite that we are standing in right now is all yours. You can enjoy living here. Just imagine, you can have all your meals here now. No more cooking or cleaning. We have all the amenities here so that you can concentrate on enjoying your life in style." Vittoria had sat down as she heard the news. It was overwhelming for her to think that all this was happening to her.

"Oh, Francesca. This is too much. I don't know what to say, but I will not refuse. For over ten years I have dreamt of living here." Vittoria, in the middle of her tears, started to laugh. "You're going to get tired of seeing me every day!"

"I would never tire of seeing you," replied Francesca, leaning over and giving her a kiss on the cheek. "Paolo, if it is ok with your Gran Mamá, that is your new name for her, isn't it? Could you run home and pick up some of her things so she can stay here tonight. I have had everything cleaned, repainted and spruced up just for her. Vittoria, what do you say?"

"I would love that. Paolo, would that be too much trouble?"

"Of course, not Gran Mamá. Anything for you. I'll be back in a few hours." With a quiver in his voice, he turned to Francesca. "This is all so unbelievable. Thank you."

Paolo kissed his Gran Mamá goodbye, walking out the door as tears streamed down his face.

On the last day of February, two weeks after his Gran Mamá had permanently moved into the Villa, Paolo made the Thursday drive for his visit. Arriving at the Villa, he was happy to see them sitting outside the bistro, busy in conversation. Francesca seemed a bit anxious, and Vittoria had noticeably been crying as they held hands.

"What is going on? Is there something wrong?"

"Nothing wrong," replied Francesca, "But you may want to sit down for this one. I finally took that DNA test and I received the results an hour ago. It seems that your dear Gran Mamá has been keeping more secrets from us."

"Really? You are a woman of many mysteries," said Paolo, smiling as he sat down. "So, what is the juicy news?"

Francesca continued. "The results show that we are all related. Apparently, according to the test, Vittoria is *my* mother," explained Francesca.

"What?" said Paolo as he looked back and forth between mother and daughter. "So, you're my aunt?"

"Exactly. When I saw my results, I almost fainted. I called your Gran Mamá and asked if we could meet before you arrived. That was an hour ago. Wait till you hear this part of the story!"

"Ok Gran Mamá, it's time to come clean. All these years and you never cared to share this little part of your life? I can't wait to hear."

Still holding Francesca's hand, she looked directly into Paolos' eyes. "I never imagined I'd find my daughter. When Francesca called me an hour ago and asked if the test could be accurate, I knew I had to confess. It was a long time ago, and a very difficult chapter in my life. After your father was born, my husband, became resentful of not being the center of attention. His behavior turned violent and unbearable. My father, not tolerating it, made sure no harm came to me or our baby. Before I knew it, my husband was sent away, and I was forced to live with my parents. Two years later, I met a handsome man who had been sailing throughout the Mediterranean. My parents hoped he would marry me and take me away, but one day, he vanished without a word, leaving me pregnant and the subject of gossip. After I gave birth to my beautiful daughter, my parents insisted I give her up for adoption. I refused. There were many arguments, but I was alone and needed their help. They didn't believe I could manage raising two children on my own. I woke up one morning, just a week after giving birth, and my precious baby girl was gone. I cried for days. I have never felt so much pain in my life. It left me weak and sad. As time went on, the memory of that little girl I only held for a week slowly faded into the past until it seemed like a mere dream." Mother and daughter held hands, smiling in contentment that they had found each other.

"This news is phenomenal and astonishing. Gran Mamá, I can't imagine how you were able to lock away so much pain. You truly are remarkable, and I love you even more for it.

3

March 2024
Tom

"Why can't you be smart like your brother?" yelled Tom's mother, smacking him upside the head. His glasses flew off, clattering onto the floor. On the far side of the room, his older brother, Fritz, smirked, basking in yet another compliment at Tom's expense.

The two brothers couldn't have been more different. Fritz was short and stocky, with a mop of curly brown hair like their father. Tom, on the other hand, was tall and lean like their mother, his dark blond hair neatly trimmed. They shared the same piercing blue eyes, but beyond that, they had little in common.

Tom fumbled on the floor for his glasses, the world around him a blur. *Why does she hate me so much?* he wondered. No matter how hard he tried to please her, it seemed everything he did was wrong.

"Tom, remember what I told you about the table for tonight's guests," his mother snapped, her voice cutting through his thoughts. "The white flower arrangements belong on the dining table, not in the entryway."

"But yesterday you said they looked better there," Tom protested, his voice barely above a whisper.

"Don't argue with me, young man! Think! You should know they're better on the dining table where our guests can enjoy them."

Tom sighed, realizing this was today's argument. There was always something to correct, always some failure to address.

"Fritz, darling," she said, her tone softening as she turned to his brother. "Go enjoy your day and get some rest. Tonight is going to be wonderful."

≈

Growing up in the shadow of his famous mother, in Düsseldorf, Germany, Tom never seemed to fit in at school, at work, or even at home. He often reflected on those days, endless cycles of criticism and chaos that left him feeling like an outsider in his own family. By the time he turned 18, he felt nothing but relief as he walked out the door, leaving behind the dysfunction and heartache. It was his chance at a fresh start, a shot at stability and independence far removed from the turbulence of his childhood.

After completing six months of military service, Tom found work as a runner for a small newspaper firm. Rejecting any help from his mother's social connections, he resolved to start from the bottom and succeed on his own terms.

His mother, Gretchen Hans Schumer, was a force of nature. Once a model whose beauty turned heads wherever she went, her willpower dominated every corner of the family's life. Her sharp words left deep scars, cutting into anyone who dared oppose her. Gretchen had leveraged her striking looks to build the life she wanted, charming men into showering her with luxurious clothes and shoes.

When her husband, Friedrich, voiced frustration, she would silence him with a steely gaze and an accusing finger. "Don't forget who made this possible," she'd say. "Without me, you'd still be a doorman at some second-rate hotel. Now, go hide in the kitchen. Dinner won't prepare itself, and our guests will be here soon."

Friedrich would bow his head, his pride swallowed by her overpowering presence. Deep down, he knew she was right. Without his wife's fame, they wouldn't have the life they did. But Tom saw it differently. To him, his father was a man undone by love, a shadow of who he might have been.

As Gretchen's modeling career took off, Friedrich was relegated to the role of househusband. What began as simple tasks, tidying up and preparing dinner, morphed into full-scale event planning. Friedrich spent his days ensuring every meal was perfect, every room spotless, and every gathering flawless, while Gretchen basked in admiration, oblivious to his exhaustion.

Tom realized at a very young age how toxic his family was; he resented his mother's self-centered behavior and wished his father would stand up to her. As her fame grew, so did her sense of entitlement. To the world, she was a star, admired, celebrated, untouchable. But to Tom, she was an absence, her glittering success casting long shadows over the boy who simply wanted a mother.

Tom's career at the Rheinische Post was firmly established after many long hours and relentless deadlines, a small price to pay for the independence he had carved out for himself. There were times when Tom would stare blankly at a half-written article, the words blurring into unspoken frustrations. He longed for time with his father, simple moments to talk, laugh, and feel understood. But every attempt was intercepted by his mother.

Fourteen years into his career, with accolades pouring in and opportunities at every turn, a rare occurrence happened; Tom received a message from his mother. He found himself back in the home he had once been so eager to leave. Sitting by his dying father's side, the familiar tension returned when his mother walked in.

"Oh, Tom," she said, her voice dripping with disdain. "You've finally decided to spend time with your papa. If only you were more like your brother. You abandoned this family and disgraced us with that newspaper job. You just don't belong."

Tom clenched his jaw. "Mother, I'm here to see Papa. Please, just go do…whatever it is you do."

"Don't speak to me that way!" she snapped. "You should respect the mother who gave you this life!"

Tom had always preferred peace over confrontation but today was different. As his mother's sharp words cut through the silence of the room, he felt a wave of frustration. For years, he'd swallowed his feelings, allowing her criticism to shape his every move. But now, standing before her, something inside him shifted. He wasn't angry, nor was he bitter. Instead, he chose a different approach.

With a calm that surprised even him, Tom spoke. "Mother, I understand you care about me, but your words have been hurtful. I'm doing what I love, and it's time you recognize that." His voice, steady and kind, held no trace of aggression, but every word carried the weight of a lifetime of silence.

His mother, taken aback by his unexpected calm, faltered. For a moment, there was no response. But Tom wasn't done. He continued, each sentence laced with a quiet strength that could not be ignored. "I am going to stay here with my Papa. For years you have interfered. Not anymore. I will stay for as long as he needs me," father and son holding hands, a tear rolling down the dying man's cheek.

As Tom finished, a sense of peace settled over him. For the first time, he had stood up for himself, not with silence, anger or harsh words, but with kindness and clarity.

Gretchen hesitated for a moment, not enjoying being outwitted. "You are such a feeble waste of space," she quickly blurted out. "Don't think that by being here you will receive any inheritance."

"I am sorry to have disappointed you. It won't be long before I am gone. Please leave us alone now," he replied, showing his mother towards the door and locking it behind her. Hours later, with the passing of his father, Tom felt the grief clinging to him like a heavy shadow. The emptiness in his heart was too much to bear. With a kiss on the forehead, he held his father's hand one last time, whispering a quiet goodbye as love and loss collided in his heart. Tom left the house for the last time, grateful that he had had the last say to be with his him.

Tom had found purpose and freedom as a journalist. His days were filled with dynamic projects, and he thrived in the fast-paced world of reporting. Just months after his father's passing, his latest assignment would bring the past roaring back. Tasked with documenting the history of Düsseldorf's iconic Portage Hotel before its demolition, Tom uncovered a chilling headline buried in an old newspaper: "Famous Actor J. Krüger Spotted Leaving Hotel Room Where Woman Secretly Gives Birth."

The whispers of the "Portage Hotel baby" that had shadowed his childhood suddenly felt real. He vividly recalled several arguments between his parents in his younger years, just before his mother's big break in the modeling industry. While Tom couldn't fully grasp the conversation at the time, the words "Portage Hotel baby, not yours" echoed repeatedly. As his mother's career took off and her paychecks grew, so did her dominance over the family. Whenever his father tried to defend Tom, she would walk past him without hesitation, coldly repeating the same phrase: "Portage Hotel baby, not yours."

Tom poured over countless reports and interviewed more than a dozen eyewitnesses to the events of 1980 before uncovering an alarming truth. Everything was falling into place; the dates, the cover-up, even the sharp words his mother used to hurl at his father whenever he tried to shield him. The pieces all pointed to one conclusion: he was the product of that fleeting affair.

Two maids, who had been present at his birth thirty-two years earlier, confirmed Tom's findings within days. His birth certificate, it turned out, was nothing more than a fabricated lie.

With his father, the one who was there during his life, now gone, Tom saw no reason to seek out his biological father nor confront his mother. His life was good, and he was on the verge of starting a new chapter with Felicia, the love of his life, as they prepared to welcome their own family.

Once the darling of haute couture, Gretchen's striking figure and face began to show the signs of aging in her mid-fifties. The modeling contracts faded at an alarming pace, and the industry that once worshipped her, now sought younger, more vibrant women. With a defiant tenacity, she clung to her persona. She would sweep into rooms with the same alluring call, remaining unapologetically herself despite her arrogance.

Following the death of her husband, she continued to cling to a lifestyle of extravagance. Designer handbags, luxury vacations, and dinners at exclusive restaurants remained staples in her life, though her income no longer justified such indulgences. She rationalized each splurge as essential to maintaining her image; she was trapped in a cycle of appearances she couldn't afford to abandon. Gretchen suddenly found herself facing the reality of her financial situation, realizing that her once, infinite stream of income was dwindling at a rapid pace.

Despite a financial crisis looming in her future, her true nature had not changed. Behind her polished facade, she belittled everyone within earshot, reminding them of their inferiority. It was no wonder she had no friends.

After years of silence, it came as a complete surprise to Tom when his mother sent him a text message.

- Tom, call me right away.

A nagging discomfort rolled up Tom's spine as he knew she needed something. "I'll call her later," said Tom out loud as he concentrated on completing the final part of his assignment.

Hours later, back at home, Tom counted over five messages from his mother, each one more demanding. After spending some quality time with his wife Felicia and their two infants, Tom proceeded to tackle the uncomfortable task. His mother picked up immediately, with no hint of a greeting.

"Tom, I need you to help me. You know things have been tough lately, and I can't manage this on my own."

"What do you mean? We haven't spoken in ages." asked Tom, baffled by her words.

"I'm in a pinch and I need you to help me out."

Tom laughed, hearing the arrogance in his mother's voice. "I have no idea what you are talking about. I think it would be best if you called Fritz."

"Oh, I wouldn't dare think of imposing my problems on your brother."

Still laughing in disbelief, Tom replied, "You mean, hashtag, not my brother. I haven't spoken to him in years."

"What do you mean, not your brother? And what's this hashtag you're talking about?"

"It's a symbol used to classify or categorize something that is a thing. I also found out about your fling with the actor and where I was born. That's all in the past now. I've moved on."

"Oh, seriously. You're still my son and I need help. Let me come over and discuss this with you. Where do you live again? I've lost your address."

Tom continued to laugh, not surprised by her response. "You really are all about yourself, aren't you mother? We moved two years ago. We are no longer in Germany."

"We?"

"Yes, my wife and our children. There's nothing more I can do now. Call Fritz or one of your friends. I am sure they can help you out. I do need to go now. Bye mother." Tom put down his phone, relieved that the conversation had come to an end, on his terms. He felt empowered.

For a split second, Gretchen felt lightheaded and out of control. How could her son have married, had children and not told me about it? "The nerve of him not keeping in touch with me. He will regret this one day."

Over the next few years, Gretchen's path was anything but straightforward. She bounced from one odd job to another, searching for the kind of help and guidance that could give her life some direction. Eventually, she found her footing in the world of brand consulting and digital influencing, a field where her knack for social media kept her hustling. Yet, despite the flurry of content creation and brand deals, her income always seemed to fall short of sustaining the lavish lifestyle she was determined not to abandon.

March 10, 2024
Undisclosed Location

A faint smirk tugged at the corner of the mysterious, elegant man's lips as he adjusted his cufflinks, each engraved with the symbol of his brand, a reminder of a genuine promise from long ago. The promise had not been broken but tragically taken away. Yet, he found the strength to carry on and now took pleasure in sharing his wealth.

Today marked the beginning of the next chapter in his social media game, crafted not merely for engagement but for triumph. Somewhere out there, his next winner awaited, and he was ready to set the stage.

With a swift swipe through the air with his gloved hands, he was drawn into the illusion of speeding through the sparkling expanse of the Milky Way, before the focus narrowed on a bright star, then zooming rapidly toward Earth, a vivid blue orb spinning in the void.

The mastermind gazed at the immersive space before him, delighted with all he had achieved, albeit alone.

With a second gentle motion of his hand, the blue orb steadily filled the screen, gradually spinning faster.

"Where will you take us this time," he murmured to himself, plucking an imaginary dart from above the table. As the Earth spun faster, he aimed and released the dart. The world completed one more rotation before coming to a stop, homing in on Europe then Germany.

"Düsseldorf," he said out loud. Let's see who our winner is today."

A row of rectangular panels appeared, flickering with rapidly changing numbers. With a swipe of his hand, each panel froze in turn, completing the sequence.

Countless magazine covers overtook the screen. Society pages and gossip columns appeared to outnumber the rest.

"Well, who do we have here?" he mused. "Gretchen Hans Schumer. You've certainly led quite the life. Let's see how this will change it."

He rubbed his chin thoughtfully, pondering what she would write on the blank line that awaited her.

"Time to call in the troops." With three deliberate taps on the table, the message was sent. Soon, Gretchen would receive her instructions.

March 10, 2024

Gretchen

Living on a tight budget was a reality Gretchen despised, and it clung to her like an ill-fitting coat. The frustration gnawed at her daily, spilling over onto anyone *unlucky* enough to cross her path.

This morning was no different. After a bitter sip of her coffee and a weary glance at the mountain of work awaiting her, her phone chirped, breaking the monotony. A smooth, confident male voice filled the room:

"Frau Gretchen, congratulations! You've been chosen as the third participant of Blank Checks. Please join us this afternoon, five o'clock at the Breuninger Department Store on Königsallee to claim and complete your blank check. Feel free to bring a few family members or friends along for the occasion. Best of luck, and remember, DREAM BIG!"

Her heart skipped a beat. Was this some kind of joke, or could this be the lifeline she so desperately needed?

Without hesitation, she opened the Blank Checks app and took note of how much the previous winners had acquired. "How dumb can these people be? Do they not know what Dream Big means? I'll show the world how this game is played. No more work nor living poorly. Time to change my life."

Pushing her obligations off to the side, she decided to treat herself to a shopping day extravaganza. With seven hours till her big payday, it was time to return to the days of the past when money was not an issue.

She made appointments at the salon first to have her hair and nails done. Next was a visit for a new striking outfit for the evening's occasion. With the millions of people who would be watching her, she had to look her best. With just two hours to spare, Gretchen returned home with armloads of designer named packages, filled with all her favorite outfits, lotions and creams. The queen was back on her throne.

Arriving early at Breuninger, the store owner, Johannes, was there to greet her. "Good evening, Frau Schumer. It's been a long time since we have seen each other. How have you been? You look elegant and dashing as always."

With a loud grunt, she pushed her way past the door. Johannes shook his head, sad to see that she had not changed. Locking the door behind him, he silently showed her towards the back area of the store where the glorious model runway stretched out over the length of the room. Gretchen's long legs had her up on the runway before Johannes could enter the room. She was busy on her phone, ignoring Johannes completely.

Typing quickly, she sent a message to her son Tom.

- You will regret not having helped me when I contacted you last.

Tom was with his wife Felicia when he received the message. "What in the world does that mean?" he asked. "My mother really cannot help herself. She has probably put a spell on a rich old man and thinks I will come running after her money."

Gretchen was so busy sending messages to her contact list that she did not notice the three tall people appear from behind the stage to stand behind her. They patiently waited as she put her phone in her purse.

"Good evening, Frau Schumer," said the first man, his voice smooth and laced with a practiced, confident warmth. A startled Gretchen turned. "In just a moment, you'll have the opportunity to write any amount you desire on this blank check."

The second man, with an air of quiet precision, retrieved a sleek, cylindrical device from his coat pocket. It unfurled effortlessly in his hands, revealing a gleaming surface that sprang to life. An image of a check materialized, Gretchen's name displayed prominently on the top.

In the upper-left corner, a polished logo glowed faintly, matching the ornate lapel pins worn by the one woman and the two men, emblems of power, no doubt. The signature scrawled at the bottom, however, was an enigma, little more than an elegant blur.

"Now, Frau Schumer," the first man continued, his tone as steady as ever, "before we proceed, you have a choice. We can film you as you write the amount, your face proudly accompanying your actions, or, if you'd prefer anonymity, we can obscure your name and record only your hand. How would you like to proceed?"

Gretchen didn't hesitate for a second. She straightened her posture, a sly smile curling at the corners of her lips. "Well, I want to be filmed, of course. The world will see me once again." The tall woman positioned herself opposite Gretchen, capturing her practiced and knowledgeable runway presence.

"It is time. With your finger, hover over the device and let your imagination guide you as you inscribe your desired amount on the glowing line. When you're ready, you may begin. And always remember, Dream Big, for the future is yours to shape."

Before positioning her hand, Gretchen looked straight into the recording device. As if on a photo shoot, she posed a few times, wrapped up in the idea that all eyes from around the world were on her. Dramatically, she positioned her hand over the device and wrote out her amount.

March 10, 2024
Undisclosed Location

The mastermind leaned back in his chair, as he scanned the check before him on the big screen. His gaze narrowed, and his jaw dropped. The numbers on screen seemed to blur for a moment, but they were undeniably clear. Each month, he had carefully deposited a randomly selected amount into an account, maintaining an air of quiet control, almost as if he were playing a game with fate. But now, as the digits flickered before him, something shifted. No one had come close to the balance, not even remotely. His eyes widened further as he processed the amount, and a slow realization dawned on him: *This month was different.* This woman had dared to dream in ways no one else had before. A smile tugged at the corner of his lips, but it was tinged with a hint of disbelief. *She's a brave soul,* he thought, his mind racing through possibilities. *Maybe a bit too brave.* The audacity of it, the boldness. It was both impressive and alarming. It was as though she had no fear of the consequences, no hesitation in reaching for something far beyond what he ever anticipated.

March 10, 2024
Gretchen

The screen froze in silent hesitation. All eyes were focused on the image. The tall woman looked up, a question in her gaze directed at the two tall men. They shook their heads not knowing what had just transpired.

Suddenly, the screen went black, a slight glow appearing around the edges that began to flicker. The message appeared, the words slapping Gretchen right in the face. "Insufficient Funds." She was in disbelief, her mind racing in anger. "How could this happen? It said to dream big, so I did. One Hundred Million is barely enough to last me the rest of my life. Let me try again," she hissed, reaching for the device that was quickly rolled up and tucked away in the tall man's pocket as he took a step back. "This is outrageous. I will sue you. Don't you know who I am? Just wait. This is not over."

The first tall man was the first to speak out as he stepped in between the two. "Frau Schumer. May I remind you that this is merely a game of chance. Unfortunately, you dreamt TOO big. There are no second chances."

Gretchen continued to yell and scold the three tall people as they stood their ground. In the background, Johannes, anticipating her behavior to escalate, called in his security. Within minutes, several security personnel surrounded Gretchen on the catwalk and proceeded to escort her away from the premises, all the while her demanding more answers.

An hour later, the world witnessed the unforeseen chain of events that was captured on video. Gretchen, her name boldly displayed on the screen with her amount and reaction, was breaking records on the internet. The model from Düsseldorf was in the news again, but not in the way she wanted. Kicking the bags and boxes of newly purchased, expensive items from earlier that day, Gretchen was furious at the headline that fanned out over the video. "Third participant of Blank Checks misses out. One Hundred Million; Check Bounces."

March 10, 2024
Tom & Felicia

It didn't take long for Tom and Felicia to huddle together, eagerly pressing play on the video. The buzz had spread like wildfire among their friends, and they were desperate to see what had everyone so riled up. When Tom's eyes landed on the screen, he was struck dumb. There, standing confidently on the catwalk, was his mother, poised as if born to model the latest high-fashion trends. The way she locked eyes with the camera, her gaze sharp and calculating just before she wrote her amount, sent a shiver crawling down Tom's spine. That look, so brimming with arrogance, was unmistakable.

It clicked. The cryptic message from earlier that day finally made sense. Tom knew his mother all too well, and it hit him like a ton of bricks: she would have already been spending money she had not yet won. A wave of sympathy washed over him, whoever crossed her path in the coming weeks was in for a storm.

4

March 10, 2024
Sean

After a short, quiet year of retirement, former detective Sean Leblanc thought his days of chasing shadows were over, until two months ago. The social media game had caught the world by storm; his curiosity being drawn back into the hunt.

Three contestants had already taken their chances in the game, each leaving behind breadcrumbs, subtle, almost taunting clues embedded in the videos. The pieces were there, scattered like a cryptic puzzle, but no one had put them together. Not yet.

With too many questions and too much time, Sean commandeered the spare room, transforming it into a war room of obsession. He stripped an entire wall bare, then methodically began constructing his Evidence Board. At its heart, a world map, stark, demanding answers. Dead center, he sketched the strange symbol that had appeared on every check, its meaning still a mystery but undeniably important.

The first thread of the web was a long stretch of twine, pulled taut from San Francisco to the top left corner. A post fluttered slightly as he pressed it into place: San Francisco, California. 20 million. A fortune. A whisper of something bigger.

Next, Mallorca. Another thread, another note. Mallorca – 10 million. The pattern was taking shape, but the answers still danced just out of reach.

At the far side of the room, he started tallying the amounts on a fresh sheet of paper; twelve checks for twelve months. A slow drip of wealth, deliberate and controlled.

The last thread traced its way from Germany, stretching toward the right of the second note. Here, the details were too important to be scribbled on a post it. Instead, Sean dedicated a full sheet of paper, drawing two meticulous lists. One side chronicled everything about the German model, her movements, connections, secrets. The other? A running dossier on the trio of unnervingly similar, tall blonde figures. They weren't just a coincidence. They were a pattern.

And patterns always led to the truth.

He moved to his computer, fingers flying as he transferred the notes, layering them with the digital evidence. The room felt different now, charged with the weight of discovery. The pieces weren't just clues anymore. They were breadcrumbs to something bigger. Something enigmatic.

And Sean was all in.

He grappled with burning questions that refused to let him rest. Who was the true mastermind pulling the strings? How did this secretive system operate so flawlessly in the shadows? And most importantly what mystifying method determined the so-called winner?

With so many unanswered questions running through his mind, he contacted a special agent friend of his to gain more information into Gretchen Hans Schumer. Recognizing that she would be one to speak out against the game, he could not waste much time. Within a few hours, he not only had Gretchen Hans Schumer personal information, but also that of her sons, Fritz and Tom. Looking at his watch, he noted a six-hour difference. He would need to call in the middle of the night to catch her early in the morning.

March 2024
Manuel

Under the golden glow of a setting sun, the vineyard buzzed with the warmth of anticipation as guests gathered to celebrate the debut of its newest wine label. Adding a touch of rhythm and soul to the evening was the famous and lively two-man band, El y Yo, effortlessly blending acoustic melodies and toe-tapping beats. Creating a rich and layered symphony of sound, their music echoed through the vines, setting the perfect backdrop for swirling glasses, lively conversation, and the first sips of the vineyard's latest creation.

The guest list for the event was nothing short of legendary, a dazzling lineup of the elite, the influential, and the enigmatic. Invitations to this exclusive affair were coveted like rare jewels, whispered about in hushed tones among social circles and sought after with an almost reverent desire. It wasn't merely a list; it was a testament to power, prestige, and an air of mystique that left everyone yearning for a spot among the chosen few.

Renowned sommeliers, celebrated chefs, and influential wine critics attended, eager to experience the unveiling of the exceptional vintage. Among the special invitees were prominent figures from the Argentine wine industry, including vineyard owners and enologists, as well as international celebrities with a passion for fine wine. The event was a dazzling celebration, blending the rich culture of the Mendoza region with the artistry of winemaking.

Experienced musical duo, Manuel and Pedro, of the El y Yo Band, were elated when they had received their invitation to perform at the most anticipated event of the year.

A decade ago, Manuel had welcomed Pedro into the family with open arms. At the time, Manuel was a man weighed down by grief, his heart still aching from the loss of his beloved Rosalinda. Keeping her cherished cosmetic shop open became his refuge, a way to stay busy, to keep the crushing sorrow at bay. But Manuel knew next to nothing about the powders, lipsticks, and perfumes that had once brought his wife so much joy.

That was where Sandra came in. At eighteen, she was the perfect heir to her mother's passion. With a natural love for beauty and glamour, she breathed new life into the shop, transforming it into more than just a business, it became a tribute, a sanctuary, a place where Rosalinda's spirit lingered in every shade of rouge and every delicate fragrance. Side by side, father and daughter found solace in their shared purpose, stitching together the torn fabric of their lives with laughter, hard work, and cherished memories.

Then came Pedro.

He had arrived at the Perez home carrying condolence flowers but left carrying Sandra's heart. The moment their eyes locked, the world around them faded. Grief made way for something electric, something undeniable. Their love story unfolded swiftly, as if destiny had been waiting for this moment. Within months, they were inseparable. And soon after, vows were exchanged, sealing a love that had blossomed in the shadow of loss but thrived in the light of new beginnings.

To everyone's surprise, at the large wedding, father of the bride, Manuel, performed an unforgettable two hours of music splendor as the guests danced in celebration for the happy couple. His multi talent with the keyboard, bongo drums, harmonica, and violin, to name a few, left the guests in awe.

Near the end of the two hours, Pedro surreptitiously pulled over a few chairs, placing them in a semi-circle close to the stage. He called over his beautiful bride and her four best friends and sat them down. Sandra and her friends were stupefied. Pedro did not utter a word. His hands alone motioned for them to sit quietly. The guests followed suit as all eyes were on Pedro wondering what magic he would bring to the end of the glorious evening.

As he strode onto the stage, a hush fell over the crowd. Leaning in, he murmured something into Manuel's ear, prompting him to silently pass over the guitar. A ripple of curiosity spread through the audience. Sandra felt a sharp nudge from her friend.

"What's going on?"

She could only shake her head, her pulse quickening. She had no answer, only anticipation crackling in the air like a storm about to break.

A single, deliberate strum, a bright, resonant chord cut through the silence, commanding immediate attention. The guitar strings, coaxed by Pedro's skilled fingers, emitted a mix of crisp, fluid, lyrical notes. The room filled with the passionate intensity of flamenco, the rhythm weaving between sharp staccato notes and smooth, cascading arpeggios.

The mournful yet romantic tone of *Bésame Mucho,* transformed into a fiery dialogue. As the intensity built, the guests felt the music reverberate in their chest, the sound brimming with both sensuality and urgency. Then, as suddenly as it began, the guitar quieted down into a tender tremolo, soft and vulnerable, leaving the room spellbound.

With a short nod of his head towards his astounded father-in-law, Manuel intuitively joined in with a few delicate, rhythmic heart-like beats on his bongos, the guitar notes began to flicker and dance, like embers in a flame. Pedro stepped up towards the microphone, looking out over a sea of eyes he now had full control over. His soul-stirring voice woke up every emotion hidden inside in the room.

The air grew electric, heavy with unspoken thoughts and feelings, as guests leaned forward in their seats, caught between holding their breath and breaking into applause.

The performance ended with a final, haunting note that hung in the air like a whispered secret. For a moment, no one moved, no one breathed, the spell unbroken. Then, the room erupted in thunderous applause, cheers ricocheting off the walls. Pedro stepped back from the microphone, his gaze locking with Sandra's across the crowd. Her heart pounded, not from the rhythm of the music but from the realization that something had shifted. Whatever story had begun on that stage tonight, it was far from over.

Tears welled in Manuel's eyes, blurring the dazzling lights above the stage. He had not expected to feel this deeply, to be so utterly unguarded. But as he watched Sandra and Pedro, something in his heart cracked open, a space he hadn't realized had been closed for so long.

Sandra, still caught in the moment, barely noticed the audience rising to their feet and move en masse towards the stage. Her eyes remained locked on Pedro's, searching, questioning, knowing. A lifetime of unspoken words passed between them in that charged silence.

Pedro stepped down, weaving through the crowd that seemed to part for him as if fate itself had cleared the path. When he reached her, there was no hesitation. He took her trembling hands and pulled her close.

The applause, the cheering, it all faded into a distant hum.

Manuel watched, his heart swelling with something deeper than pride, heavier than joy. Love, in all its raw, untamed beauty, had found its way back into his family. He had not only gained a son that evening, but he had also been reminded of what it meant to truly believe in love.

And as Pedro leaned in, whispering something only Sandra could hear, Manuel let his tears fall freely, unashamed.

Because on that night, a story had begun, one that would not end with the closing of a curtain, but with the promise of forever.

During their honeymoon, Pedro's phone buzzed with an unexpected call, his father-in-law, Manuel, on the other end, his voice brimming with warmth and an intriguing proposition.

"Would you be interested in performing with me at a few upcoming shows?"

Manuel had never let his love for music fade, his weekends devoted to filling the air of Mendoza city, with melody and soul. Pedro, drawn by the rhythm of fate, eagerly joined him.

Before they knew it, audiences were enchanted, and a question kept surfacing; "What's the name of your band?"

Pedro chuckled, shaking his head. "It's just him and me playing, nothing more."

But as if by magic, those simple words took root. Overnight, 'El y Yo' was born.

Sandra was elated that her father had found joy in his life once again. He would find additional joy four years later when the couple gave birth to quadruplets. It was a surprise for the entire family and coping with four newborns at once was a whirlwind of sleepless nights, endless diapers, and a symphony of tiny cries, but it was also the most beautiful chaos Pedro and Sandra had ever known.

Manuel, overjoyed to be a grandfather, became the babies' biggest fan, rocking them to sleep with his guitar and humming lullabies late into the night. As the children grew, their home was always filled with music. Sandra often found herself watching in awe as Pedro and Manuel played their guitars in the living room, with four tiny pairs of hands clapping along in delight.

'El y Yo' became more than just a duo. It became a legacy. As the years passed, the family's bond deepened through music. The quadruplets developed their own love for melody, often grabbing tambourines, maracas, or even wooden spoons to join in. Their house in Mendoza was filled with laughter, music, and an overwhelming sense of love.

It felt like only yesterday when Manuel and Pedro first played together, their melodies intertwining like old souls reconnecting through song. Now, years later, their lives had blossomed in ways they once only dreamed of. The four children thrived in school, their laughter echoing through the house, filling every corner with warmth and joy. Sandra, radiant and ambitious, poured her heart into her flourishing cosmetic store, transforming it into a cornerstone of the community.

And Manuel and Pedro? Their bond had only deepened. What began as casual sessions had evolved into something profound, weekends spent igniting stages with a passion that left audiences spellbound. Gone were the days when Pedro ran deliveries at the flower shop; now, every performance with his father-in-law was a symphony of trust and unspoken understanding, their music an electric dance of soul and skill.

So, when the invitation arrived from Bodega Norton, one of Argentina's most prestigious wineries, it felt like fate. With a multitude of countries eagerly awaiting the latest release of Malbecs and Blends, this year's unveiling was a grand affair. To be invited was an honor; to perform was a privilege.

The moment they stepped onto the sprawling veranda, the beauty of the land enveloped them. Neatly lined rows of grapevines stretched into the horizon, their deep green leaves shimmering under the golden sun. Beyond them, the Andes stood like silent guardians, their snowcapped peaks piercing the endless blue sky. The crisp mountain air carried whispers of oak barrels and ripe fruit, an intoxicating promise of the night to come.

Manuel and Pedro exchanged a glance; no words were needed. This was more than just another performance. Tonight, their music would not just fill the air; it would become part of the land, woven into the very soul of the region.

As the evening progressed, Manuel and Pedro would occasionally replace their live music with a backdrop of gentle jazz and tango. While sipping and sampling the latest wines, the duo was approached by the guests, each with praise and respect for their performance. Surprisingly, much of the talk throughout the evening was not on the wine but on the game that had taken the world by storm. Even those who were well off, found the allure of a blank check most enticing. The mysterious competition had captivated the world with its promise: write your own fortune.

Manuel chuckled as he tuned his guitar. "Strange, isn't it? People are more interested in a game than the finest wines in Argentina."

Pedro swirled his Malbec thoughtfully, the candlelight catching the deep ruby hue of the wine. "Not so strange," he mused, plucking a slow, melancholic note on his bass. "Everyone wants a taste of something greater than what they have, even those with everything."

The murmurs of the guests ebbed and flowed like the tide, carrying snippets of speculation about the game. Fortunes were being rewritten overnight, lives turned to legend with a single stroke of a pen. Who among them would dare to play?

A woman in a crimson dress approached the stage, her eyes gleaming with curiosity. "You're both artists," she said, her voice, smooth and rich with the weight of fine liquor. "Would you, do it? Would you wager your music for a chance at limitless wealth?"

Manuel strummed a few soft chords, his gaze flickering to Pedro before landing back on the woman. A slow smile curled his lips. "Ah, señora," he said, "music is already a gamble. Every song we play is a bet that someone will feel something."

Pedro leaned in, his voice lower, edged with something unreadable. "What if the stakes were higher? What if the price of losing was more than a missed note?"

The woman studied them both for a moment before leaning closer. "Then I hope you play well," she whispered. "We have already witnessed both win and loss. Your music *does* make us feel. It moves something in me. I believe I speak for every guest here. You are the music of the heavens. Thank you for sharing with us your talent. Good evening gentlemen." With a slow twirl, her dress flaring out as she floated back to festivities on the veranda.

The euphoria of the evening spilled into the wee hours of the morning, with over half the guests still sipping wine and reveling in the magic of the night beneath a sky dusted with stars.

Laughter rang out like a melody, twirling through the crisp night air as candles flickered, casting golden light on flushed cheeks and sparkling eyes.

The vintner gave the last call for drinks and song around three a.m. With glasses held high and a chorus reaching up into the sky, the last of the guests toasted to the marvelous soiree.

Applause thundered through the vineyard, rolling like a warm breeze over the endless rows of grapevines. Laughter and cheers lingered in the dusk as guests slowly drifted away, their spirits lifted by the evening's melodies.

Under the soft glow of lanterns, Manuel and Pedro carefully packed up their instruments, the magic of their performance still shimmering in the air. Just as Manuel reached to tuck his guitar into the van, a voice with an air of intrigue, rang out.

The woman in the crimson dress stood at the edge of the fading celebration, her eyes alight with something unspoken. "One more," she murmured, tilting her head ever so slightly. "Just one last song."

Manuel hesitated only for a moment before his fingers found the strings. A gentle strum, a lingering note, then another, and another, delicate as whispers in the night. The melody rose, weaving through the cooling air, until suddenly.

A tinny voice crackled from his pocket. His phone, unbidden, had begun to speak.

'Manuel Perez. You are our fourth selected participant of the Blank Checks. Please meet us at four o'clock later this afternoon at your daughter's cosmetic shop to fill out your blank check. You can bring a few family members and friends along if you wish. Best of luck to you. And remember, DREAM BIG."

The guitarist's hand froze over his strings. The air turned electric.

Pedro leaned in, whispering so only Manuel could hear, "You never told me you entered."

"I didn't," Manuel replied, his voice barely audible.

March 11, 2024
Manuel

The woman lingered, watching as Manuel stood frozen, his fingers hovering over the strings of his guitar. Her sharp journalist instincts tingled, she knew a story when she saw one. But tonight was not the night to pry.

Instead, she simply smiled and disappeared into the lingering mist of the vineyard, her heels clicking softly against the stone pathway.

Manuel, still in a daze, looked at Pedro, his pulse hammering. "This has to be a joke," he muttered.

Pedro shook his head, his grin widening. "Manuel, if this is a joke, it's the best damn one I've ever heard."

The two loaded their instruments in silence, the hum of the night settling around them. But Manuel's mind raced. A blank check? His daughter's shop. DREAM BIG?

By the time he got home, sleep was impossible. He sat at the kitchen table, staring at his worn guitar case. What could he even ask for? A new guitar? A studio? No, he had spent a lifetime chasing melodies, but there were bigger dreams buried deep in his heart.

When the afternoon sun finally climbed high, Manuel found himself standing outside his daughter's cosmetic shop, hands clammy, his family and Pedro by his side. Sandra opened the door and quietly let everyone in.

The moment he stepped in, a trio of tall, elegantly dressed people greeted him, their expressions unreadable. One of them, a poised man with silver-rimmed glasses, extended his hands, in them a device that shimmered with the image of a check, made out to Manuel Perez.

"Señor Pérez," the tall man said, his voice smooth as silk, his knowing smile hinting at secrets yet to unfold. "In just a moment, you will have the opportunity to write any amount you desire on this blank check. But before we continue, you must decide. Will you remain anonymous, or shall the world witness this moment?"

Manuel's breath caught in his throat. He turned to his daughter and Pedro, searching their faces for guidance. "What do you think?" he asked, his voice barely above a whisper.

Sandra didn't hesitate. "Let them film you, Papá. You're already a legend here." Her eyes sparkled with excitement. Pedro nodded firmly in agreement.

The tall man's smile widened. "Then the moment has arrived." He gestured toward the sleek, glowing device before them. "Simply hover your finger over the screen and write your amount. The system will translate it into numerals in the designated box. And remember…" His voice dropped to a near whisper, reverberating with promise. "Dream big."

Manuel exhaled, clutching his hands as he stared at the device before him. He swallowed hard and finally wrote out his amount.

And just like that, the music of his life was about to change forever.

March 11, 2024
Undisclosed Location

"Bravo, Señor Perez. You have earned this."

Leaning back with deliberate grace, the man slowly peeled off his gloves, his fingers lingering over the fine leather before setting them aside. With a practiced push against the black, moon-shaped desk, a hidden drawer slid open, revealing a black satin lining that swallowed the gloves like a whispered secret. The drawer silently sealed itself.

Turning smoothly in his chair, he reached for a crystal decanter, pouring a generous stream of deep red wine into his glass. He lifted it to his lips but paused, letting the rich aroma swirl around him. Beyond the towering screens, the ocean of stars unfurled endlessly. He savored the moment, the taste of victory mingling with the taste of the wine.

March 11, 2024

Sean

At two in the morning, Sean made the call to Germany. It was no surprise when Gretchen snatched up the phone with a sharp breath, her fingers tightening around it like a vice. "Who is this? She snapped; her voice laced with irritation and a desperate hunger for acknowledgment.

For over an hour, Sean listened as Gretchen bragged about herself, interrupted him before he could get a word in, and complained about not getting special treatment after the check bounced. Recognizing the classic signs of a self-centered narcissist, he let her ramble, knowing every bit of information could prove invaluable in his search for answers.

After his exhausting, one-sided conversation with the German model, he stepped back and added more notes to the "Evidence Board." He had learned that Gretchen had been given only a few hours' notice to meet at a specific time and place, all via a single text message. It wasn't much, but every small clue helped piece together a clearer picture.

His next call was to Tom Schumer, who had little to say and knew even less about his mother. After the brief but polite conversation ended, Sean was left with more questions than answers about the Schumer family. But he reminded himself that his focus was on the mastermind behind the game. Digging too deeply into the lives of those chosen would only complicate things. The basics would have to suffice.

Tired, he crawled back into bed. The day was going to be another wonderful day in paradise.

March 11, 2024
Manuel

Time seemed to stand still, the weight of the moment pressing down like a held breath. The only sounds drifting from their home were the carefree echoes of laughter, four children playing with their friends in the backyard, blissfully unaware that their world had just changed forever.

Inside, silence stretched, thick and uneasy, until Pedro finally spoke, his voice hesitant, threading through the tension.

"What I don't understand is… how did you win if you never even signed up to play?"

Manuel exhaled shakily, running a hand through his graying hair. His heart pounded in his chest, as if still trying to catch up with reality.

"I don't know. It's all so overwhelming." The words felt foreign on his tongue, unreal. His hands trembled as he clenched them into fists. "What in the world are we going to do with all that money?"

A voice, soft but steady, cut through the fog.

"I have a confession to make, Papa," Sandra said, shifting nervously. Her dark eyes held a flicker of guilt, but also something else, hope. "I entered your name in the game a month ago. I... I hope you're not angry with me."

Manuel's gaze snapped to his daughter. For a moment, there was only silence. Then, his face softened, his expression melting into something unreadable before he finally chuckled, a breathless, incredulous sound.

"Oh, my darling child, mijita… how could I ever be angry with you?" His voice thickened with emotion. "Not when we've just won thirty million dollars-tax-free. But Dios mío, I still can't believe I had the nerve to write such a large amount when they asked me to. I only started believing it when you got the message on your phones after I made those few deposits. That's when it hit me... this wasn't some game. This... this is real."

Pedro had been quiet, too quiet. His hands were clasped tightly together, his jaw set. Then, without warning, he bowed his head, his shoulders shaking.

"Pedro?" Manuel's voice was laced with concern as he reached out, placing a firm, reassuring hand on his son-in-law's shoulder. "What is it, mijo? What's wrong?"

Pedro let out a heavy breath, his voice raw as he finally spoke.

"You know that money has never been the most important thing in our lives. We have love. We have each other. In my world, we are already rich." He looked up, his eyes glistening. "But money... it brings trouble. It changes people. And my worst fear is that it will change you. That you won't want to continue "El y Yo." That you'll have bigger dreams now, ones that don't include us. That this will take away the life we love."

The room held its breath.

Then, Manuel, eyes shining with conviction, pulled Pedro into a deep embrace.

"Mi querido Pedro, listen to me. I would never abandon 'El y Yo.' It is my soul, my home. And as for our family? We will be fine." He pulled back just enough to meet Pedro's eyes, gripping his arms firmly. "In fact, I have an idea, something we can do together. Something that will help so many in our community. Imagine what we could build. Imagine the lives we could change."

Pedro searched his father-in-law's face, and for the first time that evening, a smile ghosted over his lips.

The weight of uncertainty lingered, but in that moment, in that embrace, they knew one thing for certain money would not break them. Their bond, their music, their love... it was unshakable.

And together, they would decide what came next.

This story was inspired by Joel and Tobie, a father and son-in-law band called
Him and Me.
They perform in and around Sedona, Arizona.
himandmeband.com

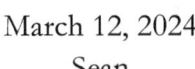

March 12, 2024
Sean

The whispering breeze gently rolled through the room as the morning sun broke over the Caribbean horizon. The salty scent of the ocean filled the air as the waves lapped rhythmically against the shore. Sean closed his eyes for a moment, letting the warmth of the sun sink into his skin, the golden light painting the world in hues of amber and sapphire. The distant cry of seagulls blended with the rustling palm leaves; a soothing symphony of nature that made him feel both at peace and alive.

After a relaxing morning, enjoying his coffee to jump start his first exciting day on the job, Sean reached for his phone and scrolled through the news. His eyes widened, his breath caught in his throat. The bold headline *'Argentine Man Wins Thirty Million in Blank Checks Game'*. His instincts screamed to find out more, but a glance at the clock made his stomach sink. Whatever secrets lay behind that headline would have to wait.

The turquoise waters of Exuma shimmered under the Bahamian sun as Sean adjusted his captain's hat, a cheap souvenir he'd bought to look the part. This was his first official day as a tour guide, and he was determined to impress. A small but lively group of tourists filled his boat, chatting excitedly about the swimming pigs at Pig Beach.

The ride started smoothly. Sean expertly maneuvered the small boat over the crystal-clear waves, cracking jokes and pointing out sights. His passengers, a mix of honeymooners, retirees, and an influencer livestreaming the experience, were all in high spirits. That was, until they reached the pigs.

As the boat approached the shore, a dozen plump, eager pigs splashed into the water, paddling toward them with determined snouts sniffing the air for treats. Sean grinned. "Alright, folks, time to meet your swimming companions! Just be careful. These pigs are friendly but very food motivated."

The tourists climbed into the shallow water, giggling as the pigs swam up to them, oinking and snuffling curiously. Everything was going smoothly until the last woman on the boat, a sprightly retiree named Marge, let out a sudden shriek.

"My snack bag!" she yelped, holding it high as a particularly large pig eyed her with laser focus.

"Just drop it!" Sean advised, but Marge panicked, spinning away and losing her footing. With a spectacular splash, she toppled backward into the water, arms flailing, the snack bag soaring through the air like a golden ticket.

The pigs were quick. One launched itself up, catching the bag mid-air, while another took advantage of the moment to chase after Marge, who was now scrambling to her feet, squealing louder than the pigs themselves. The influencer's phone was shaking from the laughter as she filmed the entire event.

Eventually, Marge was safely back on her feet, albeit soaking wet, and the snack-thieving pig was happily munching on its loot.

As his first tour successfully ended, Sean took a final headcount. "Well, folks, they say every tour is an adventure. I'd say we nailed that one."

The boat erupted with cheers and laughter. Sean may have been a rookie but judging by the delighted faces of his guests, and the sheer amount of laughter shared, he knew one thing for sure: he'd never forget his first day on the job.

≈

At the sun slowly moved down towards the horizon, Sean stood in his home, eyes locked on the masterpiece that was his 'Evidence Board'. The twine cords jetted out like a web of secrets, each thread a connection, a clue. He stretched one taut from Argentina to the right, past Gretchen, the striking model in Germany, before pressing a fresh Post-it-note into place. *Male, Argentina, 30 million.* The words, scrawled in his hurried script, pulsed with significance.

Moving swiftly to his desk, he scanned through a handful of news reports in under ten minutes: a single article, written by a journalist who had stood mere feet away when Manuel Perez's world tilted on its axis. The moment the shocking announcement was made. Sean's fingers tightened around the page. *This* was it. The golden thread he needed.

April 2024
Nozomi

When Nozomi stepped into the restaurant, the familiar hum of chatter and the occasional burst of laughter wrapped around her like a warm embrace. The scent of freshly baked bread and simmering broth filled the air, but it wasn't the food that drew people here. It was the people themselves, the ones serving, the ones being served, and the beautiful, unpredictable chaos between them.

Her mother, Kimora, moved between tables, her simple uniform neatly pressed, though she had already forgotten who handed it to her that morning. There was a delicate waver in her step, but her smile, bright, eager, never faltered. She stopped at a table; pen poised above a notepad and listened to the couple's order with furrowed concentration.

"Two coffees and a slice of..."

Kimora nodded. "Yes. Two lemonades and a whole cake."

The couple laughed saying that would be fine as well. She chuckled along, scribbling something down, though Nozomi knew it wouldn't make much difference. By the time Kimora reached the counter, the order was soup, a single slice of bread with five egg rolls.

And that was okay, because, for just one day this week, in this little restaurant located in Yokohama, Japan, mistakes were part of the charm.

The servers all had dementia, and instead of that being a flaw, it was a feature. Patrons didn't go there for perfection; they went for the joy of imperfection. They went to be surprised by a meal that wasn't quite what they expected but was somehow perfect anyway.

Nozomi watched as one waiter absentmindedly sat down with a family, chatting away as if he was part of the gathering. Another server handed a menu to a guest and asked them to take the table's orders, momentarily forgetting their own role. No one minded. In fact, they embraced it. They laughed, they adjusted, they made space for the unexpected.

It wasn't always easy for Nozomi to see it this way. When the diagnosis first came, when her mother started forgetting birthdays, burning toast, calling Nozomi by her sister's name, it felt like watching the foundation of her world slowly crumble. But here, in this space where confusion wasn't a burden but a shared experience, she saw something else.

She saw her mother, not as someone slipping away, but as someone still here, still laughing, still serving, still connecting in the most human way possible.

The restaurant didn't just provide meals. It provided moments, sweet, strange, heartwarming moments that reminded everyone who walked through the door that life was unpredictable, that mistakes were inevitable, and that sometimes, getting coffee with a saltshaker was the best thing that could happen to you.

And as Kimora delivered a plate of wonton noodles to a man who ordered a Sushi Bento box, beaming as if she'd done the job perfectly, Nozomi found herself smiling too.

Because maybe, in this little corner of the world of Yokohama, Japan, she had.

≈

Stepping out of the restaurant, Nozomi felt a quiet warmth settle in her chest. At last, she could breathe easy. Her mother was cared for; her days painted with laughter and light. The weight of worry that had once pressed against her heart had lifted, replaced by something far sweeter: peace.

It all began with a simple mistake; a dumpling served instead of a burger. A Japanese television director*, visiting a nursing home, had smiled at the mix-up, but something deeper stirred within him. He saw not just an error, but a truth; in a world that often rushes to correct, there was grace in acceptance. If he could embrace these small confusions, why couldn't others? If kindness outweighed precision, what possibilities could unfold?

And so, the idea took root. One by one, restaurants, cafés, and bakeries opened their doors, dedicating a day each week to an extraordinary experiment. Patrons arrived knowing that their order might not be what they expected, perhaps a coffee instead of tea, or cake instead of bread, but that was part of the magic. The beauty wasn't in the accuracy; it was in the experience, the shared smiles, the simple act of inclusion.

Word spread like wildfire. Soon, lines curled around corners, eager customers waiting to see what surprise might land on their plates. News outlets covered the phenomenon, praising its heart and humanity. But beyond the headlines, beyond the viral stories, was something even greater: a world learning, ever so gently, that imperfection could be a gift, and that in embracing it, everyone could find a little more joy.

April 2024
Dee

She didn't know if it was luck, life's mysteries, or karma at play, but whatever it was, she found it almost comical. Amazing, wonderful things were happening all around her, yet she was struggling to hold on to the happiness and joy she was now experiencing in fleeting moments. *'If only I could hold on to that joy just a little longer...'*

As the final days of the year had slipped away, tragedy struck. Mark, her beloved husband, had fallen ill: just a fever, he had insisted, nothing more than a stubborn flu. But as the days dragged on, his strength waned, his body betraying him in ways neither of them had expected. For a week, Dee watched over him, hoping, praying he would shake it off. But when his breathing grew shallow and his skin turned pale, a dreadful certainty settled in her chest. It was no longer just a fever. It was time to get him to the doctor, though, deep down, she feared it might already be too late.

"Damn you, Dee. I'm fine. It's just a bad case of the flu. Go get me some more pills. I'll be better in a few days."

Irritated, Dee shook her head. "I'm just trying to help. I hate seeing you in such pain and misery. What can I get you?"

"Pills. That's all. Now leave me alone. I just want to sleep."

He never woke up.

The next morning, after finishing her coffee, Dee decided to check on Mark. *He should have at least gotten up for a glass of water by now.*

She knocked on his bedroom door. Nothing. A chill ran through her body. Slowly, she opened the door and stepped into the dark, solemn room. The air was stale and cold. Her heart skipped a beat as she flipped the light switch. She gasped for air.

There, on the large bed, lay Mark, pale, with bluish-purple tinges in his skin. She stared. No breathing. No movement.

In shock, she walked over to the side of the bed, her hand trembling as she reached out. "Mark... Mark..." she whispered, touching his arm. It was ice-cold. She yanked her hand back, now shaking beyond her control. Her breathing quickened, and a wave of dizziness washed over her. "Oh my... what do I do?"

She turned and rushed out of the room, her feet carrying her to the kitchen on instinct. Grabbing her cell phone with trembling hands, she dialed the first number that came to mind.

"Please answer," she whispered, each ring feeling unbearably long.

"Morning, sunshine! To what do I owe this early call?" Claire's cheerful voice filled the silence. "Shouldn't you be out on your walk right now?"

Silence.

"Dee? You there?"

Claire could hear her friend's ragged breathing. "Dee, what's up? I can hear you. Do I need to come over?" More silence. Shallow, shaky breaths. "Okay, I'm coming over."

Claire moved fast shoving her feet into shoes, grabbing her jacket and purse, and racing to her car. The hood of the car barely cleared the garage door as she backed out in a hurry.

Within minutes, she pulled into the Dees' driveway. Dee stood outside in the crisp fall air, wearing nothing but her nightgown, hyperventilating. She was pale, visibly distraught.

Claire threw the car into park, jumped out, and ran to her. "Oh, my dear Dee. Let's go inside. Was it another argument with that husband of yours?" She reached out, wrapping Dee in a hug, only for Dee to collapse into her arms.

"Whoa, there, girl. Let's not both fall over." Claire tightened her grip. "Come on, let's get inside, sit down, and you can tell me what's going on."

Helping Dee into the house, she guided her onto the loveseat. Dee began shaking uncontrollably, sobbing into her hands. Claire pulled a cozy throw blanket over her friend and held her close.

Gradually, Dee's breathing steadied, but her head shook back and forth. "I just don't understand. How could this have happened?"

Claire's brows furrowed. "Slow down. How could what have happened? You're worrying me. Take a deep breath and tell me."

Dee struggled to form words. Her eyes were red and puffy, her voice barely a whisper. "Mark... gone... asleep..."

Claire frowned. "Where did Mark go? Did he leave while you were asleep?"

Dee just shook her head. "No... he never woke up," she finally muttered. "He's still in his room. He's gone."

The realization hit Claire like a ton of bricks. "Wait… to be clear, are you saying he's dead?"

Dee choked on another sob, nodding. Claire knew she had to take charge. "I'll call 911 first. They'll tell us what to do next. Before I do, can you tell me exactly what happened? They'll ask when I call."

Dee's voice quivered as she recounted the morning's events, rocking back and forth as tears streamed down her face. Claire, dreading what she might find, wasn't eager to verify the story herself.

"Alright," Claire said, steadying herself. "One thing at a time. Let me make that call."

Sitting beside her friend, Claire dialed 911. Emergency responders arrived twenty minutes later. Neither Dee nor Claire was prepared for the extensive questioning that followed. Paramedics and officials asked Dee about Mark's medical history, medications, injuries, work, lifestyle, and much more.

When they questioned her about the infection on his leg, Dee's expression turned blank. "What injury?" she asked, dazed. "He told me he had the flu. He's been taking cold and flu medicine all week. He never said anything about an injury."

April 2024
Nozomi

Contentment warmed Nozomi's heart as she left the restaurant, knowing her mother was basking in its peaceful ambiance. She strolled through the familiar streets, each step drawing her closer to the cozy bakery where her father worked, a place that always smelled of warmth, sugar, and home.

The moment she stepped inside, he spotted her, his face lighting up as he hurried over, wrapping her in the same embrace he had since childhood. It was the kind of hug that made the world feel safe. After placing her order, she settled by the window, her gaze drifting to the park across the street, where cherry trees stood in full bloom, their soft pink petals dancing on the breeze.

A few moments later, her father approached with her order, his smile brimming with the quiet joy she had always known.

"You're looking good today, Dad," she said, her voice light, affectionate.

But his smile faltered. His brows knit together in confusion. And then...

"Do I know you?"

The words slammed into her like a physical blow. Nozomi's breath caught, the air around her turning thick, heavy. She searched his face, willing, pleading, for a flicker of recognition, for something, anything, that told her this was just a cruel joke. But his eyes, once so familiar, so full of warmth, were distant. Unknowing.

The scent of fresh pastries curled around her, suddenly suffocating. The soft murmur of customers faded into a hollow hum, drowned out by the deafening roar of her pulse.

"Dad..." Her voice trembled. "It's me."

He frowned, as if reaching for a memory just beyond his grasp.

Outside, the cherry blossoms swayed, their petals falling like tiny whispers of time, beautiful, fragile, slipping away before she could catch them.

April 2024
Sean

Sean had struck gold just weeks ago, quite literally, and he wasted no time seizing the moment. Without hesitation, he dialed Isabella Díaz, the sharp Argentine reporter whose article had merely skimmed the surface. But her voice on the other end of the line? That was where the real story began to unfold.

Isabella was more than willing to spill the details, her words weaving a picture far richer than what had been printed. The much-anticipated wine label reveal had been overshadowed by an unexpected frenzy, the buzz surrounding the Blank Checks app. Yet, behind the glitz of the event, there was something far more intriguing: the quiet power dynamics within the Perez family and their deep-seated ambitions.

Mr. Perez and his son-in-law, owners of 'El y Yo', were at the heart of it all. Pedro, the reporter revealed in a hushed, knowing tone, had little interest in his stake in the family fortune. He had always kept his distance from the world of wealth and power. But Manuel? He was a different story. Brimming with restless energy and a vision for change, he was eager to transform Mendoza and the surrounding regions.

When Sean finally got Manuel on the phone, the conversation flowed effortlessly. Manuel, a dreamer with fire in his soul, spoke passionately about his plans. The $30 million now at his disposal wasn't just a number. It was the key to a better future. Mendoza, nestled in the heart of Argentina's wine country, was his canvas. He painted a picture of modernized transportation, aid for the impoverished, and a thriving community reborn under his watch.

Pedro, on the other hand, had been a tougher nut to crack. His reluctance wasn't just disinterest. It was something deeper, something Sean hadn't quite put his finger on yet. But one thing was clear: the Perez family, despite their differences, was bound by loyalty. And no matter what storm was brewing, they would stand together.

Manuel's vision for Mendoza was nothing short of transformative. He spoke of sleek, modernized roads to connect the sprawling vineyards with the bustling city, an upgraded public transportation system to make life easier for workers and tourists alike, and funding for local schools to ensure future generations thrived. He envisioned revitalized marketplaces where artisans and winemakers could showcase their craft, a network of support for struggling families, and even a state-of-the-art cultural center to celebrate Mendoza's rich history. With $30 million at his disposal, Manuel was determined to turn his hometown into a beacon of progress, where tradition and innovation could finally walk hand in hand.

Sean managed to pry a few more details from Manuel, though they came in fragments. He learned how the app reached out to him, the brief window of notice he was given before the meetup, and just a sliver, hardly anything at all, about the three towering figures who had orchestrated the entire encounter.

Cross-referencing the online app with the tangled web of notes pinned to his 'Evidence Board,' Sean's pulse quickened. A pattern emerged, one so subtle, so meticulously hidden, that only a trained investigator would catch it. The dates. Every selection of a new contestant aligned with the new moon. That meant the next video drop wasn't random, it was scheduled. April 8.

His mind churned with unanswered questions, but one loomed above the rest: where was the IP address originating from? He had exhausted every tool, every trick in his arsenal, only to hit a digital dead end. Whoever was behind this was using an advanced cloaking technology, one so impenetrable, so ahead of its time, that it might as well be a ghost.

April 7, 2024
Nozomi

As the world buzzed with excitement over the upcoming total solar eclipse of April 2024, the Japanese would be watching with a mix of fascination and admiration. Though this eclipse wouldn't pass over Japan, many space enthusiasts followed the news closely, captivated by the sheer wonder of celestial mechanics. For some, witnessing a total eclipse was a bucket list dream, an awe-inspiring moment of cosmic alignment that felt like a "now or never" experience. Japan's deep-rooted appreciation for astronomy and the mysteries of the universe fueled the intrigue, as social media lit up with images, live streams, and reactions from those lucky enough to stand in the moon's fleeting shadow.

The rare cosmic spectacle was set to darken the skies over Mexico and parts of the United States in just eighteen hours. The world felt suspended in time, waiting. Nozomi and her friends were amongst those eager for the event that would occur in the middle of the night. The group sat together beneath the vast, inky sky, chatting not only about the upcoming event, but about life and their dreams.

Her best friend, Ekiko, grinning with the mischief of someone who had just thought of something absurdly brilliant, turned to the group. "Let's all make a wish," she said. "Let's see if our wishes will come true before the eclipse. My wish is for the Blank Check."

A few friends chuckled, but Nozomi scoffed, shaking her head. "You're crazy," she said. "Do you even know what your chances are of getting chosen? Wish for something real, something that means something. You never know, it might just come true."

Her best friend arched an eyebrow. "Oh yeah? Then what's your wish, smarty pants?"

Nozomi hesitated, her gaze lifting to the sky. She closed her eyes for a second, feeling the universe hum around her. And then, with a deep breath, she whispered,

"I wish to live my passion. I want to be a photographer."

The words sent a shiver through her, as if the universe had heard. In the hush of the moment, silent wishes were sent into the void, carried by the whisper of the eclipse's upcoming magic. Nozomi clasped her hands together, her heart echoing a quiet longing. Becoming a photographer felt like an impossible dream, one she hardly dared to voice, but even that seemed more within reach than winning the app game's impossible lottery.

Her job as a computer analyst was stable, predictable. It paid the bills. But it never set her soul on fire. Not like photography did.

She still remembered the weight of her very first digital camera, a gift from her father on her twentieth birthday. Eighteen years had passed since then. Eighteen years of weekend pilgrimages into the heart of Japan's countryside, chasing light and shadow, capturing the land she loved through her lens. She had sold a handful of her best shots, small victories in a world that often felt impenetrable. But breaking into the mainstream had proven elusive, and with time, she had retreated. Photography became hers alone again, a private joy shared only with herself and the small, devoted circle who followed her work online.

Yet, standing there beneath the darkened sky, she couldn't help but wonder: what if?

April 8, 2024
Sean

Sean jolted upright in bed, his breath ragged, his mind racing. The darkness of his room felt suffocating, thick with the weight of realization. How could he have missed this? The cosmic event was imminent, its significance undeniable. And now, a gratifying possibility took over his thoughts. Was the mastermind deliberately going to choose the next contestant to coincide with the solar eclipse?

His heart pounded against his ribs like a frantic drum. Fatigue threatened to pull him back into its grasp, a cruel reminder that in just a few hours, he'd be guiding another group of giddy tourists to the infamous Pig Beach. But sleep was out of the question now.

He collapsed back onto the mattress, staring at the ceiling, his mind a whirlwind of theories and anticipation. The patterns were revealing themselves, the puzzle pieces clicking into place. He was getting closer. Closer to unraveling the mystery. Closer to deciphering the rhythm of The Game.

April 9, 2024
Nozomi

Nozomi and her friends had gathered in their beloved park in Yokohama; their eyes fixed on the digital screen as the universe prepared to perform one of its most breathtaking spectacles. The computer screen flickered with a live feed, an astronomical ballet unfolding in real time, the moon inching ever closer, poised to eclipse the sun in a celestial embrace that had played out for eons.

Excitement crackled through the group like lightning before a summer storm. Across the globe, news outlets blazed with reports, the eclipse had already cast its shadow over Mexico and was racing toward the United States and Canada. But here, in this fleeting, ethereal moment, none of that mattered. Time seemed to hold its breath, the air thick with an almost sacred stillness. It was more than an astronomical event, it was a whisper from the cosmos, a reminder of the infinite wonders just beyond their reach.

The eclipse came and went in the blink of an eye. Nozomi and her friends, bleary-eyed and heavy-limbed, parted ways in the quiet aftermath, each retreating to the warmth of their own beds, desperate to reclaim what little sleep they could before the demands of the day took hold.

Nozomi barely had the strength to slip under the covers before sleep pulled her under. But just as she drifted into that dark abyss, a voice, soft yet insistent, whispered her name from the shadows of her room. Her drowsy mind dismissed it as a remnant of some fleeting dream, and she surrendered once more to slumber.

The relentless chime of her alarm shattered the illusion of rest just hours later. Groggy but determined, she rushed through her morning routine, eager to grab a coffee and a flaky pastry, small comforts before plunging into the monotony of her uninspiring job.

As the city stretched and yawned into wakefulness, she scrolled absentmindedly through her messages. Nothing urgent. Nothing exciting. Just the usual digital clutter. With time to kill, she tapped open a social media app, expecting idle distraction.

Then, her phone spoke.

The voice, the same one from her dream, called out to her again.

Dazed and sluggish, Nozomi listened carefully, instantly becoming alert when hearing the end of the message; "**This afternoon, at Kogane Studio.**" A slow chill ran down her spine. *That's where my photos were displayed years ago... How strange.*

She sat motionless, the weight of the moment sinking in. Should she bring her parents? Her friends? The thought nagged at her, but in the end, she knew. This was something she had to face alone. The bigger question loomed: *How much should I write on the check?*

The realization sent a shiver through her. *This wasn't just a meeting. This could be a life changing moment.*

The hours at work crawled, each second stretching unbearably long. How was she supposed to focus knowing that, by sundown, everything could be different? Eventually, she made an excuse. Her father had just moved in with her mother at the Dementia Housing and she needed to go visit. It wasn't a lie, but it wasn't the reason she needed to leave.

When she arrived at Kogane Studio, her heart pounded. Outside, waiting for her, stood her friend, Katsuro, the studio's owner, a knowing smile playing on their lips.

"Nozomi, you made it. This is exciting."

Her stomach twisted. "You know?"

"I got a call earlier. They explained everything. Even paid me to close the shop for an hour." Her friend gestured toward the door. "They said you'd arrive at three. And here you are. Come in, they're waiting."

"They?"

The single word barely escaped her lips. Her pulse throbbed in her ears. Her mind, once sharp, began to blur, lost in a whirlwind of possibilities. What do I write? Any number, even the smallest, would be more than her parents had earned in a lifetime. More than she herself could ever dream of making. And yet... this could mean everything.

A future where she didn't have to work for survival. Where photography wasn't just a side passion, but *the* passion. Where she could create, free of worry, free of limits.

Nozomi took a breath and stepped inside.

As Nozomi followed Katsuro into the dimly lit back room of the studio, she was met with a sight that sent a ripple of unease through her. Towering over six feet tall, three figures stood in silent formation, a striking duo of men and a woman, all impeccably dressed in black and white. Their presence was commanding, their height an anomaly among her people. To see one so tall was rare. To see three at once felt almost surreal.

"Welcome, Nozomi-san." The first man's voice was smooth, deliberate. "Congratulations on being the fifth chosen contestant. Soon, you will have the opportunity to inscribe your desired amount on this digital check."

With a practiced flourish, the second man unfurled a sleek device, its screen glowing with the image of a virtual check. "You will write your amount in the air over the display," he continued. "But before we proceed, you must decide, do you wish to remain anonymous when the video is posted?"

Nozomi's mind swam. The weight of the decision pressed against her ribs. She had studied the past winners, traced the staggering sums they had dared to claim, millions, every one of them. Her fingers twitched, her thoughts scattered like leaves in a storm.

"Yes... you can film me," she murmured, her voice barely above a breath.

The second man stepped forward, and the tall woman mirrored his movement, lifting a small, modern recording device with meticulous precision. Nozomi swallowed hard. Her pulse pounded in her ears as she raised a trembling hand and began to write, tracing invisible numbers in the air. Seven million. The moment the last digit appeared; a chime rang out.

As her phone chimed in her pocket, the blank check device darkened, then erupted in a cascade of virtual fireworks. A golden banner flashed across the screen: Congratulations to Nozomi from Yokohama, Japan. Seven Million.

A tingling sensation spread through her limbs, cold and electric. The room spun. Shapes twisted, stretched. She saw Katsuro's face, his expression frozen in shock. The tall woman blurred, her body tilting unnaturally to the side. Then, sharp pain. A searing jab to her shoulder. And then, darkness.

The hospital room was flooded with an almost blinding light as Nozomi's eyes fluttered open. A familiar blur of faces surrounded her:

Ekiko, Hatsumi, Lian, and right beside her, Katsuro. Their expressions shifted from anxious anticipation to overwhelming relief as she stirred.

"Nozomi, you're awake!" Ekiko's voice, as lively as ever, filled the room. "How are you feeling?"

A dull ache pulsed in Nozomi's shoulder as she tried to sit up, and before she could fully grasp where she was, Lian jumped in. "You had us riding a rollercoaster of emotions! First, we were all shocked, thrilled, then suddenly worried sick when you didn't answer your phone. Katsuro called us back to say you fainted. Honestly, I probably would have too: seven million dollars! That's an absurd amount of money!"

Seven million dollars. The words slammed into her like a wave, making her dizzy all over again. The hospital walls seemed to tilt.

"Water... can I have some water, please?" she murmured weakly.

Katsuro was already there, holding a glass steady as she sipped through a straw. The cool liquid soothed her throat, but not the whirlwind of confusion inside her.

"So, it wasn't a dream?" Her voice was barely above a whisper. "I still don't understand."

Katsuro's gaze softened. "I think you're in shock. You collapsed so fast that I could not catch you before you hit the floor. The doctor says it's going to hurt for a while, but no broken bones. That's the good news."

"It's all on video," Hatsumi added matter-of-factly.

Nozomi's breath caught in her throat. "Wait... you mean they filmed everything? Including me fainting?"

Panic set in as fragments of the moment replayed in her mind. She had agreed to let them film her, but she hadn't thought, hadn't realized, they'd capture the entire incident. Her vision blurred as tears welled up.

Katsuro, sensing her distress, spoke gently. "The Blank Checks app only posted up to the moment before you fainted. But... I did record the whole thing. Don't worry, no one else will see it except us."

Her heart pounded against her ribs. It was too much, too surreal.

Then, as the weight of everything settled, Lian broke the silence with the question that hung in the air: "What we all want to know is… what are you going to do with all that money?"

Nozomi stared at her hands, at the life-altering reality now at her fingertips. The possibilities stretched before her like an open road; one she never dared to believe she could walk.

A slow, determined smile touched her lips.

"I'm going to travel. Be a photographer. Publish my own book capturing the pure beauty of Japan," she said, the vision taking form as she spoke. "I'll explore all eight regions, show the world the magic hidden in every corner."

Her voice steadied, her heart lightened.

"It's hard to believe… I don't have to work anymore. I am free."

*Japanese television director, Shiro Oguni, created this business to change perceptions about aging and progressive cognitive impairment. mistakenorders.com

6

May 2024
Matteo

Matteo stepped off the bus in Baruffini, inhaling the crisp northern Italian mountain air, tinged with the scent of woodsmoke and fresh bread. After ten years in the nonstop chaos of New York City, the quiet charm of his childhood village felt almost unreal. He walked the familiar, winding road toward his mother's house, the same stone cottage where he'd grown up, now framed by the deep green of the Valtellina hills. Before he could even knock, the door flew open.

"Ah! Look who it is!" said his mother, Mamma Alessandra, arms flung wide. "Ten years in America and what do you bring me? Wrinkles! Gray hair! A mother's suffering!"

Matteo laughed, sweeping her into a hug. "Mamma, you had gray hair when I left!"

"Shh! Details," she said, smacking his arm lightly. "Come inside before you freeze, city boy."

The house smelled like rosemary, garlic, and something baking in the oven. Matteo took his usual seat at the wooden kitchen table as his mamma bustled around, pouring him a glass of red wine before sitting across from him with a knowing smirk.

"You're too skinny. Do they not feed you in America? Or are you on one of those silly diets?"

Matteo laughed, shaking his head. "Mamma, I eat just fine. But I have missed your cooking."

"Aha! So that's why you're here," she said, wagging a finger. "Not for your dear mother, but for my lasagna! Typical man, always thinking with his stomach."

Matteo laughed as he sat at the cozy kitchen table, surrounded by a feast fit for royalty, silky prosciutto, aged cheeses, briny olives, honey-drizzled figs, and crisp nuts, all laid out like a painter's palette. With a glass of wine in hand, Matteo savored every bite, but his gaze kept drifting to his mother. She moved through the kitchen with effortless grace, tossing ingredients into the pan as if composing a symphony, each sizzle and stir a note in the melody of home. He grinned, watching her work.

"You know, Mamma," he said, swirling his wine, "in New York, people pay a fortune for pasta like yours."

She snorted. "Then they are fools! Good food should not cost your whole paycheck."

As they ate, stories tumbled out between bites. Matteo spoke of skyscrapers and Broadway shows, and Alessandra countered with tales of the latest village gossip, who had eloped, whose chickens had mysteriously vanished, and which neighbor had suddenly found religion after a lifetime of cursing. The house filled with laughter, echoing through the wooden beams, as if time had never passed at all.

"So, tell me, does New York have lasagna like mine?"

"Not even close," he admitted, taking a sip of his wine.

She threw her hands in the air. "Finally! The boy has learned something in America!"

They laughed, their voices echoing off the stone walls, filling the little house with warmth.

Matteo's return home was a bittersweet symphony, a tug-of-war between nostalgia and longing. He adored the village's timeless charm, the way it perched on the mountainside like a secret whispered through generations. Baruffini was a place where history clung to every weathered stone, where slate-roofed houses huddled together beneath the watchful gaze of the Church of St. Peter Martyr. Vineyards cascaded down terraced slopes, their emerald rows a lifeline for the families who had tilled this land for centuries.

Yet, the very essence of this place, its steep, winding paths, its relentless inclines, set his city, softened legs on fire. There was no such thing as flat ground here; balance was a perpetual battle, a dance with gravity that he had long since forgotten. It was the cruel irony of home; it embraced him with one arm while pushing him away with the other.

And then, there was New York. His pulse quickened at the mere thought of it. The city wasn't just a place; it was his muse, his electricity, his rebirth. Every street corner hummed with possibility; every skyline silhouette felt like a promise. More than that, it was where fate had intervened, where, in the dim glow of Zia Maria's candlelit tables in Little Italy, he had met the love of his life, just one week into his arrival. New York had not only awakened him; it had claimed him. And no matter how picturesque Buraffini might be, his heart still beat to the rhythm of a city that never slept.

At fifty and still flourishing, Matteo never believed in fate until the evening he met Tony. The warm glow of the candlelit Italian restaurant cast soft shadows on the walls as he stirred his espresso, lost in thought. Then, Tony walked in, dark curls tousled, eyes gleaming with quiet mischief, and suddenly, the world shifted. Their gazes locked across the room, and in that instant, Matteo knew. The clatter of plates, the murmured conversations, the scent of basil and wine, all faded into the background. Only Tony remained, a presence so magnetic that Matteo couldn't help but smile, knowing his life had just changed. Ten years later, their partnership still intertwined as they strolled through the same busy streets, laughter dancing between them like an old, familiar melody. Love, Matteo realized, wasn't fate, it was a choice, made every day, and with Tony, it was the easiest one he'd ever made.

As Matteo returned from his walk, he lifted his gaze to his mother's home, a place etched into his very bones. His legs throbbed with every step, and he shook his head, exhaling sharply. How had he never considered what this unforgiving terrain demanded of his ninety-year-old mother?

The house stood resilient against time, its thick stone walls whispering tales of generations past. The entrance loomed above him, reachable only by a steep, uneven flight of stacked stone stairs, each step worn by decades of footsteps, yet still defiant against nature's grasp. Midway up, a weathered wooden ladder jutted out awkwardly, its uneven legs precariously balanced between two stairs. It offered access to a small, wooden balcony, the planks warped and aged by countless seasons.

Matteo had never dared to use that frail, looking balcony to reach his room. The thought alone made his stomach tighten. No, he always chose the safer, more familiar path, the sturdy stone stairs leading to the grand front door. That door, one of the oldest in the village, was a relic of craftsmanship lost to time. Made of thick, darkened hardwood, its intricate carvings had long been obscured by the years, yet it still opened effortlessly, as if the house itself welcomed him home.

As he stepped onto the cool slate floor of the entryway, the scent of his childhood enveloped him. The rich, warm aroma of freshly baked bread transported him back to simpler days, he and his twin sister, Angelica, racing to be the first to steal a bite of their mother's golden-crusted loaves.

He stared at the photograph, his fingers tracing the edges as if touching it could bring her back. His beloved sister, his other half, gone too soon, ripped away by fate's cruel hand. Their bond had begun in the quiet sanctuary of the womb, where they floated together in warmth, whispering secrets only they could understand. The world had welcomed them with cold indifference, their first breath taken without the soothing presence of their mother. Complications from the home birth had stolen her away before they even had the chance to know her, leaving their father shattered and adrift.

It was Alessandra and Alfonso Iantosca, a childless couple with open arms and aching hearts, who stepped in when their father could not. They scooped up the grieving twins and wove them into the fabric of their family, giving them a second chance at love, at belonging.

Angelica was wild and free, a spirit that refused to stay put. She danced through life like a gust of mountain air, drawn to the untamed beauty of the outdoors. Matteo, ever the quiet observer, found solace in stillness, painting the very landscapes his sister longed to lose herself in or getting lost in the crackling voices of the radio. They never quarreled, only exchanged playful jabs, their teasing a language all their own.

And then came adolescence, the years of transformation. Angelica bloomed first, a radiant wildflower catching every gaze, laughter spilling from her like sunlight. Matteo followed at his own pace, trailing behind by a year, until suddenly, the world noticed him too. The angles of his face sharpened, his once, boyish features sculpting themselves into something striking. But no matter how much they changed, they were always halves of the same whole, an unbreakable bond.

Until the world broke them apart.

Some whispered of a tragic accident, others swore it was envy's cruel hand at play. But none of it changed the truth. Angelica was gone, stolen from this world far too soon. And Matteo? He was a man undone, his soul fractured, his heart a ruin of what once was.

May 2024
Sean

They all said it was impossible. That no outsider could waltz in and build a thriving business in a month. But that's exactly what fueled Sean to defy the odds.

Armed with nothing but a simple website offering boat tours to Pig Beach, he assumed he'd have time to ease into things, maybe sip a few cocktails on the shore while waiting for the first reservations to trickle in. Instead, he found himself booked solid, months in advance. Tourists clamored for a seat on his modest eight-passenger boat, eager for a front-row view of dazzling white sand beaches, hidden tropical enclaves, and, of course, the world, famous swimming pigs.

Sean had planned an easygoing gig, just three tours a week to keep his mind engaged and his social life afloat. A loner at heart, he refused to slip back into the shadows of solitude. He was not going to become the burned-out workaholic of the past. For two months, he had thrived on the excitement of his tours and was glad it had all fallen into place.

But his mind was fixated on something far more unnerving. Someone had sent him a message, from an untraceable IP address, and it contained just one thing, his birth name.

Stewart O'Cleary. A name he hadn't heard in many years.

Twenty-five years prior, with the dawn of Y2K just a year away, he was only twenty, young, eager, and freshly hired at Tillman Investigations in Boston. The team had insisted: he needed an alias, a name that wasn't his own, a shield to protect both himself and his parents from the unseen dangers that came with the job. A new identity. A new life. And with it, the weight of secrets he hadn't yet begun to understand. They assured him his birthname would be buried so deep in redacted files that no one could ever dig it up.

And yet, someone had.

May 2024
Undisclosed Location

The thrill of the moment surged through him, electrifying his senses beyond anything he had ever imagined. The world's insatiable hunger for wealth and power was a force he understood all too well; people believed that to have it all was to grasp happiness itself. If only they knew.

His fingers absently traced the engraving on his pen, a cherished symbol of love and devotion. As he stared into the distance, his mind slipped effortlessly into the past, a tide pulling him back to the golden days of his youth. Eighteen. The kind of love that others dismissed as fleeting, a passing infatuation. But they had known better. Bound by an unbreakable bond from the moment they met at the International School of Zurich, those two years were a whirlwind of joy and heartache. He clung to the memories, each one a vivid echo of what once was, yet an ache remained, an unshakable longing for a feeling he had never found again.

Then, as swiftly as a summer storm, she was gone. No note, no explanation, just an empty space where she had once been. He returned from his family's vacation expecting the warmth of her presence, only to be met with an unbearable void. It shattered him. His heart, his soul, his very will to keep moving forward. But they had made a promise, one he vowed never to break.

Years passed, and the path he had charted took longer than he had imagined, but here he stood, on the precipice of a dream they had once whispered to the stars. A dream not for riches or recognition, but to uplift others, to leave the world better than they had found it. Never in a lifetime would he have believed it would grow to this magnitude.

But *she* would never see it. Never marvel at what they had dreamt of building together. The truth, discovered far too late, was a cruel dagger. Tragedy had stolen her away, along with her family, long before he had returned on that fateful summer. The silence, the unanswered questions, had been a shield, a mercy from those who loved him. They had kept the truth from him to protect his fragile heart.

And yet, as he stood here now, he smiled. Because promises, true promises, never die.

A soft but deliberate knock echoed through the fortress of his encrypted world, a whisper against an iron-clad silence. Someone was trying to break through, not for riches, not for power, but for the sheer thrill of the game itself.

Intrigued, he dove headfirst into the hunt, his voice commanding searches, eyes scanning lines of data like a predator tracking its prey. And then, there it was. The answer he sought materialized before him, taunting and undeniable.

"Well, well… Detective Leblanc, or should I say, Stewart O'Cleary? It seems you've taken quite an interest in me. How delightful."

The message dripped with amusement; a challenge wrapped in mystery.

"This is going to be fun. Keep digging. You'll have to overturn a mountain of stones before you unearth the truth but trust me, there's far more to find than you ever imagined."

May 9, 2024
Alessandra

He glanced around and sighed. "Mamma, you really should think about updating this place," he said, his voice laced with both concern and nostalgia. "It's starting to look like an artifact from another time. And that balcony off my room…" He let out a low chuckle. "It doesn't look safe, but I have to admit, the view of Tirano from up there still takes my breath away."

Mamma Alessandra barely looked up from her work in the kitchen, her hands steady, her expression unreadable. For a few moments, silence hummed between them, filled only by the rhythmic chopping of vegetables. Then, as if gathering invisible threads of courage, she set down her knife and exhaled deeply.

"My dear son," she said at last, her voice calm but carrying a weight that made Matteo sit up straighter. "Come with me to the bench. There is something I must tell you."

His brow furrowed. "Mamma… are you alright? Is something wrong?"

"No, nothing is wrong." She wiped her hands on her apron and met his gaze with an unwavering steadiness. "Just walk with me."

There was something about her tone, something firm, yet fragile, that silenced any protest. Though confusion gnawed at him, he rose and followed her out the door, his legs still aching from his earlier walk. They moved through the quiet streets, past stone cottages and shuttered windows, until they reached the start of the forested hiking path.

Matteo eyed the incline warily. "Mamma, shouldn't we have our hiking sticks? If I remember correctly, this path is steep."

She scoffed, waving a hand. "You silly city boy. It's only two minutes to the bench."

He wanted to argue, but there was a nervous energy about her, something unspoken pressing at the edges of her movements. He swallowed his questions and trudged after her. The rugged path, uneven and slick with old leaves, forced him to focus on each step, but his ninety-year-old mother moved with the nimbleness of a mountain goat.

And then, just as the trees thinned, he saw it.

Perched on a flattened stretch of earth, a massive bench, a brilliant, almost comically large red bench, stood against the backdrop of the valley. It was so out of place, so unexpected, that for a moment, Matteo could only stare.

With surprising agility, his mamma Alessandra climbed up the side of the oversized bench, her tiny frame dwarfed by its grand proportions. Matteo followed, struggling a bit but managing to hoist himself up beside her. When he finally settled, he let out a slow breath.

Before them, the valley unfurled like a painting. Tirano's rooftops nestled in the basin below, framed by the snow-dusted peaks of the Alps standing like silent sentinels in the distance. The sky stretched endlessly, a masterpiece of soft blues and gold-tinged clouds.

"This…" Matteo exhaled, still drinking in the sight. "This is new." He turned to her, curiosity burning in his chest. "What's the story behind this?"

His mother's lips curled into a knowing smile, her eyes glinting with something that made his stomach tighten.

The moment had arrived. But first, the bench. Placed there in 2022, it wasn't just a seat, it was an invitation. A portal for grown-ups to slip back into childhood wonder, to drink in the landscape with fresh eyes, to share a quiet moment or rediscover themselves. A place to surrender to the art of doing nothing, utterly and blissfully.

The vision had taken root in 2009, a designer's dream* to uplift local communities by placing these oversized benches in breathtaking, hidden away corners of Italy. Each one, a reason to wander off the beaten path, to pause, to marvel.

This one, majestic, waiting, was #218.

Alessandra took in the landscape as she gathered her wits at the news she was about to share with her son. Patiently, he waited.

"Many, many years ago, when I was just a child during the dark days of World War II, our quiet little village of Baruffini and the town of Tirano, nestled below us in the valley, fell under the iron grip of the Mussolini regime and the Nazi forces. Life became a series of hardships, empty cupboards, whispered fears, strict curfews, and the distant, terrifying echoes of bombs shattering the night."

"But the greatest danger wasn't just hunger or the soldiers patrolling our streets. It was the desperate hunt for those who were marked for death. Friends disappeared. Families were torn apart. And in the shadows of fear, my own family became part of a quiet rebellion, we hid those who were being hunted, guiding them toward the hope of freedom across to the Swiss border just over the mountain behind us."

"At just ten years old, I unknowingly became a smuggler of souls. For an entire year, I played the most dangerous game of hide and seek. Every week, I was given a simple task: take two children up into the mountains to "play." We would follow the secret animal trails, giggling and darting through the trees as if it were all just a grand adventure. Somewhere along the way, we would meet another group of children, and together, we would run through the fields and hide in the forests. And then, as the sun dipped behind the peaks and the sky bled into twilight, I would return home, alone."

"I didn't understand then what I was truly doing. To me, it was just a game, a strange ritual I had come to accept as normal. It wasn't until many years later that I realized I had been leading those children to safety, to life, to a future free from fear."

Matteo listened in quiet awe, the weight of the story settling over him like a heavy snowfall. He had heard whispers before, stories murmured by his grandparents, of a brave little Alessandra and the lives she had saved. But now, hearing it in her own words, it was no longer just a story, it was history, woven with courage, innocence, and the silent heroism of a child who had played a game that meant the difference between life and death.

"That's one heck of a story, mamma. I can only imagine how much courage it took to tell me that. Are you feeling any better now?"

She paused for a moment, then, with a mischievous glint in her eye, her lips curled into a knowing smile.

"There's more," she said, her voice thick with intrigue.

Matteo raised an eyebrow. "More? Mamma, your life is already wilder than a soap opera, and you haven't even left this tiny village!"

She chuckled. "Something... rather unusual happened the day before you arrived. And you won't believe where. Right here, on this very bench."

Matteo leaned in, a mischievous glint in his eyes and a grin stretching across his face. "Oh, this should be good. Come on, hit me with another one of your legendary escapades! Wait, let me guess. Someone from the big city sneaking off for a secret rendezvous with you?"

"You silly boy. You know that no one can ever replace your dear father. Alfonso was my world. No, my dear son, this is so much bigger than I could ever have imagined."

Matteo waited in silence, understanding the unspoken rule. His mother needed space. The gentle spring breeze moved around them, carrying the scent of wildflowers and the rustling whispers of the trees. The world stood still, draped in quiet beauty.

Alessandra turned to him, her eyes shimmering, a single tear slipping down her cheek. She inhaled deeply, steadying herself. Then, with a voice laced with disbelief and excitement, she said, "I don't know how else to tell you this, but... we've won the lottery."

Matteo erupted into laughter. His mother, the most practical woman he knew, would sooner throw money into a fire than waste it on a lottery ticket. The very idea was absurd. "You're hilarious! Have you ever considered stand-up comedy?"

But Alessandra's expression remained unchanged. No smirk, no wink, no hint of jest.

Matteo chuckled even harder. "You should play poker, mamma. No one would ever know when you're bluffing."

Her lips quivered slightly, but her voice was firm. "The joke is on you, my dear son. I didn't buy a lottery ticket. I was chosen as this month's contestant for the Blank Checks app. They came the day before you arrived, and I played their game. I used your lucky number seventeen. And it worked. We won." She paused, her voice catching. "Seventeen million dollars. Tax-free. Ours. I've been dying to tell you, but I didn't want to take away from the joy of having you here after all these years."

Matteo froze, his laughter dissolving into stunned silence. His mind reeled. The sum alone was staggering, but the real shock was his mother, of all people, winning a fortune through some app he had never even heard of.

Seeing the skepticism etched on his face, Alessandra reached for her phone. "Look," she urged, pulling up the site. The list of past winners, their videos, their stories, it was all there.

Matteo scanned the page, searching for this month's name. Nothing.

"There's no winner listed yet," he pointed out, crossing his arms. "Are you pulling my leg?"

She exhaled a soft laugh, her eyes twinkling. "That's the funny part. I asked them to wait until after you arrived before making the announcement. The news goes live this afternoon. I also chose to remain anonymous. I want us to keep our quiet, comfortable life, just you and me."

Matteo stared at her, his thoughts a storm of disbelief, excitement, and suspicion. It was too much to process. He needed proof. He needed to see it, feel it. Even the sight of the bank balance in her name wasn't enough. They'd have to spend some of it. Test it. Make sure it was real.

As he grappled with this surreal reality, his gaze drifted over the valley. And then, like a tide returning to shore, the longing for Tony swept over him. Even after ten years together, two weeks apart seemed like an eternity.

Matteo exhaled, letting the weight of it all settle into his bones. His mother's voice broke through his thoughts, gentle yet brimming with quiet anticipation.

"So, my son… what should we do with all this money?"

He had no answer. Not yet. He had two weeks before his return to New York, time enough to let it all sink in, to confirm this wild dream was real. And once he knew for certain, then he would decide.

For now, all he could do was wait.

May 9, 2024
Sean

The system was broken. Fractured in ways Sean hadn't yet grasped. Was the blank check really tied to the New Moon each month? If so, then the reveal should have happened two days ago. And yet, nothing. He raked a hand through his hair, frustration gnawing at him. Something was off, something he couldn't quite put his finger on. But he couldn't afford distractions. Not now.

Two pieces of the puzzle mattered most: the shifting IP address and the unsettling fact that someone had uncovered his name.

Four months of chasing shadows had left him empty-handed. The IP location was a mirage, constantly shifting, morphing into scrambled text and bizarre symbols. Gibberish, at least, to the untrained eye. But Sean refused to believe it was meaningless. There had to be logic buried in the chaos.

Determination settled in his bones. He would crack this. He had over a hundred days' worth of data, fragments of a bigger picture waiting to be pieced together. He cleared another wall, spreading the information out in a desperate attempt to make sense of it. Service provider details, internet protocols, everything changed, every single time he checked. There had to be a pattern.

No tours for the next two days. No distractions. No rest.

Sean leaned in, eyes narrowing as he scoured the symbols, searching for something, anything, that made sense. And then, like the first glimmers of dawn breaking through a fog, a pattern began to take shape. The letters, numbers, and symbols weren't random after all. They had an order. A rhythm.

He worked tirelessly, using every method he knew, every trick he had learned over the years. The realization hit him like a bolt of lightning, this wasn't just a code. It was a cipher.

Not just any cipher, but an intricate fusion of Sumerian, Pagan, and Viking runes. A language of its own, steeped in both artistry and mathematical precision. Someone had crafted this deliberately. Someone who knew exactly what they were doing.

Sean exhaled, sitting back as he studied the symbols he had deciphered. His mind buzzed with possibilities, but he needed a break. A moment to breathe, to clear the static in his head.

Pushing away from the desk, he decided, ocean first, lunch later. A swim to wash away the tension before diving back into the unknown.

May 9, 2024
Alessandra and Matteo

Alessandra could see it in Matteo's eyes, doubt, skepticism, the quiet resignation of someone humoring a tale he could barely believe. But she was determined to shatter that disbelief. Back at the house, she deftly followed the instructions given to her by the three tall, enigmatic men, transferring funds, making payments, proving that the money was real. Matteo sat at the table, stunned. It would take time for him to come to terms with his 8.5-million-dollar bank account.

It was a rare occasion, almost unheard of, for Alessandra to skip preparing a meal at home. But today wasn't just any day. Today, she would treat Matteo. She would indulge them both. And what better place than Trattoria del Simone, the heart of the village, the only restaurant in town, and a place filled with memories. Before the world caught wind of what was coming, before the news went live and everything changed, she would show her son that this was no illusion.

As they stepped into the cozy trattoria, the warm scent of simmering tomatoes and fresh basil wrapped around them like an embrace. Behind the counter, Luca, the ever-smiling owner and an old family friend, turned in surprise.

"My dear Alessandra! Is that really you?" His voice boomed with affection. Then, spotting the young man at her side, his face lit up with recognition. "And who do we have here? Matteo? Dio mio, it's been too long. What a joy to see you!"

Hugs were exchanged; kisses pressed to cheeks in the customary village way.

"Luca, today, Matteo and I are here for a meal," Alessandra announced with a proud smile. "A proper one. No pots, pans, nor dishes to wash. Just us, enjoying a well-earned break."

Luca beamed. Hosting the village's beloved matriarch was an honor. He took their order himself, and soon, mother and son found themselves on the vine-draped porch, gazing down at the familiar rooftops of their home, glasses of deep red wine in hand.

The courses arrived in their slow, delicious procession, an antipasto of glistening olives, marinated artichokes, and thinly sliced prosciutto; then the primi, a delicate ricotta-stuffed ravioli bathed in butter and sage. The secondi followed, rich and hearty, each bite a symphony of flavor.

Alessandra, savoring the moment, teased Luca with a playful grin. "This is almost as good as my cooking. Almost. Perhaps I should give you a lesson or two."

Luca let out a deep, knowing laugh. No one, absolutely no one, could rival Alessandra in the kitchen, and they all knew it.

Two hours later, satisfied and blissfully full, Alessandra leaned back with a contented sigh. It was time to head home, to retreat into the languid embrace of an afternoon nap. She waved Luca over, handed him her debit card, and when he returned with the bill, she added a tip, one so generous that his eyes widened in shock.

"Alessandra... cara mia, this is far too much! Surely, this is a mistake?"

She reached out, squeezing his hand. "No mistake, dear Luca. Consider it payment for all the years I foolishly hesitated to come and enjoy your food. Times have changed." She exhaled; a weight lifted from her shoulders. "I'll be back every week now. It will be my honor to finally enjoy your food."

Luca's eyes softened, understanding passing between them. "Then we'll have a table waiting for you, always."

And as she and Matteo stepped out into the golden afternoon, the village stretching out before them, Alessandra knew. Life was going to be relaxing and easier for her.

Mother and son wandered through the forest, their footsteps crunching softly against the leaf-strewn path. They passed the large red bench, then veered onto the narrow shortcut that would lead them back home. The air was crisp, carrying the scent of pine and damp earth, and for a moment, it felt as if time had slowed just for them.

"Promise me you'll visit more often," his mother said, her voice warm yet laced with longing. "And next time, bring that darling Tony. I'd love to meet him properly. He completes you. I can see it in your eyes."

Matteo smiled, squeezing her hand. "Maybe you should visit me instead," he countered, picturing her navigating the bustling streets of the city. He could already hear her delighted laughter as she soaked in the vibrant chaos of urban life, if only for a week.

After carefully splitting the money between their accounts and ensuring everything was settled, Matteo wasted no time changing his flight back, this time, indulging in a well, earned upgrade for a more luxurious journey home.

In the quiet moments before his departure, he threw himself into an exciting new venture: finding the perfect home for him and Tony. Within days, they had set their hearts on a breathtaking condo on Park Place, its floor-to-ceiling windows offering dazzling views of the New York City skyline, the Hudson River, and the historic charm of TriBeCa.

The building's white-glove concierge service promised effortless luxury, catering to their every need.

Within the week, Tony had given his enthusiastic approval, the contracts were signed, and the funds transferred. Their future was officially in motion. And with an extra room waiting, Matteo knew his mother would always have a place to stay, a promise of more visits, more shared moments, and more memories yet to come.

*Big Bench Community Project (BBCP), an initiative started in 2009 by American designer Chris Bangle and his wife Catherine. bigbenchcommunityproject.org

7

May 9, 2024
Sean

The ocean embraced him like an old friend, washing away the weight of his thoughts and the knots of tension in his muscles. The rhythmic pull of the waves guided him forward, a steady ten-minute swim from his floating platform to the enchanting Thunderball Grotto. The crystal-clear waters and diverse marine life melted away the hours as Sean navigated the intricate network of tunnels and chambers.

But then, the hum of approaching tourist boats shattered the tranquility. It was time to vanish. With a smirk, he reached for his latest toy, a sleek water propulsion scooter. Fingers tightening around the handles, he squeezed the throttle, and in an instant, he was no longer just swimming, he was flying. The scooter roared to life, surging him forward with a power his weary arms could never match, slicing through the water like a torpedo on a mission. The ocean was his playground, and for now, he was untouchable.

Back home, Sean trudged up the winding, stone-walled path, the sand still clinging to his skin, his mind buzzing with the day's discoveries. The scent of salt and tropical blooms mingled in the humid air as he stepped under the cool stream of the outdoor shower, nestled within a tangle of banana plants. Water sluiced over his sun-warmed skin, washing away the grit.

Relaxing into his hammock under the thatched-roof porch, he chose the musical rhythm of a guitar, lulling him into a heavy-limbed slumber. The world melted away, until the distant roar of jet skis shattered the silence. He stirred, stretching lazily as hunger gnawed at him.

Minutes later, he was weaving through the narrow coastal roads on his scooter, the wind crisp against his face. The yacht club was alive with quiet indulgence, the clinking of glasses, the murmur of moneyed voices, the soft lap of waves on the beach. He ordered a chilled glass of white wine, and when the Ahi Tuna Chop Salad arrived, he savored every bite. The food, the rest, the change of scenery, each element worked its magic, sharpening his focus, reigniting his drive. There was more to find, more to uncover.

Back at his bungalow, the notes, photographs, and pulled string connections adorned the room that only he understood. He stood in the dim light, eyes scanning the evidence like a hunter sizing up his prey. Something was clicking into place.

He grabbed his phone, scrolling through his contacts with a purpose he hadn't felt in years. His finger hovered over a name, a ghost from the past. A hesitation, a breath.

A notification pulsed onto his screen.

Female, Buraffini, Italy, Wins 17 million.

His pulse spiked. He pulled up the video, watching, waiting, only to be met with the all-too-familiar disappointment. Another winner, another shroud of anonymity. He understood the desire to stay hidden.

But for him, anonymity was just another obstacle. One he was more than willing to tear apart.

June 2024
Jason

The Marble Bar, deep beneath the hotel and Sydney's bustling streets, bathed in the golden glow of its stained-glass panels. The scent of whiskey and old wood lingered in the air, mixing with the low hum of jazz from the back center stage.

At the bar, a man sat alone, his fingers tracing the rim of an empty glass. His suit, though tailored, looked slightly lived-in, like a man who had worn it through too many nights of unresolved thoughts.

He wasn't waiting for anyone. Not anymore.

The bartender, a woman with knowing eyes, set another drink before him. "On the house," she said.

He nodded, lifting the glass to the mirror behind the bar. In its reflection, he saw the ghosts of the past, the lover who left, the deal that fell apart, the man he used to be. He would not be undone. He would continue his struggle to make things right. He just needed to make better decisions.

Somewhere in the room, laughter rang out, detached from his world. He let the bourbon burn down his throat, a silent toast to all the things that never were.

And then, just as the ice clinked softly in his empty glass, a woman slid onto the stool beside him.

"Looks like you could use a better distraction," she said, her voice warm with amusement.

The man turned, his lips curling into the faintest smile. Maybe tonight, the past could wait.

Tucked beside an ornate marble pillar, Jason Young sat alone in a black leather booth by the fireplace, touching the pattern of his empty glass between his fingers. He was waiting. Watching. Calculating.

His next game had to be smarter. Bigger. He had spent the last week bouncing between high-rolling joints, sizing up Sydney's elite, searching for the right mark. Some desperate businessman drowning in debt, an overconfident trust-fund kid eager to prove himself, Jason could smell the type a mile away.

Tonight, it was Aidan Harrington III, a venture capitalist who had been throwing cash around like confetti. Jason had already made small talk, feigned admiration for the man's supposed "genius," and planted the seed of a too-good-to-miss investment opportunity. A vintage watch deal, rare pieces straight out of Europe. All he needed was a "small" upfront investment to secure the lot.

Now, all that was left was to reel him in.

Jason caught the bartender's eye and lifted his glass. "Another Old Fashioned."

Sydney was a playground of marks, and Jason? He was always two steps ahead. By the time the ice in his drink had melted, Aidan's money would be halfway into an untraceable account, gone before the fool even realized he'd been played.

Leaning back, he watched as Tanya glided through the room towards the bar, her smile all invitation, her eyes all distraction. She'd keep Aidan occupied, dazzled, unaware.

Human nature was laughably predictable. And Jason? He lived for the game.

Aidan felt the pull of the woman's presence before she even spoke. When she did, her voice was silk and smoke, winding through his senses like a slow-burning fuse. A drink. Some small talk. Then the inevitable invitation. The dance, as old as time itself.

He played along, knowing full well the game wouldn't last. It never did.

Heartache had carved its lessons deep into him. His wife, his partner of years, his love, had walked away, not for wealth, but for something more damning. Love. True, reckless, unapologetic love with his best friend. Aidan had wealth beyond measure, the Harrington fortune securing his every step. But none of it had been enough to stop what had been happening for years behind his back. He had never seen it coming.

That was then. Now, he was wiser. Sharper. More attuned to the undercurrents that others missed. He had learned to trust his instincts, and they had yet to fail him.

And that's why, weeks ago, as he sat in this very bar, something had set those instincts on high alert.

Two men. One conversation. A casual yet careful discussion about a rare timepiece, a relic poised for a black-market silent auction, its origins as murky as the deal being pitched. The older man had been interested, but hesitant. The younger one? Confident, aggressive. Polished in a tailored suit, his words dripping with the kind of practiced persuasion only a seasoned manipulator could wield.

It was the mention of the Swiss ring watch that snagged Aidan's attention. Supposedly discovered in a sealed tomb in Shanxi, China during a documentary filming in 2008, only one had ever been publicly acknowledged. But whispers in the collectors' world suggested more had surfaced, priceless artifacts slipping through the cracks into the hands of those who could afford the shadows.

The conversation ended abruptly. Too abruptly. The interested buyer had left in a hurry, and within minutes, the tailored suit had turned his attention to Aidan. The pitch began again, smooth, tempting, carefully spun.

But Aidan had been listening. Watching.

He had played along, asked the right questions, letting the man believe he was circling the bait. An hour later, he had walked out of the Marble Bar with all the information he needed.

Jason, ever poised, ever in control, had been left waiting. Told to be patient.

Aidan was in no hurry. Not anymore.

Once, he would have tossed money at a deal without hesitation, blinded by impulse, reckless in his hunger for the chase. But that had been before, before the sting of betrayal, before the lesson carved deep into his pride and bank account. He'd lost millions. And he had sworn, with every ounce of resolve in his body, that it would never happen again.

So now, he waited. He watched. He dictated the game's rhythm, his own tempo.

And Jason? Jason had no idea who he was really playing with.

Back home, Aidan had reached out to a few friends, collectors of rare antiquities, men of wealth and taste. Two had already fallen prey to the same trap, lured by the golden promise of investment, only to watch their fortunes vanish into thin air. Fake. A scam. We were all deceived. The words were always the same. The description of the man behind it, identical.

Aidan was ready.

Three days later, he made the call. Jason Young took the bait like a starving fish, eager, cocky. They would meet at the Marble Bar to finalize the deal. Jason, convinced he had snared yet another gullible millionaire, felt invincible. His days of hustling for scraps were long gone. He was swimming in millions now, and he had no intention of slowing down.

The exchange was seamless. In the mirror, Aidan watched Jason lean back into the leather sofa in the corner, savoring his victory as Tanya moved in, her presence the well-practiced distraction.

But Jason had no idea that Aidan was five steps ahead.

The money, transferred from a seemingly simple account, was anything but ordinary. Layered with sophisticated tracking software, it followed every move, every shift. The moment it touched an unsecured, false, or suspicious account, the flow would halt, reversing course, snapping back into the Harrington special reserves like a viper recoiling before a strike.

As Tanya made her move, Aidan watched Jason in the mirror over the bar. He saw the smirk, the telltale grin of a man who believed he had won. The smug confidence of a seasoned thief reveling in yet another perfect con.

But Aidan only smiled to himself.

Because Jason Young had just made the worst mistake of his life.

Tanya wasted no time in convincing Aidan to retreat from the bar. They checked into one of the many rooms that towered above the bar. Aidan was in no mood to play games. Excusing himself for a moment and retreating to the master suite, he took out a special wallet he had hidden away and put it in his coat pocket. He ran a hot towel over his face, letting the heat flush his skin then splashed water on his cheeks for effect. Emerging from the suite, he clutched his stomach, voice weak but measured.

"I don't feel well," he muttered, draping his jacket over the chair with calculated care. "Give me an hour to rest."

Tanya hesitated, then nodded.

He closed the door to the master suite and sat down wondering how long it would be before he heard the horrifying realization of her wrongdoing. Thirty minutes passed and nothing. He thought maybe he was wrong about her. Then, without warning, the anticipated cry was heard. "What in the world?"

He could hear Tanya at the door, frantically trying to open the locked doors, yelling the whole time. "What did you do to me? How could you? I'll be marked forever!"

Aidan waited, knowing that in a few more seconds the heightened panic would set in as the mark would increasingly get darker. And then it happened. As Tanya screamed, furniture started to fly around the room. Aidan reached for the phone and called security.

Within minutes, security entered the suite, police detaining Tanya who was feverishly trying to hide her bright blue, stained hands. Looking at Aidan, she yelled out, "How could you do this to me?"

"Let's see," said Aidan very calmly. "First you lure me up here to distract me from your friend Jason." Tanya was shocked upon hearing his name. "Second, you tried to steal from me. Either money or information from my wallet. Either way, it was a trap which I knew you would jump at when I left my jacket on the chair. Oh, don't worry. That stain will go away, in a few months. As it penetrates your skin, it will get darker. Where you are going, there will only be so many people who will see your hands. Good luck."

Security escorted Tanya out of the suite.

"Mr. Harrington, Sir. If you don't mind me asking. How did you know to set all this up a few days ago?" asked the bellman.

"That was easy. Human nature is predictable. The secret code I used when booking the room, alerted the staff that something fishy was about to happen. I was correct. The code worked and here we are. Half of the puzzle has gone down in flames. Now I will wait for the other half to burn."

Below, Jason swirled the amber liquid in his glass, watching as the ice surrendered to the warmth, melting just as he had planned. Across the room, he had watched as Tanya and Aidan slipped out of the bar, their departure as smooth as the execution of his plan, at least, it should have been. Thirty minutes. That was all it would take for the funds to be safely nestled in his ever-growing offshore account. But the confirmation never came.

Silence.

A gnawing unease crept into his chest. He checked his phone. Nothing. He made a few calls. Still nothing. The transfer had started, then, vanished. No trace, no explanation. The walls of the dimly lit bar seemed to close in around him, the once, soothing hum of conversation now an unbearable drone. He needed air. He needed space.

Pushing through the heavy stained-glass doors, he stepped into the hotel's pristine white-marble hallway, its sterility a stark contrast to the storm in his mind. He climbed the grand staircase to the main lobby, his thoughts spinning in tangled knots. And then, a disturbance.

A flash of movement. Raised voices.

Jason turned, his pulse hammering in his ears.

Tanya.

Flanked by officers, her hands, painted a shocking, almost surreal shade of blue, were bound in steel cuffs. Her frantic eyes found his, desperate, pleading. "Jason!" she screamed, her voice cutting through the hushed murmurs of the crowd.

He didn't move.

He couldn't.

To do so would be a mistake. They were watching, whoever they were. So, he remained still, his expression unreadable, nothing more than another face in the sea of onlookers. Just a spectator.

But inside, his mind was racing, twisting through every possibility, every miscalculation. Something had gone wrong.

Terribly wrong.

June 2024
Sean

Over the past four weeks, Sean had immersed himself in every scrap of information he could unearth about the secluded village of Baruffini. With only a few hundred residents, identifying the mystery woman wouldn't be a Herculean task, just a matter of patience and precision.

Leveraging his extensive network from years past, he managed to extract crucial details from the cryptic video, though at first glance, it had revealed frustratingly little. After painstaking decryption, a vital clue emerged: the location was perched on a hillside, marked by a lone red bench. A quick search on Google Maps confirmed its existence. Step one: complete.

Next, he needed eyes on the ground, street cameras, home security footage, anything that might have captured movement between May 7th and 9th. And then, a stroke of luck. A local farmer, plagued by livestock theft, had recently installed a security camera on his land.

As Sean sifted through the footage, the usual comings and goings of farmhands filled the screen, routine, predictable. But then, someone stood out. A woman. She appeared multiple times, sometimes alone, sometimes alongside a man, always heading toward the forest. Toward the red bench.

A few well-placed phone calls later, he had her name.

Alessandra Iantosca.

Sean was elated. The elderly woman had graciously gifted him two full hours of her time, recounting every detail with a clarity that painted the past in vivid strokes. And just like that, the nagging mystery of the off date unraveled before him. The two-day delay, which had gnawed at his confidence, now fell neatly into place. He never should have questioned his instincts.

Piece by piece, the puzzle mirrored what he had already gleaned from the limited videos. The same symbol adorned their lapel pins, this time worn by three imposing men, all unmistakably local.

Then, finally, something new, something that made his pulse quicken. Alessandra had requested the two-day delay. They hadn't balked, hadn't questioned. Instead, they had made a call. And on the other end of that line was someone they referred to only as Sir.

A single word, but a seismic revelation. Somewhere out there, a man was pulling the strings. And Sean was one step closer to finding him.

He turned back to the map pinned to the wall, his gaze tracing the web of dates and destinations. His pulse quickened June 6 was next. Another name, another fate sealed in ink.

June 2024
Dee

During the first part of the year, Dee had been thriving. The laughter of her grandchildren filled her home, their little hands grasping hers, their joy a remedy to the wounds time had never quite healed. She held onto that light, clinging to it like a lifeline. But as it always did, the weight of memory crept in with the changing seasons. The anniversary loomed, and with it came the relentless tide of pain and fear, drowning her once more.

Claire sensed the shift before Dee even spoke a word. Conversations grew hollow, her once, bright presence dimmed into a shadow of itself. Then, one day, Claire found her, out by the gravesite, hands clawing at the earth as if sheer desperation could summon the dead. A raw, aching grief poured from her, an agony Claire had never witnessed so unbridled.

Without hesitation, Claire rushed to her side, wrapping her arms around Dee, whispering soothing words until the sobs softened. She helped her into the car, but instead of driving her home, she took her somewhere else, somewhere special, a sanctuary Claire had meticulously crafted for the purpose of healing and wellness.

Dee was too lost in sorrow to notice the journey, too hollowed out by grief to care where she was. But over the course of two months, Claire poured her love and healing into her, tending to her spirit as one would a fragile bloom struggling to break through the frost. The first few weeks were an uphill battle, shadows clung to Dee, refusing to release her. But little by little, she began to breathe again. The fresh air filled her lungs. The whisper of the trees, the warmth of the sun on her skin, it all started to matter again.

Slowly, the fog lifted. Dee found herself in the present, no longer shackled to the ghosts of her past. She could not change what had been, and the future remained unwritten. But here, now, in this moment, she was alive, and for the first time in a long time, that was enough.

It was time for Dee to return home, to solitude, to the echoes of an empty house, to the thoughts she had been dreading. The realization settled over her like a heavy fog, thick and unrelenting. Claire saw it instantly.

It was easy to move through life when someone else set the course, just follow the path, step after step, no choices, no risks, no moments of uncertainty. But home… home was different. At home, Dee would have to decide. What to eat. When to rest. How to silence the intrusive thoughts that threatened to pull her under. It was terrifying.

Claire, ever steady, reached for her hands. "You're ready," she said with unwavering certainty. "But remember, if you focus only on the hard moments, your life will become just that hard. Shift your gaze, Dee. Focus on the light, on the small joys. That's where life is waiting for you."

Dee swallowed hard, a knot of emotion rising in her throat. But Claire wasn't finished. She handed Dee a carefully structured plan, a roadmap, a rhythm, a way to make each day feel intentional and safe. A way to make home feel like something other than a void.

Dee blinked at her friend, suddenly seeing her in a new light. "When did you put all this together? And how... how did you even know you could?"

Claire's eyes sparkled with something between pride and nostalgia. "I've been building this for years. The idea was simple: a spa-like retreat, a place for people to escape the weight of their own lives." She chuckled softly. "It took off faster than I expected. People didn't just want an afternoon of peace; they needed days, weeks... a place to breathe again. So, I built a village."

Tears welled in Dee's eyes, an ache of realization blooming in her chest. "Why didn't I know about any of this?" Her voice trembled, laced with something close to betrayal. Had she really been so lost?

Claire squeezed her hand. "I did tell you. But you were drowning, my dear friend. Losing your children, then everything with your husband... your mind was in survival mode. You weren't ready to hear it." She smiled then, the kind of smile that carries a lifetime of understanding. "But now? Now you've seen it, felt it. And look at you. You're ready to step back into the world."

Dee exhaled, absorbing it all, letting it settle. "But how did you know?" she whispered. "How did you know you could do all this?"

Claire tilted her head, amusement flickering in her eyes. "Funny," she mused, "I never once thought I couldn't."

There was more to say, so much more, but some truths are best saved for the right moment. And for Dee, the moment would come when she was ready.

June 2024
Jason

The spectators lost interest in the cuffed blue handed lady as she was dragged through the back doors of the hotel. The spectacle faded, swallowed by the usual hum of lobby life, room reservations, dinner plans, and the thrill of Sydney's nightlife reclaiming center stage. Jason remained composed, slipping unnoticed into the current of guests and stepping out onto George Street.

A brisk twenty-minute walk later, he was back at the Wharf Terraces. That's when the unease crept in. First, a whisper of doubt. Then, full-blown panic. Had someone figured him out? Someone sharper, someone faster? Aidan was still nowhere to be seen. Had he been caught too? Jason clenched his fists, forcing himself to stay in control. Details could drive a man mad. It had to be Tanya. She must have slipped up.

Inside his home, his gaze flicked to the list before him, and a slow smile curled his lips. Two wealthy Australians had already taken the bait. One had gotten cold feet. Another hit a dead end, no money, no deal. Not every con would be flawless. That was the nature of the game. He inhaled deeply, refocusing.

He zeroed in on his next target. **Oliver Bailey**.

June 2024
Aiden

Aidan moved through life like a shadow, never flaunting his wealth, never betraying the truth of his lineage, the heir to a multimillion-dollar empire. He preferred it that way. Blending in. Watching. Calculating. Days ago, he'd overheard that his friend Marcus had walk away from the so-called "deal of a lifetime", a Swiss ring watch proposal that reeked of deception. And now, it was his turn. The con artist had set his sights on him, circling like a vulture. Aidan made him wait. He needed to be sure. And now, certainty burned through him, this was the same man who had swindled millions from his two other friends.

But Aidan wasn't just another unsuspecting target. He was playing a different game; one designed to bring the con artist to his knees and recover every stolen cent.

In a soundproof chamber deep within the Harrington estate, Aidan convened his most trusted circle, twenty of Australia's elite, men and women who had built fortunes and commanded power. Each had received his call, an invitation devoid of digital footprints, extended only through his secure landline. That was Aidan's way. Mysterious. Unpredictable. It had intrigued them enough to bring them all here, to this clandestine gathering.

As he spoke, the room stirred. Murmurs rippled through the air as a few confirmed his suspicions; they too had encountered the same man, the same smooth-talking deceiver. Aidan's plan was simple, yet razor-sharp in its precision. If the con artist reached out to any of them, they were to stall, make him wait a day, maybe two. Then, they would alert Aidan, who would equip them with a special wallet, one designed for contingencies. The wallet would contain a stain, marking any person eager enough to steal identity or cards. He had even devised a method to freeze the funds mid-transfer, ensuring that not a single cent escaped into the fraudster's hands.

Yet the true challenge remained: catching him in the act. Aidan knew that con men thrived on illusion, slipping through the cracks of legality like smoke. But he wasn't worried. He had patience. He had a strategy. And soon, he would have justice. This was no longer a con artist's game. It was Aidan's. And he never played to lose.

June 2025
Oliver

The days dragged on like weeks as Oliver Bailey anxiously awaited word of the con man's next victim within the elusive circle of wealth and trust. Restless, he decided to step away from the meticulous planning of his upcoming voyage to Tasmania. He left his yacht moored in the marina and made his way to Pelican's Landing for lunch, in Melbourne, Australia, hoping a change of scenery would ease his mind.

Before departing, he lingered over his most treasured collection, rare coins and exquisite jewels salvaged from the depths of long-lost shipwrecks. Each piece had a story; an echo of history recovered at great cost through auctioned relics meant to fund the perilous expeditions that unearthed them.

Settling into his usual seat by the window, he swirled a glass of Shiraz, his gaze drifting over the water where yachts danced in rhythm with the tide. The gentle hum of conversation around him was nothing more than background noise, until a hushed exchange from the table behind him caught his attention.

A shipwreck. Off the coast of Israel. 3,300 years old.

His pulse quickened. He leaned in slightly, straining to catch every detail, irritated when the waiter arrived with his meal, disrupting his focus with needless pleasantries. By the time the interruption passed, the conversation behind him had dwindled, voices lowering to a whisper before falling into silence.

Damn.

Feigning casual indifference, Oliver devised a plan. He coughed, shifting in his seat, then rose, strolling toward the restroom with deliberate ease. As he returned, he noted that only one man remained at the table.

He finished his meal in record time, eager but controlled, then settled his bill. Rising slowly, he walked past the man, hesitated, and then turned back.

"Excuse me," he said smoothly, masking his excitement. "Did I overhear something about a newly discovered shipwreck off the coast of Israel?"

The man looked up, his expression unreadable. "Indeed, you did. I hope we didn't disturb your lunch. It's a rare find, and we're keeping it under wraps until we can safely recover the artifacts."

Oliver's heartbeat drummed in his ears. "Is there any chance I could learn more about the discovered pieces?"

The man smiled, polite but guarded. "I'm afraid not. It's currently under private funding with a dedicated research team. But if you give me your contact details, I'd be happy to reach out once more information is available."

Oliver barely contained his excitement as he handed over his business card, already lost in the tantalizing possibilities of this newfound discovery.

Outside, as Oliver strode toward his yacht, mind spinning with anticipation, Jason leaned back in his chair, watching him go.

A slow, knowing smile curled across his lips.

His web of lies and conversation had worked just as planned, hook, line, and sinker.

Lure them in rather than approach for the kill. The tide had finally turned.

Jason marveled at the sheer predictability of human nature. It was almost laughable. He had studied Oliver, dissected his every move, his every impulse. Hooking him would be effortless. All it took was patience, a few days, nothing more. Then, just as the hunger clawed at Oliver's insatiable need to be first, Jason would strike. The offer would be irresistible, tantalizing, a golden key to the kingdom. And by then, money? Mere numbers on a screen. Oliver would part with millions without a second thought. That was not a gamble. That was a guarantee.

June 6, 2024
Aidan

Aidan hadn't heard a peep from anyone since their last meeting. The silence gnawed at him, an unsettling quiet that only deepened as he reached out to each person, only to learn that none had been contacted. Odd. Too odd. His final attempt was Oliver, but his calls went unanswered. Then, an hour later, the shrill ring of his landline shattered the hush.

Oliver's voice, casual as ever, drifted through the receiver. He'd been preoccupied planning a trip to Tasmania, he explained, and had no immediate plans to return to Sydney. The conversation meandered through small talk until Oliver mentioned something peculiar. Had Aidan read about the shipwreck recovery off the coast of Israel? An ordinary topic between them, perhaps, given their shared history. They reminisced about their last dive in Madagascar, where they'd helped a team recover coins and silver bars. Not the grandest treasure, but still, the sheer exhilaration of pulling relics from the ocean's grip was a prize in of itself.

They wrapped up their call, exchanged goodbyes, and went their separate ways for lunch.

But two hours later, Aidan froze mid-step, his stomach twisting with realization. Why hadn't he pressed Oliver about that shipwreck? Something about it nagged at him, an itch he couldn't scratch. Without hesitation, he redialed, but all he got was Oliver's curt, familiar voicemail: Call me later.

Aidan hung up, uneasy. The con artist's game had always been in Sydney, so why did this feel like something much, much bigger?

June 6, 2024
Jason

The days of waiting, stretched taut like a bowstring, had only sharpened their hunger for knowledge. At last, the moment had arrived. Even Jason, usually composed, could feel the electric charge of anticipation crackling in the air. His pulse quickened as he sent the message, tomorrow, Pelican's Landing, the final step to seal the deal.

For Oliver, the thrill was intoxicating. He felt like a child once more, heart pounding with the joy of an impending treasure, a rare find just within his grasp.

Jason wasn't about to let a single detail slip through the cracks. He leaned forward, scanning his strategy with the precision of a chess master, his focus now razor-sharp on the flow of funds. One misstep could unravel everything. He adjusted the sequence of transfer points, inserting an extra stop, a clever decoy to throw off anyone watching too closely.

Back in his studio residence hotel room, he mulled over Oliver's eagerness. The man had been the first to approach him about this shipwreck deal, he was hungry to be involved from the start. That meant leverage. Jason smirked. *I'll start with two million. Just enough to bait him in. Then I'll dangle a bigger opportunity, make him think it's his idea.*

With hours to kill, he decided to clear his mind. A walk along Steve Bracks Promenade, the salty breeze teasing at his thoughts, followed by a cold plunge at Williamstown Beach. The water jolted his senses, awakening something primal; anticipation, hunger for what lay ahead. Lunch was an easy choice: fish and chips from the Rotunda. The crunch, the warmth, the comfort of an all-time favorite, it all settled him.

Then his phone spoke.

A crisp, unfamiliar voice cut through the stillness.

"Mister Young, congratulations! You've been chosen as our next participant of Blank Checks. Please join us this afternoon, four o'clock at the Sebastian Restaurant to claim and complete your blank check. Feel free to bring a few family members or friends along for the occasion. Best of luck, and remember, DREAM BIG!"

Jason froze. His pulse quickened.

Sebastian Restaurant was right there, mere steps away. His world tilted, shifting under the weight of the moment. Hours ago, he was strategizing how to scrape together a few million. Now? Now, the universe had cracked open, pouring fortune straight into his lap.

His mind raced. This changes everything. No more scheming. No more cat-and-mouse. This is it. Millions. Just a few more hours, and I walk away free.

He exhaled, a slow, disbelieving grin spreading across his face. Unbelievable.

The clock inched toward four, each passing minute thick with anticipation. Sheila still couldn't wrap her head around the surreal reality, soon, right there in her restaurant, a contestant would be sealing their fate with the stroke of a pen on a Blank Check. The details were sparse. All she knew was that three people; two men and one woman, would arrive around that time, needing exactly one hour. For her cooperation, she'd been offered a staggering ten thousand dollars. An amount too good to refuse.

At precisely ten minutes to four, they arrived. Sheila's breath hitched. They were tall, almost unnervingly so, their presence commanding the space the moment they stepped in. Their attire was immaculate, sharp black and white with an almost nautical precision. But it wasn't just their appearance that left her momentarily spellbound. There was something else, something intangible that prickled at the edges of her consciousness.

With a composed smile, she led them to the private dining room. They didn't sit. Instead, they stood, poised, waiting. A quiet intensity filled the air.

She hesitated, then asked, "Are you new in town?"

The first man turned to her, his voice deep and deliberate, his Australian accent thick.

"We are from Perth."

"Is this your first time in Melbourne?"

"It is," he replied, crisp and measured, offering nothing more.

Sheila, ever the gracious host, offered them a drink, but they declined with polite detachment. She pressed on with a few more questions, hoping to draw them out, but conversation felt like prying open a locked box. They were here for business, nothing more, nothing less.

The clock inched past 4:10, and still, the contestant was nowhere to be seen. A flicker of impatience crossed Sheila's face. "How long do we wait?" she asked.

The answer was as unsettling as it was vague.

"We don't know."

Then, without another word, the second man, silent until now, unfurled a peculiar device from his hands. He traced an enigmatic symbol in the air above it, his movements precise, deliberate. As he turned away, murmuring in hushed, almost indecipherable tones, Sheila strained to catch even a fragment of what he was saying.

Moments later, he returned. "We wait until five. Then, instructions will follow."

A tense silence fell over the room, thick and unyielding. To ease the weight of it, Sheila fetched water and an assortment of her signature appetizers. This time, they indulged, the smallest crack in their austere composure.

As the final minutes crept by, the air shifted. The three strangers, so restrained before, now engaged in a fevered discussion with the unseen voice on the device. Words sharp, decisive. Tension bristled between them.

Then, resolution.

The verdict was clear: tomorrow, a new contestant would be chosen.

June 6, 2024
Undisclosed Location

Of all the contestants the system had marked, Jason Young was the hungriest, the most ruthlessly ambitious. He was the type to arrive early, eyes sharp with calculation, dissecting every angle, every opportunity to squeeze the most money from the game. But tonight, the tables had turned, not on Jason, but on the mastermind himself.

Something had shifted. The system had pulled vast streams of data on Jason's recent movements with unsettling ease. He was still in Melbourne, his phone darting north at a relentless pace. Was he running? Or simply refusing to play by the rules? Perhaps Jason didn't believe in the game at all. None of that mattered now. Another day, another contestant.

Leaning back, the mastermind let his gaze drift over the endless sprawl of the Milky Way shimmering across the screens. This game was a beast of its own, chaotic, untamed. Even he, the architect of it all, relished the moments that veered from expectation.

Tomorrow, the chase would continue. For now, he'd wait. The system would call him when Jason Young made his next move.

Hours later, the beeping notification woke the mastermind up.

"Utter Chaos": Shocking Footage Shows Stolen Car Plowing into Man in Wealthy Melbourne Suburb. Panicked Bystanders Flee as Tragedy Unfolds. One Dead.

The footage was chaotic, grainy security clips and shaky phone recordings pieced together a scene of reckless destruction. A stolen car, a roaring beast of metal and speed, tore through the streets, bouncing over curbs, flattening lawns, and slicing across walkways. Pedestrians scattered in terror. A man, caught in the path of its fury, went down hard. Screams filled the night. And then, just as suddenly as it began, it ended. The driver abandoned the wreck, bolting into the darkness, only to be dragged into the light moments later by the relentless hands of the law.

The victim remained unnamed, but the mastermind didn't need a report to put the pieces together. His gut twisted as he stared at the last known location blinking on his screen. The Royal Melbourne Hospital.

It must be Jason Young.

June 7, 2024
Aidan

Aidan could hardly believe his ears. It felt almost surreal, too perfect, too poetic, that karma had finally caught up with the con artist.

Oliver's voice buzzed through the phone, laced with confusion. "He never showed," he said, referring to the man desperate to be part of the shipwreck discovery. But Aidan already knew why. His fingers trembled slightly as he pulled up a photo and sent it over. Silence hung in the air before Oliver exhaled sharply.

"It's him," Oliver murmured. "Jason Young."

The very same Jason who had spun his web of lies, now silenced by fate. And in a final twist, even his family seemed to embrace the irony, sending Jason off on his greatest and most permanent adventure yet.

Obituary
Young, Jason
1984 - 2024

After years of enduring Jason's mischief, pranks, and general chaos, we regret (and sigh in relief) to announce that he is now officially God's problem. May the Almighty have better luck than we did.

Jason's grand finale, also known as his funeral, will take place on Tuesday, June 11th, 2024, at 10 a.m. at Williamstown Cemetery in Melbourne. The family encourages you to dust off whatever outdated or inappropriate combination of clothing you have available to attend.

A tip jar will be provided, and we strongly urge you to contribute anything except money. If you were ever on the receiving end of one of Jason's shenanigans, you'll understand why, payback is, after all, a dish best served petty.

P.S. If you hear laughter during the service, don't be alarmed. It's probably Jason, already haunting us.

N.B. If you fell prey to Jason's tangled web of deceit, drawn in by the allure of sky-high returns, don't lose hope. Our representative holds the key to reclaiming what's rightfully yours. You will be contacted to begin the recovery of your investment. Justice is within your grasp!

8

June 2024
Leah

For the two weeks, Leah had been living in what could only be described as a tragicomedy of leaks, drips, and unexpected indoor water features. First, the kitchen faucet developed a mind of its own, spitting water sideways like it had a personal vendetta. Then, the guest bathroom pipes started making noises reminiscent of a haunted accordion. She had learned the fine art of plumbing basics from YouTube videos and developed an entirely new form of cardio sprinting between leaks. Her home was no longer a house; it was an avant-garde water park, and she, its unwilling lifeguard.

And just when she thought the madness had peaked, the toilet, that last stronghold of sanity, betrayed her in spectacular fashion. The constant sound of running water turned her bathroom into a taunting, stress-inducing meditation soundtrack. Instead of a gentle babbling brook, it whispered problem, problem, problem. With steely determination (and another frantic search), she replaced the flapper. Success! A small victory in her war against H2O.

But there was still one more battle to fight. The hose to the water supply valve looked ancient, frayed like it had seen things it wished it could forget. Leah, now armed with Plumbing 101 skills, figured it couldn't be that hard to swap out.

Except…the space was tiny. Unforgiving. An impossible nook designed by an architect with a cruel sense of humor. Leah wasn't exactly large, but she wasn't a contortionist either. Fitting herself into that tight corner and watching a tutorial at the same time? Not happening.

Then, an idea. Travis. Her son. Her tech-savvy, mechanically inclined, far more patient than she was son.

Balancing her phone beside her on the floor, she put him on speaker video. "Alright, talk me through this before I flood the place."

Travis sighed, already resigned to the chaos. "Okay, Mom. Step one, don't panic."

Easier said than done.

Leah took a deep breath, bent over, and wedged herself further into the impossibly small space between the toilet and the wall. "Alright, I've got this," she muttered, maneuvering the wrench into position.

Travis sighed on speaker. "Mom, are you sure you don't want to call a plumber?"

Leah scoffed. "Please. Plumbers are like unicorns right now, magical, elusive, and way out of my budget."

She grunted as she twisted the wrench. The hose refused to budge. "Come on you ancient, crusty..." She put her entire weight into it.

And that was her fatal mistake.

The hose, which had been hanging on to its last shred of dignity, chose that exact moment to give up on life. It snapped free with a victorious POP, and Leah, completely unprepared, lost control.

With a yelp, she tumbled forward, gravity pulling her into the last inches of available space. Leah was already feeling the rush of blood in her head. Not only was her nightgown bunched around her waist, to make matters worse, the now, detached hose began spraying water directly into her face like a miniature fire hose.

"OH, FOR THE LOVE OF..." she sputtered, blinking water out of her eyes.

"Mom?!" Travis's voice crackled through the speaker. "What was that?! Are you okay?"

"No," Leah coughed. "I am not okay. The toilet is trying to drown me." She was able to turn off the water supply but quickly realized the real problem. She was stuck.

Wriggling didn't help. The angle of her fall had wedged her firmly between the toilet and the vanity. And that's when it hit her. She had one option left. The dreaded option.

She groaned. "Travis...I'm calling the emergency service."

There was a beat of silence. "Mom. You did not just say that."

"I did," she grumbled. "And before you ask, yes, this is the lowest point of my life."

Ten minutes later, Leah heard the sirens approaching. A fresh wave of humiliation washed over her as she braced for what was coming.

And then came the knock. "Ma'am, it's the fire department! Are you alright?"

No. No, she was not.

"I'm in here," she called weakly.

The bathroom door swung open, and in stepped not one, but two firefighters, both alarmingly good-looking, like they'd been pulled straight from a calendar titled Hot Heroes 2024.

Leah groaned internally.

One of them, a chiseled blond with dimples, crouched down, struggling not to smile. "Well, this is a first."

"I don't want to talk about it," Leah muttered.

His partner, a dark-haired, muscle-bound Adonis, cleared his throat. "Uh, ma'am? Would it be ok if we adjust your nightgown?"

Leah's mind swirled in bewilderment, a fog of confusion clouding her senses, until a slow, creeping awareness sent a jolt of heat through her. Her nightgown, bunched carelessly around her waist, had left her bare bottom shamelessly exposed, not just to the open air but to the very eyes that were meant to rescue her from this predicament. Horror dawned in waves, mortification wrapping around her like a second skin.

Leah let out a sound that could only be described as part wheeze, part mortified shriek.

It took just a minute and two swipes of petroleum jelly to get Leah greased up enough for the two firemen to slowly free her from the confines of the most embarrassing day of her life.

Slowly, she rose to her feet, hands gripping the steady support offered on either side. "This never leaves this room. You hear?" she commanded, her voice sharp yet weary. A heavy silence filled the space as she lowered her head, a quiet storm of emotions flickering across her face. Then, barely above a whisper, she murmured, "Thank you."

Blondie grinned. "Well, we will have to fill out an indecent exposure on your report…"

The tension was broken. The first laugh came from her phone.

"Travis, FOR CRYING OUT LOUD. Have you been listening this whole time?" cried out Leah, completely embarrassed.

"Mom, that was priceless," still chuckling as he talked. "And guys, thank you for helping out my mom."

"Just doing our job."

As they helped her take a seat at the kitchen table, Blondie gave her a wink. "Look at it this way. You may have wanted a plumber, but you got firefighters instead. I'd call that an upgrade."

Leah groaned, still feeling humiliated as she heard Travis chuckle. She quickly picked up her phone, "I'll call you later Travis. AND don't you dare go telling everyone what happened today." Without waiting for his reply, she ended the call.

Her toilet had betrayed her, and her dignity was completely gone.

Blondie broke the heavy tension in the air. "I have an idea," he said. "Get us a glass of water and we will repair your toilet hose. On the house of course."

Hours later, Leah finally decided to share her harrowing experience with her best friend, Frank. As she recounted the moment, the sheer terror, the heart-pounding rush, she realized how absurd it all sounded in hindsight. What had once gripped her with fear now seemed almost comical, and soon, laughter bubbled between them, filling the quiet of the night. They laughed until their sides ached, and tears streamed down their faces. The weight of the world felt just a little lighter.

It had been months since Frank had laughed, truly laughed. His beloved wife, Dianne, the love of his life for thirty-six years, had passed away not long ago. After a grueling, merciless battle with ALS, God had finally granted her peace, freeing her from the pain that had bound her for so long. But while she was at rest, Frank was adrift, lost in the emptiness she left behind.

Leah understood loss all too well. She had walked that same road when her own husband left this earth years ago. She had learned how to bear the sorrow, how to keep moving forward, even when the grief felt unbearable. But Frank was different. He carried his pain like a heavy chain, refusing to let go, refusing to embrace life again. And that broke Leah's heart.

But tonight was different. For the first time in what felt like forever, she saw a flicker of light in his eyes. His laughter wasn't just sound; it was life, cracking through the sorrow, reaching for something more. And that, more than anything, made Leah's heart swell.

"We must get together again soon. It's good to see you laugh again." Frank agreed. It had been too long, and he was ready to enjoy continued moments of happiness.

From the very moment Frank entered the world, fate had played out its cruel hand. Frank was not the rosy-cheeked cherub parents dream of. He was not "precious" or "darling", not even in the way that kind-hearted liars might describe an unfortunate looking child. No, Frank was an unvarnished spectacle, a living testament to nature's occasional miscalculations.

Born in 1955 to Walter and Betty Stein, he arrived in an era when God, perhaps feeling mischievous, decided to shatter the mold, then clumsily attempt to sweep away the pieces. The result? A newborn so astoundingly ugly that the hospital staff struggled to keep their horror discreet. Nurses whispered in hushed, scandalized tones, exchanging glances as if the very walls should be shielded from the sight of him. Some swore the lights flickered when he let out his first cry.

His younger siblings would be lovingly named before their arrival; their existence anticipated with warmth and excitement. But Frank? He had come as an unscripted surprise. When a nurse inquired about his name, his mother, caught off guard and unprepared, simply turned to the nearest male nurse and blurted out the first thing she could think of: "What's your name?"

"Frank Nathanial," the man replied.

And just like that, with all the ceremony of a shrug, he was named into a world that had already decided to make his life one hell of a ride.

As Betty held her son for the first time, she forced herself to love the ugly bulbous forehead and scrunched up eyes that stared at her. It was a labor of love that was too much for her to continue. Betty, instead, focused her attention on Frank's fingers and toes which were adorable. It only took a matter of minutes before she gasped, tears of sadness rolled down her cheeks. Her newborn's wrist band said it all. Frank N. Stein. How could she have not thought that through when naming her son?

The weight of her mistake settled in her chest like a stone. She looked up at the nurse, hoping for some reassurance, but the woman only gave her a sympathetic smile, as if she, too, understood the cruel joke the universe had played.

Betty considered calling the hospital staff back, demanding a name change right then and there, but exhaustion pinned her to the bed. Instead, she cradled Frank closer, whispering apologies into his tiny ear. He didn't know it yet, but the world would have its fun with his name.

And so, with a sigh of resignation, Betty made a silent promise. If her son was going to grow up as Frank N. Stein, then by God, he would own it.

June 2024
Dee

Claire witnessed an astonishing transformation in Dee, both in her demeanor and in her life, since spending two months at her Sanare Spa. Though the road ahead was still long, the tide had shifted. Change was no longer a distant hope; it was happening.

Before Claire could even suggest the next step, Dee had already made up her mind. It was time. Time to shed the past, to untangle herself from the weight of old wounds. Her decision was bold, final, sell the house and start fresh. A new beginning.

But before she could leave, there was one last room to face. Mark's room.

Taking a deep breath, Dee stepped inside. The air was thick with memories, but she pressed forward. One drawer at a time, she sorted through his things, each item a small piece of the man who had left her with more debts than memories. Mark had always been a collector of odds and ends, of secrets. Tucked inside socks, stuffed into jacket pockets, and hidden between book pages, she found small stashes of cash. It wasn't much. Just enough to enjoy a few meals in town.

By the time she reached the last drawer, the room felt different, lighter, as if it had exhaled along with her. Now, only the desk remained, standing naked in the corner, stripped of its past. It had taken her several days to clear the space, and with every discarded relic, she felt herself growing freer.

And yet, the hardest part still loomed. The stark truth of what Mark had left behind.

Nothing.

Anger surged through her, not just at him but at herself. How had she let things get this bad? How had she spent years in the background, with nothing to show for it? No career, no real security, just an empty house and a trail of overdue payments.

With a weary sigh, she returned to her task, sorting through the last of the papers, filing away what mattered, shredding what didn't. And then, in the very back of a bottom drawer, she found something that made her breath hitch.

A wooden box.

She pried it open, and her stomach twisted. Hundreds of lottery tickets.

"SON OF A..." Her voice caught in her throat as the realization hit. All those years of him preaching about saving money. The sacrifices, the debts, the tight budgets. And meanwhile, he had been gambling it all away.

Her hands trembled as she grabbed her phone. "Claire. You won't believe this."

An hour later, the two women stood side by side at the local supermarket, scanning stacks of tickets into the lottery machine. The minutes dragged, the pile barely shrinking, but with each beep and clink of winnings, Dee felt an unfamiliar thrill, something like justice, something like liberation.

By the time they hit $300 in winnings, Dee exhaled, shaking her head with a wry smile. "I'll come back tomorrow to do the rest. Right now, I need a drink."

Claire grinned. "Margaritas?"

"Margaritas."

And so, with the weight of the past beginning to lift, Dee and Claire toasted to new beginnings over tacos and tequila, laughing into the night.

June 2024
Sally

At just eighteen, Sally had already witnessed more cruelty than a heart so young should bear, especially from those who should have known better. Her family, the people meant to embody warmth and wisdom, instead wielded their disdain like a blade at her Uncle Frank, cutting deep with every withering glance and hushed whisper.

The mere sight of him twisted their faces into masks of disgust. To them, his very existence was an offense, an ugly stain on the fabric of their name. They would rather erase him than acknowledge his quiet kindness, his longing to belong. Every word he spoke was met with sneers, his attempts to join their world drowned beneath waves of contemptuous laughter.

They did not see his heart. They did not care for his goodness. To them, he was nothing, a mistake, an embarrassment, a shameful secret best left in the shadows. And with their every cruel dismissal, their every unspoken rejection, they made sure he felt it. That he knew, in their eyes, he was unworthy of love.

But Sally loved Uncle Frank, wholly, fiercely, without shame. And that love made their scorn even more unbearable.

Her father could never comprehend the unshakable bond between his hideous brother and Sally. Even as an infant, it was Frank's arms that soothed her cries, his voice that lulled her into peaceful slumber. As she grew, no warnings from her parents could keep her away from the man they branded a monster, the pariah at family gatherings. While others kept their distance, Sally sought him out, nestling into the quiet corner where he and his wife, Dianne, sat. There, she found warmth, wisdom, and conversations that made the rest of the world feel dull.

Now able to drive and freely move around as she pleased, Sally didn't hesitate to go visit them in their own home, for the first time. Months had passed since Christmas, and she already knew what awaited her. Uncle Frank had kept her updated, Aunt Dianne's battle with ALS was nearing its cruel end. For six months, Sally devoted herself to them, offering care that transcended words, love only they could understand.

Then, Dianne was gone. And in the void, she left behind, uncle and niece clung to each other. If not for Sally, Frank might have been swallowed whole by grief. With Leah's help, the three waded through the wreckage of loss together, holding on to each other when the weight of absence became too much to bear.

Not once did Sally's parents ask about Frank or Dianne. She wasn't even sure they knew she had been there. It didn't matter. What they didn't know couldn't touch what was sacred.

When Dianne passed, Frank decided to keep the news private, just between the three of them. The rest of the family would learn in time, but when they did, it was met with nothing more than indifference. No outrage, no grief. Just another passing event in the march of their lives. And so, life went on, except for Frank and Sally, it would never be the same.

June 7, 2024
Sean

The wall map initially had six spaces above and below the continents. Sean was having to adjust those spaces as the first six months now demanded eight. He exhaled sharply, frustration creeping in as he studied the latest update on the Blank Check App.

Melbourne, Australia. No Show.

That was it. No explanation, no details. Just two words that sent a ripple of uncertainty through his calculations. If he was right, and he usually was, it could only mean one thing. Somewhere, at this very moment, another contestant was being chosen.

Sean leaned back in his chair, fingers drumming against the desk as he stared at the words on his screen. Melbourne, Australia. No Show. It didn't make sense. Every contestant who had been chosen before had shown up, eager to claim their shot at the grand prize.

Opening his laptop, he started digging. First, he checked social media. The hashtag #BlankChecksChallenge had been trending for a while. Yet not one contestant had documented their experience in real-time. Most of the posts were speculation, nothing concrete. Next, he searched news reports, nothing unusual in Melbourne over the last few days. No missing persons, no suspicious activity. But then, the headline hit him. He trusted his gut.

Utter Chaos: Shocking Footage Shows Stolen Car Plowing into Man in Wealthy Melbourne Suburb. Panicked Bystanders Flee as Tragedy Unfolds. One Dead.

It was worth a try. Minutes later, he found Jason Young's obituary. *Looks like the Universe had other plans for Mr. Young.*

Sean was convinced it was him. He would wait till the next post announced the June winner. It wouldn't take long.

June 2024
Dee

Dee woke to a pounding headache, the bitter price of one too many margaritas. Grimacing, she swallowed an aspirin and forced down a glass of lukewarm water, wincing as the Arizona summer heat pressed against the walls of her home. It was already creeping in, thick and oppressive, but she had no plans to venture outside. Today, she would stay in, sorting through closets and clearing out the garage, one step closer to putting the house on the market. In just a few days, she would say goodbye to this place for good.

By noon, the doorbell's sharp chime cut through the silence. The realtor arrived, all business and efficiency, spreading paperwork across the kitchen table and walking Dee through the process. It all felt distant, like a conversation happening to someone else.

But then, the missing documents. A simple question about the home's finances turned into a call to the lender. A routine inquiry, until it wasn't.

The truth hit her like a gut punch. Her husband had refinanced the house. Without her knowing. The numbers didn't lie. There would be little to nothing left for her once the sale was finalized.

Dee gripped the edge of the table, the weight of it sinking in. What was supposed to be her fresh start had just crumbled into another painful betrayal.

Before the realtor could even close the door behind her, Dee was already dialing Claire, her hands shaking, her breath coming in ragged sobs. Panic and fury tangled in her chest, the weight of it all crashing down at once. Claire answered on the first ring.

An hour later, they sat across from each other at lunch. This time, Claire stuck to water, she needed a clear head. Dee's eyes were red, her hands still trembling as she clutched her glass.

"For now, you can manage about a year," Claire said gently, running numbers in her head. "If you budget tightly."

A year. That wasn't much time. But Claire had a plan.

"Come with me to the spa," she offered suddenly, leaning in. "Sanare. You can live there. Work there."

Dee blinked, stunned. "What?"

"You'd have a place to stay, some stability."

Tears welled up again, but this time, they weren't from fear. Relief flooded through her, melting away the suffocating anxiety. She had no real skills to offer, but Claire wasn't deterred. This was a lifeline Dee had not seen coming.

Claire grinned, reaching for her purse. "First things first. Let's go back for your stash of lottery tickets. Might as well give yourself a little cushion for meals, right?"

For over an hour, they scanned ticket after ticket, the anticipation mounting with every beep and whir. Each time the screen lit up with a dollar amount, a thrill ran through them. The stack of lottery tickets in the box was shrinking, but their pile of winnings was growing, over $500 so far. Dee stretched her arms above her head and let out a satisfied sigh.

"Let's take a break," she suggested, glancing at the dwindling pile. "Besides, I really need to hit the restroom."

Claire smirked. "Go ahead. I'll keep scanning a few more. We can finish up later, after you've officially moved in with me."

Dee didn't need to be told twice. She practically sprinted toward the restroom, relief already within reach. But just as she settled into her moment of solitude, a piercing scream echoed through the air.

Claire.

Dee's stomach lurched. She had noticed a couple of sketchy onlookers lingering nearby, their presence nagging at her instincts. No. No way.

Bolting out of the restroom, her heart pounded against her ribs. And then she saw Claire.

She was sitting on the floor, knees drawn to her chest, rocking back and forth, her face buried in her hands.

Panic seized Dee. "Are you okay? Do you need help? SECURITY!" Her voice cut through the buzzing sounds of the supermarket.

Security rushed over. "Miss, are you hurt? What happened?"

Claire didn't answer right away. She just rocked, her breath ragged, until finally, she lifted her head. Tears streamed down her cheeks. She took a deep breath. "I'm fine. Really. Just… got scared."

As they walked out to the car, Dee pressed her for answers. "Claire, tell me the truth. Did those guys take the box? Look, it's just money. What matters is that you're safe."

Claire wiped her eyes. "I'm fine. Let's just go home." She hesitated. "And Dee… I'm sorry."

Sorry? Dee's brow furrowed in confusion, but she let it go. Whatever had happened, Claire clearly wasn't ready to talk about it. And if the tickets were gone, so be it. Nothing mattered more than her friend being unharmed.

Back at Dee's place, Claire lingered. "Mind if I use your bathroom?"

"Go for it. I'll be here waiting for you."

When Claire returned to the kitchen, her face was fresh, her nerves seemingly settled. But there was something else, something unreadable in her expression.

"Claire, I've never seen you like that before. Those guys must have really freaked you out."

Claire exhaled slowly, then reached into her back pocket with deliberate slowness. Her fingers curled around a single ticket. She pulled it out and slid it across the counter.

"You won, Dee." Her voice was barely above a whisper, but it was laced with something electric.

Dee's breath caught. "How much?"

Claire met her gaze, a sly smile playing at her lips. "One and a half million."

Silence stretched between them.

Dee's eyes widened and her jaw dropped. With trembling fingers, she picked up the ticket, staring at the numbers, the weight of the moment crashing over her.

"IN HEAVEN'S NAME. Are you telling me this is the winning ticket?!"

Claire grinned. "Oh yeah. You're rich, my darling friend."

June 2024
Frank

Frank and his siblings would say that they grew up without a father. With only the loving guidance of his mother, Frank, very much a loner, left home at eighteen and never looked back. Over the next decade, Frank made do with odd jobs here and there, eventually becoming a semi-professional truck driver, not to be confused with a professional semi-truck driver.

A man of many interests, Frank, had a penchant for fashion. When not out driving his truck making deliveries, he was frequently seen about town wearing the latest trend in homemade leather moccasins, a wide collection of unconventional hats, and boldly mismatched shirts and pants. The ladies were drawn to his style until they found out he was a mere truck driver. Frank did not care. He knew that looks were awfully deceiving and he loved luring in the interested ones. Once they realized that there was no PhD nor other distinguishable initials after the name, they lost interest and moved along. He remained a bachelor until his precious Dianne appeared and filled his life with joy.

Through the years, Frank and Dianne became experts in the art of the swift exit from family gatherings, slipping away unnoticed from the forced smiles and hollow small talk. These gatherings were a parade of pretense, where only a rare few extended genuine warmth. But there was always Sally; she was their unwavering beacon of kindness.

After Dianne's passing, she had been there when Frank needed her most, offering unconditional love and most of all, laughter to his lonely dark days. Those months together were precious but short lived.

Just a day after Leah had witnessed Frank's rare, fleeting laughter, his first in what felt like an eternity, his long, held wish came true. He was reunited with his beloved Dianne. And so, hand in hand, Sally and

Leah stood alone, bidding their final, heartfelt farewell to their dear friend and uncle.

No other family members came. They had no words, no tears, only a quiet celebration. Frank and Dianne were gone at last, leaving them free of the burden of having to lay eyes on the outcasts, the ones they mockingly called Frank N. Stein and his wife.

The Will

However, the last laugh was with Frank. Just as the family were gathered around for the joint June birthday celebrations, the doorbell rang. Sally was the first to the door followed by her father, Frank's brother.

At the door stood a distinguished gentleman holding a manila envelope. "Hello, my name is Gordan Zilinski. I am Frank Stein's attorney, and his instructions were for me to read his will tonight in front of the family. May I come in?" Jeff, in shock, did not move nor utter a word.

Sally poked her dad hard, "Dad, Mr. Zilinski would like to come in."

"Oh, I am sorry. Please, come in."

Mr. Zilinski was shown into the family room where all eyes and ears were on the envelope and the unexpected guest.

"Hello everyone. I am Gordan Zilinski, Frank's attorney. I am here to read you his will as per his instructions."

"What? Frank has a Will? He didn't have anything. For crying out loud, he was just a truck driver," laughed Frank's sister. "Go on, I'm sure it's just a few trinkets and his crazy wardrobe nobody wants anyway. Hurry up as we have birthday gifts to open."

Without missing a beat, the attorney broke the wax seal on the envelope and pulled out its contents. Sure enough, it was just one page.

"See, I told you. Just one page full of nothing but crap," burst out Franks sister.

"Please aunt Heather. Why do you have to be so mean? Uncle Frank was a kind person. You really should have given him a chance," responded Sally with deep sadness in her eyes.

"You really are a naïve little one. Go ahead Mr. Attorney, let's get to it."

Gordon cleared his throat and began reading.

"Dearest family. In the event that you are hearing my will being read to you, I have finally departed this mortal coil. DO NOT DESPAIR. Oh wait, only a few of you will." The room broke out into a fit of laughter as Gordan paused. He continued. "I know that the majority of you avoided me in life because of my looks…"

"No kidding," said little Johnny. "He *was* Frankenstein, literally." The room once again erupted into uncontrollable laughter. Sally was saddened by the lack of maturity in the room.

The attorney continued. "I would have liked to have been a bigger part of the family, but that was not to be. My darling niece, Sally, was the only one that saw and accepted me for who I really was. She loved me unconditionally." A few chuckles were let out. "Sally, I told you not to hang around your uncle. He has been nothing but bad news for our family. No one ever took us seriously because of him," said Sally's mother.

"Mother, I can't believe you are still so upset just because of how Uncle Frank looked. I loved him. He was kind and funny," she said as tears rolled down her reddened cheeks. The family continued to mock poor deceased Frank.

The attorney cleared his throat once again and picked up where he left off. "To my precious niece, Sally, I leave the home where my darling Dianne and I lived and my full inheritance of $8 million dollars."

The air in the room seemed to disappear as everyone gasped. "WHAT?" cried out Sally's mother and father. "He had money? How? He was just a measly truck driver. Don't worry Sally, we will help you invest that money."

"Not so fast Mr. and Mrs. Stein. Frank has given specific instructions that will allow Sally to move into the home when she wishes.

The money will be placed into a bank account that has already been set up in Sally's name only. Increasing amounts of her inheritance will be deposited each year until she turns thirty. Frank and Sally have already set up a plan for her future. Your assistance will not be needed."

"You and Uncle Frank talked about this? Why didn't you tell us?" asked Sally's parents as they fumed.

"Because he knew you would act this way. He was much smarter than you think," said Sally, saddened yet empowered.

"How did he make all that money anyway?" grilled her father.

"That's our little secret that I promised Uncle Frank to never reveal," replied Sally, boasting a very proud smile.

Sally could feel the weight of her parents' curiosity pressing down on her. They wouldn't stop digging, wouldn't stop prying, but there were some things she would never, could never, share with them. Uncle Frank had entrusted her with a glimpse into the secret behind his astonishing wealth, and even though she now understood how he had built his fortune, she was still shaken by the sheer scale of it.

His method was deceptively simple: pay yourself first. Every month, he had tucked away ten percent of his earnings. At first, it was a pittance, hardly noticeable. But with patience, smart investments, and the magic of compounding interest over four decades, that small habit had blossomed into something extraordinary.

Her mind raced. She needed clarity, a voice of reason, Leah. Instead of returning to her family after speaking with attorney Gordon Zellinski outside of the family gathering, Sally made a choice. She walked away, pulled out her phone, and called Leah. Minutes later, they were seated at their favorite Italian restaurant, the scent of garlic and basil curling around them like a warm embrace.

"The family has lost their minds," Sally sighed. "Now they're all obsessed with Uncle Frank. Did you have any idea he'd built up that kind of fortune?"

Leah's eyes widened. "Not a clue! I mean, I knew he was a saver, but that's next level. Guess he knew exactly what he was doing, and now, you're the one he's passed it to. Just imagine, soon, you and I will be neighbors! If you need any help making it feel like home, say the word. Have you thought about when you're moving in?"

Sally blinked. Had she? The reality of it all was still sinking in, but as they talked, it became obvious. This wasn't something to hesitate over. It was hers. Uncle Frank had meant for this to be her home. And why wait?

By the time they finished their meal, the decision was made. Sally would move in as soon as possible. After all, it wasn't just a house. It was the beginning of something entirely new.

Sally didn't breathe a word of her plan to anyone else. Instead, she spent the next three days quietly ferrying her clothes and toiletries over to Uncle Frank's house, her every move deliberate and unhurried. With Leah by her side, the two transformed the main bedroom, clearing it out and painting the walls anew, a fresh start, as much for the room as for Sally herself.

By the end of the third day, she knew it was time. She picked up the phone, her fingers trembling only slightly as she dialed her parents. The moment she told them she was moving in immediately; their reaction was swift and furious. They didn't ask why. They didn't ask how she was feeling. They demanded, no, ordered, her to come home. And if she didn't? They would come and get her.

The conversation didn't last long. It ended with a single question from her father, a question that landed like a stone in the pit of her stomach.

"By the way, where is your new home?"

Sally hesitated only for a breath. Then, with a quiet strength she hadn't realized she possessed, she answered.

"If you never cared where Uncle Frank lived all these years, it doesn't seem important for you to know now."

Silence. Then a click. He had hung up on her.

The weight of it all hit her at once. She crumpled onto the bed, tears spilling freely, her chest tightening with the painful truth, how could people be so selfish? So cruel?

Just then, the door creaked open, and Leah stepped inside. "Sally, what's wrong?"

One look at her face, and Leah knew. She sat beside her, wrapping an arm around Sally's shoulders, her own heart aching for her friend. They had been through so much together, and nothing would change that.

After a few moments, Leah's lips curled into a soft, knowing smile. "I have an idea," she said, squeezing Sally's hand. "How about we take a little trip? Let's drive up to Canada this weekend. I'd love to show you my hometown, Montreal is only an hour away. We can leave the day after tomorrow. That gives you another day to finish up here and clear your head. And if your parents do find out where you are? Well... you won't be here."

Sally blinked through her tears, a spark of hope flickering in her chest. Maybe a change of scenery was exactly what she needed.

"What do you say?" Leah asked, her voice warm and inviting.

Sally inhaled deeply, then nodded. "I say...let's go."

June 7, 2024
Montreal, Canada

Friday unfolded in a golden haze of sunshine; the kind of day that made the world feel wide open and full of promise. The drive to Montreal was smooth, the miles slipping by effortlessly, and even the border crossing, so often a tedious ordeal, was surprisingly swift. Leah couldn't help but marvel at their luck.

Their first stop was Mont Royal Park, a lush oasis perched above the city, where towering trees swayed in the breeze and the skyline stretched endlessly before them. It was the perfect balance of adventure and serenity, a breath of fresh air after being on the road.

By the time they reached their cozy apartment in town, excitement buzzed beneath their fatigue. A little rest was in order, but soon, the city's electric pulse would call them out into the night, ready to embrace all the magic Montreal had to offer.

Just as Leah had put her head down on the pillow, the phone in her purse across the room started to make a funny noise. *I should have silenced the darn thing. It can wait. I need just ten minutes. A quick cat nap.*

Soon, she was rested, quietly going into the kitchen and pouring herself a glass of water. On the porch she enjoyed the lush backyard while Sally continued to relax.

Thirty minutes later, Sally joined her, ready for the afternoon and evening ahead.

"That park is amazing. I really enjoyed the climbs, views and lake. Can we go back again this weekend?"

Leah agreed it would be a good time to visit again with the beautiful weather ahead of them. "Let's get ready to go into town. I have a surprise for you. I bought us tickets to go see your favorite show, but this time live, The Phantom of the Opera. Show starts at eight so that gives us time for a relaxing dinner and then the show."

"You are amazing. Thank you. This weekend could not get any more exciting. I'll be ready in a jiffy."

Sally, upon entering her room, noticed her phone lighting up more than usual. Over ten messages from her parents. Several missed calls from her school. A sigh escaped her lips as she rolled her eyes and tossed the buzzing device into her purse without a second thought. Whatever it was, it could wait. This weekend was hers, and she wasn't about to let anyone ruin it.

An hour later, she and Leah wandered the streets of Old Montreal, the city humming softly around them. The scent of warm pastries drifted through the crisp evening air, wrapping Sally in a sugary embrace. Then, like a magnet, her gaze locked onto a pastry shop window. She stopped dead in her tracks.

Inside the dimly lit display case, only a few treats remained. But there, gleaming under the golden light, were caramel and chocolate éclairs that practically begged to be devoured.

Leah chuckled, recalling the first time she had ever craved an éclair with such desperation. "Oh no," she teased. "You've got the look."

Minutes later, they were inside, clutching the last two éclairs. They split them in half, the first bite sending Sally straight into confectionary nirvana.

"Oh. My. God." She moaned dramatically. "This is what happiness tastes like."

Leah licked the last trace of chocolate icing from her fingers, glancing at the time. "Alright, we've got forty minutes before our dinner reservations down the street."

Then, her phone began to talk to her.

"Leah Appleman. You have been selected as this month's participant of the Blank Check. You must have missed our original invitation for tonight's rendezvous. You have thirty minutes left before forfeiting your chance at the game. We are at Théâtre Sainte-Catherine, not far from you. Best of luck. And remember, DREAM BIG."

Sally let out an ear-piercing squeal, clutching Leah's arm. "Leah. LEAH. This weekend has just gone from amazing to insane."

Leah's eyes widened in shock before realization struck like lightning.

"We have to run."

Halfway to the theater, Sally glanced at Leah with a spark of curiosity. "Is this the same place where we're seeing Phantom of the Opera?"

Leah shook her head, a knowing smile playing on her lips. "No, but it's just around the corner. Come on, just a few more blocks."

The city lights shimmered as they approached the entrance, where a strikingly tall, elegant woman awaited them. She stood poised beneath the marquee, wrapped in a flowing white dress adorned with delicate black patterns. Her presence was magnetic.

"Miss Appleman, I presume?" Her voice was smooth; her French laced with quiet authority. "Please, step inside. We have been expecting you." Then, her gaze shifted to Sally. With effortless grace, she switched to English. "Miss Stein, I presume? Welcome. We are delighted you could both join us. Do come in."

The two women followed her inside, moving past a polished wooden bar and rows of neatly arranged chairs on the red floor. The soft glow of stage lights bathed the space in an almost dreamlike hue. As they neared the small stage, Leah turned to speak, only to realize Sally was no longer beside her.

"Sally?" Leah's voice carried a note of confusion.

"Just a minute," came the distant reply.

Sally was rooted to the spot. Behind the counter stood a young man, where time seemed to fold in on itself. Their eyes met, and something electric crackled between them, a pull, deep and undeniable. Her breath hitched, her pulse quickened.

Later, the young man would confess he had felt it too.

"Sally!" Leah's voice cut through the fog, sharp with impatience as she hurried toward her friend. "Please, focus."

Sally barely heard her. She turned, dazed, her voice a whisper. "Leah... do you believe in love at first sight?"

Leah let out a short laugh. "Oh, come on. Of course not. That éclair must've had some kind of magic in it. We don't have time for this." She grabbed Sally's arm, tugging her along. But Sally moved as if in a trance, her gaze never breaking from the young man's.

Backstage, Leah came to an abrupt halt.

The elegant woman in white stood waiting, flanked by two tall men in crisp white shirts and black suits. Their presence was commanding, their expressions unreadable.

A voice spoke, low and deliberate, but Leah barely registered the words. Her heart pounded as her gaze locked onto the second man.

"Leah," Sally nudged her gently. "You're not listening."

Leah couldn't move, couldn't speak.

The man's dark eyes held her captive, pulling her into something unknown, something vast.

Then, with a slow, deliberate motion, he unfurled a sleek, gleaming device.

And just like that, the night took a turn neither of them could have ever imagined.

"Miss Appleman," the first man's voice shattered the silence like a crack of thunder. "When you're ready, you may enter your amount into the device, any amount you wish."

Numbers were the last thing on Leah's mind. Her thoughts felt distant, tangled in something unfamiliar, something she couldn't name. She turned to Sally, her voice barely a whisper. "I think I believe now."

Sally's eyes flicked toward her, urgent but unwavering. "Leah, we'll talk later. Focus. Write your amount. There are only five minutes left."

Leah wrenched her gaze away from the dark, hypnotic eyes that had ensnared her. The tablet gleamed before her. Pick a number. Just pick a number.

From the depths of her mind, a whisper, no, a command, repeated itself. *Five. Five. Five.* The number pulsed like a heartbeat. Before she could second-guess herself, her hand moved, tracing the digits in the air. But as her fingers quivered, the tablet misread her intent.

Fifty million.

A chime rang from her phone, unfamiliar and final.

"Congratulations, Miss Appleman," the first man announced smoothly. "Your new bank account has just been created, with fifty million dollars, tax free. Here are two debit cards for your convenience."

Leah's breath hitched. She wasn't looking at the cards. Her eyes were locked on *his*, the man before her. He smiled, nodding slightly, as if they shared some unspoken secret.

Her stomach twisted. *What is happening?*

Leah was in a whirlwind, her mind racing to process the events of the past week, no, the past hour. Everything had unfolded so fast, so unexpectedly, that her senses were still catching up, struggling to separate reality from the dreamlike state she found herself in.

The poised and elegant woman interrupted her thoughts, her voice smooth and professional. "Miss Appleman, please review the video so we may post it on social media. Any changes you wish to make, we will gladly accommodate."

Still dazed, her body thrumming with an unfamiliar yet electrifying energy, Leah nodded. Together, they watched the footage, and with a quiet certainty, she gave her approval.

In a fleeting moment, the first man and woman slipped through the backstage doors, Sally's attention was elsewhere. Her heart pounded as she searched for him, the man who had set her soul ablaze. Leah and the remaining man lingered in the hush of the empty backstage.

His voice, deep and deliberate, cut through the stillness. "Forgive my forwardness, but I believe you feel it too."

Leah's breath caught. She melted under his gaze, her body betraying her with a silent nod.

"Can we meet soon, see where this leads?"

Her lips parted, hesitant but hopeful. "I would love that. But I don't live in Montreal. I'm from Plattsburgh, New York, just an hour south."

A slow, confident smile spread across his face. "That's no obstacle. I can be anywhere, anytime." He reached into his pocket, producing a slip of paper. "Here's my number. Let's exchange details and go from there."

Leah's heart raced. "We're here until Sunday. Let me check with my friend. Perhaps lunch tomorrow?"

His eyes held hers, warm and certain. "I would love nothing better."

A sudden realization struck him, and he chuckled, offering his hand. "How impolite of me, my name is William. William Dumas." He took a step closer, his presence intoxicating. "It is both a privilege and an honor to meet you, Leah Appleman."

Before she could respond, he placed both hands gently on her shoulders, leaning in with the effortless charm of a man who knew exactly what he was doing. His lips brushed her cheeks in the customary double kiss, sending heat rushing to her face.

As he pulled away, her skin still tingling from his touch, she knew, this was only the beginning.

"Till we meet again, Leah Appleman." It took a minute for her to realize that he had left. Her mind was racing. *Sally, oh my, Sally.*

She spotted Sally and her young suitor deep in conversation at the wooden counter, their voices weaving together like a melody.

"Leah," Sally began, a hint of hesitation in her voice, "would it be terribly rude of me to ask if we could skip our lunch together tomorrow? Henry has invited me out so we can get to know each other better." Her eyes sparkled with anticipation, though a flicker of guilt lingered.

Leah couldn't help but smile, a soft chuckle escaping her lips. If only Sally knew how perfectly this evening had unfolded.

"Not a problem at all," Leah replied, amusement dancing in her tone. "I'm sure I'll find some way to keep myself entertained."

Over morning coffee, Leah took a deep breath, clutching her cup as if it were the only thing grounding her. She had a confession to make, no, two.

"I was supposed to write five million," she admitted, her voice barely above a whisper. "But my hand was shaking so badly that the tablet registered fifty. I just... I couldn't think. My mind was somewhere else, no, with someone else." She exhaled, her eyes distant yet alight. "Is that why you asked me about love at first sight? Because the moment I looked into William's eyes, I knew. It wasn't a question; it wasn't a possibility, it was certainty. Even now, I feel it in my bones. We're meant to be."

Sally smiled, a knowing glint in her gaze. "It's impossible to explain, but when you know, you know." She reached across the table, giving Leah's hand a squeeze. "Funny, isn't it? We've both fallen into wealth and into love at the same time. Today is going to be grand. And you know what? I think Uncle Frank is watching us, smiling from above. He always believed in fate, and I think, my dear, fate is finally smiling back at us."

June 7, 2024
Sean

Just as Sean had suspected, the video had been released.

Montreal, Canada. Fifty million.

He leaned in, scrutinizing every frame, his fingers absently pinning the first scrap of information onto his ever-growing 'Evidence Wall'. Something about this video felt... off. A subtle shift, a detail just out of reach. And then, there, his sharp gaze locked onto it.

The contestants face.

She wasn't looking at the tablet. She was looking at the man holding it. And that look was unmistakable. A silent message, a flicker of something unspoken passing between them.

But there was something else.

Sean replayed the footage multiple times, his mind chasing an explanation that refused to form. It didn't make sense. Not yet.

A frustrated sigh escaped him. He needed a break, and besides, there was a fresh batch of eager tourists waiting for their first swim with the pigs. The investigation would have to wait.

But one thing was certain, this time, the video had revealed more. Clues that would help him untangle more of the mystery.

9

July 2024
Undisclosed Location

The room pulsed with an almost supernatural glow, charged by the sheer electricity of the latest winner's triumph. The mastermind leaned back, his eyes locked onto the screen, watching the replay once more. He had seen it, the delicate tremor in her hand, that fleeting hesitation that made the device register a number far greater than Leah Appleman had intended. Exhilarating. Every blank check was a jolt of pure adrenaline, even for him. But then, there was the look. That look between William and Leah. And he recognized it instantly. Once, long ago, he had felt it himself, that brief, electric moment that had sent his heart spiraling into a world he could never quite leave behind.

One hundred and thirty-four million dollars. That was the total so far. And it was only the beginning. His lips curled into a slow, knowing smile. How many more lives would be irrevocably altered? Some would rise to greatness, seizing their windfall with wisdom and precision. Others would drown in their own excess, victims of their own desires. That was the beauty of it, human nature, so predictably unpredictable. But the aftermath wasn't his concern. He was only the architect, the unseen hand shaping their fates.

July 5 was just days away. As an added thrill, he watched as the system he had meticulously designed selected the next unclaimed bank account, its algorithm weaving fate into numbers. The digits flickered, the tension mounting, then, a decision.

Sixty-five million.

A chuckle escaped him, deep and satisfied. He was brilliant. He was unstoppable. His mind drifted back to where it all began,

COMDEX, the legendary **COM**puter **D**ealers **EX**hibition, Las Vegas. He was a twenty-six-year-old man, eyes wide with wonder, surrounded by the future. The keynote speaker had been none other than Bill Gates himself, painting a vision of a world at one's fingertips, where information was limitless, boundless. Tim had been enthralled.

Windows '95 had stolen the spotlight that year, alongside a new era of software, APPS, they called them. The tools of the future laid bare before him. Touchscreens, digital assistants, multimedia wonders, whispers of the revolution to come. And Tim had seen it. Had understood it. Had been ready for it.

Now, decades later, he wasn't just riding the wave. He was the wave.

1994 was Tim's rebirth, a thrilling escape from the shadows of nearly a decade of despair. It was the year he seized his second chance, plunging headfirst into the electrifying world of technology. No longer just a spectator of innovation, he became the architect of his own digital creations, a master of code and possibility. As the twenty-first century dawned, he remained relentless, breathing new life into his existing applications while dreaming up fresh ones. The horizon stretched endlessly before him. Even when his time on this earth would pass, his imagination, his legacy, would live on, pulsing through the very software he had crafted.

July 2024
Sean

Driven by curiosity and a gnawing need for answers, Sean jotted down a few urgent notes, his pulse quickening at the weight of the mystery before him.

One hundred and thirty-four million dollars. A staggering sum, and six more months left in the game.

Find Leah Appleman. She held some interesting, personal insight.

Reach out to the theatre. Sean had no doubt that somebody would reveal a bit more information

With a final glance at his scribbled words, he set his pen down. This was far from over. Time for another tour to Pig Beach.

≈

The boat rocked gently as it neared the shore, the turquoise water so clear that tiny fish could be seen darting between the ripples. Pig Island, an almost mythical place where friendly pigs roamed freely, its sandy beach speckled with shade from the swaying palm trees.

As soon as the tourists stepped onto the warm sand, a group of adult pigs trotted toward them, their pink snouts wiggling in curiosity, but the real stars of the day were the baby piglets. Tiny, round, and full of energy, they stumbled over their own hooves as they dashed toward the group, their little tails wagging.

Laughter filled the air as the tourists knelt, offering small pieces of fruit. One piglet, barely bigger than a coconut, nudged against one of the tourists' legs and let out the softest oink before flopping onto the sand, belly-up, demanding a rub. It was an irresistible scene.

After a while, the group waded into the shallow water, and to their delight, the piglets followed, paddling clumsily but determinedly beside them. Sunlight glinted off their wet fur as they splashed around, turning the ocean into their personal playground.

The afternoon drifted by in a haze of relaxation, lounging on the beach and watching playful piglets dart across the sand. Here, time moved slower, the worries of daily life dissolved into the rhythmic crash of waves and the occasional contented snort.

As the day came to an end, the piglets took one final, joyful trot along the shore, as if offering a fond farewell. Sean lingered for a moment, savoring the tranquility before it was time to go.

Back at his beach bungalow, it was time to get some real work done. Contact Leah Appleman.

July 2024
Aleena

The bitter wind whispered through the trees as the last light of day faded into a dusky glow. Aleena stood at the window, her breath fogging the glass, lost in dreams of warmer days and tasks that would take her beyond the confines of her family's guesthouse. She longed for the freedom of the wild, envying the older girls who spent their days by the lake, deep in the forest, their hands busy with work that let them breathe in the untamed beauty of the land.

Every summer, when the July sun kissed the rugged northeast landscape of Russia's Kamchatka's volcanoes, fearless adventurers arrived, fifteen groups over the course of three fleeting months, to embark on the grueling yet exhilarating nine-day, trek through Russia's volcanic region. Every four days, sixteen new faces would appear in Kozyrevsk, a tiny village cradled by dense forest, its population a mere fifteen hundred. Exhausted from the bone-rattling nine-hour journey, the hikers would sink into the steamy embrace of the guesthouse sauna, their muscles aching but their spirits soaring. A hot meal, lovingly prepared by the field cooks, awaited them before they collapsed into a well-earned rest, eager for the challenge of the Kamchatka volcanoes that lay ahead.

For years, Aleena had been tethered to the guesthouse, a role thrust upon her not long after marriage. With no child to occupy her, her father and husband had quickly found other ways to fill her days. She scrubbed floors, washed dishes, made up beds, her world confined to the wooden walls of the inn. Yet, through the revolving door of travelers, she caught glimpses of something bigger. English echoed through the halls, a language that seemed to bridge every corner of the world. Aleena listened, learned, and, before long, spoke. She delighted in conversations with visitors, but none more than with Owen and Ingrid, a vibrant couple from Alaska whose laughter was as boundless as their love for adventure. They returned every year, carrying with them stories of places Aleena had never seen, sparking a hunger in her that she could no longer ignore.

She wasn't unhappy. But she wasn't content, either. The walls of her life felt smaller with each passing season, and her heart ached for more.

Then, overnight, everything changed.

The news had sent her pulse racing; no more endless cleaning, no more scrubbing dishes. In just four months, she would step into a new role, one filled with skill, tradition, and meaning. Owen and Ingrid were going to be elated.

Each day became a flurry of learning. In the dim glow of the rustic wooden smokehouse, Aleena watched her Aunt Marina move with effortless grace, slicing thick salmon into delicate ribbons and laying them onto wooden boards. The air was rich with the scent of smoldering birch, the fire crackling as though whispering secrets of generations past. Her aunt's voice, warm and patient, guided her through each motion. Aleena's fingers fumbled at first, but soon, muscle memory took over. Side by side, they worked in a rhythm as old as their Cossack ancestors, bound by tradition, bound by blood.

Mistakes were met with gentle laughter, corrections given with love. In two months, Aleena was no longer the student, she was the master. If her mother had been alive, she would have been proud.

Then came May, carrying with it the gift of sixteen-hour days, sunlight stretching long into the night. Now, Aleena turned her focus to the sauna, nestled in the forest just a short walk from the guest house. The crisp morning air bit at her cheeks as she carefully stacked birch logs in the firebox, striking the perfect balance for a slow, steady burn. She carried water, cold and pure, from the spring-fed lake, pouring it in careful measure over the heated stones, releasing a fragrant cloud of steam that wrapped around her like a warm embrace.

With every flickering flame, every wisp of rising steam, Aleena felt it, something stirring deep within her. A fire just as fierce as the one she now tended.

This summer, she would not simply watch the world pass by. She would be part of it.

During those four months, Aleena had immersed herself in learning, absorbing every detail of the family's traditions. Then, one evening, she made a bold suggestion, one that would change everything. She envisioned an entirely new setting for their guests' evening meal, something rustic, something authentic. With excitement gleaming in her eyes, she proposed transforming the forgotten structure at the edge of the forest into a dining hall unlike any other.

Her husband, Alexei, was stunned. He had always known Aleena to be creative, but this was inspired. Her father, Boris, however, dismissed the idea outright. The building was nothing but a useless relic, filled with rusting machinery and decades of dust. It was a fool's errand, he insisted. But Alexei saw the fire in his wife's eyes and sided with her. Begrudgingly, her father relented. They could have their project, but only in their spare time.

The building stood humble and unassuming, its weathered wooden frame bearing the weight of countless seasons. Yet, within its walls a quiet marvel awaited, a vast, square opening in the ceiling, its edges framed by thick, timeworn beams stacked with purpose. This open skylight was more than just an architectural feature; it was a portal to the sky, where sunlight poured in by day and stars cast their silent watch by night. Alexei envisioned a central stone fire pit; Aleena delighted with his idea.

For three grueling months, Aleena and Alexei toiled away, clearing out decades of clutter and debris. The dirt floor, once buried under discarded wood and rusted tools, slowly revealed itself. Every moment spent inside that building brought Aleena's vision closer to life. She wanted something raw, something immersive, a Cossack style indoor campfire experience that would captivate their guests.

The finishing touches were no less spectacular. From the shadows of the old storeroom, they unearthed a treasure trove of over a hundred bear pelts, now repurposed to line the walls and floor, their rich textures adding a primal luxury to the space. Three long wooden tables, each seating six, flanked the room, waiting for the first feast to be served.

Then came the night of the grand reveal. Aleena and Alexei invited the villagers to witness the transformation, and as they stepped inside, gasps of astonishment filled the air. The central firepit crackled, its flames licking skyward in shades of crimson and gold, illuminating the space in a flickering, mesmerizing glow. Overhead, the last remnants of the summer sun streamed through the towering skylight, casting an ethereal warmth upon the scene.

At the edge of the three tables stood six of Aleena's pièce de resistance, the salmon display, consisting of two tripod like wooden supports with a horizontal wooden rod span between them. The rich aroma of the draped glistening salmon fillets filled the air. Around them, the tables overflowed with platters of traditional Cossack dishes, rustic loaves, and an array of fresh vegetables.

It was a spectacle, a masterpiece born from passion and perseverance. What had once been a forgotten ruin was now the heart of their home, a place where fire and feast intertwined, where tradition met ingenuity, and where guests would gather, enchanted, for years to come.

Most of the villagers stopped by to just look, others stayed to enjoy the festivities till the wee hours of the night.

July 2024
Sean

Over five relentless months of investigation, Sean had carefully gathered a tight-knit circle of trusted contacts, individuals just as hungry for the truth as he was. Together, they were determined to peel back the layers of secrecy surrounding the elusive social media game and the enigmatic mastermind pulling the strings.

His gaze lingered on the chaotic sprawl of his 'Evidence Board', a testament to his obsession. Eight recorded Blank Check events. Only six victories. And with the rare occurrence of thirteen new moons in 2024, the numbers painted a clear picture: if no unexpected disruptions occurred and every player won, the game would play out across fifteen high-stakes events. Methodically, he scrawled the remaining dates along the bottom of his wall map:

July 5

August 4

September 2

October 2 – Solar Eclipse

November 1

December 1

December 30

The puzzle was finally offering him glimpses of a bigger design. But he needed more than fragments, he needed answers. And for that, it was time to call Leah Appleman.

≈

Sean's first aha moment came the instant he noticed the inconsistency; Leah's phone number linked to the Blank Checks event didn't match the country where it had taken place. A small detail, but potentially seismic. He filed it away, a mental red flag waving wildly. He'd make sure to confirm it with Leah.

≈

Hours later, Sean leaned back in his chair, Leah's revelations sinking in. He took a slow, deliberate sip of his stiff drink as he sifted through the intricate web of details she had laid out.

The game's software wasn't just tracking movements, it was following the players, pinpointing their locations with precision. Leah's last-minute decision to drive not just across the border, but to Montreal, had confirmed it. She had ignored and slept through her first notification, only to receive a stark reminder with just thirty minutes to spare, her meeting pointing eerily close, mere blocks away.

Then there was William. A hometown man pulled into the chaos at the last second. He couldn't name the mastermind, but he did reveal something else, he had been a cog in the machine of 2T Technology Corp for years. His job? Managing and updating APPS, keeping them sharp, feeding the insatiable beast of the digital world.

But none of that compared to Leah's surprising win fall. The shock still clung to her. Her own trembling hand. One tiny slip. A quiver. A five twisted into a fifty, rewriting fate in an instant.

Sean felt the shift. His vision sharpened, his instincts ignited. Another layer of the puzzle had crumbled away, revealing something deeper. And one thing was certain; this game was bigger than he had ever imagined.

Now, they had a target. A name to chase. 2T Technology Corp. And Sean was ready to sink his teeth in.

July 5, 2024
Aleena

The first wave of guests trickled into the village on July 5th, their laughter and chatter weaving through the crisp summer air. Among them, much to Aleena's astonishment, were Owen and Ingrid.

"Aleena!" Ingrid's voice rang out like a melody as she rushed forward, arms flung wide. She enveloped Aleena in a fierce embrace, squeezing tightly before pulling back to study her friend. "It's so good to see you! Owen decided to come earlier this year, completely last-minute. We had no way of letting you know, hope you don't mind the surprise! And look at you! You're glowing."

Aleena beamed, her heart swelling. "I missed you both. Your letters and postcards mean the world to me, you know how much I love them." She turned to Owen, her face still alight with joy. "And you!

Hello, stranger." She wrapped him in a warm hug, feeling the familiar comfort of old friends reuniting.

Owen grinned as he stepped back, a playful glint in his eyes. "So, I see you are part of the welcoming committee now. Does this mean they've finally recognized your brilliance and given you a better role? I certainly hope so."

Aleena laughed, nodding enthusiastically. "They have! I'm in charge of cooking and preparing the sauna for our visitors. It's perfect, I spend my days in the forest, and by the lake now... it feels like a dream." She gestured for them to follow. "Come, let me show you to your room."

From a distance, her husband watched, his heart brimming with quiet pride.

As they walked toward the guest house, Owen exchanged a knowing glance with Ingrid and gave her a subtle wink.

After settling the guests into their rooms, small groups of four were led through the forest to the lake for their fifteen-minute sauna sessions. Ingrid and Owen chose to go last, eager to catch up with Boris and Alexei. When their turn arrived, the two hikers scheduled to join them decided to stay back at the guesthouse to rest.

"Alexei, why don't you join us? We have a little something for you and Aleena."

"Sure."

The four walked through the forest path and out into the opening by the lake.

Owen could barely contain his excitement as he nudged Ingrid, their shared anticipation evident in their expressions. Ingrid took a deep breath, closing her eyes momentarily to steady herself before speaking.

For the past six months, she and Owen had been closely following the online social media game that had captured global attention, though it remained largely unknown in the remote Russian countryside. The premise of the game was astonishing: once a month, a randomly chosen participant received a blank check, allowing them to name their own sum of money. At first, the concept seemed unbelievable, but as the months passed, six individuals had already filled out their checks and secured their fortunes.

Owen and Ingrid had eagerly signed up, including their friends, Alexei and Aleena. Understanding how the game operated, they had discreetly entered Aleena's name, purchasing a phone in her name to ensure eligibility. Since the winner was determined by the location of the phone rather than the actual participant's whereabouts, they had carried it with them throughout their travels.

What they hadn't expected was for fate to intervene so dramatically. That morning, as they departed from their hotel in Paratunka, Russia, a message arrived on the phone. The words on the screen were clear and direct: Aleena had been chosen as the July recipient of the Blank Check. She was instructed to meet the game's representatives at six the following morning, near the sauna by the lake in Kozyrevsk, and was welcome to bring family and friends.

The revelation left Alexei and Aleena stunned. The implications of the message were overwhelming. Aleena would be presented with a sleek, futuristic device, allowing her to write the desired sum of money in the air with a mere movement of her hand. No recipient had ever received less than seven million dollars, a sum that translated to over six hundred million rubles.

The weight of the moment was too much for Alexei. His legs gave out, and he sank to the cold earth, struggling to process the enormity of what had just been revealed. His mind reeled, searching for logic in something that defied explanation. How could such wealth be given away so freely? Why had they been chosen? And how had the game's organizers known the exact location of the phone?

Owen remained composed, understanding their disbelief. He and Ingrid had once felt the same skepticism. But the accounts of past winners were undeniable, it was real, life changing. By morning, they would have their answer.

A heavy stillness settled over them, broken only by the whisper of the wind through the trees and the rhythmic ebb and flow of the water against the shore. The weight of the unknown pressed down on them, vast and inescapable.

Taking a steadying breath, Aleena forced herself to refocus. There was no use in getting carried away just yet. For now, there were tasks to complete, dinner needed tending, and the evening's routine had to continue. Whatever awaited them in the morning, they would face it when the time came.

As Owen and Ingrid lingered by the lake, taking in the quiet serenity of the water, Alexei and Aleena made their way back through the forest, lost in their own thoughts. Upon returning to the guest house, they slipped into their familiar roles, Aleena heading to the kitchen, Alexei tending to the fire in the new wooden dining hall, each silently preparing for whatever the next day might bring.

Aleena found it difficult to concentrate as she gazed out into space, lost in thought. *How much am I going to write on the check*? Her head could not comprehend the numbers that Owen and Ingrid had spoken of. Her Aunt Marina asked her a time or two if anything was wrong, but Aleena managed to fudge the truth by explaining that she was overwhelmed with Owen and Ingrid showing up so soon for the tour.

Aleena pushed the crazy thoughts from her mind and focused on the task at hand. *I'll talk to Ingrid and Owen later tonight and figure this out.* This was the first night that the new dining room was going to be used for guests, and she wanted it to be flawless.

At seven that evening, the large bell outside the guest house was rung. The sixteen guests followed Aleena, Boris, and Marina out to the new dining room.

"Where are we going?" asked Owen and Ingrid in unison.

"You're not the only ones with a secret. We have a surprise for you. Alexei and I have been working on it for the last three months. You are going to be amazed," smiled back Aleena as she continued towards the wooden square building.

The awe and delight expressed by each who entered the enchanted, rustic Cossack room brought much delight to Aleena and Alexei. Owen and Ingrid were the last to enter. They gasped at the attention to detail. Ingrid was utterly intrigued with the bear pelts that covered every inch of the walls and most of the floor. Owen drooled over the food presentation displayed on all three tables, especially the draped salmon filets, seemingly suspended in the air.

"Oh, Aleena and Alexei. This is beyond words. You have created a perfect haven. What an honor to your Cossack ancestors. This is…." Ingrid choked on her words. Owen put his arm around his wife and took in the amazing transformation himself. He remembered the mustiness and dampness of the dark room filled with machinery and forgotten items of the past. "It is very impressive. You both have done a fabulous job," said Owen, also a bit teary-eyed.

Distant music played from the adjacent building, adding that extra touch of ambiance to the delightful evening. Aleena and Alexei sat by the door, now and then tending to the empty glasses, or refilling the plates with bread and vegetables. Some of the new hikers were taken by Aleena and enjoyed asking her questions about life in rural Russia. Alexei watched as his wife moved with ease, tending to their guests throughout the evening. How she was able to contain her excitement was bewildering. Her graceful and non-assuming movement amongst their guests was a sight to behold. Their life could dramatically change at sunrise and yet, she hosted the dinner as if nothing was about to happen.

"I hope you have all enjoyed this fabulous evening of rest as the next two days are going to be less relaxing as we hike through the valleys amongst the volcanoes," explained the tour leader. "Get your rest tonight as we embark on our journey by foot at nine. Rest well and we will see you in the morning."

Once Alexei and Aleena had finished cleaning up from the evening's successful dinner, they met with Owen and Ingrid. Aleena quickly started the conversation. "First, I want to know if this is true."

"Yes, my dear, it is true. Tomorrow morning you will get the chance to change your life, not only for yourself, but your family, friends, and even your village if you wish," replied Ingrid.

"Please help me. I just don't know what to write down. It all seems so unrealistic. What would you do?" she asked, trying not to sound too desperate.

"That's a hard question to answer. However, let us take it one step at a time. What you would like to do that you cannot do now. Then we can attach an amount onto each item."

"That sounds like a good start. Of course, you know that I would love to travel. Seeing your pictures and postcards makes me want to go and experience those places for myself. Alexei, you would go with me, wouldn't you?" Alexei was a man of few words. "Yes, my love, I would love to explore with you."

For over an hour, the four discussed dreams, visions, and ideas as their imaginations gave way to unimaginable possibilities. Their newfound wealth would allow their village to rebuild the airport, allowing for easier access to them. They could pave the two main roads in town to help reduce the mud and dust throughout the year. New vehicles and appliances throughout the village would be a welcome addition to everyone's personal life. Once those numbers were all tallied up, the figure was still a very small percentage compared to the lower winning amounts. More numbers were added so that Aleena and Alexei could travel off-season. With their vast travel experience, Ingrid and Owen were able to put together a figure for a twenty-year plan of two annual trips for the couple. Secretly, they overestimated each trip. The final figure came out to two and a half million dollars, over two hundred and fifty million rubles. They were both again in disbelief.

Although it was not sinking in, Aleena and Alexei agreed on the number. It was a sleepless night for the two couples.

July 6, 2024

Aleena was out by the lake, sitting on the bench lost in thought before sunrise. It was 4:30 in the morning and she hadn't slept a wink. An hour later, Ingrid and Owen showed up by the shore. "Only another half hour," said Owen in a whisper.

At six o'clock on the dot, two men and a woman, elegantly dressed in black and white, walked through the opening in the forest. The two couples were startled by their arrival.

"Greetings to you all," said the first man, his voice very calm and soothing. "We are delighted to begin your adventure Aleena Vovkodav. In a few moments, you will write in your desired amount on this blank check," pointing towards the second man who pulled out a rolled-up device. He unrolled it and placed it on the nearby bench. Displayed on the sleek device was the image of a check with Aleena's name. Owen noticed the modern lined logo at the top of the check that matched the lapel pins worn by the three people. The signature at the bottom of the check was illegible.

"Now, Mrs. Vovkodav, before we proceed, you have the choice to be filmed as you fill out your amount, or we can block out your name and just film your hand. How would you like to proceed?"

Aleena could not think straight. She turned to Owen and Ingrid. "What do you think?"

"You could blur out your name and have this moment filmed. Just a thought." Without a moment's hesitation, Aleena agreed. She had made up her mind. *I'll be famous for a few days. Why not,* she told herself.

Instantly, with a graceful swipe of the hand over the device, Aleena's name became a blurry translucent rectangle.

"It is time. With your finger, simply hover over the device and write your amount on the line. When you are ready, you may begin. Remember, Dream Big."

Standing on the other side of the bench, the tall woman began recording Aleena from a distance with a slim device.

Aleena focused on the shiny device sitting next to her on the bench. Then she proceeded.

Five Million.

Immediately, the phone chirped in Owen's hand. He handed the phone over to Aleena.

"Congratulations Mrs. Vovkodav. You are July's big winner," said the first man calmly. "An additional app has just been installed on your phone. This app is a private bank account where the Five million has been placed in your name, tax-free. On the app, you can access and transfer however much money you would like to whomever you would like. Simply follow the instructions. Also, here are two debit cards for this account for your convenience."

No one spoke as the man handed over the two cards to Aleena.

The tall woman walked over and sat beside Aleena. Owen, Ingrid and Alexei watched as they viewed the video. It ended with a bright white burst of light, and the words "Congratulations to our July winner in Kozyrevsk, Russia. Five Million Dollars."

"Before we leave, Mrs. Vovkodav, we would like for you to transfer an amount of your choosing to your bank account. We want to make sure you are comfortable with how the system works."

"I don't have a bank account. We…" looking over at her husband, "…don't have a bank account.

"Then you can open up a separate account within the system for someone else, your family for instance?"

"Can I have a minute with my husband please?"

"Yes please. We are in no rush."

Aleena and Alexei entered the cold sauna building. Overwhelmed by the whirlwind of recent events, Aleena struggled to gather her thoughts but knew one thing for certain, she wanted to share half the money with Owen and Ingrid. Without hesitation, Alexei embraced her in agreement.

Turning to the screen, they typed in Ingrid and Owen Johnson, Anchorage, Alaska. A single match appeared, prompting them to input the transfer amount. After a brief exchange of glances, Aleena made the decision to send half of the money. Alexei nodded, and she carefully typed in the amount: Two and a half million dollars. A moment later, the transaction was complete.

Stepping out of the sauna, they walked over to the bench where everyone had gathered. As they arrived, Aleena was handed two additional debit cards. Both Owen and Ingrid received notifications on their phones but paid them no attention.

Aleena, overwhelmed with gratitude, embraced the couple warmly. The enormity of everything that had transpired still felt surreal. Ingrid reassured her, reminding her that she now had the freedom to put her ideas into action and decide how to share the news with her loved ones and the village.

Back in their rooms, Ingrid and Owen had two hours before their trek into the mountains. After repacking their backpacks, they headed downstairs to the small breakfast room for a cup of coffee. The morning was quiet, and they took their drinks out to the patio, enjoying the stillness of the early hours.

As Ingrid sipped her coffee, she pulled out her phone to check her messages. The peaceful silence didn't last long.

"Oh my..." she murmured, her voice sharp with surprise.

Owen looked up, waiting for an explanation. "What is it?"

Ingrid didn't answer right away. Instead, she glanced at him, then back at her screen. "Check your phone," she said. "See if you got the same message."

Owen pulled out his phone. Within seconds, his eyes widened as he stared at the screen. "My, oh my."

10

August 2024
Sean

There simply weren't enough hours in the day for Sean to lose himself entirely in his private investigation, not the way he wanted to. Clues had been scarce in those first few months, slipping through his fingers like grains of sand. And the contestants? Too entranced by the game itself to notice the world shifting around them.

But then, he'd found it. The biggest clue yet. A name he could sink his teeth into. 2T Technology Corp.

For the entire month of July, he had thrown himself into the chase, digging deeper, pushing harder, determined to unearth the truth. His former contacts, now his allies in this relentless pursuit, had burned through countless hours of research, only to uncover a frustrating reality: 2T Technology Corp. was just one of thousands of faceless, anonymous entities, its true nature hidden behind a labyrinth of corporate obscurity.

This wasn't going to be easy. It was an uphill battle, steep and unforgiving.

But Sean had never been one to turn back.

August 2024
Celeste

The weather across the globe had grown erratic, unpredictable, a relentless force of nature that paid no mind to the lives it disrupted. Sharm El-Sheikh was no exception. The looming storm on the horizon was the last thing Celeste needed as she prepared, yet again, to take her mother to the doctor. The desert's relentless summer heat had already drained the life from the city, pressing down like an unforgiving weight. And after three long years in her mother's hometown, Celeste had yet to grow used to it.

They said it took years to acclimate, but Celeste wanted no part of that. The heat was a living thing, suffocating and merciless, slowing people down until they moved as if wading through 115°F (46°C) degree scorchers. Even the nights refused to offer respite, the air heavy and oppressive, never dipping below a stifling 95°F (35°C). The earth itself seemed to trap the heat, radiating it back like an endless exhale of fire.

Celeste felt stretched thin, fraying at the edges. She had enough battles of her own to fight, but her mother's care came first. Always.

The doctor's appointment was at 9 a.m. a short, ten-minute drive, but the real challenge lay in the time it took to get her mother ready. Thirty minutes, at best, just to settle her into the wheelchair and navigate their way to the car. And then there was the storm. It was coming, thick clouds pressing in like an unspoken threat. If they were lucky, they could be home before the downpour began.

"Ommi?" Celeste called, glancing at the clock. She set her coffee cup down, her fingers tightening slightly around the ceramic. "It's time to get ready. I'll bring the wheelchair in a few minutes. Looks like we might just dodge the rain today. Want something to drink before we head out?"

She waited, listening. Nothing.

Frowning, she rinsed her cup in the sink, placing it beside the other breakfast dishes.

"Ommi?" she called again, this time with a touch of urgency.

Silence.

A hollow feeling swelled in her chest.

Celeste stood on the narrow balcony of her mother's modest apartment, watching the Red Sea shimmer like liquid fire beneath the morning sun. The air was thick with salt and jasmine, wrapping around her like a memory. In the distance, the hum of a dive boat setting off for Ras Mohammed reef echoed across the water, a quiet reminder of why her mother had chosen to come home.

"One day, we will live by the water," her mother used to say, tracing invisible waves in the air with graceful fingers, her voice full of longing. That dream had remained just that for most of her life, until, after sixty-five years of marriage, Celeste's father passed away in his native Italy. Grief had a way of shifting the tides, and so Celeste honored her mother's final wish: to return to the sea, to the place where she had been a girl, wild and free beneath the Egyptian sun.

Now, standing there, Celeste felt the world pressing in, the heat, the weight of loss, the ache of displacement. Egypt embraced her as one of its own, yet something in her soul tugged toward her father's land, toward the other half of her history.

She let herself drift with the rhythm of mourning, spending her days snorkeling through world-class reefs, enjoying meals prepared by the old Bedouin men who cooked with stories as much as spices, and watching the sky bleed into dusk. The quiet softened her grief, but it also carried ghosts, her mother's laughter, the scent of her perfume, the stories she told of places she never got to see.

One evening, as she wandered the shores of Naama Bay, the weight of absence grew too heavy to bear. She exhaled into the wind, her voice barely more than a whisper. *"Ommi, I miss you."*

A warm breeze curled around her, lifting a strand of her hair, soft as a touch. And for the first time in a long while, she wondered if, perhaps, she wasn't alone after all.

Leaving Sharm El-Sheikh was easier than Celeste had expected. When her mother's family expressed their wish to buy the apartment, to keep it within their lineage, the decision felt less like a choice and more like fate revealing its hand. The desert heat pressed against her, coaxing away the last traces of hesitation, until all that remained was a startling sense of clarity. Her family rejoiced over their newly claimed home, while Celeste took comfort in knowing that soon, the relentless sun would set on this chapter of her life.

On her final night, she sat cross-legged on the bedroom floor, surrounded by empty boxes, after her fingers had brushed against something unexpected, the old leather-bound diary that had been buried in the back of the closet amidst the clothes. She hadn't been searching for it, only packing up her mother's belongings, but now, as she traced the cracked spine, an unshakable pull gripped her.

The pages, worn and yellowed with time, were filled with her mother's familiar curled handwriting, a cascade of memories spilling across the paper. Celeste turned the pages, absorbing snippets of youth and longing, until one entry made her catch her breath.

It was dated her mother's twenty-first birthday.

"How will I be able to keep this secret? I must, I must. A promise is a promise. He would never forgive me if I didn't."

The words burned into her mind, unraveling something deep within her. Page after page of flowing Arabic script begged to be deciphered, a mystery waiting to be uncovered.

But exhaustion weighed heavy on her eyelids, dulling her focus. With a sigh, she let sleep claim her, the diary slipping from her grasp. As it tumbled to the floor, a hidden page fluttered open, a revelation left waiting for the moment she would wake and dare to uncover it.

August 2024
Sean

The endless search through countless companies was wearing Sean down. Frustration gnawed at him, growing sharper with each passing day. The stress he thought he had conquered was creeping back, a shadow from the past he couldn't afford to let in. He knew where this road led, spiraling into exhaustion, teetering on the edge of relapse, drowning in pills meant to keep him steady. His body had betrayed him before, and he wasn't about to let it happen again.

He needed an escape. A reset. Without overthinking, he made a snap decision, a retreat into the lush, untamed jungles of Jamaica, where the world could quiet down, and maybe, just maybe, he could breathe again.

August 2024
Celeste

The sharp chime of the doorbell jolted Celeste awake. Disoriented, she sat up, blinking against the pale morning light streaming through the curtains. The room was a disaster, clothes strewn across the floor, and empty boxes waiting to be filled. A sinking weight settled in her chest. The family had expected the apartment to be ready by now.

Barefoot, she hurried to the door, smoothing down her tangled hair. When she opened it, she didn't bother with excuses. "I'm sorry," she murmured, voice still thick with sleep. "I haven't finished packing. I..." She hesitated, then let out a breath. "I just... I couldn't."

The family members exchanged quiet glances, their eyes filled with understanding. "It's okay," one of them said gently. "We'll come back later."

As soon as the door closed, Celeste pressed her forehead to the wall. There was no time to drown in emotion. She had a flight to catch in the morning, back home to Italy, back to her life. And yet, this place, her mother's place, still felt like an unfinished chapter.

Shaking off the haze of sleep, she forced herself into motion. A quick shower washed away the grogginess but not the ache in her chest. Then, one by one, she folded her mother's clothes, tucking them into the empty boxes. The scent of lavender lingered on the fabric, a ghost of memories she wasn't ready to part with.

It wasn't until she moved the last heap of pillows that she saw it, worn, leather-bound, and tucked away as if hidden for safekeeping. Her mother's diary.

Her fingers hovered over it, the weight of it heavier than it should have been. A lifetime of secrets, thoughts, emotions, all pressed between those pages. For a moment, the world around her faded, and all that remained was the quiet hum of her own heartbeat.

But there was no time. Not now.

She exhaled, slipping the diary into her suitcase.

With one final glance around the apartment, she dialed the family's number. "I'm ready," she said, though she wasn't entirely sure she meant it.

July 2024
Molucca Sea

Tim had stepped away from the game, from his secret lair, from the relentless pulse of his double life. July had always been his sanctuary, a time to disappear into the world with the people who mattered most. And in 2024, he had chosen the Molucca Sea.

The invitations had gone out early in the year, nine, to be exact. Every single one had been accepted. A three week escape on a private yacht, sailing through the untouched beauty of Indonesia's Spice Islands, awaited them.

For 21 days, they lived in a dream. The yacht, sleek and luxurious, was their floating paradise. Sun-drenched decks stretched beneath an endless sky. A private chef transformed the day's freshest catch into feasts worthy of royalty. Every detail, every indulgence, was curated for pleasure.

Their days unfolded like poetry, kayaking through secret lagoons, hiking volcanic peaks for jaw-dropping views, wandering through remote fishing villages where time stood still. Some chased adrenaline, plunging into the deep with hammerhead sharks in Halmahera or drifting weightlessly over untouched coral walls in Morotai. There were no crowds, no tourists, just them and the vast, boundless blue. Tim savored that exclusivity.

Nights were pure magic. Impromptu dance parties on deck, laughter echoing beneath the stars. Midnight swims, the ocean swallowing them whole. Bonfires on secluded beaches, where stories spun and secrets slipped through the cracks of flickering flames.

There was no outside world here. No emails, no meetings, no schedules, only the sea, the sky, and the people he trusted most.

And yet, even here, the game found a way in. Conversations buzzed with excitement over the social media phenomenon gripping the globe. Even his friends, wealthy, powerful, seemingly untouchable, were enthralled. They had signed up, eager to claim their piece of the ever-growing fortune.

Tim played along, amused. Not one of them suspected the truth.

$139 million had been shared already. More than sixty percent of the world was waiting, desperate for their turn.

And he, he was the architect of it all.

August 2024
Undisclosed Location

Rested and ready for the return of the game, with only days left before the next new moon, Tim moved with a quiet confidence, his senses sharpened by anticipation. Then, he all but froze. A whisper, barely more than a breath against the unseen currents of the world, reached him. Somewhere out there, someone with relentless stamina, someone starving for the truth, had begun prying into the companies.

A slow grin spread across Tim's face, a glint of mischief in his eyes as he murmured to himself, *"Ah, so the hunt begins."*

He chuckled, the sound low and knowing. "Good luck, old chap," he said to the nameless seeker, amusement curling through his words. Let them try. The game was afoot, and Tim had played it far longer than most.

August 2024
Celeste

Back in her hometown of Tivoli, nestled on the outskirts of Rome, Celeste enjoyed the cool morning breeze. The oppressive desert heat was now a distant memory. With her coffee in hand, she gently turned the worn pages of her mother's diary, picking up exactly where she had left off.

And there it was, what she had set out to find.

"It has been months now. He has asked me to marry him. I think I will. Our adventure in Venice was supposed to be just a fleeting romance, a moment in time. But then I found out I was pregnant. Gianluca was elated. My family, however, will not honor me. I may as well stay. I do love him, but it is all happening so fast. People think I am Italian. I find that funny. I do look like the local girls, and my Italian is perfect."

Celeste's fingers trembled as she read on.

"This secret, I can only tell you, my dear pages that allow me to speak what is in my heart. Gianluca wishes to never speak of it again. But he chose to share with me his true family history. They do not come from Tivoli/Rome as everyone has been told. Gianluca and his family are Sicilian. He does not explain. He seemed to have had the world lifted off his shoulders after telling me this. I do not understand, but I do not pry either. Our child is what matters. She will be named Celeste, or if he's a boy, Celestin."

Celeste closed the diary, holding it to her chest as her heart raced. A flood of emotions surged within her, longings, questions, the weight of the unknown. But now, she had a name. A place. A beginning.

And deep within, she knew what she had to do.

Celeste was going to Sicily.

August 2024
Rodolpho

In the quiet town of Castelbuono, nestled in the hills of Sicily, Rodolpho started his day before the sun fully rose. The mist still clung to the cobblestone streets as he walked to the stables on his farm at the edge of town, where the donkeys, the local garbage collectors, waited for him. These weren't just any donkeys, the small group of female donkeys had replaced the loud trucks, providing an eco-friendlier way to collect garbage six days a week. His bond with the animals was a special one, built over years of shared trust and understanding.

Rodolpho, with his gentle demeanor, and kind eyes, knew all the town's secrets, even the ones left unspoken, and his quiet presence often felt like the steady pulse of the village itself.

As he made his way through Castelbuono's narrow streets, he stopped at each house, placing the garbage into the wooden boxes that straddle the blanket and leather cover on the donkey's back.

Though he was beloved by the town, there was an air of mystery about him. Rodolpho had his own secrets, things he kept hidden in the quiet places of his heart. The donkeys knew these secrets, in a way, they were the only ones who heard the soft confessions whispered during quiet moments in the stables, when no one else was around.

Late that afternoon Rodolpho visited the local café. He remained silent, watching the new lady in town. At first, all was going well, until it wasn't. He had seen how the town had turned on her in just two short days. Soon, he would set things right.

Celeste arrived in Castelbuono with a heart full of anticipation. Her roots were here, somewhere beneath the ancient stones of the town. This was where her ancestors had lived, where they had once walked the same cobbled streets. But there was something more, something hidden in the whispers of the village, that Celeste could not quite place.

She spent two days wandering the narrow, winding alleys, each one with its own history, frozen in time. Every corner, every cobblestone seemed to hold secrets, waiting for her to discover them. But no matter how much she explored, the town held its silence.

Hungry and weary, Celeste stopped at a small Osteria just around the corner from her hotel. She sat outside, beneath the shade of an old olive tree. The quiet comfort of the place was interrupted when a grizzled old man, his weathered face etched with the years, emerged from the café. His eyes scanned her with a suspicion that felt almost palpable.

"You want something to eat, I presume?" His voice was thick with an unsettling tone, as if his words carried weight she couldn't understand.

"Yes, please," Celeste replied, her voice uncertain, but polite.

The man narrowed his eyes, sizing her up. "What do you want?"

Without a menu, she hesitated, then ordered a simple pizza margherita. The man's eyes flashed with irritation. "No pizza," he said curtly, as if her request had offended him.

She tried again, listing three more items, each met with the same terse reply. Confusion crept into her mind. "Can I just have a glass of water?" she asked, hoping for something, anything.

The man's face darkened, and he spat on the ground with a sharp, audible snap. "Leave, before you regret it. Your family's name is not welcome here."

Taken aback, Celeste's heart began to race. "What do you mean?" she asked, her voice trembling.

He stepped closer, his presence imposing and cold. "Your ancestors... *THEY* are your problem, girl. They left this town in disgrace. It's better you don't dig any further. Leave before you find yourself in trouble."

Celeste's mouth opened to protest, but the man held up his hand, silencing her with a finality that struck her to her core.

"Don't bother. Go back to your life, wherever you came from. This place, this town, will never welcome you. You are better off forgetting your name and leaving the past buried."

The weight of his words was suffocating. Tears welled up in her eyes, but she fought to hold them back. She turned to leave, her legs heavy, as if each step away from him was a step deeper into a cold abyss. His voice rang out behind her, chilling and final.

"Never come back."

The words burned in her ears as she walked back to her hotel. It felt as if every eye in the town followed her, burning holes through her, whispering threats she did not understand.

Across the cobbled street, Rodolpho watched in grim silence. His heart sank as Celeste, shoulders hunched in sorrow, disappeared into the hotel. He waited, knowing something was terribly wrong. When she emerged again, she stopped first at the bakery, then the pastry shop, and finally at the local food store, only to be turned away at each door. No one would serve her. No one would even let her in.

It was time for him to act.

He approached her quietly, his voice soft with an apology. "Please forgive them. It is hard for them to let go of the past." He saw her confusion, her pain, and knew he couldn't let her face it alone.

"Why?" she whispered, her voice breaking. "What is happening here?"

"I think it's better we speak away from prying eyes," Rodolpho suggested gently, leading her down a quieter path. "Come with me."

Celeste broke down in his arms, her tears flowing freely now. "They want me to leave my hotel. They won't let me stay another night. I have nowhere to go, and it's already late."

Her words were a jumble of panic and pain, barely coherent. But Rodolpho understood.

"Come with me," he said firmly, his voice soothing. "I live just outside of town, where it will be safe. There, I'll explain everything. But for now, let's gather your things quickly."

With her small suitcase in tow, they walked out of the town together. The evening air was cool, and the donkeys greeted them as they arrived at Rodolpho's farmhouse. The animals were calm, savoring the last light of the day, as Celeste, exhausted and broken, was led to safety.

Rodolpho gently guided Celeste to the guest room, offering her a moment of solitude to collect herself. In the kitchen, he warmed a bowl of soup, the comforting aroma filling the air. He carefully arranged a plate with warm bread and butter, the simplicity of the gesture meant to soothe. A glass of wine added a promise of calm, a subtle hint at the weighty conversation that was about to unfold.

Rodolpho wasted no time. After confirming her family name was indeed Rizzo, he immediately began explaining the troubling state of the town.

For years, the citizens of Castelbuono had lived in fear, trapped in a cycle of silence and submission to the Mafia that ruled over them. The Mafia's grip on the town was suffocating, tightening with each passing day.

What began as small extortions, shop owners paying for "protection" in exchange for a semblance of safety, grew steadily more oppressive. Over time, the Mafia took control of the town's resources, the local construction projects, and even the schools. They manipulated the local government, bribing officials to turn a blind eye to their criminal activities.

Those who dared to speak out were swiftly silenced, either through threats or more sinister means. Families were torn apart as people vanished, only to be found years later, their bodies discarded in quiet corners of the mountains.

Gianluca Rizzo had become a pariah, along with his family. The whispers had escalated into open condemnation. The doors that once welcomed them now remained firmly shut. The people of Castelbuono had made their judgment, the Rizzo family was no longer one of them. With the mountains looming behind them and exile awaiting ahead, three generations of Rizzo's took a final, lingering look at the cobbled streets of their hometown, knowing they would never again call them home.

Celeste Rizzo's breath hitched as the words sank in, her pulse pounding in her ears. She gripped the edge of the table, her knuckles white, eyes wide with disbelief. *La Cosa Nostra. The Sicilian Mafia*? Her family, the people who raised her, loved her, were part of that world? A cold shiver crawled down her spine as memories twisted into something darker. Sunday dinners, whispered conversations, the heavy presence of men she once thought were her uncles. The room felt smaller, the air heavier. "No…that's not possible," she whispered, but deep down, a terrible truth had already settled in."

Rodolpho could see the pain in her eyes. He understood. His little secret was also about to be revealed. "Celeste, I understand. I have lived in this town, hiding in the shadow of what *my* family left behind. To this day, the town has not discovered my true identity. I was fortunate that my youngest aunt took me in when my own family was exiled, pretending that I was her child. My name was changed, and I survived. It has not been an easy road since I have had no communication with my family. But two days ago, something happened that changed my life, and now I believe, can change yours."

Celeste Rizzo began to think the man was crazy. Tomorrow she would have to find a way to escape not only the town but a man that she was starting to think might be delusional.

Rodolpho could sense that she was beginning to feel uncomfortable with the situation she found herself in.

"Have you heard of the social media game "Blank Checks?"

Celeste nodded wondering where this conversation was going. Nothing was making sense. She kept picturing the family gatherings, their faces now mafiosos, sitting around hatching out plans. She shook her head. Rodolpho broke the silence, his voice steady yet charged with something almost electric as he explained the game.

"Two days ago, on August 4th, the very day you arrived in Castelbuono, I became the tenth contestant on Blank Checks. I had only a few hours to study what others had won, my mind spinning with numbers and possibilities. And then, in a daze, I wrote down my age.

Forty-five. Somehow, it felt lucky. Forty-five million dollars. It's still hard to believe."

"Five minutes after I became rich, I saw you. Walking the streets like a ghost from a past neither of us chose. In a town this small, gossip moves faster than the wind, and the hotel clerk had already taken note of your last name. That's where it all began."

"You and I, we share a similar, unfortunate past. But I refuse to let the past dictate my future anymore. Until two days ago, I never imagined I'd have a choice. But now? Now, I can go anywhere. Do anything. Be anyone."

"I was never an educated man, and I never thought I'd be more than a garbage collector. But fate had other plans. My first wish two days ago was to simply find my family, but now, I also want to share it with you. No strings attached. No expectations. Just a gift, freely given."

"We both have roots in a town that refuses to welcome its own past. I refuse to be trapped by that history any longer. Today was my last day collecting garbage."

"Take this, please. Because truthfully, I don't even know where to begin spending such a fortune. My only wish now is to find my mother, my family, the ones who had to leave when I was just a year old."

"Maybe, just maybe, this money can buy me the one thing I've wanted my whole life. My family reunited."

Celeste could see the pain in his eyes, the generosity he wished to share with her and the desire to find his family. She asked if she could think about the offer for another day. All the information had been too much for her to take in and she was not thinking clearly. The night kindly wrapped itself around Celeste, affording her the rest she so desperately needed.

Celeste woke to the braying of donkeys, their voices tearing through the morning stillness like rusty hinges on a forgotten gate. The sound jolted her from sleep, her heart pounding in protest.

Outside, Rodolpho moved with quiet purpose, securing the animals for their journey. He had gifting them to a friend down the road, a man eager to trade his monotonous years of dishwashing for the lively, if odorous, work of a garbage collector. It would be a change, a fresh chapter.

Back inside the farmhouse, the aroma of coffee curled through the air. Celeste, wrapped in the lingering warmth of sleep, handed Rodolpho a cup. She looked different this morning, more at ease, as if the weight of uncertainty had finally lifted.

For the next hour, they spoke of dreams. Celeste had always longed to walk the ruins of ancient civilizations, to trace her fingers over the stones of history. And now, impossibly, that dream was within reach.

Rodolpho pulled out his phone, his fingers tapping with quiet finality. Then, with a small, knowing smile, he handed her a debit card.

"Your own account," he murmured, eyes glinting. "Five million dollars. Go see the world, Celeste."

The room fell silent, the weight of possibility hanging between them.

Tears welled in Celeste's eyes as she stared at the screen, the zeroes blurring together. "Rodolpho… how?" she whispered.

He simply smiled, "Dreams should never stay dreams."

The donkeys brayed again in the distance, their voices carrying on as if announcing the turning of a page. Celeste let out a breath, her heart light. The world was waiting, and for the first time, it was hers to explore.

11

September 2024
Dee

Dee was lost in a haze of disbelief for what felt like an eternity during the first week of June, when the stunning revelation hit her; one of the many lottery tickets her husband had tucked away in secret had unlocked a world of endless possibilities. For the first time, she found herself standing on the edge of a life she never thought she could have.

Claire, watching with pride, couldn't help but marvel at Dee's newfound clarity. With a heart full of hope, Dee chose to purchase a home nestled near Claire's spa wellness center, a sanctuary tucked in the serene foothills of Black Mountain. It was more than just a change of address; it was a bold step into a new chapter. Together, they gently guided Dee away from the shadows of her past and toward a future filled with peace, tranquility, and the promise of harmony.

It filled Claire with joy to see her friend stepping forward, and she decided it was time for them to do something special, something bold. A vacation. Maybe Bermuda. The very thought sent a thrill through her. There was something almost mystical about being near the Bermuda Triangle, a place tangled in myths and mysteries. She had always wanted to stand on the edge of the unknown, even if just one of its points.

Dee had been throwing herself into new hobbies, trying to fill the spaces once occupied by her children's laughter and chaos. Claire knew this was part of the healing, but maybe, just maybe, Dee could carve out some time for an escape. Sun-drenched days, salty ocean breezes, cocktails by the shore. It sounded perfect.

To Claire's delight, Dee responded almost instantly. *I'm in. Let's talk dates and details.*

Excitement bubbled in Claire's chest. Finally, something fun to look forward to. She quickly suggested meeting up to plan, but Dee's next message stopped her cold.

I'll be auctioning kids for a few days. After that I'll be free. Claire blinked at the screen, then read it again. *Auctioning kids? What in the...*

Without hesitation, she called Dee. The second her friend picked up, Claire demanded, "What in the world are you doing auctioning kids?"

A confused pause. "What?"

"That's what you just texted me!"

Dee sighed, already exasperated. "Claire, I have no idea what you're talking about." But even as she said it, she flipped back through her messages. A second later, a sharp burst of laughter erupted from her. "Oh my. Autocorrect strikes again! I meant *auditioning* kids. The school is bringing the magic of Christmas to life with a spectacular musical talent show! Our stage will shine with the incredible talents of our students, and it's bound to be an unforgettable, heartwarming celebration of music, joy, and holiday spirit!"

Claire groaned but couldn't help laughing too. "I was about to report you to child services."

Dee snorted. "Please don't. I'd like to make it to Bermuda without a criminal record."

And just like that, the stress of the day melted away, replaced with laughter and the promise of an adventure.

September 2, 2024
Lilith

Lilith breathed in the fresh Reykjavik air, the scent of salt and seaweed wrapping around her like an old blanket. And tonight; tonight was the night her dream would finally come to life.

Her restaurant, *Volcanic Glacial Cuisine*, stood proudly on a quiet street near the harbor. The windows glowed against the drizzle of the September evening, the promise of something both new and deeply rooted in Icelandic tradition.

Lilith had spent the last year testing, inventing, and dreaming of the moment she could bring the true flavors of her homeland to life. Not just the touristy, picture-perfect versions, but the real tastes of Iceland. The dishes that reminded people of their grandmothers, of windswept fishing villages, of stories whispered over late-night coffee.

Inside, the tables were set, the candles flickering, and her small but eager team moved like dancers in the kitchen. The menu was her greatest joy, a love letter to Icelandic cuisine with a playful twist:

• Loki's Little Lye Cakes – Traditional hákarl (fermented shark), served with Brennivín (Icelandic spirit) and a daring grin.

• Sheep's Whisper – Smoked lamb (hangikjöt) on warm flatbread, with a tangy rhubarb compote.

• Viking's Midnight Snack – A modern take on plokkfiskur, creamy fish stew with crispy rye bread chips.

• Geysir's Delight – Hot spring-cooked eggs with black lava salt and smoked trout roe.

• Troll's Treat – Skyr cheesecake with crowberries (blackberries) and caramelized whey.

True to herself, every night there would be the Chef's special. Only those that knew her story would understand their meaning. On her opening night, the Chef's special was proudly posted at the entrance:

Laufabrauð → Laugh Bread – *Crispy holiday bread, now bringing you uncontrollable giggles.*

Her heart raced as the first guests stepped through the door, friends, old neighbors, curious newcomers. As they settled in, murmurs of delight filled the space. A man laughed after daring to take a bite of the Loki's Little Lye Cakes, while an elderly woman wiped away a tear after tasting the Sheep's Whisper, murmuring that it tasted just like Christmas in the old days.

Lilith moved between tables, her heart swelling with pride. This was it. She was not only representing Reykjavik, but herself.

And as the night deepened, as glasses clinked and the warmth of the hearth mixed with the laughter of her guests, she knew, *Volcanic Glacial Cuisine* was a success.

It all had begun on a whim, twelve months ago, a spontaneous decision to enter a cooking contest just for the thrill of it. Lilith hadn't planned on competing; her days were already consumed by the relentless pace of her job at the fish market. The work was grueling, fast paced, and left little room for indulgences. But something about the challenge called to her.

Each morning, before the first light kissed the horizon, Lilith suited up in her signature bright orange waterproof gear, heavy-duty apron, thick gloves, and sturdy rubber boots, her armor against the cold, damp world she moved through. The air was thick with salt and the fresh catch as she wove her way past the chaos of forklifts and workers hauling crates of fish, their voices blending into the symphony of an industry that never truly slept.

At the long, gleaming stainless-steel tables, she took her place. The ritual began. Her gloved hands worked swiftly, sorting the morning's haul with precision, cod, haddock, mackerel, and, on lucky days, the elusive monkfish or halibut. Hours slipped by, lost in the rhythmic sorting, the cold biting through even the toughest gloves.

By the time her task was done, exhaustion pressed down on her, but there was still one final duty, to clean. With methodical efficiency, she hosed down the tables, scrubbed every surface, and disinfected each tool, ensuring the space gleamed, ready to face the next relentless wave of work.

And then, the quiet reward. Each day, every worker was presented with a small box, a humble offering; four fish that didn't quite meet the market's exacting standards but were still good, still worthy. She cradled her box, already imagining the warmth of her kitchen, the sizzle of fresh fish in the pan, the flavors she would coax out for her family.

Lilith hadn't expected a contest to change anything; one her family had urged her to enter. But as she walked home, the salty wind tangling in her hair, she felt it, something stirring, something more.

Maybe, just maybe, this was the beginning of something unexpected.

Taking home first place at the Reykjavík Culinary Championship had been nothing short of a shock, a breathtaking, pulse-racing shock. The judges' announcement of a possible tie for first place had already sent ripples of astonishment through the crowd, but what truly left everyone reeling was the revelation that Lilith's victory hinged not just on the flavors dancing on the judges' palates, but on the sheer originality of her dish's name. It was an unexpected twist, a moment of triumph laced with disbelief, as whispers and murmurs filled the room. How could a name hold such power? Yet, there she stood, golden medal in hand, a smirk tugging at her lips, knowing that sometimes, creativity extends far beyond the plate.

Overnight, Lilith became a household name. With an insatiable hunger to innovate her motherland's cuisine, she decided to combine her two passions: cooking and storytelling. Late at night, after preparing her family's meals, she started posting daily on social media, sharing her bold fusion creations with the world. But it wasn't just the flavors that captured attention, it was the dish names that pulled people in.

Her first viral hit? "Taco-fiskur", crispy fried cod wrapped in rúgbrauð (rye bread) tortillas, topped with fermented shark aioli and pickled red onions. The fusion of Mexican zest and Icelandic depth sparked intrigue. People had to know more.

Next came "Volcanic Pizza". A Neapolitan-style sourdough crust topped with smoked Arctic char, skyr-based white sauce, and ghost pepper honey, symbolizing the fiery contrast of Iceland's land and sea.

Then she dropped "Kung Pao Puffin", a controversial but ethically sourced dish where the tenderness of puffin met the bold spices of Sichuan, leaving followers divided but engaged.

Her followers skyrocketed when she introduced "Butter Chicken Björn", an Indian Icelandic twist on butter chicken but made with slow-braised reindeer, served over lava-baked flatbread.

She even took a playful jab at fast food with "McViking". A towering lamb burger drenched in béarnaise sauce, served with seaweed-seasoned fries.

Each post came with a short, poetic description of the dish's origins, its cultural blend, and a tantalizing close-up shot. Soon, food influencers and chefs around the world started recreating her dishes. Restaurants reached out. A TV producer slid into her DMs.

And one day, as she watched her follower count tick past a million, she realized: this was no longer just a passion project. She was rewriting Icelandic cuisine, one eccentric, mouthwatering name at a time.

September 2024
Karl

An accomplished baker and sous chef, Karl had spent months perfecting his dishes for the Reykjavik Culinary Championship. Every spice, every garnish, every technique, meticulously refined. His flavors were bold, his textures exquisite, but there was just one problem.

His dish names were boring.

The judges praised his slow-braised lamb with wild Arctic thyme and lava salt but winced at the name: "Lamb and Potatoes." His tangy fermented shark was masterfully balanced, but the title. Dull and boring. "Fish Bite."

In the end, he came in second.

First place went to the unknown, fish sorter Lilith, whose presentation was flawless, her flavors adventurous, and her dish names... well, memorable.

Her winning entrée, a crispy cod fillet in black garlic sauce, had been named "Crispy God with Dark Mystery." The judges laughed and called it genius branding.

Sous Chef Karl had been devastated by his loss to an unknown in the industry. He had mastered delicate emulsions, the art of butchery, and the poetry of plating. His skills were second to none, or so he believed.

When the moment of truth arrived, the judges tasted each dish in silence, their faces unreadable. Then came the announcement. Karl could not understand how someone so young and inexperienced could have created a dish equivalent to his masterpiece. He swallowed his pride and accepted the runner up position.

Soon, he found himself captivated by Lilith's online presence, watching in awe as her creations flourished before his very eyes. Then came the cookbook, the one misstep that should have been her downfall. But instead, it propelled her to unimaginable heights, turning her into a superstar. And Karl? He was left lingering in the shadows, a forgotten figure in her meteoric rise.

But he wouldn't stay there. No, he had a plan. He wouldn't fight her, why struggle against the tide when he could let it carry him forward? He would ride the wave of her success, slipping into the limelight on her heels. What a stroke of brilliance. Her so-called mistake would be his golden opportunity. And Lilith? She wouldn't even see it coming.

September 2024
Sean

Fresh from the lush rainforests of Jamaica, Sean returned with a newfound sense of calm, his mind sharper, his vision clearer. The relentless mass of corporations awaited him, an ocean of intrigue and tangled motives he was eager to plunge back into. His colleagues, ever resourceful in their stolen moments of free time, had spun a web of theories, each clever, yet none struck the perfect chord.

To Sean, a person willing to give away vast sums of money must either have everything they could ever desire and be chasing the thrill of generosity, or be standing at the twilight of their days, determined to control their legacy before fate took the reins. Were they truly hiding? It didn't seem so.

Sean wasn't one to let a puzzle lie unsolved. He would press on, dig deeper, and refuse to rest until he uncovered the story that whispered its truth just beneath the surface.

September 2024
Undisclosed Location

On the binary grid, it was clear: thousands of corporations, each meticulously arranged, were being subtly nudged from afar. At first glance, it might appear as though Tim had orchestrated these setups to serve as a diversion or, perhaps, to cloak his own presence in shadow. But the truth was far simpler, yet far more brilliant. Each APP demanded the establishment of hundreds of corporations, each one strategically positioned across the globe. With every new APP, a complex web of systems unfurled, each one crucial to maintaining the delicate balance of the whole. It wasn't about hiding; it was about control, an intricate dance of management and coordination. Even if someone were to breach the core of it all, they would be left bewildered, lost in a labyrinth of operations that made no sense. Only Tim, the Mastermind, could comprehend the full scope of the masterpiece he had woven, a web of such complexity that even those closest to it could never truly unravel its secrets.

September 2024
Lilith

Lilith was a force of nature, an unstoppable whirlwind of creativity and passion. She danced on the edge of exhilaration, pouring her soul into the grand adventure of launching her new restaurant. And all this, after narrowly escaping the most laughably disastrous blunder a cook could ever conjure, a misstep so outrageous, it was almost legendary. Yet, here she was, undeterred, turning chaos into culinary magic.

Her cookbook, *The Modern Icelandic Alchemist,* had been released over the summer, one that her eager viewers had been clamoring for. Known for her instinctive cooking style, she never bothered with measuring spoons or writing down recipes. The kitchen was her canvas, and she cooked from the heart. As she set out to perfect each dish and measure every ingredient, the challenge became an intricate dance of precision and memory, each step a piece of art. What once flowed effortlessly from her hands now demanded her full attention and meticulous care, but she was determined to bring her culinary vision to life, piece by piece.

It would be her masterpiece, a collection of unique dishes blending tradition with modern flair, not forgetting those eye-catching names her viewers loved so much.

Her cousin had showered her with guidance, offering meticulous, step-by-step instructions on refining spelling, grammar, and punctuation. Not that a cookbook required much correction, but for Lilith, perfection wasn't just a goal; it was a promise to her readers. She wanted every word to be just as precise and flavorful as the recipes themselves.

"One click, and perfection," she murmured, sipping her coffee as she hit 'Auto Correct All.'

She should have known better.

The first sign of disaster came from her best friend Katrín.

"Lilith," Katrín texted, "what are *'crushed ghosts'*?"

Lilith frowned. "What?"

"In your Viking Harvest Stew. It says, *Add two tablespoons of crushed ghosts for a smoky depth.*

Lilith's blood ran cold. She checked the document. *Ghosts.* It was supposed to say **garlic**.

Panicked, she scrolled through the recipes. The chaos was widespread.

"Fresh basil" had become "Fresh **betrayal**" in her Pizza of the Northern Lights.

"Whipped cream" had turned into "Whipped **screams**" for her Lava-Licious Hot Cocoa.

"Chopped nuts" was now "Chopped **nuns**" in Yule-icious Crunch of Icelandic Joy.

Her stomach plummeted, a sinking weight of dread pressing against her ribs. And the worst part? The book was already out there live, spreading like wildfire, purchased by countless eager readers. Every flaw, every overlooked mistake, frozen in digital permanence. Fixing them wouldn't just take hours, it would take days, maybe longer. And the cruelest twist? She hadn't saved a backup. Not a single failsafe to turn to. Now, she would have to claw her way through the errors, one painstaking recipe at a time, knowing that with every moment, more copies were being sold, more imperfections exposed to the world.

The internet had seized the catastrophe with glee. *The Modern Icelandic Alchemist* went viral overnight, with social media chefs dramatically questioning where to source "crushed ghosts."

A famous food critic even called it "a cookbook for the brave." Sales skyrocketed. Instead of humiliation, Lilith became a sensation.

The online mockery was swift, but Lilith knew better than to panic. Instead of retreating in embarrassment, she owned the disaster.

She filmed a video of herself reading the funniest typos aloud, barely holding back laughter. "Today, we're making my famous 'caramelized onions', or as my book calls them, 'traumatized onions.' Honestly, they are one in the same. Tomorrow we will be creating cinnamon buns which call for two tablespoons of ground sins. We all have at least a cup of those hidden somewhere in our kitchen!" Her laughter was infectious, and her viewers loved her.

The internet exploded with delight. Fans embraced the chaos, posting their own videos of how to find those *'ground sins', 'whipped screams', 'sesame needs', 'baking sofas'* and so many more... Within days, her cookbook, errors and all, became a bestseller, with people calling it the most accidentally hilarious culinary masterpiece ever.

And so, Lilith learned a valuable lesson: Sometimes, even a disaster can be delicious.

She was so consumed by leaning into her blunders with her online videos, that she failed to see Karl's unshakable urge to outshine her by plotting his own triumph. Not just any restaurant, but one mere step away from hers. Not just any opening, but a grand debut set for the exact same day as hers. The battle lines were drawn, yet she remained blissfully unaware.

September 2, 2024
Karl

Karl watched in shock and amazement at how such a blunder could become a success. Not only had she come from nowhere, but she had succeeded in areas that one could never imagine. Humiliated but determined, he devised a plan.

Instead of sulking, he was going to open his own restaurant. But instead of fighting Lilith's branding magic, he leaned into it by using her unintentional, spellcheck, induced disasters.

He called his restaurant "*Eaten Mistakes.*"

Menu items included a few homages to Lilith's auto-correct mistakes.

- "Cursed Bread with Lava's Tears" (a sourdough with smoked sea salt and Icelandic butter)
- "Smoked Whale's Cry" (a minke whale tataki with horseradish foam)
- "Caramel Misery" (a salted caramel skyr cheesecake)

Thrilled and amused, Karl was ready for his inspired competition, one he knew he would win.

His morning produce inspection routine was interrupted by an unexpected phone call, one that left him momentarily stunned. The proposition was as bizarre as it was intriguing. A contestant in Reykjavik was to be handed a Blank Check, an opportunity to write their own destiny. But there was a catch. Karl's restaurant would need to close for an hour, and in return, he would receive a hefty sum for the inconvenience.

The call was brief, yet it sent Karl's mind into overdrive. The voice on the other end was direct, efficient, leaving no room for questions. Karl decided to pass on the opportunity, suggesting they contact Lilith just down the street. If she accepted, then it would give him the upper hand in attracting her clientele to his restaurant during that hour. That's all he needed.

A spark of ambition ignited within him. By turning the tables, he would turn this into an advantage. He would take the spotlight while the *Volcanic Glacial Cuisine* was closed shut.

A heartbeat of silence passed before the caller accepted. A polite thank you, a click, and the line went dead. Karl stood amidst the vibrant colors of his carefully curated ingredients, the weight of opportunity settling on his shoulders. Monday had certainly taken him by surprise.

September 2, 2024
Lilith

Lilith's fingers hovered over her notebook in the damp late morning hours, her mind an infuriating blank as she wrestled with the perfect name for her opening night creation. Frustration prickled at her, but before she could sink too deep into it, her phone rang. The timing was impeccable, almost eerie.

The voice on the other end delivered an offer so unexpected, so outlandish, that she had to replay the words in her mind before she fully grasped them. A game. A gamble. A social media spectacle. Lilith had heard whispers of it before, but she was too engrossed in her menu and opening night. Yet this? This was different. This was exhilarating. A win-win.

Delay the grand opening by an hour, they said. Just an hour. The mere suggestion sent a thrill through her. Anticipation, she understood its power. The longer the wait, the greater the hunger. A slight delay would only amplify the excitement, heighten the experience for her eager customers. Offer accepted.

She glanced at the clock. Five hours until the trio from 2T Technologies arrived, along with the enigmatic contestant. As she ended the call, she let out a laugh, rich and full of delight. Opening night hadn't even begun, and she had already pocketed a massive amount of cash.

Stepping outside, she inhaled deeply, letting the cool moist air spark inspiration. She needed the perfect words to announce the delay. And then, like lightning, it struck.

Delay your excitement.
The best things in life are worth the extra hour.

A slow grin spread across her lips. Yes, that would do. And to sweeten the wait, she'd offer her waiting guests a little indulgence. After all, what was pleasure without just a touch of teasing?

Laufabrauð → Laugh Bread – *Crispy One Hour Wait Bread, now bringing you uncontrollable giggles.*

That was when she noticed the new sign down the street being inspected by Karl; *Eaten Mistakes*. Lilith, amused and slightly horrified, paid him a visit. She laughed as she read the menu, shaking her head.

"This is my mess, Karl!" she said.

"And now, it's my success," he replied with a smirk.

She had no choice but to tip her hat. The competition wasn't over, but this time, it wasn't fought only with dishes. It was also fought with words.

Lilith caught her reflection in the polished glass of her restaurant's front window and allowed herself a small, satisfied smile. Tonight was the night. The culmination of months of planning, sleepless nights, and boundless ambition, the grand opening of her dream. But with last-minute changes piling up, she needed backup.

Without hesitation, she reached for her phone. Katrín. Her rock. She kept her request simple. Could she come an hour early to help smooth out a few final details? No mention of the surprise contestant. No hint of the Blank Check event.

Katrín, ever the enthusiastic friend, had agreed immediately. And when she arrived at five o'clock, she wasn't alone. Her husband, Viktor, walked in beside her. Lilith blinked, caught off guard, but quickly recovered. More hands meant more help, and tonight, every extra moment of preparation mattered.

The three of them moved seamlessly through the space, fine-tuning every detail, the table settings, the humming energy of the kitchen, the plates prepared and waiting to dazzle. The online buzz had reached a fever pitch, with eager guests practically breaking down the digital doors to be part of this moment. Lilith had even arranged for extra food, sensing the rush that was about to unfold.

As they completed their final circuit of the restaurant, the quiet murmur of their conversation was interrupted by the sound of footsteps. Three figures, tall and poised, elegantly dressed in black and white, emerging from the back delivery entrance like shadows slipping into the light.

Lilith turned, her heart quickening.

"Good evening, Miss Sigurdsson." The speaker's voice was smooth, brimming with importance. "Thank you for allowing us a moment of your time on such a momentous occasion. And before we go any further. Congratulations on your book's success. On this extraordinary opening night. We have followed your culinary journey, watched your online videos with admiration. And now, we hope to experience your artistry firsthand. If you would permit us, we would be honored to stay as your guests this evening, once our contestant has had their chance at reshaping their future."

Lilith's heart pounded. Fellow countrymen, here, to taste her craft. She felt the heat of pride rise in her chest, but before she could form a response, the speaker continued, this time with words that sent a chill racing down her spine.

"I also see that you have already met our eleventh contestant, Viktor Ólafsson."

Lilith froze. Her gaze darted to Viktor, then to Katrín, searching for an explanation. The words refused to come.

Katrín exhaled, her expression tender, apologetic. "I wanted to tell you," she said, her voice soft but steady. "When you called, we had just received the announcement, the instructions. It was surreal, like fate aligning itself before our eyes. But we didn't want to steal your moment, your night. When we saw that the meeting place was here, your restaurant, we knew. This was meant to be."

Lilith stood motionless, the weight of it all settling over her. Her best friend's husband. The surprise contestant. Destiny, threading its way through her grand opening in ways she never could have foreseen.

And the night had only just begun.

September 2, 2024
Karl

Karl could barely contain the thrill bubbling inside him. Every nerve in his body buzzed with anticipation, his grand plan was about to unfold. Opening night was creeping closer, the tension thick in the air. Down the street, the competition sat in eerie silence, its lights extinguished, its windows dark like abandoned dreams. The once bustling rival restaurant had become a ghost of itself, and soon, its loyal patrons would have no choice but to step into *Eaten Mistakes*. They would surrender to his culinary genius, and at long last, Karl would rise to the fame and recognition he knew he deserved.

Inside, the atmosphere was electric. Karl stood before his assembled army-cooks, waiters, bartenders, his voice steady but charged with energy as he ran through the final preparations. The menu had been crafted to perfection, the specials honed to tantalize even the most skeptical of tongues, and the drinks curated to ignite conversation and delight. Beyond the frosted windows, a growing crowd huddled under the drizzly September sky, their umbrellas forming a sea of black and navy. Their hunger was palpable, their silhouettes eager. But which establishment were they waiting for? Karl knew the answer.

Then, finally, it was time.

He took a deep breath and strode toward the entrance. With a flourish, he pulled open the grand doors, his heart hammering with exhilaration. And there it was, a queue that stretched endlessly down to the water's edge. A hundred seats, barely enough to contain the feverish demand. He drank in the sight, his chest swelling with pride, his gaze flickering briefly to the void of darkness down the street where his competition lay dormant.

The first guests were friends, family, smiling, reassuring presences. Then... nothing.

Karl's breath hitched. The line outside stood still, unmoving, almost defiant. Inside, only six tables were occupied, their conversations hushed, their cutlery barely scraping against the fine porcelain plates.

His stomach knotted. A strange unease clawed at the edges of his excitement. With forced calm, he signaled one of his staff to step outside and assure the waiting crowd; *Eaten Mistakes* was more than ready to welcome them.

Moments later, the answer came back.

They weren't coming.

Not yet.

They were waiting, waiting with patience, with unwavering loyalty, for *her*.

Karl's blood ran cold.

Volcanic Glacial Cuisine wasn't truly closed. No, she had unknowingly outwitted him with a simple trick. Her waiting guests had been treated to a warm, mouthwatering Crispy One-Hour-Wait Bread, a clever, tantalizing snack, a thank-you for their patience. And they were loving it. The street was alive with the crunch, the murmurs of delight, the camaraderie of shared indulgence.

Karl's hands clenched into fists as realization crashed over him. His masterstroke had collapsed in on itself, his triumphant moment stolen.

Seething, he stormed back to his office, slamming the door behind him.

How could she?
How?

September 2, 2024
Lilith

Viktor stood tall, his heart pounding with exhilaration, as he exchanged a knowing glance with his wife, Katrín. The plan they had meticulously crafted, a bold, daring leap into the unknown was about to unfold before their eyes. They had whispered about this moment in the quiet hours of the night, and now, their gamble was teetering on the edge of destiny.

A hush fell over the room as the numbers flickered onto the flat screen. The tall woman behind the camera captured every fleeting second. Time seemed to slow, the air thick with anticipation. Then, there it was. His name, their number.

Viktor and Katrín froze. A single beat of silence before the realization struck like a lightning bolt. Sixty-five million.

Tears welled in their eyes, their bodies trembling with a mixture of disbelief and overwhelming joy. Their carefully laid plans were no longer a distant hope. They were a reality, unfolding faster than they had ever dared to dream.

Lilith, standing just a few feet away, felt her own breath catch in her throat. The sheer magnitude of the win left her reeling. Sixty-five million. The kind of figure one only heard about in far-fetched stories. Yet here it was, real, tangible, theirs.

But there was no time to linger in shock. Hungry eager patrons awaited them out in the damp evening. What should have been an hour-long delay in Lilith's grand opening was reduced to just fifteen minutes, an impossible feat, but tonight, impossibilities were being rewritten.

The lights flickered back on, the restaurant door swung open, and cheers erupted, rolling through the streets like waves against the harbor. Within moments, every seat was filled, the hum of excitement blending with the clinking of glass and the sizzle of hot plates in the kitchen.

Lilith, ever the mastermind, had already anticipated the chaos. While enthusiastic guests had patiently stood outside, she had orchestrated a seamless ballet of efficiency. Orders had been taken in advance, ensuring that as soon as the doors opened, meals landed on tables as if by magic.

And yet, it wasn't enough. The line outside stretched longer, restless and hungry. Lilith glanced at them, at the faces of her loyal viewers who had waited for this moment, and without hesitation, she made her next move.

Grabbing a tray of four steaming plates at a time, she stepped outside into the crisp night air, her arms steady, her heart full. She moved through the crowd with purpose, handing out dishes one by one, looking each guest in the eye as she thanked them for their unwavering faith in her dream.

Midnight had finally arrived. Lilith exhaled, her body tired from the relentless pace of the evening. Yet, beneath the exhaustion, a quiet pride warmed her chest. She had done it. The service had been seamless, the dishes exquisite, and the guests had left satisfied, their laughter and praises still echoing in her ears.

What made the night truly remarkable, however, was that her staff, her friends, had taken the reins, executing each dish with precision and passion. Months of guidance, of long hours perfecting sauces, tempering heat, and plating with finesse, had led to this moment. They had found their rhythm without her hovering. They had thrived. And Lilith, though an ever-watchful presence, had trusted them. It had paid off beautifully.

Now, the kitchen stood pristine, gleaming under the dim golden glow of the overhead lights. Lilith slumped into a chair at the back table, Viktor and Katrín joining her, her loyal companions, her unwavering support. They had been her eyes and hands throughout the night, ensuring every detail was flawless.

Katrín grinned, as she leaned forward. "What a successful evening, indeed! I think we ran out of every single bit of food in that kitchen.

Your staff even got creative, whipping up plates from whatever ingredients were left for the last-minute guests. You'll have to give those dishes a name someday!" She laughed, her eyes sparkling with mischief.

Lilith chuckled, shaking her head. "It's been a wild day. And I couldn't have done it without you both."

Viktor exchanged a glance with Katrín, a secret glimmer passing between them. He cleared his throat, reaching into his jacket. "Actually… we have something for you."

Lilith's brows lifted as he slid a small envelope across the table. She picked it up, flipping it between her fingers, her curiosity piqued. The logo embossed on the card inside was unfamiliar. She frowned.

Viktor smirked realizing she had not noticed the debit cards from earlier on.

Lilith gave him a blank look, and Katrín snorted in amusement.

"Scan the QR code on the back," Viktor instructed, amusement lacing his tone. "When you have the time, of course." Lilith tucked the card into her apron pocket, thinking little of it at that moment.

It wasn't until days later, when exhaustion had finally loosened its grip and curiosity won out, that she finally scanned the code.

Her breath caught.

The numbers stared back at her, incomprehensible at first, then shocking. A bank account in her name. A balance of ten million dollars.

Her hands trembled as she reread the screen, her mind racing. Her heart pounded against her ribs.

Somewhere, Katrín and Viktor were probably laughing, knowing this moment would leave her speechless. And for the second time in a week, Lilith had no words.

12

October 2024
Johanika

Every morning, just as the sun stretched its golden fingers over the water, Johanika slipped on her sandals and stepped onto the cool sand of Boulders Beach. The rhythmic whisper of the waves greeted her, a familiar song she had come to cherish in her years of living by the South African coast.

She walked slowly, savoring the salty air, her steps in sync with the gulls flying overhead. The sand was damp beneath her feet, and tiny shells glistened like forgotten pearls in the early light. This was her ritual, her time of peace before the world fully awakened.

As she neared the smooth granite boulders that framed the secluded cove, she caught sight of them: the penguins. A blanket of black-and-white figures waddling about the shore, their flipper-like wings held slightly away from their bodies.

Johanika smiled. She had been coming here for years, watching them live their little lives, their colony growing and shrinking with the seasons. The penguins had become her silent companions, a presence more comforting than any human crowd.

One penguin caught her eye, a young one, still molting, its patchy feathers giving it a scruffy charm. It stood at the water's edge, hesitant, the way it did every morning. "Go on," she murmured. "The ocean is waiting."

As if understanding, the penguin finally took the plunge, bellyflopping into the waves before righting itself with a determined paddle. Johanika chuckled, as a gust of wind passed by.

With one last lingering look at her tuxedoed friends, she turned back toward home. Tomorrow, she would return, just as she always did, to greet the sea, the sand, and the ever-faithful penguins of Boulders Beach.

That was when she instinctively turned. It wasn't just the wind but the sound of the waves crashing on the boulders was getting louder. In the blink of an eye, one hapless penguin found itself torn from the safety of its group as the relentless waves surged with sudden ferocity. Like a forsaken surfboard caught in the chaotic dance of the ocean, the little bird was lifted, tumbled, and flung across the frothy crests, its flippers flailing in a desperate bid for control. Tossed and tumbled by the ocean's relentless grip, it careened toward the exposed boulder, a helpless passenger on nature's wild ride.

For a breathless moment, all was still. Then, with an unceremonious shake of its slick, salt-drenched feathers, the penguin staggered forward, wobbling like a tipsy sailor on unsteady legs, each step an awkward struggle against its lingering disorientation. Each movement was a battle against the lingering dizziness, its tiny, webbed feet slipping awkwardly over the damp sand. Yet, despite its disoriented state, instinct drove it forward, toward the familiar warmth of its colony, where a sea of black-and-white figures basked lazily beneath the golden afternoon sun.

Finally reaching solid ground, well beyond the reach of the sea's mischievous pull, the little survivor paused. Its head swiveled in slow, uncertain circles, as if piecing together the absurdity of its impromptu oceanic adventure. With a final shake, perhaps of defiance, perhaps of exhaustion, it waddled forward, disappearing into the embrace of its fellow penguins, as if nothing had ever happened.

Johanika knew that disoriented, breathless sensation, the way the world spun after being tossed by the unrelenting force of a wave. It was a feeling she understood all too well. But relief warmed her chest as she watched her little companion make it back safely to its colony.

Today, anticipation hummed in her veins. She was leaving work early, something she rarely did. But this wasn't just any early day off.

This was a leap into the unknown. For the first time ever, she had dared to dip her toes into the unpredictable waters of online dating. And this wouldn't be an ordinary first date. She had orchestrated the meeting with meticulous care, choosing Kalk Bay Harbor as the rendezvous point, just far enough from home, a buffer in case the magic failed to spark in person.

But first, there was the ocean. Only one tour for the day, a group of eager kayakers ready to be swept away by the breathtaking landscapes of Simon's Town. The wind had picked up, promising a challenge, demanding every ounce of strength from her and her group. It would be a battle against the elements, a final test before she embarked on something even more nerve-wracking: meeting an online friend who could possibly change her world.

October 2024
Dee & Claire

In just a few short weeks, Dee and Claire would be basking in the sun-drenched paradise of Bermuda, an island where pink-sand beaches kissed the turquoise sea and gentle breezes carried whispers of adventure. The thought of waking up to the rhythmic lull of waves and the scent of salt and hibiscus was almost too much to bear.

Dee had finally settled into her new home, embracing the rhythm of her new life while successfully casting every role for the much, anticipated Christmas musical. But beyond her work, a new world was unfolding before her. Living closer to Claire and her spa sanctuary, Sanare, she was beginning to understand, though not fully grasp, the magic woven into its essence. Each day spent preparing the individual pods for guests awakened something inside her. The spa wasn't just a place of relaxation; it was a living, breathing network of tranquility. The soft rustling of palm fronds, the delicate blend of lavender and eucalyptus in the air, and the distant chime of wind bells all worked together to create an atmosphere unlike any other. Even without understanding how it worked, Dee felt it. Sanare wasn't just a destination. It was an experience; a retreat people longed to return to.

Curious by nature, Dee had prodded Claire time and again for the secret behind Sanare's enchanting pull. Claire only ever smiled, promising that, in time, all would be revealed. But for now, their focus was on something even more thrilling. Their upcoming two-week escape to Bermuda.

October 20 couldn't arrive fast enough. The very thought of it sent a rush of excitement through them. The choice to book two rooms at Surf Side Beach had been effortless. With its secluded shores and crystalline waters over the reef, it was the perfect haven for two ocean lovers like themselves. From the moment their toes sank into the powdery sand, they would be home. Mornings would be spent gliding through the waves, swimming out to the coral reefs where a dazzling underwater world awaited, graceful sea turtles, shimmering parrotfish, and hidden grottos just waiting to be explored. Afternoons would be for sipping rum swizzles in the shade of swaying palms, and as the sun dipped into the horizon, they'd lose themselves in the vibrant island nightlife, where the pulse of Bermuda's culture beat strongest in its music and laughter.

Adventure, relaxation, and the irresistible pull of the sea. It was all just weeks away. And Dee and Claire were ready.

October 2024
Cosmo

Meeting someone online was the last thing Cosmo had ever wanted to do, much less on the other side of the world, but he was tired of repeating the same tired relationships that had nothing new to offer him. He planned his dream safari along with a face-to-face week of adventure with the dynamic South African girl. Johanika. Even her name was mysterious.

Their first meeting was nothing short of cinematic. They had arranged to meet at Kalk Bay harbor, a place teeming with old fishing boats nestled inside a large protective break wall, lazy seals, and the briny scent of the ocean. Cosmo spotted Johanika first. Her dark hair whipped by the wind, a mischievous smile playing on her lips as she leaned over the edge, tossing scraps to a bellowing seal.

He opened his mouth to call her name when, out of nowhere, a rogue wave reared up beyond the breakwater. The ocean roared, and before anyone could react, a wall of seawater crashed over the harbor, drenching them both. Cosmo staggered back, blinking through the salty spray, while Johanika let out a breathless laugh, shaking the water from her arms like a drenched cat.

She looked up to see the familiar online face of the Kiwi she had been interacting with over the last few months.

"Welcome to South Africa!" she shouted over the wind, grinning.

Cosmo couldn't help but laugh. So much for a composed, first-date, worthy introduction. Instead, he was soaked to the bone, standing before a woman who seemed to belong to the sea itself, wild, unpredictable, and utterly magnetic.

Basking in the golden warmth of the sun, they lingered outside Kalky's, the salty scent of the sea mingling with the crisp aroma of freshly fried fish and chips. Between sips of cold beer and bursts of laughter, time unraveled effortlessly, their conversation stretching for hours like the endless horizon before them.

October 2024
Sean

Sean replayed the video countless times, his sharp gaze shifting beyond Viktor to two women whose reactions spoke volumes, one utterly astonished, the other only slightly less so. Armed with a name, he reached out to Viktor Ólafsson in Iceland, and what he uncovered was nothing short of a gold mine. Viktor's wife, Katrín, and her best friend, Lilith, had been there that day, and through them, Sean pieced together a crucial thread of information.

His conversation with Viktor led him straight to Lilith, the store owner, who eagerly shared what she knew. How 2T Technology had approached her and what they had promised. While it didn't unlock the full mystery of the company, it confirmed something just as important: the three towering figures in the video weren't outsiders. They were locals. The realization suddenly hit him that it was not just in this instance, but in every location where that blank check had surfaced.

A pattern emerged, undeniable and vast, a network of employees, seamlessly woven into the fabric of thousands of corporations across the globe.

Sean stepped back from his "Evidence Board," tacking up the latest revelations. The pieces were falling into place. The picture was still incomplete, but for the first time, he could see the shape of something bigger, something far more intricate than he had imagined.

October 2, 2024
Cosmo

Cosmo stirred from the depths of sleep, the remnants of dreams still clinging to him like mist on the morning sea. The world outside was hushed, the sky just beginning to shake off the weight of night. He slipped out of bed with a quiet determination. Today, he would greet the dawn from the tidal pool just across from his hotel.

Anticipating solitude, he was startled to find Woolley's Tidal Pool already alive with movement. The secluded picturesque natural rock pool that had been filled at high tide by the sea, was alive with a handful of swimmers, their strokes fluid and rhythmic. Their dedication was admirable, a silent communion with the sea as the first blush of sunlight stretched across the horizon.

Cosmo stepped to the water's edge, inhaling deeply. The briny air filled his lungs, sharp and exhilarating. He walked down the stone stairs into the cool embrace of saltwater shocking his skin awake. Each stroke sent a cascade of silver droplets into the air, the ocean's ancient heartbeat pulsing against him. As he glided through the liquid sapphire, his thoughts drifted to Johanika. The easy laughter, the unspoken understanding, the kind of effortless joy that made yesterday feel like a dream he never wanted to end.

As the golden afternoon light had faded the previous night, Johanika's eyes sparkled with excitement as she proposed an adventure, a day immersed in the wild beauty of the Cape of Good Hope and the breathtaking expanse of the Cape Peninsula.

Invigorated by his morning swim, with the scent of the ocean lingering in the crisp air, Johanika arrived early to fetch him. She insisted on starting their journey the right way, with a lavish, soul-warming breakfast. Fuel for the unforgettable day that awaited them.

The spring air was crisp, the landscapes were alive and colorful with blooming fynbos, a natural shrub, and the promise of adventure lay ahead as they drove along the Cape Peninsula.

Their first stop was Boulders Beach, where a colony of African penguins waddled between the smooth granite boulders. Johanika laughed as one particularly bold penguin strutted up close, eyeing her with an air of curiosity.

"He's jealous of me," Cosmo joked, wrapping an arm around her.

From there, they followed the winding road through the Cape Point Nature Reserve, spotting ostriches pecking at the sandy terrain and a family of baboons casually lounging near the roadside.

The wind howled as they reached the Cape of Good Hope, the southernmost tip of the peninsula. Waves crashed violently against the jagged cliffs, a reminder of the explorers who had once braved these treacherous waters.

Cosmo took Johanika's hand as they stood by the famous sign. "I can't believe I am actually here."

She smiled, the salty breeze tangling her hair. "It feels like standing at the edge of the world. I love coming here. Are there places like this in New Zealand?" she asked as they gazed out beyond the turquoise waters, rugged coastlines, and the vast Atlantic merging with the Indian Ocean.

He watched her as the golden light of dusk kissed her skin. "Yes," he said softly. "There are cliffs where the sea sings just as fiercely, where the wind tastes of salt and freedom. But no place is quite like this."

She turned to him, curiosity and something deeper flickering in her eyes. "Will you take me there someday?"

He hesitated, not because he didn't want to, but because moments like these, so perfect, so fleeting, made promises feel fragile. "If you want me to," he finally said, the words slipping between them like a quiet vow.

A gull cried overhead, the waves crashing against the rocks as if answering for him. She reached for his hand, her fingers warm against his own. "I do," she whispered, her gaze steady.

And just like that, standing at the meeting place of oceans, with the wind as their witness, something unspoken shifted between them, something vast, like the sea itself.

Their romance hung in the air, delicate and fleeting, until a voice, distant yet undeniable, shattered the moment. Their eyes met in startled unison before snapping toward the source. But there was nothing. Just silence. Just emptiness.

"It must be 'The Whisperers'. They love to come out during the New and Full Moon," explained Johanika, a speck of concern written across her face.

"Should I be afraid? And what are 'The Whisperers'? They sound a bit ominous."

Johanika explained that there was a legend that spoke of voices carried by the wind, murmurs in forgotten tongues that seemed to rise from the waves. Sailors who rounded the Cape often claimed to hear them. Some believed they were the souls of lost mariners, warning others of the dangers ahead. Others whispered that they were the voices of an ancient people, long vanished, whose secrets were swallowed by time. Cape of Good Hope was known not just for its treacherous waters but for something more mysterious, the whispers.

"It seems that the spirits of the Cape have spoken to us," she said.

As the wind wrapped its fingers around them with each gust, Johanika clung to Cosmo, her embrace both shelter and urgency. "Let's head back into town," she muttered. Cosmo agreed, more than eager to leave the whispers of the wind behind.

Moments later, as the car hummed to life and the wind became a distant roar beyond the glass, a sound slithered through the silence, a voice, muffled yet unmistakable. **"Cosmo Baker...... you have been...."**

Cosmo stiffened. Slowly, he reached into his jacket, pulling out his phone. His expression darkened.

"That," he murmured, his voice edged with something between fear and certainty, "was neither the wind nor *The Whisperers*."

Cosmo and Johanika listened to the message several times. Venus Pool, a hidden gem where the ocean cradled a crystal-clear tidal basin, was just minutes away down the winding, unnamed road. Upon arrival, Cosmo recounted his morning swim, in a pool much like the one before them, describing the serene, weightless world beneath the water's surface.

Time slipped through their fingers as they delved into the latest social media frenzy, watching the viral clips that had the world enthralled. They traded dreams, dissected ideas, and let their thoughts flow freely, weaving an unspoken connection between them. But just as the moment deepened, a sudden shift in the air made them pause. Three tall figures emerged, their presence cutting through the tranquility like a blade.

It had all happened so fast that reality and fantasy became indistinguishable. Johanika was now sitting next to a multi-millionaire whom she had gradually fallen in love with over the last twenty-four hours. She froze as they drove home, her instincts telling her that he would not stay around much longer. With money and freedom, what reason would he have for sticking around?

Cosmo was utterly shaken, his mind reeling with disbelief. Here he was, standing beside the woman of his dreams, a woman who valued neither riches nor fame, standing beside him as he anonymously wrote a check worth forty million dollars. It wasn't the fortune that troubled him, but the fear that it would drive her away.

She had already turned her back on a life of luxury, walking away from affluent parents who wielded their wealth like a weapon, suffocating her under the weight of their power. He knew, without a doubt, that she would never willingly tread that path again.

And yet, here they were. Six months of building something real, something beautiful, through the quiet intimacy of online conversations that had led to this one perfect day, a day now threatened by the very thing he wished to keep hidden. Money. And an overwhelming amount of it.

He had to come up with a plan that would draw her closer to him rather than to push her away. The weight of the silence pressed down on him, thick and suffocating. He glanced at her, Johanika, her profile illuminated by the passing streetlights. She looked serene, but deep down, he knew the war was waging inside her mind.

He swallowed hard and finally spoke.

"I know what you're thinking."

Without taking her eyes off the road, her expression was unreadable. "Do you?"

He exhaled. "You're thinking that money changes everything. That maybe I'll become someone different now that I have forty million dollars. That maybe... we won't work."

Her silence confirmed his fears.

Her eyes began to well up. She could not continue driving. She pulled off to the side of the road, cutting the engine. She turned to face him fully. "I'd like to hear more," her voice cracking through the words.

"I don't care about the money. I never have. And I know you don't either. That's why I love you." The words tumbled out before he could stop them, but they felt right. True.

Johanika's breath hitched. "Cosmo..."

"I'm not going to let money come between us," he continued. "If it helps, I'll donate every cent. Or I'll keep just enough to live comfortably and give the rest away. Whatever it takes. You mean more to me than any fortune ever could."

Johanika searched his face, her eyes brimming with emotion. Then, to his surprise, she laughed, a light, genuine laugh. "You're ridiculous."

His heart clenched. "What?"

She reached for his hand, lacing her fingers with his. "I never said I was going to walk away. I just needed a moment to process. Money terrifies me because I've seen what it does to people. But you? You're different. You don't let it define you."

Relief washed over him, and he squeezed her hand. "So... we're, okay?"

She smiled, the warmth in her gaze making his chest tighten. "We're okay."

Cosmo let out a breath he didn't realize he was holding. Maybe money had the power to change lives, but love; love had the power to make them worth living.

And for the first time that day, he knew, without a doubt, that he hadn't just won the lottery, he had won something far greater.

October 20, 2024
Sean

The sun had barely begun to pierce the eastern horizon when the first warnings crackled over the airwaves. Hurricane Oscar was no longer a distant threat; it was a fast-growing monster closing in, swelling with a ferocity no one had anticipated. A group of tourists, basking in their Bahamian paradise, found their dream vacation abruptly shattered by the urgent call to evacuate. The storm, an enigma in its early formation, had eluded detection until a hurricane hunter aircraft pierced its heart on Sunday, October 20, revealing a beast far more powerful than forecasters had feared.

Oscar was already unleashing its wrath on Cuba, feeding on the warm waters and growing stronger with every passing hour. When evacuation orders swept through the islands, panic and tension thickened the humid air.

Sean, a recent island resident, had only ever witnessed hurricanes through the flickering images of a television screen and on social media. But here, in the face of an encroaching tempest, he knew better than to second-guess the islanders' urgency. *Better safe than sorry.*

As travelers frantically stuffed suitcases, the only two events taking place on the island were outgoing flights and boarding up of homes. The sky had taken on an ominous shade, bruised with rolling clouds, and the once gentle waves now surged hungrily against the shore.

Then came an unexpected lifeline. An American couple, whom Sean had bonded with over conch fritters and rum punches the day before, offered him a seat on their charter flight to Fort Lauderdale. He hesitated. This was his home, his world. But the ocean had turned restless, the winds howling their warning, and hesitation was a luxury he couldn't afford. With a last glance at the swaying palms, he grabbed his backpack and climbed aboard.

From the small jet's window, he watched as the Bahamas, his paradise, his refuge, vanished beneath the swirling storm clouds.

An hour and a half later, they touched down in Fort Lauderdale, where the couple graciously offered to drop him off at the Miami Airport. He had nowhere to be, no plan beyond escape, so he booked a last-minute ticket to Nashville. If a hurricane was going to upend his life, he might as well turn it into an impromptu visit to his sister. An unexpected detour, a temporary shelter from the storm.

Sean had time to burn before his flight, a handful of restless hours stretching ahead of him like an unwelcome guest. After devouring a hearty meal, he wandered through the terminal, turning the sterile corridors into his makeshift walking track. It was a habit; getting his steps in, keeping himself moving, as if stillness might invite thoughts he wasn't ready to entertain.

Every so often, he paused at a departure board, not to check his own flight but to indulge in a game he had played for years: find a destination he couldn't place on a map. It had been easy once, back when the world was vast and mysterious, but time and travel had shrunk it down. Now, the challenge was rare. Today was no exception. Every city, every airport code, was familiar.

With a quiet sigh, he continued toward his gate, only to find every seat occupied. Across the way, however, rows of empty chairs beckoned, a small reprieve from the press of bodies. He settled in, close enough to hear the announcements but far enough to be alone with his thoughts, unfortunately.

And there it was. That creeping, unwelcome sensation. Anxiety, slithering in like an old adversary, wrapping itself around his ribs. It had ruined years of his life, this ghost of worry, this weight he could never quite shake. Medication dulled it but never erased it. He didn't want sedation. He wanted a cure. But finding one always felt like chasing smoke.

You'd think a private detective would be better at solving his own mysteries.

Instead, he sat there, staring at nothing, his mind drifting back to the hurricane looming over his new life. If it swept everything away, then what? He felt the old fear coil tighter. It was happening again.

Sean clutched his boarding pass, his fingers damp with sweat. He could feel the airport terminal buzzing with movement, people rushing, and announcements blaring. His chest tightened. He swallowed hard, but his throat felt like sandpaper. Now it was building, his pulse hammering, his breathing turning shallow.

Not now. Not here.

A baby wailed somewhere nearby. A man behind him sighed loudly. The walls felt like they were closing in. His vision blurred for a second, then snapped back, too sharp, too bright.

Sean pressed a hand against the strap of his backpack, trying to ground himself. *Just breathe. In for four. Hold. Out for four. Hold.* But his lungs weren't cooperating. His body was in full rebellion.

He was losing control.

And then, soft, warm fingers brushed his wrist.

"Hey," a woman's voice said quietly. Startled, he opened his eyes, everything still a blur before him. "You, okay?"

He couldn't speak, but he shook his head.

"Breathe with me," she said, inhaling deeply, exhaling slowly. He followed. Once. Twice.

The ground steadied beneath him. The world didn't feel so loud. His vision started to become clear, and he had more control of his breathing.

"Okay," she continued, her voice warm and steady, "I want you to try something with me. Can you name five things you, see?"

Hip lips parted, but no words came. His fingers tightened around his legs. She tried again. "Anything. It doesn't have to make sense."

After a moment, his voice rasped. "Chair, window, shoes, floor." He paused, struggling. "Your hair." He smiled.

He continued to follow her instructions by naming four things he could touch. His shoulders relaxed, and his breathing calmed down as he exhaled deeply, rubbing his face. Embarrassment started to creep in. He hated his weak, uncontrollable side he was forced to live with.

"Thank you," he murmured, casting his eyes away from her. "I...I couldn't control it." He could see her long blond hair moving as she nodded. "Panic attacks feel very scary, but they always pass. Are you headed to Bermuda as well?"

Sean was confused. He thought he heard Bahamas, but then did she say Bermuda? His mind was a mess, and the fog was so thick. Not sure what to say, he simply pointed to the other side of the room and whispered. "Nashville."

She rested a gentle hand on his shoulder; her eyes filled with something that felt like both sorrow and promise. "If only you were coming to Bermuda," she murmured. "I could help you." There was a sincerity in her voice that cut through the noise of the terminal, through the final boarding call echoing overhead.

Just as he was preparing to let her go, he felt something slip into his palm, cool, firm, deliberate. A card. Then her voice again, soft yet unwavering. "Come find me. I can help you."

The golden light of the gate flickered and dimmed as the jetway door inched shut. He looked down. One word stared back at him in clean, simple print: *Sanare*. A jolt ran through his veins. His breath caught. No. It couldn't be.

"Wait...wait!" he called, his pulse hammering, his vision blurring with the finality of the closing door. His fingers quickly turned the card over. *Claire Baines*.

And just like that, the fog lifted. The name struck his memory like a spark catching dry tinder, igniting something long buried. Claire Baines.

Years ago, she had consumed him. Every lead, every whispered rumor of miraculous recoveries had led him back to her, to Sanare, a name that had sent ripples through the medical world before vanishing beneath the surface. His relentless pursuit had unearthed more questions than answers, a mystery that rattled even the most seasoned experts. Then, just as abruptly as his obsession had begun, it had been taken from him. The board of directors had shut the door, handed him a new case, and redirected his focus. Within days, Claire Baines and Sanare had become ghosts of his past.

Yet here she was, just moments ago. Not a rumor. Not a fading name in an old file. Real.

And in mere minutes, she had accomplished what months of medication had failed to do for him. The pain that had clung to him like a second skin had simply... dissolved.

Sean exhaled slowly, his mind reeling. Who was this woman?

As certainty settled deep in his chest, he knew one thing for sure. Nashville wasn't his final stop.

It was time to experience Sanare for himself.

13

November 2024
Undisclosed Location

In his sophisticated circular room, hidden away from the world, Tim, the mastermind, had tracked the hurricane close to the Bahamas with an almost obsessive focus, his eyes glued to the swirling storm that had ripped Sean, the retired investigator from his island home. Though not a monstrous tempest, it had been disruptive enough, knocking Sean off course and fracturing his concentration on the intricate web of secrets behind the game. Sean hadn't just left the island; he'd extended his exile, choosing to linger on the mainland, visiting his sister in Nashville. The system had remained eerily quiet in his absence, as the next new moon was upon them, November 1st, it seemed certain that Sean wouldn't be returning just yet.

The high-stakes, adrenaline-fueled game had already surpassed every wild expectation Tim had envisioned, and yet, as its inevitable conclusion loomed, he found himself unwilling to let it end. Somehow, some way, he would find a way to stretch it further, to keep the game alive. But for now, his mind pivoted toward the close of the year, and the luxurious escape he had planned for the start of the next.

Twelve players had entered the arena, but only ten had walked away with fortunes, bank accounts overflowing with staggering wealth. To date, a jaw-dropping $289 million had been given away, yet the real thrill remained. The final two players were out there in the world, and Tim could hardly wait to see just how far they'd go. The end was near, but the most electrifying moments were yet to come.

November 2024
Sean

After a restorative week under his sister's care in Tennessee during the last week of October, Sean exhaled a breath he hadn't realized he was holding. His home was still standing, untouched by the hurricane's fury, and for a fleeting moment, peace settled over him like a warm blanket. The gentle rhythm of life at his sister's ranch soothed his nerves, offering him a reprieve from the relentless buzz of his mind. But it wasn't the 'Evidence Board' or the faceless mastermind that haunted him now. It was Claire Baines, and the enigma that was Sanare. His focus had shifted, quietly, irrevocably.

It all began to change with a panic attack he never saw coming, ambushing him like a ghost, snatching his breath and clarity in an instant. He had believed to be in control. How wrong he was. But then, in the middle of the chaos, there was Claire. She appeared, not with fanfare, but with the kind of presence that calms storms. Her touch, her voice, whatever it was, it anchored him. No medication. No ER. Just her. Had she not been there, no doubt he'd have been driven away in an ambulance.

Just a few years back, after twenty years in the field, Sean had stared down mortality and felt its icy breath. At forty-two, a heart attack had split *his* life into a before and after. Years of suppressed stress and unresolved anxiety had turned on him, leaving scars deeper than any case ever could. He had tried to be the stoic figure his job demanded, the "tough guy" in a trench coat, battle-worn and brooding. But that wasn't Sean.

At twenty-two, and fresh out of university, his life took a sharp turn into shadows and secrets. He stepped into the world wearing wire-rimmed glasses and ambition, his closet lined with neatly pressed shirts that still smelled of starch and hope. On that first day at Tillman

Investigations in Boston, the bureau opened its doors to Stewart O'Cleary.

But within a week, Stewart was gone. His name was erased, his past buried beneath layers of fabricated history, and an alias was born.

On paper, stood someone new, Sean Leblanc. A man without a history, born not in a hospital, but in the dim-lit backrooms of bureaucracy and espionage.

His weapon was his mind, razor-sharp and incisive, though it often fought to rise above the dull ache of ever-present panic. He was brilliant, yes. But also, human. Terribly, achingly human.

By day, he was methodical, composed. He solved cases with an elegance that made clients think he had some kind of superpower. His first years were focused on missing persons, stolen heirlooms, and cheating spouses. He handled them all with a steady hand and a calm voice. What no one knew was that every knock on his office door made his chest tighten, that every phone call set his mind spiraling into a hundred what-ifs. Anxiety was his shadow, always walking a step behind, whispering doubts in his ear.

The thing was, in the detective world, masks were part of the uniform. Everyone had something to hide, and Sean was no different. He hid his shaking hands behind folders and fast-typing fingers. He hid his racing thoughts beneath silence, which people mistook for mystery.

One case, though, threatened to crack that calm exterior. A young girl had vanished from a college campus, leaving behind only a cryptic journal entry: "I think someone's watching me." Her parents were distraught; the police were stumped. Sean took the case.

The investigation led him down corridors of secrets, surveillance footage, and half-truths from nervous classmates. At every step, Sean's anxiety clashed with his instinct. When he walked into the empty dorm room she'd vanished from, the air heavy with absence, he felt the panic rising, cold sweat on his neck, a quake in his fingertips. But he focused. He did what he always did: followed the facts.

It was a single overlooked note tucked behind a poster that gave him the lead he needed. A strange drawing of eyes. And one word: "Labyrinth."

Sean traced it to a hidden chat group, a student-run underground society obsessed with urban exploration and psychological games. The young college student had been trying to outsmart them. But they were smarter.

He found her in the tunnels beneath the old campus library, weak but alive. She'd been trapped in a dare gone wrong, the game spiraling into something cruel. When Sean carried her out into the daylight, blinking and gasping, the paramedics called him a hero. Reporters came. Cameras. Flashes.

He smiled and nodded, heart pounding like a trapped bird in his chest.

Later, alone in his apartment, Sean sat on the floor in the dark. He let the panic have him, just for a moment. Then, slowly, he typed out the details of the case, every word anchoring him. The anxiety never left. But neither did his purpose.

Sean's rise was nothing short of meteoric. In no time, he evolved into a master of unraveling mysteries, his instincts razor-sharp and flawless. Before long, he was plunging headfirst into chilling abduction cases, infamous murders that gripped the nation, and relentless pursuits of high-profile fugitives. Each case etched itself into his story, a story of grit, brilliance, and an unshakable pursuit of justice.

In a world of lies and misdirection, Sean Leblanc had found his place, not despite his anxiety, but in defiance of it. The quietest man in the room, solving the loudest mysteries.

For years, medication had dulled the edges of fear, fears Sean had never dared to trace back to their source. He hadn't had the time, the clarity, or the courage. But everything shifted after the heart attack. Retirement, recovery, quiet days in the Bahamas, the sudden stillness of life; they cracked him open. For the first time, he felt calm. He felt joy. Life became a gentle rhythm, a warm breeze brushing against his once, battered soul.

Then came the airport, and Claire Baines.

That brief encounter had ignited something. A spark. A hunger. Questions bubbled up with a ferocity he hadn't expected, and he couldn't ignore them anymore. Instead of flying home, Sean boarded a different flight, one that led him to Arizona.

He was chasing an unsolved mystery that had quietly shaken the medical world in 2018. Terminal diagnoses, reversed. People once deemed untreatable now living full, vibrant lives, not through scalpels or pills, but something else. Something unexplainable. And all signs had pointed to a place called Sanare.

A place that didn't exist on any map.

But Sean knew it was real. And he was determined to find it.

November 2024
Aarav

In the mysterious village of Kodinhi, India, known for its unusually high number of twins, two mischievous brothers, Aarav and Arav, made life endlessly confusing for the villagers. They were just one pair amongst hundreds of sets of twins nestled within the village, a mystery so profound it left doctors and scientists utterly bewitched. No logic could untangle this enigma that stretched back three generations. No formula could pin down its origins. Some pointed to the diet, others to the water, but proof remained as elusive as the secret itself.

Identical in almost every way, their main difference lay in the spelling of their names, a detail few ever noticed. On their tenth birthday, their parents, caught between love and practicality, made a simple yet heartfelt choice; to ease the everyday confusion of two nearly identical names. And so, Arav became A1, the first spark, and Aarav followed as A2, the echo with a twist.

With their quick wit and love for pranks, they delighted in switching places and baffling everyone around them.

One day at the village tea stall, A2-Aarav, or perhaps it was A1-Arav ordered a cup of chai from their elderly uncle. A moment of confusion followed, as their uncle was certain he had just served one of them. But minutes later, the other twin appeared, also expecting his chai. Perplexed and muttering to himself, he was left shaking his head at the mischief of the indistinguishable brothers.

Even with their tricks, the villagers adored Aarav and Arav, knowing that life in Kodinhi would be far less entertaining without them.

≈

A1-Arav had always been the smarter of the two, quickly finding life in Kodinhi stagnant. His love of archeology grew from years of playing in the nearby secluded caves filled with ancient carvings and inscriptions. With a desire to learn more, A1-Arav applied to the Indian Institute of Science at the age of twenty.

His acceptance letter arrived on a dry monsoon day, the words sharp and clear. A1-Arav read it once, twice, and then sprinted to the banyan tree to share the news with his family. They didn't say a word. They saw it in his eyes. Pride, fear and something like guilt.

"I'll write," he promised. "Every week."

The Institute was everything the village of Kodinhi wasn't, buzzing with minds, stories buried not in caves but in books, labs, and dusty artifacts. A1-Arav thrived, but he never stopped thinking about home. Five years later, his thesis took him back to the very soil of his childhood, the ancient carvings and inscriptions in the secluded caves, long overlooked.

He returned, not just a scholar, but a seeker of something deeper.

The dark cave entrance, once beckoning the twins to enter, was no longer visible beneath the thick jungle canopy. What the twins had once discovered, nature had quietly reclaimed. The first year was a battle of machetes and willpower, as the twins hacked through the relentless jungle, each swing of the blade met not with triumph, but disappointment. Every path led to a dead end, never the elusive cave they were searching for.

Yet, the village buzzed with life, thanks, or no thanks, to A2-Aarav. With the return of his brother, mischief poured from his fingertips like rain in monsoon season. Every prank, every sly trick bore his signature grin, while his twin, A1-Arav, had already outgrown such games. Quietly, almost invisibly, A1-Arav hatched out a master plan, one his brother would never notice. It would be his proof, his secret badge.

By the third year, their persistence bore fruit. The cave revealed its mouth at last, dark and wide like a secret waiting to be whispered. Documentation began, studies took shape, and A2-Aarav, true to form, lost interest the moment discovery gave way to diligence. He abandoned the painstaking site survey and measurements, leaving A1-Arav in solitude with shadows and science.

Back in the village, trying to recapture the thrill of deception, A2-Aarav found himself outwitted by almost everyone in the village. Suddenly it appeared that the twins were different. Despite his practiced mimicry and newfound skill at mirroring his brother's quiet intensity, people could always tell them apart. No more stolen lunches. No more elusive games of pretending he had already paid. The game was up. He was confused and he hated it.

So, he pivoted. At twenty-eight, he chose love, the only thing that had ever truly anchored him. He married Oviya, his other partner-in-pranks, whose heart had always belonged to the whirlwind that was A2-Aarav. She had waited for him, through the mischief and the mayhem, through the years his attention was divided by the brother he could never quite shake.

Oviya's world had once held a twin, too, a sister lost too soon, so she knew the ache of the missing half. She knew what it meant to long for a whole. Now, she dreamed of children. Of noise. Of life.

And life answered. Within two years, their home echoed with laughter, tiny feet, and the miracle of not one, but two sets of twins. It was a first in the village's memory, a wild blessing. With four little mouths to feed and endless small hands to hold, A2-Aarav was finally forced to stand still. To plant his feet. To become, at last, the man his family needed.

But it wasn't easy.

The weight of responsibility chafed like an old scar. He envied his brother's solitude, his cave, his calm. The quiet hum of research seemed, suddenly, like freedom. While A1-Arav wandered ancient corridors of stone, chasing mysteries and meaning, A2-Aarav was at home folding diapers and trying to outwit tantrums.

≈

Inside the cave, working alone, he carefully brushed away centuries of dust, tracing the intricate symbols with his fingers. The cave was the protective womb from the outside world that A1-Arav embraced. The ancient site held secrets of lost civilizations, etched in peculiar engravings, symbols, and carvings left behind from past cultures.

His brother's interest had faded, and to A1-Arav, that fading was a quiet mercy. He welcomed it like a soft wind after a storm. The silence of the cave, its steady, echoing calm, suited him far more than the noise and clutter of the world beyond. In time, the cave became less a refuge and more a home. He lived there, embraced by stone and shadow, venturing out only when he missed the laughter of his nieces and nephews or needed a handful of essentials before retreating once again into the stillness he had come to cherish.

≈

That was the moment when everything shifted. As A1-Arav's steady taps against the rock reverberated through the ancient chamber, a sudden rush of cool air sliced through the crack he had just found. He froze; breath caught in his throat. Water. He could hear it, faint but unmistakably moving, on the other side of what he had assumed was merely a wall of engravings. A wall that had for centuries concealed nothing more than a forgotten past.

His hands trembled as they carefully brushed away layers of dust and time, revealing what lay hidden beneath a stone door, ancient and eerily smooth. A passage. A portal to something that should not exist in the known world. The weight of it pressed upon him, but it was not fear he felt. It was the pulse of something ancient, something lost. This was no ordinary discovery. He had uncovered the door to a forgotten realm.

Months passed, and with each day, he pieced together the puzzle, unlocking the intricate codes, the cryptic symbols carved deep into the stone. Then, with a triumphant final movement, the door groaned open, revealing a vast cavern far beyond anything he had ever imagined. His crude lanterns flickered, casting long shadows that danced over what could only be described as a world long past, a civilization that had vanished into myth.

But even in the dim light, the enormity of the cavern whispered secrets he could not yet grasp. He would need more than just the lanterns to illuminate the truth of this place. It would take months, years, perhaps, before he could piece together a proper lighting system, one that stretched from the village to the heart of the cavern. But for now, he knew he could not share this with anyone. He could not trust anyone with the weight of this discovery, not yet.

What had he found? An ancient civilization? Or something far more mysterious, something that could rewrite everything? A1-Arav's pulse quickened, but he held his silence. Until he could understand the depth of what lay before him, the world would remain in the dark.

Oviya and A2-Aarav couldn't ignore the shift in A1-Arav's behavior any longer. It was subtle at first, an overlooked tool here, a forgotten item there. But soon it became impossible to ignore. He was leaving behind the essentials: his food, his clothes, even his water. At first, when they asked him about it, he seemed as sharp and present as ever. His eyes were clear, his responses quick, but the things he left behind told a different story, one of quiet neglect, a sign that something deeper was amiss.

A2-Aarav, however, didn't have the luxury of time to delve into the mystery of his brother's strange new habits. But a promise he made long ago bound him in silence. The cave was not a topic for discussion, and his trust in his brother's well-being ran deep. He believed, perhaps foolishly, that A1-Arav would be fine on his own.

He had promised his wife something else, too: if A1-Arav's health were ever in jeopardy, if the line between concern and intervention ever blurred, only then would they step in. Only then would they tear him away from the work that consumed him. Until that moment came, his faith in his brother, and in the promises, he had made, was all that held him steady.

≈

Within months, A1-Arav had surreptitiously created a unique solar powered lighting system for the cave. The day he flipped the switch to illuminate the vast cavern, it not only took his breath away, but his knees collapsed under him. He fell to the ground, tears rolling down his face as he peered into the past before him. Large elaborate temple facades were carved into various areas of the rock that surrounded the lake. With the beauty now exposed, it was time to begin the real task of exploring. The documentation and analysis would come later.

The ancient craftsmanship and spiritual artistry of the temples featured intricate carvings and sculptures, telling stories from bygone mythology, depicting deities, animals and symbolic motifs.

The carvings were masterfully chiseled directly into the rock walls, showcasing ornate pillars, archways and reliefs. The expressions of the gods and goddesses in their dynamic poses were frozen in time. Though hidden from the world above, its' very essence echoed the ancient traditions that had shaped the land. The temple's facades seemed to rise organically from the stone itself, an effortless fusion of architecture and nature that left one breathless in awe.

New light, softly introduced, cast its glow across the tranquil underground lake, mirroring the profound stillness of the place, lending an almost otherworldly glow to this underground sanctuary. Off in the distance, slow moving water calmed and relaxed the senses.

He discovered rooms carved into the stone behind the facades, some square, others rectangular, each able to hold twenty souls in stillness or movement. The walls and ceilings were bare yet gleaming, catching the light, creating a shimmering, ethereal glow that illuminated the space in a way he had never witnessed before.

There was something magical about the space, something that went beyond the artistry of stone and light. It wasn't merely an architectural marvel, it was a spiritual refuge, a place where art, religion, and nature had intertwined in a delicate, flawless dance. Every stone whispered a secret; every beam of light carried a message. A1-Arav stood in awe, entranced by the mystery that unfolded before him, feeling the heartbeat of something ancient, something eternal.

During his five years at the Institute of Science, not once had he come across anything remotely close to what he was now witnessing. This would shake up the archeological world as well as the history of India. Before letting the world know, A1-Arav was going to enjoy this ancient find for a while.

Leaning over to brush the dirt off what appeared to be a symbol etched into the stone, a small hammer fell from this tool belt onto the floor in the room where he stood. It was not the usual metal impact sound A1-Arav was expecting. Rather, it was a musical note that hummed, the vibration bouncing off the walls creating an iridescent visual light to dance around the room. The sound continued for minutes causing A1-Arav to feel calm and almost sleepy. He sat with his back to the wall, allowing his body to relax. Time ceased to exist, and A1-Arav was floating through a space he could only imagine to be heaven.

With no sense of time, he woke up from what felt to be a good night's sleep. His eyes focused on the iridescent light that continued to shimmer along the walls and ceiling holding him in a trance. The beauty was captivating. He was not sure how he would explain the sensation within him, but he knew this was deliberately crafted and he would take his time to discover the mystery.

Each week, he had sent in samples of his finds, keeping the unusual and intricate discoveries to himself. Thus far, the institute had paid him handsomely for his research and finds, and with the discovery not being out of the ordinary, they had left him alone.

Excited by his new discovery of the sound and light, each day, he let the hammer fall, deliberately, into one of the six rooms. Each space sang a different note, shimmered with its own peculiar light. And yet, for A1-Arav, the ritual never changed. The echo of impact, soft, resonant, inexplicably soothing, washed over him like a lullaby from another world. Time slipped through his fingers. He drifted, not asleep, but somewhere deeper, somewhere brighter. When he came to, hours later perhaps, he felt reborn: alert, electric, more *himself* than he had ever been.

But to his brother and sister-in-law, he was simply slipping. They saw only the forgetful, absent-minded person who constantly left items behind. They didn't hear the music. They didn't see the light.

Each time his brother slipped silently out of the house and vanished into the ancient cave, chasing after those carvings, symbols, and timeworn engravings, A2-Aarav couldn't help but scoff. It all felt so pointless wading through dust and shadows when entire libraries overflowed with studies and scripture on the temples that embroidered the Indian countryside like forgotten jewels. Still, a flicker of envy gnawed at him. His brother moved with a freedom A2-Aarav could only observe, never touch.

The room they once shared, once a sanctuary for secrets, arguments, and midnight giggles, had long since surrendered to the demands of A2-Aarav's family. With the arrival of the twins, the space that once felt infinite had shrunk overnight. There was no room for nostalgia now. No room for A1-Arav. And so, whenever his brother returned briefly, only to vanish again without warning, A2-Aarav collected what little was left behind, and tucked them away in the bottom drawer of his bedside table like fragile relics of a fading presence.

November 1, 2024
A2-Aarav

Friday had finally rolled around, and A2-Aarav could almost taste the freedom. Just one night, one precious evening, away from the whirlwind that was life with four energetic infants. It wasn't just noise and mess anymore; it was a full-blown circus, and for the first time, he truly understood what he and his brother had once put their own parents through. The realization hit hard: the storm had only just begun.

But tonight wasn't for worrying. Tonight was for breathing again. For laughter and lazy conversation. For tea that wasn't reheated four times. He was heading out to the local tea house, where his friends would already be gathering, the buzz of the week's biggest soccer match pulsing in the air.

He clocked out of his dull, soul-sapping job a little early, the thrill of escape in his step, only to pat his pocket and freeze. His wallet. He was becoming just as forgetful as his brother. *The twin essence must be rubbing off,* he thought, as he chuckled to himself.

The house greeted him with silence, a rare, unsettling kind of quiet. His wife and kids must have gone to visit her parents. That explained the stillness. Yet even in the absence of chaos, it took longer than expected to search their compact home. He combed through rooms, opened drawers, checked under tables… until, at last, buried behind a mountain of sofa cushions, his wallet peeked out like a mischievous child playing hide and seek.

Just as relief settled in, a sound, strange, metallic, and out of place, echoed from the bedroom. His body went rigid. Without a second thought, he sprinted toward the noise, instincts kicking in. The sound was coming from the bedside table. Specifically, the bottom drawer.

He opened it. His brother's phone was speaking. Talking.

A2-Aarav froze.

That voice, it was from The Blank Checks Game. His eyes darted to the screen. There it was. His brother, A1-Arav, had somehow been chosen as a participant. A sick, surreal joke, and the punchline was hitting home hard. A2-Aarav cursed under his breath. He knew how this had happened. It had started as a prank, a little mischief. Just a laugh between brothers, or so he thought.

But A1-Arav, obsessed with that damn cave and its riddles, had never noticed. And now he was a contestant in the most mysterious, and most lucrative game the world had ever whispered about.

A2-Aarav stared at the screen, mind racing. He couldn't ignore this. Not now. Not when the stakes were this high. The soccer match he'd planned to attend evaporated from his mind. He'd have to return to the cave. It had been a long time, but if his brother was still there, or in another nearby cavern, he'd find him.

Because this... this was everything.

The amounts winners had claimed were staggering numbers that could make anyone vanish into a better life. He'd stopped following the news after life had become a storm of diapers, and late nights. Four infants didn't leave much time for dreams.

But now? He did the math, choosing a number high enough to shock his village, yet just believable enough to slip under suspicion. His pulse quickened. This was it. Finally, he could stop pretending to be the responsible one, the provider, the "grown-up." Finally, he could breathe.

The rendezvous was set: 5 o'clock, just beyond the edge of town. Strange, yes, but oddly perfect. Far from prying eyes. As the sun dipped, the jungle began to swallow the light, shadows creeping like rumors through the underbrush.

He waited.

And then, they came.

Three tall figures appeared from the depths of the forest, moving like ghosts. A2-Aarav jumped to his feet, startled. After curt introductions, an unnatural silence wrapped around them. Something about the way they looked at each other, but not at him, made his skin prickle.

The tallest man unrolled a sleek device, light dancing across his fingertips. A2-Aarav's heart stuttered. This was it. It was real.

His nerves buzzed with electric hope.

The device lit up with a flicker. A second man answered a call, his voice measured and cold.

"Yes, sir. We'll verify now," he said, casting a glance toward the glowing screen. "What exactly are we looking for?" Silence. Then a nod. He beckoned to the first man, and together they examined the screen, shielding it from A2-Aarav.

"Give us a moment. Please stay on the line."

The third stepped forward, stone-faced, receiving quiet instructions before turning to A2-Aarav.

His body thrummed with anticipation. Blood roared in his ears. He could barely think, barely breathe. This was the moment.

"Mr. Ram. Aarav Ram. That is you, yes?"

"Yes...yes, that's me. I got the message just a few hours ago." He fumbled for the phone, showing it to the man. "Look. It's right here."

The man studied the device carefully, then gave a small nod.

"Yes. This is the correct message. We just need one final confirmation. You understand, identity matters in a game like this."

"Of course."

"One more thing before we proceed. Kindly show us your tattoo."

The words hit him like a slap.

Tattoo. His mind spiraled. That was how his brother made himself different.

Aarav's blood boiled. His brother had branded himself as the player and hadn't told him. Betrayed him without even knowing it. But it wasn't over. Not yet.

He forced a calm expression. "My twin brother has a tattoo. He's inside the cave right now. He gave me the phone and asked me to stand in for him. He found something... something he doesn't want interrupted."

The three men exchanged a look. Finally, one nodded.

"You cannot play in his place. But... we can wait. You have thirty minutes to bring him here. After that, the offer expires."

Hope surged again. He could still win. He would win. A slow, determined smile spread across his face.

"I'll be back," he said. "With my brother."

And then he was gone, disappearing into the shadows, chasing fate through the jungle, heart pounding with purpose. Tonight, everything could change. Forever.

Two hours had passed, and the jungle had swallowed A2-Aarav whole. Darkness pressed in on him, not just around him, but inside him, thick and suffocating. He slumped against a twisted tree, the damp earth cold beneath him. He was lost, not just in place, but in purpose.

Betrayal burned in his chest like a fresh wound. His own brother. His mirror. His other half. A single act of rebellion had shattered the symmetry they were born into. How dare he?

Now A2-Aarav was the one left behind, tethered to a life of gray repetition, where every step was predictable, every breath another sigh. No freedom. No change. Just duty, sameness, and the gnawing ache of resentment.

And now, on top of it all, he was lost in the godforsaken jungle.

A rhythmic rustle broke the stillness. Leaves shifted. A2-Aarav's ears twitched. Footsteps, too steady to be the wind. He snapped upright, tension locking his spine.

"Hello?" he called out, voice a trembling mix of hope and warning.

A flicker of light pierced the canopy, dancing like a firefly. Then, through the thick green, a face emerged. His face.

"What are you doing here in the dark? I thought you hated it out here," his brother said, voice tinged with surprise and something softer.

Emotion surged through A2-Aarav like a live wire. Rage and relief collided. He sprang to his feet, threw his arms around his brother in a sudden, fierce hug, then socked him hard in the arm.

"Ow! What the hell?"

"What's gotten into you?" A2-Aarav snapped back, but the fire in his words faltered under the weight of confusion.

A2-Aarav had never learned to face the truth of his own decisions. He had always played the game, pushed blame, dodged consequence, spun the wheel hoping for a better ending.

But games have endings. And for him, this was the cost.

It took A1-Arav only a matter of days to understand why his brother had ventured so deep into the jungle, lingering near the mouth of the ancient cave. The secret lay in the ink behind his ears, A1 etched behind one, Arav behind the other, a quiet code the villagers used to tell the two apart. But as the days passed, and the truth of his brother's choices settled into his bones, A1-Arav came to accept what he had always known deep down: his brother would never change.

So, with a heavy but resolute heart, A1-Arav moved into a modest home on the village's edge, a place where the wild whispered and the cave's mysteries beckoned. There, he continued the work he'd begun, unraveling secrets the earth had buried long ago. And though he kept his findings close for now, the time would come when he would share them with the world, when the story was ready, and so was he.

November 1, 2024
Sean

Sean found himself once again drifting through the familiar hum of an airport, this time bound for the dry, sun-soaked reaches of Phoenix, Arizona. He had booked a week at a place called Sanare, a name whispered more than advertised. It had no website, no digital footprint, no pin on the map. Just a cryptic little card handed to him by Claire Baines, its edges worn like an invitation to another world. Strangely, the cost had been almost suspiciously affordable. A bargain, or a trap?

As the final boarding call echoed through the terminal, a shiver of recognition ran through him. Today was a new moon. Which meant, somewhere, someone else was being chosen. Another player pulled into the fold.

He powered down his phone and stepped onto the plane, the hum of anticipation mixing with fatigue. Four hours in the sky, and he slept through most of it, the kind of sleep that feels like falling between the cracks of consciousness.

Outside the airport, under the punishing Arizona sun, he waited for his taxi. Out of habit, or maybe instinct, he opened the Blank Checks app. A new entry glared back at him.

November 1, 2024: False identity eliminates contestant.

Sean's pulse quickened. His fingers gripped the phone tighter. The game, if that's what it was, had shifted. Someone had been denied for pretending to be someone they weren't. No one he'd spoken to had ever hinted at that kind of consequence. Until now.

But those questions could wait.

Sanare, and the enigma of Claire Baines, were just on the horizon.

14

November 1, 2024
Sean

The drive through Phoenix was swift and mercifully timed, just ahead of the daily flood of traffic. Sean's driver was a native to the area, knowing when and where to exit, allowing Sean time to enjoy the Arizona desert region. As the city slipped away behind him, Sean turned his gaze toward the horizon where jagged peaks rose like ancient sentinels from the vast, sunbaked expanse. The desert unfolded on either side of the road in a tapestry of warm earth tones, sandy browns, burnt oranges, and pale, sun-bleached tans. Towering saguaros stood with arms lifted to the sky, solemn and regal beneath the endless blue, as if saluting the heavens.

A sudden flicker of movement caught Sean's eye, a roadrunner darting across the road, vanishing into the brush just as the terrain began to shift. They were nearing the foothills of Black Mountain, where nature had carved granite into monuments of time: colossal, weathered boulders shaped into unlikely formations, balanced rocks teetering on impossibly narrow bases, rounded spires that looked more sculpted than formed. The landscape wasn't just scenic, it was theatrical. It felt like an entrance cue, a dramatic welcome from the desert itself.

As they turned into the estate tucked within those ancient hills, Sean felt like he was entering a dream, silent, sun-drenched, and slightly surreal. The road wove upward in soft curves, the stones looming larger with each bend, demanding reverence. These weren't just rocks. They were relics, storytellers, frozen mid-gesture by eons of wind and time. Some were so delicately balanced, Sean half-expected them to tumble with the next breeze. Around them, homes emerged from the earth like whispers, their architecture molded into the landscape. Boulders weren't obstacles, they were embraced. Walls were shaped around them; roofs framed their silhouettes. Nature wasn't pushed aside; it was honored.

Sean's pulse quickened as the car climbed higher, the homes growing scarcer, the silence more profound. Finally, the road forked. They veered left, guided by a modest wooden sign half-hidden in the dust, Private Residence. No house in sight. Just desert.

The car crunched slowly down a dirt road, ending at a solar-powered gate. The driver rolled down the window, letting in a breath of warm desert air thick with the scent of dry mesquite and sunbaked dust. With a soft beep, he entered the code Sean had provided. The gate opened, revealing nothing but more winding gravel, and they pressed on.

The tires whispered over crushed rock as the road rose and dipped gently into a secluded canyon. Then, finally, civilization emerged, though barely. Nature still ruled here. A trio of monumental boulders marked the entrance: two massive stones at the base, and one impossibly balanced overhead, forming a natural portal to the man-made world beyond. It felt like entering a hidden temple rather than a home.

Driving through the entrance of nature's balancing act, a wide, manicured gravel court opened, flanked by two sweeping carports, each topped with elegant terracotta-colored solar tiles. Palo verde trees rose strong and full in the background.

The driver eased the car up to the main entrance. The granite boulders towered, silent and sublime. The door seemed carved from the rock itself, a deliberate invitation into a place shaped by both human hands and nature's will.

Sean stepped out, his luggage set gently beside him. The car turned and disappeared, leaving only the whisper of gravel and the heartbeat of the desert.

The instructions had been clear enough, enter through the main door, follow the marked path. But nothing could have prepared him for the wonder that lay beyond that unassuming threshold.

The moment he stepped inside, the world shifted. It was as if he'd walked into an oasis, cool, crisp air washed over him, tinged with the scent of earth and greenery. His senses sparked to life. Somewhere, water trickled softly, and the palette of nature, soothing greens, sun-warmed browns, the occasional bloom, beckoned him deeper.

He found himself in a vast, circular room that breathed serenity. Tall potted trees stretched skyward, their branches nearly brushing the two-story ceiling, where sunlight spilled through lofty transom windows in golden shafts. Beneath them, lush ferns unfurled like dancers' mid-pose, palms fanned the air, and rubber plants added depth with their glossy leaves.

Nestled within this verdant sanctuary were havens of comfort, loveseats and deep chairs hugged by cushions, low ottomans waiting to be claimed, each with its own quiet corner. Side tables held ceramic curios and small sculptures, and shelves were tucked with a collector's delight of oddities. A bookcase, heavy with literary treasures, invited pause and pleasure.

At the very heart of it all lay a circular reflecting pool, still and mesmerizing. A smooth stone sphere, perched in a shallow dish off-center, released a steady trickle of water that flowed in delicate ribbons down its sides. The overflow spilled into the pool below, whispering a soft symphony that seemed to hush even his thoughts.

A pathway of rectangular steppingstones cut across the pool, a poetic illusion of walking on the surface itself. He crossed, each step a meditation, his gaze drawn to one of three doors that stood at equal intervals around the room. One was ajar. Two remained closed.

Guided by the glowing map on his phone, he made his way toward the open door. Just beyond its frame, a winding path unfurled, snaking gently around natural boulders. Above him, a canopy of triangular wooden beams interlaced with glass panels embracing the sunlight. He had entered something sacred.

Keeping to the main hallway, a beautiful honey colored wooden archway welcomed him into an opened domed room. The dome structure consisted of multiple arched wooden beams that radiated from a central pillar. The six elegant, curved beams of the pillar resembled the skeleton of a tree, the trunk, tall and thick, the base fanning out like a sturdy root structure. Five, floor to ceiling arched skylights nestled themselves between sections of the natural wood dome structure.

A masterfully carved spiral staircase of polished wood curled elegantly around the central column, a sculptural centerpiece that seemed to float in the air like a ribbon of warmth and grace. Light poured in through the windows, casting golden reflections across the open-plan living area below. At the far end, just beneath the landing, a woman rose from behind a sleek wooden desk, her presence serene yet striking.

"Good afternoon, Mr. Leblanc. Welcome to Sanare," she said, her voice a gentle melody as she extended a graceful hand. "My name is Seraphina."

There was something instantly calming about her, perhaps it was the warmth in her smile, or the way her name seemed to echo softly in the space around them.

"Your week is entirely yours to shape," she continued. "We are here to make your stay not just comfortable but deeply rejuvenating. The dining hall is always open, and our meals are served buffet-style, offering a rich assortment of flavors. If there's anything special you crave, culinary or otherwise, please, let us know. It is our wish to offer you an experience you won't soon forget."

Sean listened intently, each word sinking in like the first sip of something soothing after a long journey.

"In your suite, you'll find details about our spa offerings, relaxing mineral baths, immersive sound therapies, and a variety of massages designed to ease body and mind. We also host nightly entertainment, and this evening, we invite our guests to gather beneath the stars. The sky will be at its clearest tonight; it's a new moon. Have you ever seen the Milky Way, Mr. Leblanc?"

"I have," Sean replied, a soft smile curving his lips. "In the Bahamas, where I live. It's always magical."

Seraphina's eyes lit up. "Then you'll appreciate what the skies have in store. During your stay, we'll witness some truly special celestial events. In a few days, on Nov 4th, the Moon will pass by Antares, and the following night, it'll appear near Venus while the Taurids meteor shower reaches its peak. Nature's own fireworks."

Sean hesitated for a beat, then asked, "Is Claire Baines here? She's the reason I've come. I was hoping to speak with her."

A knowing nod followed. "She's expected to arrive later tonight, or perhaps early tomorrow. If you can be patient just a little while longer, I promise, she'll give you all the time you need."

A hush settled between them, thick with anticipation and something unspoken. Sean exhaled, his gaze drifting toward the ceiling, where soft shadows played among the beams.

Something was beginning. Something he hadn't quite named yet, but he could feel it.

November 1, 2024
Claire & Dee

The dream had ended, but its echo lingered like salt on sun-kissed skin. After a blissful, soul-soaked week in the turquoise waters of Bermuda, the girls returned, fully awakened. For Dee, it was more than just an escape. It was the emergence of something new. A spark that ignited what she had long buried. And for Claire, it was a continuation of the journey she'd started years ago.

In those warm, weightless days, something within Dee had shifted. For the first time in what felt like forever, she felt calm. Centered. Alive. Gone was the fear that had once gripped her, the quiet despair that colored her every move. In its place bloomed a fragile but fierce peace. And Claire, radiant, and grounded, had shown her the way. Not just how to enjoy life again, but how to step into her own skin, unafraid.

It was during a quiet moment beneath the surface, snorkeling through the endless blue, that Dee knew. She would join Claire at Sanare Spa. But not just to help. To heal. To be someone.

Bermuda had revealed a secret neither of them had known: Dee had a rare and gentle gift. She didn't just listen, she felt people. They sought her out without knowing why. Strangers became confidants over cocktails, beachside swims, or stolen moments in the shade. They poured their stories into her hands as if she'd been waiting all along to catch them. And she never flinched. With patience and grace, she offered words that soothed like balm.

Claire had watched in awe. It was like watching a new self-emerge from Dee's shell, vibrant, empathic, magnetic. She hadn't seen this side of her before. Neither had Dee. But it was real. Powerful. Conversations that began with a simple hello turned into soulful exchanges, and people left lighter, brighter, as if something deep within them had been quietly rearranged.

This wasn't just a new chapter. It was Dee's true beginning.

Returning home came with a breath of pure excitement. The two friends were ready to tackle their new journey together. They hatched out a plan to create a walking path from Dee's new home to the Sanare Spa. They studied the maps online and came up with a few viable paths. They would start immediately hiring out the grunt work so that they could focus on a new line item on the spa offerings.

They arrived home just before midnight with the next day offering them a new beginning of partnership.

November 1, 2024
Sofia

Sunlight spilled through the open window like liquid gold, relentless and blinding. Sofia turned her face away, her thoughts spinning in a storm of frustration and grief. The bitter taste of yesterday's exchange with her heartless boss still lingered on her tongue, each word a bruise. Whether Peter's attack had been deliberate or not no longer mattered. A quiet but fierce resolve began to settle in her bones. Enough. Enough of the humiliation. Enough of the pain.

Dragging herself from bed, Sofia's limbs trembled with weakness, a harsh reminder that her body still hadn't forgiven her. She would not be leading the one-day trek through the Andes, not today. And perhaps not for a long time.

Her mind drifted to the moment everything changed, a moment that should've been ordinary. She was stepping out of the Tamir Bakery, the aroma of a freshly baked chicken empanada still clinging to her clothes. Then, screeching tires, the thud of metal, the blur of a panicked tourist clutching his map behind the wheel. Her body crumpled on the sidewalk like paper. Her legs shattered. The surgeries were long, the recovery even longer. And then the words she could never unhear: "You may never walk again."

That wasn't the life she'd imagined, not the life she had built.

In her early years, she had become a rising star among high-altitude trekking guides. Young, fearless, and female, Sofia had carved her place in a male-dominated world with nothing more than grit, grace, and a voice fluent in Spanish, Quechua, and English. Born of the mountains, she belonged to the Andes. By twenty-four, she wasn't just guiding treks, she was shaping dreams.

That's when Edward had found her.

In 2013, as he planned his first trip along the Inca Trail, her name kept surfacing like a legend. Curious and a little weary of researching, he booked a spot under her leadership. Four days and three nights later, he was in awe, not just of the mountains, but of her. Sofia's spirit left an imprint on him deeper than any mountain trail ever could.

A year later, they were married, their love as sure-footed as the stone steps of Machu Picchu. Edward became her partner on and off the trail, humbly taking on the role of porter on every expedition. He fumbled through Spanish and Quechua with quiet charm, his kindness disarming everyone he met.

Children did not come easily, and the ache of waiting became its own kind of journey. After many conversations and quiet tears, they found their answer in surrogacy. Marisol arrived like a miracle, blue-eyed like her father, crowned with her mother's midnight hair. Perfection.

While Sofia and Edward led travelers up ancient paths twice a month, Rosa, Sofia's mother, watched over Marisol with the strength only grandmothers possess. The rhythm of their lives beat in sync with the mountains, providing, healing, enduring.

But the only place that could ever rival the Andes in Sofia's heart was Hawaii.

Every year, for one sun-kissed month, they escaped to its shores. There, on the sand, with waves whispering secrets and Marisol laughing in the distance, Sofia would press her head against Edward's shoulder and breathe, "One day, maybe just one day, we can live forever in paradise."

And Edward, ever the gentle realist, would only smile, knowing that sometimes, a single month of paradise had to be enough.

Peter Klein was a cunning man with ambition hardwired into his bones and empathy notably absent. A shrewd operator with a self-serving streak, he ruled his professional world with icy precision. But long before he wore tailored suits and barked orders from corner offices, Peter was a boy with a bruised ego and bloodied arms.

Back in Germany, in the adolescence of life, Peter's family uprooted him to Cusco just as he was beginning to forge his identity in secondary school. He was smart, driven to excel, and far too young for his class, thrust a year ahead, a fourteen-year-old among fifteen-year-old wolves.

"Hey, look at short little four-eyes over there," sneered the class tyrant. "Think he can even find his way to class without those ridiculous glasses?"

Peter said nothing. He never did. Instead, he walked, slowly, blindly, through the thorn bushes, toward the gilded façade of the Bavarian International School. Its mansion walls echoed with silence as he stepped into the marble hallway, blood streaking his arms from fresh scratches and cruel jabs.

The Director was the first to spot him. "Good heavens," she gasped. "What is this?" Her voice turned stern. "This behavior is unacceptable. This time, Peter, you *will* tell us who's responsible. But first, to the nurse. Then we talk. Do you hear me, Peter Klein?"

He nodded, mute and stoic, all the while cradling a storm behind his calm expression. Revenge had begun to form in the quiet chambers of his mind.

But vengeance would have to wait.

Two months later, summer began to appear across Bavaria. Peter's father earned a promotion, and the family packed up their lives and flew south-crossing continents and hemispheres, to settle in the high-altitude cradle of Cusco, Peru. Peter left without enacting his carefully plotted retaliation. "No one will ever treat me that way again…" he murmured, his voice coiled with unfinished business.

Then something extraordinary happened.

Perhaps it was the altitude. Perhaps it was destiny. Peter's genes surged into overdrive. In the first two months in Cusco, he shot up six inches, his body aching with a vengeance his fists never delivered. By the end of the Andean winter, an additional four inches had been added to his frame.

On his first day at the Andean International School, Peter Klein entered as a towering figure, blond, striking, and fifteen years old, but already bearing the air of myth. His new classmates, all shorter and darker-haired, stared as if some Germanic god had wandered down from Olympus. Even the teachers paused, caught for a moment in admiration.

Peter, for the first time, felt adored.

The move had been a rebirth. In the vast space between continents, he shed the battered, bespectacled boy and stepped into power. He mastered languages with unnerving speed and conversed with students and staff from every corner of the globe. By sixteen, he stood at six foot five. Tall. Golden. Unshakable.

And Peter milked it for every inch, every glance, every flicker of awe. After all, hadn't he earned it?

Sofia had already surrendered so much more than anyone should ever have to. After her last surgery, a fragile thread of hope had begun to stitch its way through her heart. For a brief, blissful moment, she let herself believe she might walk again. But hope, as always, proved fleeting. Her legs refused to cooperate, and each step with the crutches felt like a reminder that the ground beneath her could give way at any moment.

Edward continued working for the Andean trekking company, guiding eager tourists through landscapes that once set Sofia's soul on fire. But his income alone couldn't sustain their lives. Swallowing her pride, Sofia had taken a job as a trek coordinator. It was dull, underpaid, and kept her chained to a desk, but at least it was something. At least it kept the darkness at bay.

Until now.

Peter, her boss in title, tyrant in truth, was the owner's son, and he carried that entitlement like a badge of honor. He was the kind of man who mistook arrogance for leadership and thought charm was measured by how many people feared him.

Before her desk job, Sofia had barely registered Peter's existence. He showed up just once a year in Edward and Sofia's life, gliding through the annual company party at the Peruvian Steakhouse like some kind of local royalty. His birthday conveniently aligned with the gathering. Peter always kept to the dignitaries' corner, far from the porters and guides. *Too good for us*, Sofia used to think with a scoff.

But in just two months, under fluorescent lights and Peter's glass-walled reign of terror, he had stripped away any illusions. His disdain dripped from every interaction, but it wasn't until that moment that he truly cut her open.

"Sofia!" His voice cracked like a whip from behind his pristine glass walls, the Andes rising in quiet, majestic protest behind him. "Come here," he barked. "And bring next week's schedule."

With a resigned sigh, she rose, slid the file under her arm, and gripped her crutches. Her legs wobbled. Peter thrived on control, and chaos. Every day he changed his mind, and every day, the office held its breath.

She placed the folder on his desk. "Here's next week's schedule. I made the changes you asked for, though I really think we should reconsider the weather conditions for those camping spots. They're not safe, not this time of year..."

And then, it happened. That look.

His eyes narrowed. "And what would you know about hiking in the Andes, you crippled woman?" he spat, loud enough for the entire office to hear. "I know these mountains better than anyone. Don't ever question me again. Ever."

The words hit her like stones. Around her, colleagues sank lower into their chairs, desperate to disappear. Nobody moved. Nobody breathed.

Sofia turned to leave, but her crutch slipped and fell. Her cheeks burned. She nudged it toward the door with small kicks, pride keeping her upright. A kind co-worker, Mario, scooped it up and handed it to her in silence.

"Does he not know you used to be our head guide?" Mario whispered.

"Obviously not. But arguing with someone who thinks they are always right is like screaming into the wind," she replied, her voice barely a murmur.

Lunch couldn't come soon enough.

At twelve-thirty, Sofia and a handful of coworkers escaped to their usual hideout. For one golden hour, laughter returned, brushing against her like sunlight after a storm. Nobody spoke of the morning. They didn't need to.

Back at her desk, she counted down the hours till she could be back home with her husband, and her daughter's warm snuggles. Peter hadn't returned all afternoon, and the peace was almost enough to forget the calamity of the morning.

But then... like a thunderhead cresting the mountains, he stormed in.

"Sofia!" he bellowed. "In my office. Now!"

Her body stiffened. She gripped her crutches, her legs trembling again. Please, not again.

"I don't even know why you're still here," he roared the moment she entered. "Sending tourists into dangerous zones? Are you trying to ruin this company?"

"What? No... I warned you against that location..."

"Then explain this!" He flung open the folder with dramatic flair. "You typed it. It's right here."

"That's not..."

"Don't lie! It's clear as day. You're not just crippled, you're stupid too."

The tears came fast this time, unbidden, stinging. Her body began to tremble as Peter's voice echoed through the halls like a cruel spell.

"Oh good," Peter sneered. "Here comes my father. Let's hear what he has to say about your incompetence."

Mr. Klein walked in, adjusting his jacket, radiating calm authority, until he opened his mouth.

"What's going on in here? I could hear you from the elevator."

Peter launched into his fabricated tale. "She wants our clients camping on a dangerous ledge next week. Look, she typed it up herself."

"But that's not wh..."

"Tsk, tsk," Mr. Klein interrupted, wagging his finger at her like she was a misbehaving child. "Did anyone ask for your opinion?"

He turned to Peter, beaming with paternal pride. "Well caught, son. Good job spotting that. Could've been a disaster. Make the changes, Sofia, and don't let this happen again. My son knows these mountains better than you ever will."

And just like that, it was done.

Sofia stood there, stunned, breathless, her heart pounding like a war drum. She turned, walked out with silent dignity, tears sliding down her cheeks as the entire office watched her limp back to her desk in paralyzed silence.

No one said a word. Not because they didn't care, but because they feared for their own retaliation.

November 2, 2024
Sean

Sean couldn't remember the last time he'd slept past nine. Maybe it was the lull of the spring's gentle gurgle outside his window, or perhaps it was the kind of night sky that makes you forget everything, that great celestial ribbon arcing over the desert, draped in stars. Whatever it was, he felt something rare and precious when he woke: peace. Deep, undisturbed peace. He stretched beneath the cotton sheets, his limbs heavy and content, not feeling the usual urgency that snapped him into motion. Today, there was no hurry.

He made his way out to the patio; a secret garden tucked into the heart of the desert. The oasis shimmered in the soft morning light, palm fronds rustling in the breeze, bougainvillea spilling bright pink over exposed boulders. With a steaming cup of coffee in hand and a plate of fruit and warm bread before him, he let himself sink into the moment.

That's when he saw her.

Claire.

Across the courtyard, emerging like some vision from a dream, her hair tousled by sleep, a robe tied loosely around her waist. She moved slowly, languidly, and yet there was something luminous about her presence, serenity in motion. She hadn't seen him yet, and he didn't call out. He just watched, struck silent by the thousand questions ricocheting through his mind.

What exactly had she done that changed the course of his life in just a blink?

Then, as if she heard him thinking, Claire looked up.

Her eyes met his. Calm, knowing.

She raised her coffee cup in a quiet salute, a soft smile curving her lips. "Good morning," she mouthed across the distance.

Sean, stunned by her presence, managed to mirror the gesture. "Good morning," he replied with a nod, his voice caught somewhere in the space between disbelief and joy.

They sat in silence for a while, separated by the gentle swaying of the tree branches in the morning breeze and sunlight, yet somehow entirely in tune, each lost in their own thoughts, sipping slowly, letting the morning unfold like a flower blooming toward the sun.

Then, from somewhere deeper in the valley, bells rang at ten o'clock, their chimes soft and echoing, like time itself clearing its throat.

Claire stood up, stretching with the kind of grace that made Sean forget how to breathe. She walked toward him with the unhurried ease of someone who knew exactly where she was going, and why.

"Good morning, sleepyhead," she said, standing in the dappled light before him. Her smile was warm, a spark of mischief in her eyes. "Looks like you finally got some real rest. I wasn't sure you'd remember me... we met at the airport about a week ago."

Sean set down his cup, heart beating faster now. "That's exactly why I'm here," he said. "You gave me your card, just before you hurried onto your flight. And… thank you, for what you did. I still don't even know how to explain it; I was sure I was heading for the hospital. You stopped that from happening. But, how?"

Claire tilted her head slightly, that same secretive smile dancing on her lips. "That's a story," she said, "one that takes more than coffee and bread to tell."

She turned, already stepping back toward the winding path. "Come for a swim with me," she called over her shoulder. "I'll meet you by the spring-fed pond. It's quiet there. We can talk."

And just like that, she disappeared behind the palms, leaving Sean staring after her, utterly awake now, and more curious than ever.

November 2, 2024
Sofia

Edward was already out, preparing for his upcoming four-day trek. In their silent cozy home, golden sunlight spilled through the open window, casting amber streams across Sofia's face, gently coaxing her from sleep. But as her eyes fluttered open, the sting of yesterday's betrayal snapped her fully awake. She still couldn't wrap her mind around the cruelty, the sheer arrogance, Peter and his father had shown her. As if she were invisible. As if their success hadn't been built, brick by brick, on her unwavering dedication. But it wasn't just her, it was all of them. Her team, her friends, her family. Side by side, they had woven something unforgettable into the wild. Each step, each story, etched into the trails they loved. Together, they created more than memories, they built a magic that repeatedly called hikers back.

She moved on autopilot, preparing Marisol's breakfast with practiced grace, masking the ache that threatened to split her chest open. She kissed her daughter's forehead and walked her next door to her mother's, the familiar path grounding her, if only slightly.

Back in the stillness of her own home, doubt crept in like a shadow. Should she even go back? She could fake a cough, a fever, hide beneath a blanket of excuses and let the day slip by unnoticed. But then, something stirred inside her, deep and defiant.

No. Not today.

Today, she would move. She would feel the earth under her feet again. She would begin the slow, determined work of strengthening her legs, not just her muscles, but her spirit. The Andes were calling her back, and she would answer, not for them, but for herself.

She followed the proper protocol, taking the day off from work. She ignored the calls that immediately flooded in. Silencing her phone, she walked around the ruins of the ancient Incan temple just outside of the city. Her footsteps echoed softly against the worn stone paths, the air cool and thin at this altitude. Sunlight filtered through drifting clouds, casting shifting patterns of light and shadow on the moss-covered rocks and intricately carved stone altars.

She paused beside a massive limestone monolith, tracing the smooth grooves etched centuries ago, ceremonial channels once used for offerings, perhaps blood or chicha, still mysterious in their purpose. The air was hushed, filled with a quiet weight, as if the spirits of the past still lingered in the labyrinthine tunnels and ceremonial chambers carved into the earth.

She could feel her past, pride beaming within as she looked upward toward the craggy outcrops and jagged silhouette of the Andes. In her eyes, awe and quiet longing brought her to tears.

She yearned for those glorious nights under the harsh, brilliant blue sky, the kind that only exists at 11,000 feet, hiking through the cloud forests, past glacial lakes, and over mountain passes where the air grew thin and ghosts were said to follow. She recalled all that her father had taught her of the Andes.

Around her, eucalyptus trees whispered in the breeze, their scent mingling with the ancient dust. The city of Cusco hummed faintly in the distance, but in the ancient ruins of Q'enqo, time felt suspended, wrapped in the stone silence of a lost empire. Sofia was beginning to feel her strength grow. It would take time, but she could see her future. It was in the mountains. And back to the mountains she would return.

Three hours had vanished in a blur. Back home, she and Edward wasted no time, they sketched out a regimen, a promise inked in sweat and grit, to ready her body for the mountains again.

But her phone loomed like a storm cloud. The messages waited, venomous things she didn't want to face. Still, Sofia Vasquez was no stranger to hardship, she had never run from it before, and she wouldn't start now. One by one, she pressed play, her jaw tightening with every word. Ultimatums. Warnings. Then the final blow: she was fired.

Edward didn't say a word. He didn't need to. In the silence, their resolve hardened. The fire in her to return to the Andes blazed higher, hotter. They'd make do with one income. She'd claw her way back, step by step, summit by summit.

And then, her phone lit up.

A synthetic voice broke the tension like a thunderclap: **"Sra. Vasquez. You have been selected as the latest contestant of The Blank Checks game. Please join us at eight o'clock tonight at the Peruvian Steakhouse for your opportunity to fill out your blank check. You may bring friends and family. Best of luck. And remember... DREAM BIG."**

The room stood still.

Sofia and Edward stared at each other, speechless, breathless, as if the universe had cracked open and whispered back.

For two intense hours, Edward and Sofia sat hunched over their modest kitchen table, their eyes wide as they absorbed each figure on the page, each amount more staggering than the last. For the Vasquez family, it wasn't just a windfall. It was liberation. Together, they crafted a plan, bold and calculated, that would launch them into the driver's seat of a life they could finally command. Control was no longer a dream. It was within reach.

That evening, under the glow of the setting sun, Edward, Sofia, their young daughter Marisol, and Sofia's dignified mother arrived early at the Peruvian Steakhouse. The small parking plaza, usually bustling, was strangely quiet, just a handful of cars dotted the lot. Sofia's eyes narrowed. Odd, she thought. A prickle of anticipation climbed her spine as they were quietly ushered to the far, secluded end of the dining hall. Tonight was no ordinary night.

Across town, Peter Klein was riding a wave of vanity and impatience. Tonight was supposed to be a showcase, the perfect night to parade his new girlfriend, Pamela, a trophy that consistently turned heads. He relished the public gaze, the whispers, the admiration. But as they pulled into the parking lot of the Peruvian Restaurant at precisely 8:30 p.m., his jaw clenched. His favorite spot, his unofficial claim, was taken.

With exaggerated flair, he guided Pamela to the entrance, only to find the heavy wooden door stubbornly shut. Locked. He slammed his fist against it.

"What the hell? It's never locked," he barked, pounding harder.

Pamela took a cautious step back, her eyes darting nervously. "Peter…"

"Open up!" he roared.

On the other side, the Maître 'D hesitated before finally cracking the door open just a few inches, his face etched with polite discomfort.

"Good evening, Mr. Klein. What can we do for you?"

"We are here for dinner. Now let us in," Peter growled, shoving the door with his large hand. It didn't budge.

"I'm afraid the restaurant is closed tonight, for a private event."

Peter's face twisted into fury. "Closed? Are you forgetting who I am?"

"I do indeed know you well Mr. Klein," said the Maître 'D calmly, "but tonight, someone else holds the keys."

Just then, two tall men appeared, holding a space at the threshold. Peter reeled, his ego smacking into an immovable wall. "What the hell is going on here? Who else can afford this place besides my family?"

From behind, Sofia hobbled forward, composed and radiant, keeping her distance as she stood between the two tall men.

"Hello, Peter," she said coolly. "Remember me? The 'crippled' employee you mocked? The one who, according to you, didn't belong in the Andes?"

Peter's mouth dropped.

"Well, not only am I going to get back on my feet, but I'm also going launching my own trekking company, with a team and sponsors who believe in me. And tonight… we celebrate."

Pamela blinked, recognition dawning. "Wait… you're Sofia Alvarez? *The* Sofia Alvarez? Do you know how famous you are back in the United States?"

Peter turned, confused. "You know this woman?"

"She's a legend," Pamela said, stunned. "She's the most talked-about guide in the America's. Every one of my friends dreams of hiking with her."

Peter scoffed. "She's nobody. Just another…"

"...Woman?" Sofia interrupted, her voice like steel wrapped in silk.

Pamela stepped forward, eyes shining. "You're my hero. Would you ever consider... maybe... having dinner sometime? When you're free?"

"I'd like that," Sofia replied with a warm smile. Peter's face turned crimson. He spun on his heel and stormed off, rage and disbelief trailing behind him like smoke.

"You dodged a bullet," Sofia told Pamela gently. "Would you care to join us?"

Pamela hesitated for just a second before nodding. "Yes. I'd be honored."

Pamela followed Sofia to the back room where the air thrummed with quiet anticipation. The three impeccably dressed strangers waited in silence. Pamela's heart pounded with curiosity that threatened to boil over.

"Come," Sofia murmured. "I want you to meet my family."

They stepped inside... and Pamela stopped cold.

Her gaze locked onto the lapel pins. That symbol. The one that had set the entire planet ablaze.

"You... you're the November winner?"

Sofia nodded, her face awash in disbelief, awe, and a flicker of quiet triumph. "The message came this morning. A blank check. A choice. I never thought it would be me."

Her voice dropped to a hush, trembling with memory. "Last April, I was lying in a hospital bed, fresh out of surgery, wondering if this was it. If that was all my life would ever be. I posted my name and number to some silly contest, something to distract myself from the fear. And now... here we are. On the edge of everything."

Pamela's voice was barely a whisper. "But... why haven't I seen this online?"

A man with storm-gray hair and eyes that had clearly seen too much spoke from the side. "The world thinks it's live. But we give the winners some time. To breathe. To vanish, if that's what they want. Freedom isn't something you rush. It's sacred."

Pamela turned to Sofia, her mind reeling. "So… what now?"

Sofia's eyes sparkled with a fire that came from deep within. "We have a vision, one that will transform not just our family, but this town we love. My husband and I are launching our own trekking company right here in Cusco, where every step of the journey will reignite the joy of purpose. We're carving a new path, and for those who believe in bold beginnings, the trail is open."

Pamela nodded, the full weight of the moment settling into her bones. "This… this changes everything."

Sofia smiled, radiant and unshakable. "Yes," she said, the word like a sunrise. "Yes, it does."

November 3, 2024
Claire

It wasn't just the crystalline shimmer of the spring-fed pond or the way the morning sun danced on its glassy surface that stirred Claire's heart into a frenzy. No, it was something deeper, something electric and impossible to ignore. A pull so powerful, so unexpected, that it made her forget all about Dee and the dreams they had promised to chase together that week. In that moment, those plans felt like faded chalk on a rain-washed sidewalk.

What was meant to be a brief conversation by the water, just a quiet exchange before the day unfolded, turned into an entire day suspended in time. Laughter echoed across the ripples, and glances held just a breath too long left Claire dizzy with possibility. She could feel it: the magnetic current between them. It surged under her skin, undeniable. And she was certain, achingly certain, that it wasn't one-sided.

But reality crept in, uninvited. The distance loomed not just in miles, but in oceans, across the country, across the water, to the islands where dreams were harder to reach. Still, she wasn't ready to let go, not yet. She would give it a week. Just one week to see if the feeling stayed, if it deepened, or if it would fade like morning mist when the sun comes to claim the sky.

November 7, 2024
Sean

The week at Sanare turned out to be more than Sean could have ever imagined, more than he dared to hope for. It wasn't just a retreat; it was a spell, a slow-burning enchantment that unraveled him in the most unexpected ways. He arrived curious, intrigued by the mystery of what exactly Claire did at the spa.

Each day with Claire felt like stitching together moments of quiet magic. They shared laughter like it was a secret language, walked for hours through the sun-dappled trails of the Black Mountain hills, and dined beneath the warm, dusky skies in the rustic charm of Cave Creek. There was something sacred in the simplicity of their time together, a rhythm that felt ancient and new all at once.

He was falling for her, no, he had already fallen.

It was the kind of week that didn't just leave him with questions, it left him changed. Dreamlike, dizzying, and more real than anything he'd known.

As the week melted into the past, they made a decision that felt like stepping into a dream. With laughter in their voices and something electric in the air, they sketched out a plan, equal parts daring and romantic. She would fly to the Bahamas, where he'd already be waiting, sun-kissed and grinning, for the better part of December. White sands, turquoise waves, and warm island nights would be their backdrop as they pressed pause on reality to explore something fragile, thrilling, and full of promise. They didn't know what would come next, but for the first time, that didn't matter. They were choosing the adventure, and each other.

15

End of November 2024
Undisclosed Location

The mastermind leaned back in his chair, a sly smile playing at the corners of his lips as he studied the Blank Checks list. The contestants' names glowed on the screen beside their chosen sums, numbers that carried vastly different meanings depending on the eyes that read them. Money, he mused, was never just money. It was legacy, freedom, revenge, rebirth. Across continents and cultures, the psychological weight of a blank check revealed more about humanity than any confession ever could.

He lingered on the latest winner, a young woman from Cusco, Peru. A mountain trekker, once known for conquering high-altitude trails, now grounded by multiple leg surgeries. She had played it safe: thirty million. A modest choice, considering the options. Still, it was more than enough for her to finally launch the eco-tourism business she'd sketched out during her long hospital stays. He admired her restraint. So many played recklessly, hungry for headlines. But she had chosen rebirth.

Tim felt a rare flicker of satisfaction. His mad creation, Blank Checks, the global social media game where contestants selected a dollar amount that could change their lives, had taken root far beyond what he'd imagined in those chaotic early days. In just eleven months, nearly 65% of the world's population had interacted with the app in some way. A cultural phenomenon. A psychological experiment. A social revolution.

And now, just one month remained. Two new moons. The last, a grand finale.

He chuckled softly, knowing that what was coming next would surprise the world.

Yet even as he basked in the success, his gaze drifted toward a different corner of the screen, one tracking a certain detective. Tim had been keeping tabs. Sean Leblanc had been relentless once, a bloodhound on the scent. But lately? Distracted. Off his rhythm. Sidetracked... by love.

Tim knew that sensation all too well.

Love, damn it, was the great saboteur. It crept in like a gentle fog, blurring logic and reason until even the sharpest minds softened. No matter how disciplined or battle-hardened, no one was immune. Love made the immovable move, the unshakable tremble. It stole hours, hijacked thoughts, twisted priorities into knots. Suddenly, purpose took a backseat to a glance. A scent. A memory.

His heart tugged him backward, through years, to his teenage days in Zurich. To Trish.

She had been his first everything. His friend, his joy, his undoing.

He was sixteen when she appeared like a vision in his life. Her eyes, soft, glowing, blue, always smiling, always knowing more than she let on. She was fifteen but carried herself like someone twice her age, shaped by a life surrounded by diplomats and dignitaries at the American Embassy. Her parents treated her not like a child, but as an equal. She was worldly, witty, and unafraid to challenge him.

At first, they were just friends, inseparable, playful, curious. But that first summer apart had changed everything. Tim returned to the Canary Islands, the yearly gathering back home, where time passed slowly under the weight of missing her. They exchanged letters, pages stained with emotion, inked with longing. When he returned to Zurich, she was different, taller, more graceful, glowing with a quiet confidence. And he was smitten beyond reason.

Their love blossomed with an intensity that made others stare. They became a legend at their international school. They spoke often of the future, of changing the world together. Of doing something that mattered.

The following summer, once again, they were torn apart, this time deeper than before. They cried not wanting to be apart, but the families carried the weight of the decision. They were told they were too young to be so serious. They knew better. Another summer of letters and endless days. For both, it was torture. Then, suddenly… silence.

The letters from Trish stopped. No calls. No replies.

Confused and aching, Tim clung to hope. His parents offered gentle excuses: Maybe they went on holiday. Maybe they had returned to the United States. But then the truth came like a thunderclap.

A boating accident. Gone. All of them. Trish, her mother, her father.

Tim shattered. The world lost color. He barely scraped through his final year of school, sleepwalking through exams and friendships. But somewhere deep inside, a spark remained, one lit by her belief in him.

He clung to the dream they had shared, to make a difference, to touch lives, to turn the impossible into a reality. And in a way, he had. He had created 2T Technology, putting their initials side by side. Blank Checks was madness, yes, but it was also beautiful. It gave people something few ever truly received: a chance.

Trish would have loved it. She would have cheered every unlikely winner and laughed at the chaos. He carried her with him in every decision. Every risk.

Blank Checks was coming to an end, but not for long. Tim had a plan, but first, he would take some time away, a visit home to the Canary Islands, his ritual journey, his annual pilgrimage to the place where he could still breathe freely. Where he could still imagine her voice in the wind.

The islands waited for him, as they always did, bathed in golden sun, crowned with whispering pine forests, scarred with haunting volcanoes. Lunar landscapes stretched under vast skies, hiding secret coves and Sahara like dunes. It was a place made for dreams, and memories.

And for a man like Tim, he was haunted by both.

End of November 2024
Max

Just two weeks earlier, Max had received an invitation that felt almost too surreal to be true, an opportunity to share his journey on one of the most prestigious stages in the world: **TED Talks**, a platform where ideas worth spreading in **T**echnology, **E**ntertainment, and **De**sign are shared. It was the kind of platform he'd only ever watched in awe, never imagining, not even in his boldest daydreams, that he would stand there as a motivational speaker, and certainly not at fifty-two.

At fourteen, Max had blended in like any other teenager, laughing too loud, chasing soccer balls, fumbling through adolescence. But something began to shift. He started tripping over nothing, fumbling with buttons, and falling behind his friends on the field. The changes were subtle at first, then unignorable. After a battery of tests and waiting rooms filled with dread, came the diagnosis: Charcot-Marie-Tooth disease. A rare genetic disorder that slowly erodes the nerves meant to carry life to the limbs.

From that moment on, Max's world became a quiet battlefield. He wrestled not just with the betrayal of his own body, but with the heavy weight of self-doubt. The leg braces, meant to steady him, felt more like shackles. He avoided gym class, avoided mirrors, avoided the parts of life that reminded him of what he could no longer do.

But Max wasn't one to stay defeated for long. By the time he was twenty, he had started documenting his journey, not just the medical parts, but the human ones. The heartbreaks, the stares from strangers, the nights spent wondering if anyone would ever truly understand what it meant to live in a body that refused to cooperate. He wrote everything down in notebooks, the dream that one day he would publish a book of his journey. What began as a personal outlet in a few magazine articles, soon turned into a beacon for others living with invisible battles.

Now, standing backstage at the TED conference in Astana, Kazakhstan, he could feel the same tightness in his chest he felt the day he took his first step with leg braces, part fear, part anticipation. The deep red curtains ahead of him were almost glowing under the stage lights. Behind them sat an audience of hundreds, and beyond that, potentially millions online. He glanced at the monitor one last time. His opening slide was queued: a childhood photo of him, mid-laugh, mid-run, back when his legs still obeyed him.

The host's voice echoed in the wings: "Please welcome Max Baker, a man whose journey will challenge everything you think you know about resilience."

The applause began as a polite murmur and quickly grew. Max stepped forward into the lights that shone brighter than the sun. As he made his way across the stage, a quiet settled over the crowd. They weren't looking at his braces or his limp. They were watching a man who had lived a hundred lives in one body and still found a way to stand tall.

"I was fourteen when my body started failing me," he began, voice steady. "But I wasn't prepared for how much louder the silence would be, the silence from friends who didn't know what to say, from teachers who expected less, and from a world that didn't have a place for someone like me."

He paused. The room was breathless.

"And yet, I'm here. Not because I beat the disease, but because I stopped trying to be someone else. I learned to walk again, yes, but more importantly, I learned to be still. To listen. To speak, even when my voice shook."

His story unfolded like a slow, powerful river, stories of falling, of being carried, of rediscovering strength in unexpected places. There was the physical therapist who taught him how to dance in the pool, the ex-girlfriend who once told him he was "too broken to love," and the audience of teenagers who wept as he told them it's okay to feel angry, lost, or afraid.

By the end of his talk, people were on their feet. Not in sympathy, but in recognition. They saw their own struggles reflected at them through Max's words. And Max, who once hated mirrors, now stood reflected in every teary eye in that auditorium.

Backstage, as the applause lingered like a heartbeat, someone handed him a bottle of water and said, "You changed people tonight."

Max smiled, tired, and a little overwhelmed, whispered, "I finally told the truth."

At the celebration party, Max and his wife Stella sat at the honorary table, surrounded by other members and their guests. Following their dinner, the lights dimmed, and the room stilled. On stage, a glow of purple and blue hues took over as white fog rolled out over the floor. A piano and its player silently and magically crossed the stage, as a hauntingly beautiful melody rolled out over the crowd. An invisible voice from another world, so perfect and angelic, began to sing. Those in the audience that recognized the voice, began to gently applaud as the man himself, simply dressed in black, no spotlight, no glitter, stepped forward. His voice weaved through the melody like a golden thread. Beginning low and warm, his baritone voice rose, not just in pitch, but in presence as he glanced at the pianist. A high note shimmered in the air, crystalline and piercing, and people forgot to breathe. Dimash, the musical legend of Kazakhstan, had women clutching their chests, men blinking away the tears, unashamed.

His voice moved like the wind through the seasons, soulful and sonorous one moment, then leaping effortlessly into ethereal heights. It wasn't just range, it was color, precision, a kind of sorcery. The piano followed him like a loyal shadow, but everyone knew this was a voice that didn't need accompaniment.

When he finished, there was a moment of silence more profound than applause. Then, the room erupted, not just in claps, but in gasps and laughter and the kind of awe that only comes when someone reminds you what it means to feel deeply and truly alive.

Dimash, in his ever-striking blend of elegance, humility and quiet confidence, tilted his head back as he outstretched his arms. Slowly, he bowed as his hands overlapped his heart.

A standing ovation. His presence alone drew people in. Max and Stella did not move. They had never experienced such a voice that pierced their very souls. They stood, clapping and admiring the man, the artist that stood before them.

Dimash let the applause die down before lifting his microphone. He spoke with a gentleness wrapped in soft charm. "Thank you, my Dears. I do hope you enjoyed the song I just sang called *The Love of Tired Swans*. It is a story of loyalty and love, without which life has no meaning." The audience erupted into applause once again.

"My next song I would like to dedicate to someone I admire very much. Mr. Max Baker," reaching out his hand to the table below him. Max tilted his head to one side looking confused. "Yes, you Mr. Baker. I understand your pain all too well, but your conviction to continue is such an inspiration to us all. My grandmother took me to my music lessons every day when I was young, *despite* the pain in *her* legs. She never complained. Rather, she encouraged and supported me. It took me many years to understand what she truly sacrificed for me. So tonight, I not only honor her, but I want to dedicate this next song to you Mr. Baker. *The Show Must Go On.* Please, will you join me on stage?"

Max stepped onto the stage with measured steps, his heart pounding louder than the applause that erupted around him. The audience rose in unison, drawn to their feet by the magnetic pull of the man who had moved them to tears just hours earlier.

Dimash, in his towering presence, met Max's eyes, and in that moment, they were equals, soul to soul. A gentle smile curled on Dimash's lips as he embraced Max, not as a stranger, but as a kindred spirit.

With a graceful gesture, he guided Max to the red stool at center stage. The spotlight softened, the air thick with anticipation, and then, the music began.

Max felt like he was being swept into an emotional tidal wave wrapped in velvet thunder. Dimash's voice, was dynamic and crystal-clear, making Max's skin prickle, his chest tighten. Reaching the climatic notes was like hearing lightning, soaring, powerful, emotional. It wasn't a sound Max could *hear,* he *felt* it, in his throat, gut and spine.

Max was left breathless on stage, a little wrecked and weirdly uplifted, wondering how one voice could hold so much soul. His legs trembled as he returned to his seat beside Stella who was noticeably moved by the kind gesture of dedication.

For the next hour, Dimash held the audience spellbound, his voice a force of nature that refused to be tamed. And then, as he finally stepped off the stage, the atmosphere shifted. The grand piano gave way to a lively band, and in an instant, the room was pulsing with an infectious, toe-tapping beat that begged for movement.

Max shifted in his seat, discomfort creeping into his bones, he'd been still for too long. But it wasn't just the ache that stirred him. It was the rhythm, bold, bright, and utterly impossible to ignore. It snuck into his bloodstream, electrifying his limbs. Before he even knew what he was doing, Max rose from his chair, his fingers instinctively reaching for his wife's hand. Together, they stepped into the music, carried by a rhythm too joyous to resist.

At first, just a sway. Then a step. Then more.

Some began to laugh, as the couple, alone on the dance floor looked less like a couple and more like a girl dancing with her favorite tree. The striking contrast in their heights turned heads as it always did. And tonight, under the golden lights, they danced in their own strange rhythm, the center of attention whether they meant to be or not.

The braces on his legs seemed to catch the rhythm, metal catching light, his body flowing with a grace born not of perfection, but of pure feeling. Those watching tapped the table with their fingers. Whispers turned to cheers.

The band noticed, too. The tempo rose, and Max met it. He danced like a man possessed by joy, arms like wings, feet pounding in time with centuries, old songs. No hesitation. No apologies.

When the music finally stopped, silence hung thick before the explosion of applause. Someone shouted in Kazakh, then in English: "The best dancer we've ever seen!"

Max and Stella laughed aloud.

People were clapping, whistling, stomping their feet. A group on the side of the room, still recording, their eyes wide, jumped up to join the couple. "It's him! The guy from the videos! He really does exist. The best dancer ever."

The crowd's energy shifted, not away from awe, but into something new. Recognition.

A woman gasped. "It's true. It's really him."

Max rubbed the back of his neck, a little sheepish now that everyone was staring at him. Stella looked up at Max who towered over her. "You're officially famous, like it or not."

The crowd began to move closer, not aggressively, but with curiosity and excitement. Some wanted pictures. Others just wanted to say thank you, to tell him how his videos had made them smile, made them dance, made them feel something.

Max looked around, at their faces, at Stella, at the wild, small Kazakh town they'd never planned to visit.

He raised his arms sheepishly and gave a small bow. "Guess the internet really is forever," he said.

And the cheers came all over again.

The band continued, every person dancing throughout the room. Max had ignited a fire from within every soul. It was joy and laughter that continued for hours.

Late into the evening, they decided to leave the celebration earlier than expected. They still had three weeks to go on *The Stans* tour, and they needed to take it easy. To ease the pain in Max's legs and feet, they lingered for a while in the hotel's indoor, serene and luxurious swimming pool, sipping pomegranate tea, occasionally dipping into the steam sauna. The quiet and calm eased itself into their muscles.

Back in their room, Max still couldn't quite believe his life. Just a few years ago, he had barely left the Midlands of England, and now here he was, speaking alongside innovators and visionaries in a part of the world he'd never imagined visiting.

His rise was the kind you only hear about in podcasts and documentaries: quiet, steady, and suddenly explosive. Max Baker's fan base had grown like wildfire, sparked by a single, raw video about resilience and identity. What followed was a cascade of shared stories, emotional truths, and a community that grew louder and stronger with every upload.

The invitation to join the TED Talks in Central Asia had arrived like a shooting star, unexpected and thrilling. For four weeks, they would trace the Silk Road, retelling his story.

December 1, 2024
Max & Stella

Their week in Kazakhstan was ending, and already it felt like a dream slipping through their fingers. It had all begun in the beating heart of the country, Almaty, a city alive with color, history, and hidden magic. For three unforgettable days, they wandered through its treasures: the surreal, turquoise shimmer of Big Almaty Lake, a gem cradled high in the mountains, and the whimsical Zenkov Cathedral, rising like a candy-striped fairytale against the sky.

They thought back to the drive they had taken, the road framed by towering pines that whispered secrets to the wind. Then, just as the mountains opened their arms, the view unfurled before them, so staggering, so achingly beautiful, it seemed torn from the pages of a myth.

"It looks unreal," Max breathed, his voice barely a whisper as his fingers found Stella's and held on tight, as if to anchor himself to the wonder before them.

Wrapped in thick coats and wool scarves, they stood in silence for a moment, gazing at the lake. It was frozen in hues of turquoise and pearl, nestled like a secret jewel among snow-dusted peaks.

They walked slowly, their boots crunching over the snow. The path wound around the edge of the lake, beneath the heavy branches of pine trees that wore thick coats of frost. Every step felt like they were falling deeper into a fairy tale.

Max stopped suddenly and pulled her close. "You know," he said, "I read that the lake changes color depending on the season. But I think winter is its truest self."

Stella smiled, her cheeks pink from the cold. "Kind of like us. We've changed so much this year. But right now... this feels like the realest part."

Despite the cold, they sat on a log dusted with snow, sharing a thermos of hot tea. The mountains towered around them, vast and silent, like ancient guardians. No phone signal. No city noise. Just the soft sigh of wind and the distant caw of a crow.

For Max, it was the Zenkov Cathedral that quickened his heart. It stood like a confection from a dream, a gingerbread house painted in candy cane stripes of lemon yellow, teal, and raspberry red, its onion domes frosted with snow. Fairy lights twinkled on the fence surrounding it as the sound of children laughing, chasing each other through the park, echoed in the distance.

"It's even more magical than I thought it would be," Stella said, eyes wide.

They stepped closer, pausing to admire the delicate wooden detailing of the facade. The cathedral looked less like a place of worship and more like a place where sugarplum fairies might hold midnight mass. Stella tilted her head, enchanted by how the stained-glass windows glimmered like jewels in the afternoon sun.

"Do you think it's warm inside?" she asked.

"Only one way to find out."

Inside, the stillness wrapped around them like a velvet blanket. The scent of incense drifted through the nave, mingling with the faintest smell of pine. Candles flickered beneath icons, their golden halos catching the light. Max slipped a coin into the offering box and lit a taper, whispering a wish.

As they sat in the back pew, Stella rested her head against his arm. "I'll never forget this," she said softly.

Outside, the sky turned violet, and the first stars appeared. The cathedral, aglow in the twilight, looked like something out of a snow globe, fragile, festive, and full of wonder.

And in the stillness of a Kazakh December, surrounded by candy-colored dreams, love felt as timeless as the snow that continued to fall.

They had slept soundly, the joy of the celebration party still lingering like a warm echo in their dreams. Now, with the golden light of morning spilling across Astana's skyline on the first day of the month, they faced their final full day in the city, a bittersweet pause before the rhythm of the road called them onward once more.

The snow had continued to fall, but they knew this was a once in a lifetime trip. It was now or never. For a relaxing last day, they decided to visit the Ascension Cathedral, a remarkable Russian Orthodox church. Max was intrigued by the mere fact that this, the tallest wooden structure in the world, had been completed without the use of nails, relying instead on iron bolts and innovative joinery techniques.

Standing beneath the kaleidoscope spires of the Cathedral, the scent of incense still lingered in the air. He had successfully completed the first part of his tour, people engaged in his story, delighted by his dance moves which he found so comical.

The day, however, hadn't unfolded quite as smoothly for Max. His braces, those stubborn, necessary contraptions, had begun to protest after a week of whirlwind adventure. The strain wasn't new. It had been building over three long years, the result of tireless days teaching math on his feet and countless afternoons chasing a little white ball across manicured greens, indulging in his lifelong love of golf.

Though the braces were rated for five years, Max had always known better. With the sheer amount of wear and tear he put them through, three years felt optimistic. If only they weren't so outrageously expensive and frustratingly hard to get, custom-molded to his feet, crafted to the millimeter, and costing more than a month's salary. If it were up to him, he'd have ordered a new pair every year, just for peace of mind. But life, and budget, rarely offered such luxuries.

He could feel it now, an ache that threaded through his knees and up his back, quietly reminding him of his age and of the years spent pretending he still had the stamina of a man half his age. The cold weather wasn't helping either. It crept into his bones with a familiarity that unsettled him, making the warmth of rest not just a desire but a necessity.

Before retiring to their room for a quiet evening and a soothing dip in the pool, Max and Stella paused to place a call home. They knew their children would be gathered, waiting, excited to hear the next chapter in this unlikely adventure their parents had embarked on.

For nearly an hour, laughter and stories flew back and forth across the Zoom call. Their boys back home spoke animatedly of their plans to go ice fishing at dawn. Meanwhile, their daughter was positively glowing, nerves and excitement twining together as she prepared for her very first marathon the next morning.

There was warmth in the digital reunion, even from thousands of miles away. And just before they ended the call, Max's eyes sparkled with that familiar sense of wonder as he shared their next destination: Turkmenistan.

Goodbyes were said with lingering smiles and promises to send photos. Then the screen went dark, the room silent once again, and Max let out a long, quiet sigh. The day had been long. The road ahead was still longer. But for now, there was rest, and that pool was calling his name once again.

In the warm blue glow of the room, the pool shimmered like glass. Stella slipped through the water with graceful determination, each stroke a quiet meditation. Max, meanwhile, floated on his back, lazily treading water before meandering to the hot tub, where the bubbles hummed around him in soothing warmth. Everything felt still, peaceful.

As they returned to their hotel room, the tranquility shattered. Their phones, tossed casually onto the nightstand, were lit up like emergency beacons, call after call, dozens of missed notifications. It was their daughter, Yvonne. Her name repeated across both screens in a digital chorus of urgency.

Max picked up his phone. Stella was already dialing. The worry was instant, sharp.

Yvonne answered on the first ring, breathless, trembling on the edge of disbelief. "Mom. Dad. You won't believe it. I... I've been chosen."

Stella's heart skipped. "Chosen for what?"

There was a pause thick with emotion on the other end. Then, Yvonne exhaled shakily. "The Blank Checks... They picked me. I'm filling it out in a few hours. I need to know... how much should I write? Zane and the kids are saying more than twenty million, but it just feels surreal. What do you think?"

Max and Stella stared at each other, stunned into silence. For a few seconds, the room was only the sound of Max pulling a pad from the drawer and scribbling down numbers. His mind, always methodical, raced to process.

"Okay, let's think," he murmured, eyes scanning his notes. "So far, they've handed out $319 million. Only one check bounced, and that was for $100 million early in the year. So... the odds are in your favor."

He paused and looked at Stella. "But the real question is, what do you want in life that you don't already have?"

Yvonne laughed through what might have been tears. "We made a list. Me, Zane, the kids. But we want to expand it, we want to share this. With you. With our siblings."

Max didn't skip a beat. "Alright then. Let's make our own list."

His pen danced across the page. "A new set of braces every few years," he quipped with a grin. Stella rolled her eyes fondly and added a few extravagant touches, why not dream big? A lake house with their own boat and dock. Trips in first class so that Max could have his leg room. A room just for her sewing.

When they tallied it up, the total came to two million. Modest in the grand scheme, but more than enough to make dreams come alive.

"Alright," Yvonne said softly. "I've got it. I'll call you after it happens. Might be late though, in Kazakhstan it'll be close to ten your time."

Stella didn't hesitate. "Call. No matter what time it is."

Max nodded. "We'll be awake. We're not missing this."

As the call ended, the room seemed to buzz with a new kind of energy, nervous, joyful, surreal. Something extraordinary was unfolding, and their world, so calm just an hour ago, was about to really get exciting.

Each minute and hour stretched on endlessly, and with three grueling weeks still left on the tour, Max and Stella could think of nothing more tempting than catching the first flight home. But Max was a man of principle, a man who kept his promises, no matter how weary his bones or heavy his heart.

He would see this tour through to the end. Every speech, every meeting, every broken soul he could lift with his words, it all mattered. He was there for a purpose: to spark hope where hope had dimmed, to remind the hopeless that the sunrise always follows the darkest night. They just had to take that next, trembling step.

Still, hope was a fragile thing, and Max guarded his own carefully. The Blank Checks game was nearing its end. One of the last golden tickets, and there was no guarantee how much the online game would give.

The wait for that call was agonizing. Ten o'clock crept by... then ten-thirty... still silence.

Stella, exhausted from the relentless pace, had already drifted off to sleep, her breathing slow and steady. Max, though, sat upright, eyes heavy, forcing himself to stay alert, his heart pounding with a quiet desperation.

Then, out of nowhere, the phone rang. The sharp trill shattered the stillness, jolting both Max and Stella awake.

"Mom, Dad," came the voice, electric with emotion. "Are you ready for this? Not only are you getting everything on your wish list, but more. So much more. I was going to put down $25 million, but then... something came over me. I went all in. $50 million. And it cleared."

There was a stunned silence.

"We're still speechless," Yvonne continued, almost laughing through disbelief. "It's the wildest thing I've ever done. I don't even know if I'll sleep before the marathon tomorrow. It's more than a dream, it's surreal."

Max and Stella could barely breathe. Tears welled up, spilling over as they clutched each other in the quiet, trembling joy of a miracle come true. This wasn't just a windfall. It was a turning point. A moment that would mark them forever.

It was everything they had dared not hope for, and more.

December 2024

Claire & Dee

From afar, Dee had watched it all unfold, the way Claire slipped helplessly into love's intoxicating snare, wide-eyed and heartsick. And yet, there was no bitterness in Dee's solitude. She carried on with their shared dream, coordinating with the landscaper to carve a path through the canyon, a quiet, winding trail that stitched their homes together not by road, but by something more intimate. On paper, miles separated them. By foot, a five-minute trail-walk over a stretch of soft earth.

Claire never even noticed when the path was done. Its entrance, nestled like a secret near the spring-fed pool, had blended into the wild landscape. That's where Dee first saw them, Claire and Sean, entwined in a world of their own, laughter echoing through the brush and trees.

And still, Dee rejoiced. She soaked in Claire's excitement, her decision to chase the tender unknown, to give love room to breathe, even all the way in the Bahamas. Before she left, they sat side by side, mapping out the road ahead. Not just for Claire and Sean, but for themselves too, for the project, for their friendship, for whatever the future might bring.

Dee would begin by adding her services as a Wellness therapist. Her sessions would take place in the room Claire called the Gifted Space. It was located at the back side of Sanare, a cave room tucked into the base of the rugged hillside. It had been used by Claire's father, transformed by his hand to form a sanctuary where nature and luxury converged. The stone walls curve inward, forming a protective, womb-like embrace, their surfaces cool to the touch and smoothed by time. Overhead, a natural skylight pierced the rocky ceiling, a wide opening created by the erosion of softer stone, allowing golden shafts of sunlight to occasionally pour into the space. Throughout the day the light shifted gently with the movement of the sun, casting delicate patterns across the uneven surfaces and creating a slow, calming dance of shadow and warmth.

The minimalist room honored the raw beauty of the stone. A few hand-woven mats and low wooden loungers were arranged around a shallow, stone geothermal pool at the center, its waters steaming lightly, infused with calming botanicals. The scent of eucalyptus and lavender lingered in the air. The natural acoustics of the cave softened every sound: a distant drip of water, the quiet inhale and exhale of breath, the gentle hum of tranquility.

Small niches adorned the cave wall, holding flickering candles, shedding a soft light to lush ferns and mosses growing in the damp, shaded corners, lending a soft green life to the earthen tones. It was timeless inside, as though the outside world had paused.

Over the years, Claire had noticed how guests emerged transformed, restored not only by the treatments they received, but by the ancient serenity of the cave itself.

Dee was delighted that this would be her new sanctuary, that Claire had believed in her to participate in the Sanare experience.

Before Claire's departure, they had decided on a much-needed getaway, one more extravagant than their recent Bermuda trip. They toyed around with a few ideas when Dee shocked Claire by suggesting, so far out in left field it made Claire wonder what all Dee had hidden in that busy, overactive mind of hers.

Dee had suggested a trip to Switzerland, to Lucerne, specifically. She could not say why, but it was calling her to visit. The picturesque photos of the deep blue irregular shaped lake, surrounded by majestic snowcapped mountains felt familiar, even though she had never been to Europe. A phenomenon known as déjà vu was happening from a distance, through photos online and through magazines.

Her next suggestion was the Canary Islands. Another surprise to Claire. Where was Dee getting all these crazy locations from in her head? But she went along with it. After all, Dee was coming into her own, finally making decisions and being the leader Claire always saw in her.

Their plan was done. They would leave in February giving Claire plenty of time to return home for a month before jetting off across the globe one more time.

Mid December 2024
Sean and Claire

Three weeks together in total was all Sean and Claire needed to know their union was one that could not be broken.

They both admired the other for their lifestyle and the calmness they had sought out in life. For Claire it came much easier than for Sean, however Sean was ever the student of life. He wanted to learn more, about life, about the mysteries behind Claire and what she was able to do for others. He was more alert and ever so cautious with what he was about to get himself into. It was a conversation that he was not sure Claire would want to engage in. But he had to know. He was biding his time to ask Claire about the secret behind Sanare and share with what he had uncovered in 2018.

To gain her trust, Sean delved into all the details he had uncovered on the Blank Checks Evidence Board. He covered month after month, the phone calls, the evidence in the videos posted online and the massive amounts of personal stories that had started to appear, of those mildly associated with the winners. Everyone seemed to want to be attached, even at a distance, with a winner. A mere "We saw them eating pizza across the street from us" gave way to countless encounters.

Claire had not heard much about the social media game; she had not even entered for a chance. To her, life was a bit simpler and easier, where money was not the name of the game. Sean, ever so intrigued, of course wanted to know more, but he knew the time was not right.

After a private day out on pig beach, they sipped a delicious mint lemon drink with some pomegranate juice that Sean had concocted himself. Under the stars, with the sound of the waves below them, Claire shared the story of how her father had bought the land in the foothills of Black Mountain in the early 60's. As a child of the 70's, Claire could only remember living in the mountains, far away from the city. She recalled her feet kicking up little clouds of red dust as she tore through the land and into the canyon.

The air would buzz with the sound of cicadas, and the saguaros stood tall like ancient watchmen, guarding the wild-hearted child with sun bleached braids and scraped knees.

Her family's land stretched far and wide, dotted with mesquite trees and granite outcroppings that shimmered in the heat. To Claire, it was a kingdom. Her kingdom. One that smelled of freedom.

The caves, her favorite places, shallow hollows tucked into the base of the mountain. Her grandfather said the caves were sacred, once used by the native Indians, but to Claire, they were secret hideouts, or magical portals depending on the day.

"Don't go past the third cave," her mama warned every time, wiping her hands on a flour-dusted apron. But Claire always did. Not out of disobedience, exactly, just curiosity too big for the rules.

Inside the cool shadows, she'd trace her fingers over the cave walls, finding ancient petroglyphs and imagining stories for each figure. One, a spiral, she decided was a map, a secret trail to treasure buried beneath the mesquite roots.

As the sun dipped behind the mountain, casting long purple shadows, Claire would lie on the warm rock outside the cave mouth, arms behind her head, watching the sky turn from flame to indigo. Coyotes would start to yip in the distance, and she knew Mama would be on the porch, calling her name.

But for a little while longer, Claire stayed still, the desert all around her, alive and ancient and hers. A wild desert child with a flashlight and a head full of stories, dreaming up her own legends in the arms of Black Mountain.

The foothills still belonged to her. Even as new homes had crept in with the new millennium, sprawling neighborhoods blooming like wildflowers after rain, Claire's claim on the land felt unshaken. Nestled deep within the canyon, their home remained a quiet haven, shielded from the noise of progress. Here, solitude wasn't a luxury; it was her way of breathing.

After her parents passed, Claire breathed life into a dream she had carried quietly for years, a sanctuary in the hills. A place where nature wrapped its arms around the weary. Where time slowed, and people remembered who they were before the world told them otherwise. Sanare, she called it. A spa, yes, but also something more sacred. A return. A becoming. It was a quiet haven where the world faded, and calm took root. Visitors never quite understood it. To them, it was all a riddle wrapped in sage-scented incense. But Claire had always smiled gently and said, "One day, you will understand. It all takes time."

Then came Dee.

A soul who had once been tethered, by duty, by circumstance, by love. But life had shifted. After her husband's passing, Dee began to unfurl, petal by petal, finding joy in her grandchildren's laughter and light in the places she'd never thought to look. She was blooming, at last.

And now, she worked with Claire. At Sanare.

This was the moment Sean had been waiting for. "So… Dee's with you at Sanare? Has she been there long?"

Claire nodded, the hint of a smile curving her lips. "Just a month. She's finding her rhythm." Then, as if reading his thoughts, her eyes locked on his. "Sean, whatever's on your mind, ask. You've been holding onto it far too long."

He blinked. How did she always know?

"Go on," she said again, her voice warm, her fingers wrapped around a glass beaded with condensation. Mint, lemon, something cool and alive.

He exhaled. "Back in 2018, I was assigned a case... unusual. Nearly classified. I spent six months on it, chasing shadows, hitting nothing but dead ends."

Claire laughed, light and incredulous. "What does a top-secret case have to do with me?"

"That's exactly what I was hoping you could tell me."

Her eyes sparkled with curiosity. "Tell me more. Let's see how deep this rabbit hole goes. Because I had no idea I was being investigated."

Sean hesitated. He was trained to be cautious, but this, this was personal. If she truly didn't know, then perhaps he had wandered down the wrong path altogether. But he was sure of his findings. "Maybe... maybe it was a different Sanare. Another spa. Somewhere in Italy, perhaps. I was pulled from the case before I could dig any deeper. They needed me elsewhere, bigger cases, higher stakes."

The air hung heavy with silence until the sky offered an escape: a shooting star, streaking silver across the darkening canvas above.

"Isn't that something?" Sean said softly. "Did you make a wish?"

"I did," Claire murmured, her gaze locked with his. And in that glance, there was something unspoken, ancient, tender, full of questions and answers neither of them was quite ready to name.

Claire's visit wasn't just a fresh beginning; it *was* the beginning. It was the future they were daring to imagine, hand in hand. They had made a quiet promise to spend more time together, to lean into this unexpected rhythm they had found. Sean, ever the skeptic, wasn't entirely convinced about settling in the Bahamas, but neither of them wanted to rush into anything. They knew better than to gamble with something that felt this rare.

Having lived a little in each other's worlds, the next step was clear: see who they were when the backdrop changed. No more cozy familiarity. No more easy escapes.

One phone call later, the plan was in motion. Europe, in February. Sean could hardly believe it, he'd be wandering foreign streets not just with his golden-haired enchantress, eight years his senior, but with Dee as well, who had already mapped out the whole escapade. Lucerne, and the Canary Islands, names that sounded like poetry to someone who'd never been. He felt the familiar flutter of anticipation, the kind that only comes when adventure calls and the heart says yes.

The Blank Checks game was ending. The chase, the riddles, the thrilling dance, it had consumed him. Even if he hadn't cracked every code, it had been his own private mission, a puzzle he gave himself permission to abandon. Now, finally, it was time to live. To stop running after phantoms and start savoring the moments that made life shimmer.

16

December 30, 2024
Undisclosed Location

A night darker than the rest, ink-black and infinite, stretched over the world like a velvet curtain. The moon, hidden, invisible to the eye, was still very much present between the earth and sun. To astronomers, this was a celestial event. To the mystics, dreamers, and seekers, it meant something far greater. It was a moment between endings and beginnings, a quiet, sacred pause. A time to close one chapter and write the title of the next.

For Tim, it was everything.

This night was his ritual. Each new moon, he gave. Quietly. Anonymously. Unconditionally. It was his way of shifting the world, just slightly, into something better. And now, on this final new moon of the year, the ritual would take on a splendor even he hadn't anticipated.

He had allocated $500 million to give away, no strings attached. So far, $344 million had found its way into the random selection of twelve individuals. There was $156 million left. And tonight, he would part with the rest.

From the heart of his secluded estate, Tim stood before the glowing screen. With a gentle swipe of his gloved hand over the slick black table, the system responded instantly, as if it had been holding its breath.

A soft chime echoed through the room as the bottom of the screen came alive with a line of rectangular shapes, numbers spinning through each one. The sequence of numbers stopped, a name appearing above it with a photo. Then another. Two. Four. Eight. Sixteen. Names multiplying like a heartbeat speeding up. Thirty-two. Sixty-four. Ninety-eight. The screen bloomed with life.

One hundred and fifty-six names. Each representing a life about to be changed forever, receiving one million dollars. No application. No explanation. Just grace, descending like snow from the sky.

The final name locked into place with a satisfying tone. Then silence. A hush. As if the universe paused to honor the moment.

And then, chaos. Beautiful chaos.

Phones began to ring from Mexico City to Monte Carlo, from Lagos to Lisbon, from small island villages to towering cities of glass. Some buzzed, on nightstands, waking their owners from dreams. Others lit up in boardrooms, back alleys, kitchens, or classrooms.

The message was the same, personalized and warm:

"You've been chosen. You are now $1 Million richer. No catch. No repayment. Just joy. Use it well. Change your life, or someone else's."

At first, disbelief. Then tears. Screams. Silence. Knees buckled. Hands shook. Laughter spilled out uncontrollably in some corners of the world, while others sat in stunned quietude, phone still clutched in hand, heartbeat wild.

In a hospital in Manila, a nurse sank into a chair, tears spilling into her mask. In a windswept village in Hawaii, an elderly man laughed so hard he dropped his phone into the sand. In New Zealand, a teacher danced barefoot in the yard, clutching her chest with both hands.

Tim watched from his perch, eyes misty, his lips softened into a smile that was part peace, part mischief.

He didn't want thanks. He didn't want headlines. This was not charity. It was a game, his game. A rebellion against despair. A flare shot into the night to remind people that miracles didn't always come from above. Sometimes, they came from systems. From secrets. From strangers who still believed in something better.

17

February 2025
Lucerne, Switzerland

The two lovers, hand in hand, stepped into the storybook charm of Lucerne, their hearts brimming with anticipation for the unforgettable month ahead. By their side was Dee, practically glowing with excitement, this trip had been her labor of love. She had poured herself into every detail, orchestrating each day from afar with a flair she never knew she possessed. From picturesque day trips to breathtaking sights, everything had been thoughtfully woven together. And yet, Dee had one more card up her sleeve, a secret surprise nestled into their itinerary, perfectly timed for Valentine's Day in the heart of Switzerland.

The first day unfolded gently, a soft landing into the charm of Lucerne. As the afternoon wore on, they wandered through the winding alleys on a walking tour, their senses wrapped in the city's quiet magic. Church bells chimed delicately in the distance, their sound floating over cobbled streets like a lullaby. A silvery mist clung to Lake Lucerne, giving the water an ethereal shimmer. At the corner of Weinmarkt, Claire, Sean, and Dee paused, scarves snug around their necks, cheeks pink from the February chill, breath rising in pale, swirling clouds, as if the city itself had extended its arms and welcomed them in.

"Welcome to the Hidden Gems of Lucerne walking tour," said their guide, Elise, with a cheerful smile. She was young, with a spark in her eyes that hinted she had secrets to share. "You won't find these places on a postcard."

Their first stop was the *Museggmauer,* the ancient city wall. Elise led them behind it to a narrow staircase none of them would have noticed on their own. At the top, the city stretched below, a mosaic of rooftops and spires with the shimmering lake like a silver coin tossed into the landscape. They took photos and laughed, as the tour continued into the secret streets.

As they wound through alleyways painted with centuries-old murals, Elise told stories of merchants, medieval intrigue, and even a ghost or two said to linger in the rafters of old timbered houses. Along a forgotten corner by the Reuss River, they paused to watch swans glide past like they had all the time in the world.

But it was the hidden courtyard near the Jesuit Church that silenced them. "Not many come here," Elise said softly, leading them past an unmarked gate. Ivy curled over stone walls, and a single fountain whispered in the center of the stillness. "A place for reflection."

Claire touched the cold iron railing. "It feels like Lucerne is letting us in on a secret," she said.

Their final stop was a tucked-away bakery on a quiet backstreet, the kind locals guard like treasure. Over warm slices of Swiss nut filled pastries and cinnamon-scented coffee, they talked about old times, new dreams, and how this city, with all its hidden corners, had quietly stolen their hearts.

As dusk settled and the mountains turned lavender, Sean grinned. "This wasn't just a tour," he said. "It was a memory in the making."

And Lucerne, timeless and watchful, seemed to nod in agreement.

Claire and Sean thanked Dee for such a magnificent start to their trip as they retired for the night, exhausted but exhilarated from the two long days of travel and sightseeing.

The following day was a much more relaxed day as Dee had planned a scenic boat trip on Lake Lucerne.

As the boat rocked gently, pulling away from the dock, the trio stood on the bow, looking out over the snowy mountains that circled the lake like ancient guardians, their reflections shimmering in the ice blue water. The sky was a watercolor wash of soft grays and silvers, promising a calm journey.

Claire tugged her scarf tighter as the wind kissed her cheeks. Beside her, Sean leaned against the railing, camera in hand, trying to capture the way the mist curled above the lake like breath from a sleeping giant. Behind them, Dee laughed as she peeled apart a pretzel, the warmth of mulled wine in her thermos keeping the chill at bay.

"I still can't believe we're here," Dee said, her voice muffled behind her cup. "This looks like a postcard."

"It is a postcard," Claire replied, pointing to a cluster of timbered houses perched at the edge of a hillside village. "Literally, I saw that view on a rack in Lucerne yesterday."

The boat curved toward the bay. Sean lowered his camera. "Feels like time slows down out here," he murmured.

As the sun broke through the clouds, a golden beam lit up the snow-dusted forest lining the shore. The trio fell into a peaceful silence, each lost in the moment, the hush of winter, the lapping of water, the quiet beauty of friendship shared in stillness.

The boat sailed on, leaving soft ripples in the heart of Lake Lucerne.

Over dinner that evening, Dee unveiled her Valentine's surprise with a quiet smile and a touch of ceremony, a fondue feast, meticulously prepared, meant for just the two of them. A gift wrapped not in paper, but in thoughtfulness and love. They stared at her, surprised.

"What are you going to do, Dee? You can't just go off on your own," said Claire in disbelief.

Her eyes sparkled with a calm certainty. "Oh, but I can," she said softly. "In fact, that's exactly what I want. Tomorrow is for the two of you, enjoy it, cherish it. As for me, I've crafted a little adventure of my own. I'm heading somewhere that feels strangely familiar. Like a dream you half-remember or a story you've once lived. There's no need to worry. I'll be just fine."

Her words hung in the air like the lingering scent of melted chocolate, bittersweet, warm, and just a little mysterious.

Dee awoke late on Valentines Day, wrapped in the rare luxury of stillness. No buzzing alarms, no pressing obligations, just the quiet hum of a day entirely her own. The kind of day that feels like a small rebellion against the pace of the world. She stretched beneath the covers, then smiled to herself. Today, she would follow the pull of curiosity rather than a calendar.

Two places whispered to her from the pages of her research; places soaked in history and shadowed with stories. She stepped out into the crisp air, the cobbled streets of the old town welcoming her with their uneven charm. As she wandered deeper into the heart of the city, the world seemed to slow with her.

Then she saw them, the medieval wooden footbridges, weathered and majestic, stretching gently over the water like outstretched arms. Covered, intricate, and impossibly enduring, one had stood for more than four centuries, bearing silent witness to time's slow dance. Dee ran her fingers along the aged beams as she gazed up to the unique paintings, in the overhead triangular frames, marveling that something so delicate could also be so strong. It felt like standing inside a memory.

As she crossed the second bridge, lost in thought, a soft voice interrupted her reverie. A man, wrapped in a wool coat and holding a steaming cup of coffee, smiled and said, "They've seen more sunrises than we ever will." His words struck something deep in her. She turned, smiled and replied. "Yes, they have."

"Is this your first time in Lucerne?" he asked, his voice low and smooth. "I only ask because... you looked so captivated by the paintings. As if you were searching for something inside them."

"Yes," Dee replied softly, eyes still lingering on the brushstrokes of the piece behind him. "But it feels like I've been here before. Not déjà vu exactly... more like a memory brushing against the edges of a dream." She hesitated, then added, "It's hard to explain."

He didn't press her. Instead, they wandered through a conversation that bloomed slowly, like a flower coaxed into opening by the sun. They traded stories about the power of art, and how it was the soul's way of communicating with the world.

Mid-sentence, he paused, brows furrowing as if a sudden realization had struck him. "I've completely lost my manners," he said, shaking his head and letting out a soft laugh. "I'm standing here, enjoying the warmth of this cup, while you're likely freezing. Would you allow me to buy you something hot to drink? I understand if you'd rather not. I'm a stranger, after all."

There was a pause, brief, thoughtful.

"Actually…" she said, with a small smile, "a hot drink sounds perfect. Do you know somewhere nearby?"

His face lit up, not just with relief, but with something else, something gentler, quieter. "Yes, indeed. Just a short walk from here. Forgive me again, I'm not usually this scattered." He held out his gloved hand in an almost ceremonial gesture. "I'm Tim."

"Dee," she replied, slipping her hand into his. "Nice to meet you, Tim."

"Likewise," he said, then offered his arm, old-fashioned but earnest. She accepted, threading her arm through his, and together they walked beneath the golden glow of lanterns that lined the cobblestone streets, leading them deeper into the heart of Lucerne's Old Town.

The world around them shimmered in a winter hush, quiet snow beginning to fall, soft as feathers. They arrived at a tiny café tucked beneath a crooked awning, its windows glowing from the warmth inside and twinkling with fairy lights. The scent of roasted coffee, cinnamon and something buttery drifted out as the door opened with a gentle chime.

Inside, the café was a patchwork of mismatched chairs and old wooden tables, each one telling its own story. A fireplace crackled in the corner, and a sleepy cat curled on a cushion near the hearth. Tim guided her to a table near the window, where they could still watch the snowfall, as if the city was tucking itself in for the night.

Over mugs of velvety hot chocolate, thick, indulgent, crowned with swirls of cream that slowly melted into the warmth, they leaned into a conversation that didn't rely on time but on trust. The kind of intimacy born not from years, but from a rare and quiet willingness to be seen.

Time slipped by unnoticed, the hours dissolving like sugar in their drinks. Words flowed freely, yet their truths remained partially tucked away. There was caution in their candor, as if both sensed the fragile nature of this encounter, something precious that might evaporate with the morning light.

Dee, with laughter in her voice, recounted the joy she found in crafting the journey, her eyes lit by the memory. And Tim, he listened. Not just heard but listened, with the reverence of someone who knew the value of presence. He was drawn in, not just to her stories, but to her essence: her grace, her ease, her quiet confidence.

For years, every woman he met had been a shadow of someone else. None could measure up to his Trish. But Dee... Dee wasn't a comparison. She stood wholly on her own. And that realization struck him like a soft bell in the distance, could it be, at 56, he was falling in love again?

Outside, snow blanketed the city in silence, softening every edge. Inside the café, something tender had begun to stir, uncertain and delicate. A flicker of something that felt dangerously close to hope.

As the café emptied and hunger began to nudge, Tim turned to Dee with a smile and asked if she'd join him for dinner. She nodded, and soon his chauffeur whisked them away, gliding through the snow-dusted streets to the quiet elegance of Lucerne's north side.

The moment they arrived, Dee burst into laughter, free and bright, like a bell chime. Tim raised a curious brow. Between soft giggles, she explained: she had gifted her friends a Fondue Valentine meal, and here they were, stepping right into that very spot. Fate, it seemed, had a playful sense of humor. Dee exhaled a breath she didn't realize she was holding, a wave of relief washing over her as they were led to a quiet table, no Sean, no Claire, just blessed absence and the sweet promise of solitude.

But what struck Tim most wasn't the coincidence, it was her. The way she remained unchanged, unmoved by the chauffeur, by the upscale restaurant, by any of it. She was grounded, gracious, unfazed. A steady presence, like the gentle stillness Trish once brought to his world.

Careful not to seem too eager after the delightful meal they had shared, Tim casually offered a private guided tour to Mt. Pilatus the next day, ending with dinner at the legendary Restaurant Pilatus-Kulm. Dee's eyes lit up, her laughter bubbling again. "You won't believe this," she said. "That's exactly what I had planned."

Something fell into place with that moment, a small, exquisite alignment of hearts and intentions.

As the night wound down, Tim walked her to the grand entrance of her hotel. He took her hand briefly, warm against the cold, and wished her a good night, promising to return by eleven to collect Dee and her friends for their mountain adventure.

When they parted, something lingered. For Dee, it wasn't just the crisp night air or the fading warmth of cocoa that clung to her, it was something quieter, deeper. She had come to Lucerne in search of history. But that evening, she left with something entirely different: a moment of unexpected connection, gentle and rare. A moment that, like the ancient bridges of the city, might just stand the test of time.

As twilight fell over Lucerne, the city's cobbled streets shimmered beneath soft lantern light, their golden glow reflected in the tranquil waters of Lake Lucerne. Snowflakes drifted lazily from the heavens, blanketing the rooftops and softening the world into a picture-perfect hush.

Claire had never imagined that Valentine's Day could feel like this, not grand or over-the-top, but warm and deeply intimate. Sean led her gently through the winding streets, their breath curling in the crisp winter air. Just ahead, nestled between the two historic wooden bridges, a cozy yet upscale chalet-style restaurant beckoned with flickering candles and the inviting aroma of melted cheese.

Inside, the air was filled with laughter, the gentle clinking of glasses, and the rich scent of Gruyère and Emmental bubbling over a flickering flame. They settled into a corner table by the window, where fairy lights danced along the edges of the pane and offered a view of the lake, glistening under moonlight.

A waiter brought their fondue pot, its golden surface smooth and steaming. Claire smiled as Sean swirled the bread into the cheese, then held it out for her with that familiar twinkle in his eyes. They laughed, shared stories, and toasted to old dreams and new beginnings with glasses of crisp Swiss white wine.

The world outside melted away. There was only the warmth between them, the quiet joy of being known and cherished, and the sense that in this moment, this small, beautiful sliver of time, everything was exactly as it should be.

And as the night deepened, the snow fell heavier, their fingers intertwined across the table, and love, simple, sweet, and slow, found a home in the heart of Lucerne.

The next morning, over steaming mugs of coffee and warm, cinnamon-kissed pastries, Claire and Sean practically shimmered with excitement as they recounted their enchanted Valentine's Day.

Claire's eyes sparkled as she described the restaurant's old, timbered ceiling arching like a cathedral above them, their cozy table perched beside the window, where the silhouette of wooden bridges danced across the glistening water. It felt like something out of a dream, timeless, serene, and stitched together with love.

Sean chimed in, his voice animated with delight as he painted a vivid picture of the fondue pot before them, a bubbling cauldron of cheeses, mingling with white wine and just a kiss of garlic. The heavy ceramic dish cradled the molten gold like a sacred treasure. He grinned, recalling how they dunked hunks of crusty bread into the cheese, their laughter ringing out when Claire lost a piece to the cheesy depths, declaring it a worthy sacrifice. Between bites, they nibbled on paper-thin slices of Grisons air-dried beef, the tang of pickled onions dancing on their tongues, a perfect counterpoint to the richness.

Then came dessert, chocolate fondue that shimmered like silk, with pears, strawberries, and little cubes of sponge cake. As Sean leaned in to gently wipe a smear of chocolate from Claire's lip, time seemed to slow. The city murmured around them like a lullaby, but within their little cocoon, there was only warmth, sweetness, and the gentle rhythm of the river beneath them.

Dee listened, her smile soft and wide. She didn't want to interrupt the spell they were under; it reminded her of something precious, something she'd almost forgotten.

When their dreamy tale finally tapered off, she cleared her throat and said gently, "You'll want to be ready by eleven. There's a special day ahead, Mt. Pilatus, followed by dinner."

Claire, crunching contentedly on a cinnamon cookie and finishing her last bite of potato pancake, looked up with curiosity. "So, what did you get up to all day by yourself?"

Dee hesitated, a slow smile spreading across her face as she traced the rim of her coffee cup. "Well…"

Claire leaned forward, eyes narrowing with mock suspicion. "I know that look. What wonderful surprise do you have for us now, dear Dee?"

Blushing just a little, Dee glanced down. "I met someone yesterday… under one of the covered bridges. We spent the afternoon together talking, sipping hot chocolate, sharing dinner."

Claire gasped. "Wait. You found someone you could talk to for hours? That's unheard of!" Sean laughed, watching the women dissolve into giggles like teenagers whispering secrets.

"What's he like? Can we meet him?"

Dee's eyes twinkled. "He's easygoing, charming, and well… fun to be around. And yes, you will meet him. He's the one taking us up to Mt. Pilatus. You can decide for yourselves what you think of him."

Sean raised his eyebrows, amused. "Well, this day just got very interesting."

And with that, the morning air seemed to shimmer with the promise of new adventures, blooming connections, and the quiet magic that only travel, and a touch of serendipity, can bring.

≈

Tim knew the feeling, the flutter of anticipation, the tug of something deeper, but with decades of life lived and lessons carved into his bones, he wasn't about to be led blindly by his emotions. He'd seen what happened when he followed a feeling too fast, too far.

No. Not this time.

He grounded himself in the present, a mantra looping quietly in his mind: *you barely know her, she doesn't even live nearby, let it be.* He held back the impulse to dive into a digital rabbit hole of clues, photos, and maybes. There would be no searching, no scrolling. He would let life happen, raw and unfiltered, like it used to, when the world wasn't compressed into screens and swipes.

The morning dragged, minutes ticking by like hours, until it was finally time. He slipped on his coat, his chauffeur dropping him off early. He made his way into the hotel lobby, letting the alpine air rush through the revolving doors behind him as if ushering in something new. As he leaned against the stone column on the side of the room, the air shifted.

There, by the fireplace, stood a man he had only seen in his shadow online. Sean. Sean Leblanc.

The detective.

The one who had been investigating from the other side, nudging at the vast array of companies, always observing, trying to piece together the invisible lines between the game and the randomly chosen contestants.

Tim froze.

His gut twisted.

What in the world was Sean doing here?

Then, as if on cue, Dee stepped out of the elevator, and in an instant, Tim forgot all about the detective. Her presence lit the lobby like sunrise breaking through fog. From across the room, she waved, radiant, her smile effortlessly stealing his full attention.

"Good morning, Tim. You're here early."

He rose to greet her, the warmth of her voice washing over him. "Good morning, Dee. Yes, I try to get a head start when I can. I hate the chaos of rushing; much prefer a calm beginning. And you... you look marvelous today. I take it you slept well?"

"I did," she beamed. "And I'm so excited about our trip up to Mt. Pilatus. My friends should be arriving any moment. Claire is always *right* on time. We still have about fifteen minutes. Would you like to sit while we wait?"

"I'd love to," he said, casting a quick glance toward the fireplace. The detective had vanished. Gone. Good. *Remember he doesn't know who you are.*

Tim focused solely on Dee. Her voice, full of color and rhythm, danced through a story of her morning walk, the quiet river, the soft creak of the covered bridges, the vivid paintings she'd stopped to admire again.

Then came her curious gaze, her questions like gentle waves lapping at the shore. She wanted to know everything, where he was from, what he did, the pieces that made up the man in front of her.

But before he could offer even a glimpse of an answer, a pair of voices chimed in behind him.

"Here we are. Right on time."

"Well, good morning again, you two. I'd like you to meet my friend Tim," Dee said, glowing with pride.

Tim rose, turned, and there they were. Claire *and* Sean. What were the chances?

Play it cool. He doesn't know who you are.

"Good morning," Tim said with a calm smile. "It's a pleasure to meet Dee's friends. Is this your first time in Europe, as well?"

In perfect unison, the couple answered, bright-eyed and eager, "It is."

Tim relaxed. Sean was just meeting a perfect stranger for the first time, and he was with someone who was completely diverting his attention away from any investigation that might get in his way. Relieved, Tim suggested they take a seat so that he could map out their plan for the day.

It only took five minutes to agree to all that Tim had decided. They were along for the ride and Tim was pleased that they were open to a new unplanned adventure.

Their first stop of the morning was to the Hammetschwand Elevator, a sleek structure that rose dramatically from the forested cliffs of Burgenstock, perched high above Lake Lucerne. The surrounding forest carried a scent of pine up into the afternoon air.

The elevator climbed the steep cliffside with alarming speed, Claire and Dee exchanging wide-eyed glances. As the doors opened at the top, they gasped. The breathtaking view of the Alps, reflected on the lake below, was nothing like they had ever seen.

Tim stood a few paces back, quietly observing them. The way the sunlight danced across their faces, the way they leaned into the view, the majestic sprawl of Lucerne below, the snow-capped peaks in the distance, it all felt unreal, like watching a dream unfold.

Claire's eyes sparkled after reading the information sheet. She gestured animatedly toward the towering steel structure behind them. "Did you know," she began, her voice alight with wonder, "this is the highest outdoor elevator in all of Europe?" Her excitement was infectious, drawing smiles from a group standing close by as she launched into the story of its origins, her voice rising and falling like a symphony of curiosity.

A crisp breeze swirled around them, sending a flutter of wind through their hair and coats. None of them moved, wanting to soak in the panorama just a little longer.

Eventually, Tim broke the spell. "Shall we head in for tea? There's a place I know, warm, cozy, and they do a lemon tart that might just change your life." His tone was light, but there was something more behind his words, an invitation not just to tea, but to linger a little longer in this world he called home.

Before heading to the table, Claire and Dee exchanged a glance and excused themselves to freshen up, giggling like schoolgirls. Behind a closed door, Dee raised an eyebrow. "So... what do you think of Tim?"

Claire's cheeks flushed. "Well, you two are clearly smitten with each other," Dee teased. "My only concern is the whole long-distance thing. But for now? We're here, the vibe is perfect, and honestly what harm can a little magic do? Just promise me you won't fall head-over-heels. Not yet anyway."

Claire laughed. "Excuse me? Coming from the woman who herself is in a long-distance relationship? Seriously."

They both burst into laughter, the kind that echoed off walls and through hearts.

The next week unfolded like something out of a travel journal, only better. The four of them were inseparable. Tim seemed to relish every moment, his energy bright and generous. He whisked them off to hidden villages nestled in the Alps, secret lakeside cafés, and winding trails that ended in panoramic views that stole their breath. One morning, they woke to find themselves headed on an impromptu trip to Liechtenstein, Tim grinning as he handed them fresh croissants and pastries.

Over lunch on a sunny terrace perched high in the Alps, the mountains stretching like gods around them, Tim leaned in. "So, what's next for you all?"

Claire and Sean both looked at Dee, who smiled, a touch of mystery in her voice. "We're heading to the Canary Islands at the end of the month. Two weeks of sun, sand, and soul-searching."

Tim raised an eyebrow, intrigued. "The Canary Islands? That's an unusual pick for first timers in Europe. No Paris, Venice, London?"

Dee shrugged, a knowing gleam in her eyes. "I followed my gut. Something about it called to me. Besides, I've heard it's spectacular. Ever been?"

Tim chuckled softly, stirring his espresso. "Actually… I'm flying to Lanzarote myself, soon, to visit my family."

Dee nearly choked on her hot chocolate. "Next, you'll tell us you were born in Lanzarote."

Another grin. "I was. How do you do that?"

The table erupted into laughter.

Later, as the sun dipped behind the peaks, casting golden shadows across the valley, Tim turned serious. "I have a proposition. The big Lucerne Carnival begins in a few days; music, parades, masks, the works. It's like stepping into a fairy tale. I'd love for you to stay a few extra days and experience it. Then… fly with me to Lanzarote. My family's guest house is empty, and there's room for all of you. No pressure, just think about it."

Claire nudged Dee under the table. "Wash hands?" she whispered. They slipped away, and in the quiet of a tiled bathroom, weighed every angle.

"I mean… what do we have to lose?" Dee asked. "He's genuine. People know him, respect him. He's no stranger here."

Claire nodded slowly. "It's another adventure."

By that evening, their decision was made.

They chose to extend their stay. Dee swiftly canceled their flight and extended their hotel stay. Fate, it seemed, had other plans that were smoothly and effortlessly playing out.

And just like that, Lucerne opened its arms to them once more, with carnival drums in the distance and the whisper of a new story just beginning.

The Carnivale was very different to what Sean, Claire and Dee had anticipated. They saw the Swiss go all out! From bankers to nurses, the town had replaced their suits and scrubs with colorful costumes and creative masks.

The cold hardly mattered as there was magic in the air. The city had transformed into a riotous swirl of color, music and masked mischief.

From the moment Claire, Sean and Dee turned into the heart of the Old Town, they were swept into a moving sea of costumed revelers. Drummers in gold-trimmed robes pounded enormous bass drums with theatrical flair, their faces hidden behind intricately painted wooden masks, some grotesque, others comical, all utterly captivating. They marched in sync, led by a stilt walker dressed as a flame haired harlequin, tossing handfuls of candy into the crowd.

The floats rumbled down the narrow streets like rolling dreams. One was shaped like a massive, fire-breathing dragon, its paper-mâché scales painted in shimmering shades of green and bronze. Its jaws moved mechanically, releasing bursts of orange confetti instead of smoke. Children squealed with delight, reaching out for the fluttering pieces of color.

Then came the celestial float, a glimmering crescent moon carried aloft on a platform of midnight blue. Figures in silver robes and glowing star-masks moved around it in a slow, hypnotic dance. The lights of Lucerne reflected in their mirrored surfaces, making them appear otherworldly.

In the parade there were jesters in neon suits juggling torches, while a brass band dressed as intergalactic travelers, played as the crowd danced in the streets. Every costume was a marvel of creativity and craftsmanship: feathered headdresses, velvet capes, LED-lit wings, patchwork gowns sewn from recycled carnival posters.

Confetti coated the cobblestones like fresh snow. Laughter and the brassy clang of Guggenmusik echoed through the alleys. Strangers handed out tiny glasses of spiced schnapps, and for a moment, under a sky lit by sparklers and streamers, the trio forgot everything but the joy of being right there, in Lucerne, in February, where the whole city danced to the beat of chaos and celebration.

As the afternoon crowds thinned for lunch, Tim extended a heartfelt invitation. "I don't entertain much," he admitted, with a warm smile on his face, "but it feels only right to host you on your final evening here. My chauffeur will pick you up at six. You'll have plenty of time to rest before our journey tomorrow. Our flight will leave around eleven or when we are ready."

Back at the hotel, the energy of the past days gently gave way to quiet reflection. Dee curled up for a well-earned nap, her dreams surely still dancing with confetti and music. Meanwhile, Claire and Sean, not yet ready to say goodbye to the charm of Lucerne, slipped out for one last walk, eager to soak in the city's beauty and tuck away a few more memories.

At precisely six o'clock, the chauffeur appeared as if conjured by the hour itself. The journey that followed was nothing short of cinematic, a winding, twenty-minute ascent through a landscape so beautiful it seemed painted by the gods. As they climbed higher, the world unfurled beneath them, a breathtaking panorama of rugged peaks and velvet valleys bathed in the golden hush of early evening.

Then, as if sensing their arrival, an elegant electronic gate began to glide open on its own. Beyond it, the driveway stretched ahead long and sinuous, like a ribbon weaving through the steep alpine slope. Towering trees stood sentinel on either side, their branches whispering in the mountain breeze, guiding them ever upward into a realm that felt suspended between earth and sky.

The world faded below as the distant whistle of the wind threaded through the trees.

Then, as the last curve opened, they saw it: a humble two-story Swiss château, nestled like a secret in a cradle of snow-dusted peaks. It was modest in scale, with pale timber beams and stone walls weathered by time and storm. The shutters were painted a deep green, peeling at the edges, and the front path was cobbled, moss creeping between the stones.

There was no grand entrance to mark the threshold of this place, no sweeping archway, no opulent fanfare. Just a weathered wooden door, its grain scarred by years of wind and rain, and beside it, a pair of lanterns, their soft flicker painting golden halos across the stone wall. It felt like something lost in time. A sanctuary chiseled into the earth itself, hidden in plain sight.

The front door creaked open, and from within, Tim emerged, beaming with a warmth that instantly disarmed his guests. "Welcome," he said, his voice calm and resonant, like the hum of an old melody.

But stepping inside was like crossing through a veil into another world.

Gone was the rustic, aged exterior, in its place was a space that pulsed with character and contradiction. A study in modern rusticity, the house was a paradox of sleek lines and raw textures. It was elegant, understated, and achingly beautiful. Claire, Dee, and Sean stood frozen for a beat, awash in wonder. The art, the lighting, the textures, it all blended with an effortless grace that made it feel like the house itself had been curated, not constructed.

"It's like the outside is a mask," Sean murmured, almost to himself, his eyes drawn toward the luminous structure in the center of the room.

The circular atrium rose like a heart encased in glass, framed in matte black metal and crowned with a gabled roof. Inside, nature bloomed wildly. Lush tropical plants, their leaves broad and glistening, creating a pocket of jungle serenity. The air near it felt warmer, and alive.

"Very perceptive, Sean," Tim said with a knowing smile, stepping forward. "The front is the past. I kept it as a kind of homage. This land, this house, it came to me when I started my company. It was falling apart, forgotten. I couldn't bring myself to erase its story completely. So, I built around it, behind it, letting the facade remain… a whisper of what once was."

He glanced upward, gesturing toward the ceiling. "Skylights with heated panels. When it snows, they stay clear, like windows into the heavens. I like knowing I can always see the stars."

He paused, the moment thick with unspoken things. Then he brightened, clapping his hands. "But enough of that. Come. Let's sit in the study before dinner. And no, before you ask, no fondue tonight."

Laughter bubbled up between them, a shared inside joke lighting the air as they followed Tim down a hallway dressed in rustic herringbone floors. The wood, reclaimed and lovingly worn, gave off a comforting warmth beneath their feet. Artworks glowed softly from recessed niches, each one a quiet marvel. Sean's eyes lingered, half-convinced these pieces belonged in galleries, not a private home.

Claire leaned close to Dee, whispering behind her hand, "We should've stayed here. This place is unreal."

Dee gently nudged her with an elbow, her polite way of saying hush.

At the hallway's end, the study opened like a dream. Settees and sofas formed cozy islands, while shelves stretched up to the ceiling, brimming with books and glinting curiosities. It was the kind of room that invited both conversation and reflection, lit softly by antique sconces and the amber glow of a crackling hearth.

"In daylight," Tim said, motioning toward the wide windows, "you can see the Alps stretched across the horizon." He gestured to the furniture. "Please, make yourselves comfortable. What can I get you to drink?"

Sean joined him at the bar, admiring the solid beauty of the mahogany.

"I've always meant to ask," Sean said, reaching for a shaker. "Your language skills… how many do you speak?"

Tim chuckled, pouring with practiced ease. "In Europe, it's not unusual to know a few. I speak… more than a few. What about you?"

Sean hesitated, just long enough for Tim to notice. "Three. English, Irish, and Swedish. My mother's side. Though I'm rusty, been in the States too long."

Tim passed him two glasses. "White Russian for Claire. Whiskey Sour for Dee. Napkins and coasters are over there, would you mind?"

Sean turned, crossing to the sideboard. He picked up the napkins without thought, but the moment his eyes fell on the wine decanter, his breath caught in his chest.

There, etched into the glass, unmistakable in its detail, was the symbol.

The same symbol he'd chased for months, obsessively, hopelessly. The same one worn on lapel pins by the tall, enigmatic figures in every video. It was here. It was real.

He blinked hard. Once. Twice. The room seemed to fade around him as he stared. Slowly, he turned to face Tim.

Tim was watching as he raised a finger to his lips, mouthing a single word; "shhh..."

Sean's voice cracked as he whispered, "It's you… am I right?"

Tim didn't stop mixing. "Yes, Mr. Detective. Or should I say, Stewart O'Cleary?"

The room shifted, like the world tilted slightly off axis.

"How do you know that? I have so many questions…" Sean began, his heart thundering.

Tim cut him off gently. "And I will answer them. Perhaps in the next few days, on the Islands, we'll go for a drive. I'll tell you everything. I've been following your work as much as you've followed mine."

"But how?"

"There's a time and place," Tim said, laying the last glass down. "Let's not spoil the night. For now, let it be our secret."

"Does anyone else know?" Sean asked, the weight of realization settling heavily on his shoulders.

"Not that I'm aware of. Not even my closest friends."

They returned to Claire and Dee as the soft strains of jazz threaded through the room, wrapping around them like silk.

And Sean, still reeling, still piecing it all together, sat across from the man he had hunted for nearly a year. The Mastermind. The creator of the game that had captivated the world. And now, here they were, sipping drinks in a quiet room, talking like old friends.

Thirty minutes later, dinner was announced by a short, stout woman whose very presence radiated the kind of warmth and confidence that only comes from a lifetime spent orchestrating magic in the kitchen. Her cheeks were flushed, her apron dusted with flour, and her eyes twinkled with mischief.

"Lina, dearest," Tim called out cheerfully, "come in and meet my new friends, Sean, Claire, and Dee, all the way from America!"

Lina let out a soft, knowing laugh as she stepped into view. "Well, it's a rare treat to see Mr. Martel in the company of guests who seem like they belong here. Come along, then, your supper is waiting, and it's not the sort you let grow cold."

The dining room was a surprise, a gentle, unexpected kind. Instead of the stiff formality they'd braced for, it embraced them like an old friend. The space glowed golden in the firelight, the hearth roaring with massive, ancient logs that cracked and popped like storytellers. Dee glanced at the flames and imagined them burning long into the night, casting shadows that danced across the stone walls.

What followed was not a meal, it was an experience. A steaming bowl of creamy potato soup arrived first, simple yet soul-soothing. Then came the salad, surprisingly hearty with earthy mushrooms nestled among tender greens. The main dish, a rustic chicken and potato lasagna, was rich, comforting, and wholly unexpected. Finally, dessert arrived: three delicate pieces of chocolate, each one melting like a secret whispered against the tongue.

For two golden hours, time seemed to soften its grip. Laughter flickered like the firelight, conversation flowed gently, and for the first time in hours, Sean felt his shoulders ease. The weight of unanswered questions dulled, tucked away behind the quiet promise of another day.

Dee couldn't resist. The kitchen called to her like an old friend, familiar, warm, alive with the scent of memories and spice. She rose from the table with a quick apology, curiosity lighting her steps as she followed the path Lina had taken after dessert.

In the heart of the home, Lina moved gracefully between pots and pans, her hands still busy with the aftermath of the feast. The conversation between them flowed easily, like old friends rediscovering one another. Dee peppered her with questions, about ingredients, spices, techniques, and Lina answered with a quiet pride, the kind that only comes from years of cooking with love.

Time slipped away unnoticed until Tim wandered in, eyebrows raised in amused confusion. "Everything alright here?"

Lina flashed him a playful grin. "Your darling friend has been trying to uncover all my cooking secrets. But don't worry, I didn't spill everything!" She laughed, light and melodious, and Dee joined in, her laughter echoing warmly through the room.

Then Lina leaned closer, her eyes twinkling. "Wait right here. I've got something for you, a little something to take home, to remember tonight by. Just need to grab it from outside. I'll be right back!"

She dashed out the door, and a sudden gust of winter wind burst into the kitchen, sending a chill through Dee and lifting her hair in a tumble around her face. She shivered, pulling her arms close.

"Goodness, that's brisk," she said with a smile. "I can't wait for warmer weather tomorrow."

Tim gestured toward the stove with a half-smile. "Come stand over here. Much better. And besides…" He paused, his voice softening. "Lina doesn't just hand out gifts to anyone. You've clearly made an impression."

He winked as Dee tucked her windswept hair behind her ear, cheeks warming under his gaze.

Then, the door creaked open once more. Another burst of icy wind howled through the kitchen as Lina stepped back inside, her arms hidden behind her back.

Tim turned to greet her but froze. His eyes locked on Dee, and for a split second, the color drained from his face.

The birthmark. Just below her hairline, now exposed.

His breath caught.

No. It can't be.

They said you were dead.

His voice, barely more than a whisper, trembled through the kitchen. "Trish…?"

18

March 2025
Lucerne

Lina's voice broke the thick silence like glass. "Here you go, dear," she said gently, handing Dee a bundle wrapped in linen. "Dried mushrooms, from my garden. For your cooking back home." She smiled, drawing Dee into a warm, maternal hug.

Tim gripped the kitchen counter, his knuckles bone white. His face was even paler. Lina's smile wavered.

"Tim? Are you alright? It's not the food, is it?"

He opened his mouth, but no words came. Only tears. Silent, sudden, relentless. Lina rushed to his side, pressing a glass of water into his shaking hands, easing him onto a stool.

"There now, love. Breathe. Just breathe."

Dee watched, tense with concern, and something more. She could feel it: a current, an unspoken truth tugging at the edge of the room.

Tim looked at her, his voice raw. "Do you have... another name?" he asked, eyes scanning her face. "Are you sure you've never lived in Europe?"

Dee blinked, startled. "I think I'd remember something like that," she said with a nervous laugh. "Though... Lucerne has felt oddly familiar."

Lina leaned in, her brows furrowed. "Tim... what are you saying?"

He turned to her, trembling. "Zurich. Do you remember when we lived there? I was sixteen. And Trish, my girlfriend. I thought I'd marry her."

Lina gasped. Her eyes shot to Dee like she'd seen a ghost.

"She has the same birthmark," Tim whispered. "Dee, would you mind letting Lina take a look?"

Dee shifted under their stares, the air growing heavy, electric as she pulled her hair to the side.

Lina slowly sank into a chair. "I considered many things," she murmured, stunned. "But never... never this."

Tim's grief boiled over. "Did you know? All this time? Did you keep her from me?"

He broke, sobbing into his hands. Lina flew to him, embracing him as tears streaked her own cheeks.

"No, my sweet boy. No. They told me she had died."

Dee's voice cut through, bewildered and small. "Who died? Why are you talking like I'm not here?"

Just then, Sean and Claire stepped into the kitchen, pausing mid-step.

"Oh," Sean said carefully. "We've interrupted something."

Dee turned, her instincts kicking in. "Stay. You'll want to hear this."

Tim straightened, still shaken. "Let's move into the study. I think we will all need a drink for this."

Minutes later, they gathered in the study, the weight of the past pressing down like fog. All eyes turned to Lina as she began.

It started in Zurich, 1984. The Martel's had moved there when Tim's father took a top post at the Lindt Chocolate factory. Young Tim was dropped into a swanky international school, where he met her. Trish. Fierce, vibrant, full of fire. They fell hard. The kind of love that consumes.

But Trish's parents, entrenched in the rigid world of diplomacy, disapproved. And when their time in Zurich ended, they made it clear: Trish would not be left behind for the sake of teenage love.

Lina, then Tim's caretaker, had seen it all.

Dee sat frozen, listening, until finally she spoke, her voice unsteady. "You must have me confused with someone else."

Tim turned to her gently. "Trish had a birthmark. On the back of her neck. Just like yours."

Claire and Sean exchanged glances, then asked to see it. Dee hesitated, then turned. There it was.

"Lina, go on," Tim urged.

Lina pressed on, recounting their first year together followed by a summer apart, one with letters and dreams... until the second summer, when it all fell apart. The families forbade them from reuniting. Letters stopped. Silence swallowed their young love whole.

Dee let out a cry, disbelief breaking through her composure. "I'd remember something like that! Wouldn't I?"

"Maybe not," Lina said softly. "If you are Trish... a head injury could explain the memory loss. Even your eyes... they're darker now."

The silence in the room turned suffocating.

"There's more," Lina whispered.

She spoke of that night. Of whispers in embassy corridors. A yacht, a drunken crash. Three pulled from the water. Two dead. A girl, badly hurt. They said she died the next day. But perhaps... she didn't.

Tim stared at her, fury and heartbreak clashing. "Why didn't you tell me?"

"I was sworn to silence," Lina said through tears. "By the Ambassador himself. It could only have meant something far darker and mysterious."

Dee leaned forward, her voice barely there. "What really happened?"

Lina's tone dropped to a hush. "They said it was the Ambassador's son. He hit the other boat. They buried it all. The money. The influence. The silence."

Sean, thoughtful, turned to Tim. "I'm sorry for changing the subject, but did you and Trish ever visit Lucerne?"

Tim nodded. "Yes. She loved the covered bridges. It's where I first ran into Dee."

Sean let the silence settle before speaking. "Tomorrow, we fly to Lanzarote. I'll call in some favors. And Dee, would you consider a DNA test? It will put to rest many of our questions."

Dee nodded slowly, still dazed.

Later, as the others stepped outside, Tim lingered with Dee. He cupped her face, his voice low and full of emotion.

"I've only fallen in love twice in my life," he said. "And I think… both times, it has been with the same girl."

Dee gave a fragile smile. "It's been a lot. I'm not sure what I believe yet. But I'm glad I'm here. And I'm looking forward to Lanzarote."

She kissed him goodnight, then turned, her mind spinning. She wasn't ready to say those words. Not yet.

March 2025
Canary Islands

The night had been long and unforgiving before they flew south. Sleep came in fitful fragments, and by the time the wheels of the sleek Learjet kissed the tarmac of Lanzarote, the travelers were worn thin, souls frayed by turbulence both in the skies and in their hearts. The island's strange, raw beauty stretched out before them under a smudged, smoky sunset, but none of them were in any state to drink it in.

Sean's mind buzzed relentlessly. Even after a few stolen catnaps and the rhythmic hum of jet engines, he couldn't shake the sense that they were on the edge of something. He had made a silent vow mid-flight: he would help Dee and Tim uncover the truth about the secret that tore them apart.

Before heading to the guesthouse, Tim proposed a detour, a sanctuary of sorts. He guided them northward, across the island's barren, lunar landscapes, to one of his most beloved escapes: Jameos del Agua, a wonder of nature with natural openings in a lava tube produced by the collapse of the ceiling.

Here, the earth had split itself open long ago in fire and fury, leaving behind cavernous tunnels of volcanic rock and a lake so still, it seemed to mirror the soul. An artist, bold enough to dream of blending creation with destruction, had turned this scarred land into a masterpiece, a living poem written in stone and water.

As they descended into the cool, whispering darkness of the caves, Dee stopped short. A jolt ran through her, sharp, electric, undeniable.

There, in the dim, dreamlike glow of the underground lake, memory collided with reality.

"I know this place..." Dee whispered, her voice trembling in the heavy air. She fumbled in her satchel, heart pounding, and pulled out a battered, sun-faded postcard. It had been tucked away in a dusty box back home, something she had found but never understood. Until now.

The photograph on the card was unmistakable: the same pools of blue, the same jagged cathedral of black volcanic stone, the same feeling, as if the earth itself had secrets to tell.

Tears pooled at the corners of her eyes as she turned to Claire, Sean and Tim, her voice barely a breath.

"This is the place."

The past was no longer just whispering. Tim looked down and gasped. The postcard, old and worn, hinted at what once was. "Where did you get that?" asked Tim.

"I found it at the bottom of a box as I was cleaning out my house before I moved last year. It was with several other postcards and items. Something about it made me want to come to the Canary Islands, Lanzarote specifically."

Tim asked if he could take a closer look. As he held it, he waited, then turned the post card over not believing his eyes. There, as clear as day, a simple message; *To my T from your T.* "It *is* you," said Tim looking straight into Dee's eyes.

"And why would you say that?" asked Dee.

"Because this is my handwriting."

With their minds still steeped in the riddle surrounding them, they found a quiet table at the edge of the restaurant, cantilevered delicately over the mirrored lagoon. Half-shaded by drooping palms and whispering ferns, it felt like the threshold between two worlds, one rooted in reality, the other adrift in dream. They lingered there, conversation ebbing and flowing like the tide, speaking in meandering circles about everything and nothing at all.

Claire sat back, letting her eyes drift over the surreal beauty of the place. The lagoon shimmered like liquid glass beneath a vaulted ceiling of volcanic rock, an ancient cavern hewn by fire and time, a forgotten wound in the heart of the island. It was a space shaped as much by nature as by reverence, and it stirred something in her, a hush, a pause, a sense of being deeply seen.

As the sun began its slow descent, the world outside the cave softened into watercolor hues, lavender melting into peach, peach deepening into molten orange, and then, suddenly, crimson, like flame caught on the horizon. Shadows lengthened across the rugged lava terrain, their silhouettes sharp against the glowing sea. The breeze, laced with salt and jasmine, stirred the waters gently, casting ripples across the mirror like surface of the lagoon.

The chill inside the cave grew more pronounced, and with it, a new weight settled over them. Dee, whose thoughts had grown knotted and heavy with unanswered questions, glanced at Claire with a tired smile. "I think I need to call it a night," she said softly, her voice edged with fatigue. The others agreed as they left the cavern behind.

The drive to the guesthouse wound through sleepy villages nestled in the folds of the countryside, their stone houses painted gold by the last light of day. At the top of a hill, the Martel ranch awaited them, an old finca bathed in twilight, its silhouette carved against the fading sky. For a moment, as the car pulled into the gravel drive, silence fell. The land breathed around them, and the quiet beauty of dusk emptied their minds.

Claire wandered slowly through the farmhouse, letting her fingertips trace the cool, timeworn stone of the three-foot-thick walls. Each room opened like a poem, arched white ceilings, sun-kissed wooden beams, and bursts of life where bougainvillea and herbs tumbled from terracotta pots. The air inside was perfumed with the scent of fig leaves and old books. It was a house that remembered things, a house with soul.

Down by the pool, moonlight spilled like silver across the water. Tim was already there, his notebook open, a bottle of local wine resting nearby. He leaned forward, eyes bright with ideas, and began outlining plans for the coming days. Claire listened, half engaged, watching as Dee's shoulders tightened.

After a moment, Dee looked up, her voice tentative. "Would it be alright if I stayed back tomorrow? I just… need to breathe, to think."

Claire didn't hesitate. "I'll stay too," she said gently. "We both could use a day of quiet."

There was a soft nod from Dee, a trace of gratitude in her eyes.

Tim smiled and raised his glass, undeterred. "Then the boys shall embark on their own little expedition," he said, his tone light. "But promise me something, don't get too comfortable. The island still has secrets waiting for you that I would like to share."

And with that, under the stars scattered like salt across the night sky, the group slowly unraveled into sleep, each carrying dreams touched by lava, legend, and the whisper of a mystery just beginning to stir.

Tim and Sean stirred before the first light crept over the horizon, the soft hush of dawn whispering promise through the windows. A sense of anticipation crackled in the air, electric and unspoken. Today was no ordinary day, it was an escape, and perhaps, a revelation.

Tim had orchestrated the experience with quiet mastery: a full day on his private yacht, circumnavigating the island in slow, indulgent loops. Though the late winter air carried a crisp edge, the sun was already beginning its ascent, and the promise of warmth shimmered on the horizon. Whether basking in golden rays on the deck or watching the world glide by from within the polished embrace of the yacht's interior, serenity awaited.

Sean was quietly brimming with excitement, and nerves. He'd long wondered what it would be like to live a life with no limits, to move through the world with the kind of effortless abundance that Tim seemed to command. But more than that, he had questions; questions that had gnawed at the edges of his mind for weeks. And today, he hoped, Tim would finally answer them.

They boarded just as the first blush of sunlight kissed the marina, where a gleaming vessel awaited, sleek and impossibly elegant, with the name Orion's Whisper etched in silver script on the hull. As the engines hummed to life, breakfast appeared as if by magic, spread about on fine linen in the glass-walled dining hall.

Sean had imagined wealth. But this? This was artful, otherworldly. Opulence wrapped in taste, not flash. The table groaned under the weight of indulgence: banana-pecan pancakes stacked high beside warm maple syrup, delicate omelets folded like silk, French toast oozing apple strudel filling and dusted with cinnamon sugar, a frittata studded with roasted vegetables and fresh herbs, and breakfast pizza topped with prosciutto and runny egg. Plump strawberries glistened beside wedges of papaya, wheels of artisan cheese, and curls of smoked salmon. Croissants, pain au chocolate, and cardamom buns filled wicker baskets still warm from the galley ovens. It was, Sean thought with a dazed smile, a meal fit for a royal court, and yet somehow just for the two of them.

But they were not alone. That much became clear as the day unfolded. Discreet hands moved in and out of view: crew members in soft-soled shoes, each performing their task with silent precision. Everything unfolded as if orchestrated by invisible strings, the music, the meals, the steady rhythm of the yacht gliding into deeper waters.

Soon they settled in the underwater dining room, a jewel-like chamber encased in glass, suspended just below the waves. There, the sea unfurled its wonders before them: schools of glittering fish danced through shifting shafts of light, a pod of dolphins skimmed the hull above, and once, just once, the majestic silhouette of a whale breaching far in the distance. The ocean felt close enough to touch, alive with secrets.

Tim, relaxed and animated, spoke of his family's deep bond with the sea. Of how he'd spent a year working with designers to craft the next Martel family yacht, a modern marvel replacing the one they had cruised on for decades. "Being on the water," he said, "is when I remember who I really am."

And just like that, Sean's questions began to fade, not forgotten but softened. In this floating world of calm seas and connection, answers seemed less important than the moment itself.

Above, sunlight pierced the skylight dome, pouring golden light into the room like a blessing. Sean looked up, something stirring inside him. He rose, drawn toward the glow, eager to step into the fresh air and feel the sun on his face.

Tim glanced over, eyes narrowing slightly as he caught the subtle shift in Sean's expression, the quiet churn of thoughts, the tightening of his jaw, the storm building behind his gaze. The moment had arrived.

Without a word, Tim led him out onto the promenade deck, their footsteps echoing softly as the ship swayed gently beneath them. They continued to the Stern Deck, where scattered seating areas overlooked the open water. The morning air was crisp, laced with salt and sunlight. Sean drifted to the railing, his fingers gripping the cool metal as he stared out across the endless blue. Tim, meanwhile, sank into a cushioned seat, letting the breeze wash over him like a memory trying to take shape.

The silence stretched, pregnant with anticipation.

Sean hesitated. There was a tightness in his chest he couldn't name, a flutter of anxiety that didn't belong to the confident man he usually was. Why was he nervous? He took a deep breath, the scent of the sea filling his lungs, and sat down across from Tim.

But before he could speak, Tim's voice cut through the stillness like a blade, calm, but with unmistakable weight.

"I can tell you've been holding questions," he said, eyes locked on Sean's. "Given everything that's happened these past several weeks, and everything you've already unearthed... I believe it's time. You've earned the right to know the full truth, about 2T Technologies, and beyond."

He leaned back, open, unguarded. "Ask whatever you need. I won't hide a thing from you. Not anymore."

A flood of relief surged through Sean. Somehow, Tim always seemed to know what was circling in his mind.

He leaned forward, voice low but urgent. "Then I need to start with the one thing that's haunted me since day one."

He paused.

"How did you uncover my birth name?" His words hung in the air, heavy with years of buried identity. "I was told the agency erased every trace of my past. Scrubbed clean. But the moment I signed up for the Blank Checks App... there it was. My name. Not the one they gave me. My birth name. It... it shook me to my core."

A slow, knowing smile spread across Tim's face.

"I never meant for it to cause such a reaction. That was never the purpose of the system I built," Tim said, his voice calm but carrying a current of regret. "From the start, its instructions were simple: verify the name and location. Then confirm the primary cell phone associated with the applicant. I anticipated some would try to cheat the system, burner phones, false identities, but those were filtered out instantly. The system wasn't just smart, it was discerning. Legal name changes? Tracked. The most recent name, cross-referenced and locked to a single device."

He paused, letting the weight of his words settle. "Your case, as well as a several others, were different."

Tim leaned back, his gaze distant for a moment. "I spent months studying every loophole, every way someone could change who they were. A close friend of mine went through something not unlike your situation. That experience gave me the insight I needed to program the system to detect fractures in identities, to look beneath the surface."

He looked directly at Sean. "It wasn't designed to scare anyone. It was meant to say, 'I see you.' A signal that the system wasn't just watching, it understood. It looks like it found a crack in the cover story they gave you all those years ago."

Sean absorbed this quietly, before leaning in with a more pointed question. "So... are you able to track someone directly?"

Tim took a sip of his tea, the steam curling into the air. "Yes," he said simply. "I've been following you for a while now. The first signal was a while back. I detected some poking around the bank systems, too many angles at once to pin down immediately. I didn't know it was you at the time. How did you get so much done so quickly?"

Sean gave a half-smile. "I have a network," he said. "People all over the world. We started digging, but we couldn't trace the signal. The IP kept jumping. Constantly moving. How were you cloaking your location like that?"

Tim chuckled softly, the kind of laugh that comes with a secret too clever to keep. "Simple," he said. "I have my own satellite. Turns out, money can buy more than just comfort, it can buy silence, shadows, and freedom."

Sean laughed, shaking his head and tapping his forehead. "Of course. Constant movement, global drift. That explains the chase. But what about the encrypted data? I've never seen anything like it."

Again, Tim's eyes lit with memory. "Ah, that. You'll laugh at this too. Years ago, when the internet was still finding its feet, I had a few friends, brilliant, rebellious minds. We were misfits with nothing to lose. After I lost Trish... I lost myself."

He went quiet for a beat.

"Let me digress for a moment. I was seventeen, and she was sixteen. We were each other's escape. Both only children, invisible to wealthy parents who barely noticed our absence. That second summer apart was hell. I invited her to Lanzarote, but her parents refused. I waited every day for her letters that suddenly went silent. When I got back, she was gone. We were going to dedicate our lives to something bigger than ourselves, something better. We'd change our families' legacy. But the future we imagined never came."

Tim's voice softened. "After the accident, I thought the world had ended. But I knew I had to continue. For her. For us."

He smiled, faint and wistful. "That fall, my friends and I took a computer class, an elective. We didn't know it then, but we were opening the door to a new universe. We learned code, built games, and played obsessively. From Pac-Man to Tetris, Star Wars to Super Mario, we were hooked. Every class, every project, we pushed further."

He paused, lost for a moment in memory.

"Then the internet began to go great guns; domain names, dot coms, we were already ahead. Our domains? Free. Instant. We knew the tide was turning, and we were ready."

Tim leaned forward now, his voice gaining strength. "In 1994, at COMDEX (COMputer Dealers EXhibition) in Las Vegas, we realized we'd only just scratched the surface. The world of tech was exploding. Apps were still a whisper, but we could feel the coming storm. We didn't back down. We doubled down. One of my friends delved deep into encrypting data. His interests in all things ancient allowed him to create his own language by combining various languages into his own symbols. If I'm not mistaken, the three main ones are Sumerian, Pagan and Viking runes. I don't know much about it. I leave it all to him. It seems though that he does his job well as you could not crack the code. I'll pass on the job well done to him."

He looked at Sean with a knowing gleam. "And now? The game that I triggered. It was our dream. My promise. We said we'd make a difference. We said we'd leave the world better than we found it. And we are."

Sean let the weight of it all settle over him, his mind spinning as the pieces began to fall into place. Across from him, Tim sat with the serene patience of a man who had long since made peace with mystery. He watched Sean closely, eyes flickering with quiet amusement as he spoke again.

"I'm curious," Tim said, his tone casual but loaded. "As an outsider, beyond chasing shadows through the online app, what else were you able to uncover?"

Sean leaned forward, compelled now to speak. He described the Evidence Board he'd begun building back in March, a madman's map, some might say. Every video was a breadcrumb, every frame a whisper of something larger. The first connection had come via the German model, cryptic and distant, offering little more than a time and place in a terse phone message. Their conversation had been more of a monologue, really, about her, not the game.

"But I kept circling back to two things," Sean continued. "How did you choose the contestants? And why did the German model's check bounce?"

Tim chuckled, the sound soft and unexpected. "Believe it or not," he said, "it's all random. A game, for them, *and* for me."

He leaned in slightly, his voice lower now, like he was sharing a secret meant for no one else. "A friend of mine created a program. Think of it like throwing a dart at a spinning globe, pure chance. Once the area is selected, the program randomly generates digits until a cell phone number is completed to whomever is in that location at the time. From there, a local team, part of the 2T Technology network, steps in. They do the research, find out who the person is, what makes them tick, and deliver the message."

He paused, letting the machinery of it sink in.

"The rendezvous is set. Then come the three agents to carry out the Blank Check moment. As for the amount? Also, random, but within limits I designed. If someone, like our German model, chooses an amount that exceeds what was loaded into that one account, the check bounces. Simple really, unless you're on the outside, trying to make sense of it all."

Sean narrowed his eyes. "The three tall people, who are they? Why three?"

Tim smiled again, this time with the air of a storyteller warming up. "Height implies power. Authority. Presence. I wanted them to loom, to be unforgettable. And as for the number three? It's everywhere. Triads carry weight in every aspect around us. Three primary colors. The Holy Trinity. Third time's the charm. The classic rhythm of three men walking into a bar. Beginning, middle, end. It's harmony in chaos."

Sean nodded slowly, mind still spinning, then pressed forward. "And the new moon? It took me four months to crack that pattern. Thirteen new moons in 2024. I had to rework my entire board."

Tim leaned back, stretched, and grinned like a man proud of a worthy opponent. "Mr. Detective," he said with admiration. "You should come work for me. You're insatiably curious, and relentless. I like that."

He continued, eyes gleaming now. "I've always been fascinated by the cosmos. The new moon is a symbol of rebirth, transformation, a blank slate. What better time to start something unpredictable and profound?"

Sean sat, absorbing it all, still trying to reconcile the man in front of him with the legend he'd been chasing. Tim, the architect of mystery. Tim, the oracle of fortune. He was giving away secrets like they were candy, and still, Sean knew there was more.

He asked a few more questions. Tim answered them without hesitation.

Tax-free money? Easy. His global network oversaw making sure the taxes were paid on every winning. It was all pre-arranged, Tim's design. He knew the game would cost him a billion dollars. And he didn't care.

"I've already had everything I've ever wanted," he said simply. "The rest? Just numbers sitting in a bank. Doing no good for anyone."

Sean stared, overwhelmed and inspired. He wasn't just talking to a man, he was speaking to a force, a living legend cloaked in charm, secrecy, and staggering generosity.

As Tim and Sean sat in companionable silence, the island lay before them like a dream, golden and still, a distant jewel glinting on the sea. The spell was gently broken by the announcement of lunch, and only then did they realize how swiftly time had slipped through their fingers. Their anticipation bloomed as they approached the table, where a decadent feast awaited: glistening seafood, handmade pasta, skewers of tender kebabs, vibrant salads, sweet fruits, fine cheeses, and crusty, warm bread. Crystal glasses were filled, ruby red and golden white wines shimmering in the midday light.

Sean, eyes wide with delight, resolved to taste everything. He took modest portions, determined to savor each flavor slowly, reverently, like a man reading poetry one line at a time. As they dined, the conversation deepened, shifting from surface smiles to the vulnerable warmth of memory and confession.

Sean spoke of Claire, his voice softened by the weight of real feeling, while Tim wove in tender recollections of his own long-lost love, Trish, painting in the gaps with boyish honesty.

"That symbol on the decanter," asked Sean, his voice almost reverent, "the same one engraved on the lapel pins your people wear all over the world... At first, I thought it was a crossroads, but now I see it differently. Two T's, standing together. Trish and Tim... am I right?"

"You are right," Tim said quietly, his gaze fixed somewhere just past the horizon. "Trish and I created that symbol... and though she may not remember, I do. It's magic, really, finding her again like this. I know deep down she's the same girl. I'll wait for your findings next week, but I don't need them to believe it's her."

"When will you tell the girls about who you are? I don't believe it is on their radar?" asked Sean.

"Soon, when the time is right." He paused, a wistful smile touching his lips. "But for now, how about a short ride on the jet skis before we head back to spend the afternoon with the girls?"

Grinning like teenagers set loose, the two launched into the waves, their laughter trailing behind them as they carved joy into the water. For over an hour, they raced across the glittering sea, dolphins leaping and twirling in their wake as if joining the celebration.

The two weeks spent wandering the sun-drenched Canary Islands had been nothing short of magical. It was the kind of adventure that stitched people together, and the four of them had, without question, begun weaving a bond destined to last a lifetime.

Just days before they were due to part ways, Sean gathered them with an expression that said he wasn't bearing ordinary news. He had uncovered new information, something significant, about Trish Berg.

No one hesitated. They were hungry for the truth.

Sean opened the file on his laptop. "Patricia Ann Berg," he began, his voice steady, "was born on August 28, 1969, in Bar Harbor, Maine."

He went on, revealing a tale that felt more like a spy novel than real life. Her parents, Anna and Gerhard Berg, were American born, of German descent. In 1983, the family relocated to Zurich after Mr. Berg was offered a role as a Diplomatic Secret Agent for the American Embassy. The twist? Their home was Zurich, while the Embassy's heartbeat pulsed in Bern. The move was strategic designed to cloak Gerhard's true identity and preserve his cover.

What followed was even more astonishing.

Sean's eyes scanned the pages. "The records are classified, but I've been granted clearance to share the essentials. It appears Gerhard Berg lived a double life, an operative not just for the Americans, but for the Germans as well."

Gasps and murmurs passed between the group like wind through leaves.

"Did you know this?" Dee asked Tim.

"Not a clue."

Sean continued, revealing that the American Ambassador, far from betraying his own country, was complicit. He benefited quietly from the intelligence funneled through this clandestine friendship. But it all unraveled after the boating accident. A search of the Berg home uncovered damning evidence, forcing long-buried truths into the light. Immediate changes were made at the American Embassy, all under the cover of night.

Then came the most heart-wrenching revelation: Patricia, just sixteen at the time, had survived the accident but with no memory of who she was. The Embassy moved swiftly, spiriting her back to the U.S., where a childless couple, the Reynolds, adopted her. They were told very little. A new life was crafted from scratch: new name, new history, new everything. Every shred of her and her family's former life, school records, medical files, yearbooks, birth certificates, passports, vanished without a trace.

Dee's voice cut through the silence like a blade. "Does any of this make sense to you?" she asked, turning to Tim.

He paused, thoughtful. "Not really but your parents always kept people at a distance. Even me. They were secretive yet loved to flaunt their wealth. Boats, cars, houses, it was all for show. We were kids. We didn't know how to read between the lines."

He looked over to Sean. "What about Dee's DNA test?"

Sean nodded solemnly. "Are you ready for this, Dee?"

She met his gaze. "I am."

He took a breath. "Your DNA confirms that you *are* Patricia Ann Berg. I traced your bloodline through the Berg family. Even though your parents do not appear in the records, other family members do. There's no connection at all to the Reynolds."

Tim instinctively wrapped his arm tighter around her.

"I know this must be a lot to take in," he said softly. "How are you feeling?"

Dee's eyes glistened, not with tears, but something clearer. Lighter.

"In a strange way… I feel free. Lighter than I have in years. Like a weight I didn't even know I carried has finally been lifted." She smiled faintly. "I've learned not to live in the past; Claire taught me that. I've lost so much already. But I made a vow to choose joy when I can. And this…" she gestured around at them all, "this is part of that joy. I may not remember our past, Tim, but I treasure what we have now. That's more than enough for me."

They decided, why not celebrate? Tim insisted on taking them out for a special meal, and none of them protested.

For hours, the little restaurant echoed with their laughter. They feasted on fragrant, home-cooked local fare, passing around bowls and bottles like old friends at a family table. The wine flowed as freely as their stories, weaving together the past and present in threads of joy and mischief.

At one point, Sean leaned across the table with a grin. "So, Tim," he said, a playful spark in his eye, "you always say you come here to visit family every year… we have yet to meet them. Are you planning to keep us your little secret forever?"

Tim smiled, a slow, knowing smile. "We can go meet them tonight, if you'd like," he said. "They'll be delighted to meet my new closest friends. We'll stop by on our way home."

A quiet thrill ran through the group. The night was far from over.

As they left the warm glow of the restaurant behind, Tim took the wheel, guiding the car along the coastal road that curled like ribbon around the island's northern cliffs. The moonlight shimmered on the sea, and the air was cool and laced with salt. After a while, he turned onto a narrow dirt path and, with a cryptic smile, murmured, "Almost there."

Ahead, perched on the cliff's edge, rose a sprawling Spanish-style estate, its white walls glowing softly under lights hidden among the trees. The gates creaked open like something from a dream. The grounds were immaculate, an elegant blend of nature and design, timeless and still. But instead of heading toward the grand house, Tim took a sharp turn, veering right down a winding road that led farther down the cliffside.

When the car stopped, they stepped out into silence and moonlight. And there it was, the family cemetery.

It was breathtaking.

The graves stood proudly overlooking the endless ocean, each one a sculpted masterpiece of marble and reverence, angels with bowed heads, carved crosses, ornate tombs that looked like miniature chapels.

Dee exhaled sharply. "Why do cemeteries always have the best views?" she asked, half-laughing, half-exasperated. "It makes no sense."

But it did. In some strange, poetic way, it made all the sense in the world.

Tim gestured with an almost reverent theatricality. "Dee, Claire, Sean, meet my family. And family, meet my new friends."

Laughter rolled through the quiet air, rich with wonder and absurdity.

Sean shook his head, grinning. "Now it all makes sense. We were so tangled up in Dee's past, we never stopped to wonder why you never left us to come visit your family."

"One day," said Dee, stifling a yawn, "you'll have to tell us everything about them. But for now... I need some rest."

The others murmured their agreement, the magic of the night softening into fatigue.

They slipped into their rooms without another word, and the silence of the island night tucked them in. Sleep that night wrapped around them like a thick, comforting blanket.

The golden morning light rose gently over Lanzarote, casting golden streaks across the sea, their final day on the island, and Tim had one last surprise up his sleeve. A day on the open water aboard the sleek, sun-kissed yacht, Orion Whisperer. The scent of salt and promise hung in the air as a lavish breakfast was served on deck. Sean and Claire lounged together, wrapped in quiet intimacy on the sun-drenched cushions, their laughter mingling with the sea breeze. Meanwhile, Dee and Tim tore across the waves on jet skis, wild and free, their laughter echoing across the water.

Then came lunch, and with it, the grand surprise reveal.

Tim stood, raising a glass, the corners of his mouth curled with mischief. "One last surprise," he said. "We're flying home in my jet. Or… anywhere you wish to go."

Silence fell, heavy and stunned. Dee's eyes filled instantly. Tears slipped down her cheeks, unbidden, the weight of goodbye crashing into her like a rogue wave.

"I didn't mean to make you sad," Tim said gently. "You know this doesn't have to be goodbye."

Dee nodded, trying to smile, but the ache in her chest only grew. The magic of the trip, the escape, the connection, the unreality of it all, was beginning to unravel, thread by golden thread.

Claire rushed to her side, arms around her, grounding her with quiet strength. Dee took a trembling breath, still sniffling. "I'm sorry. I didn't mean to fall apart. It's just... this has been more than a vacation. It's been a dream. And I'm not ready to wake up yet."

Tim sat beside her, pulling her close, his arms a fortress against the tide of sorrow. "Then don't," he said softly. "Stay. Stay with me a little longer."

Dee looked up at him, searching his face. "You're serious? I can stay?"

"As long as you like," he whispered. "I'm all yours."

A slow smile spread across Dee's face. "Then that's what I'll do. One more month. Time for you and me to get to know each other without all the waves and whirlwinds. And then I'll head back. My grandchildren are waiting. I miss them dearly."

Across the deck, Sean and Claire were deep in conversation, voices hushed but hearts alight. Claire had responsibilities in Sanare, but Sean… Sean just wanted her. And so, a decision was made. They would return to Sanare together, hearts aligned.

Dee excused herself, giving the pair space as they mapped out their plans with Tim. When she returned, she was breathless with laughter, eyes sparkling like sunlight on water.

"What on earth is so funny now?" Claire asked, raising an eyebrow.

"You are not going to believe this," Dee said, clutching her phone. "Remember that wild social media craze last year? The Blank Checks game? Well, guess what, it's back. Just launched. Look at your phones!"

One by one, the group read the simple, cryptic message:

Welcome, Blank Checks applicants.
To continue the game, enter the Blank Checks Lottery for one dollar.
A limit of 10 entries can be made before March 31, 2025.
The first Blank Check will be presented on April 27, 2025.
Follow the instructions below.
All your dreams can come true,
if you have the courage to pursue them.
And remember to
DREAM BIG. REALLY BIG.

Dee's laughter bubbled up again. "Can you believe it? It's absolutely insane. Who does this? Who gives away that kind of money? People are going to lose their minds all over again!"

Tim turned, an amused glint in his eyes, and shot a look at Sean. "Actually… I think I can answer that."

Sean gave a sly, knowing smile.

"I'm that man you speak of. I'm the Mastermind behind the Blank Checks."

Epilogue

SINCE WE LAST SAW THEM...

As the dust settles and the final chapter closes, the path
each character has chosen begins to unfold,
marked by bold decisions,
quiet departures, and
the promise of new
beginnings.

– 1 –

After three soothing summer months in Singapore, Anthony and Carol found it hard to believe how swiftly their life had turned a corner. It felt surreal, like walking into a beautiful dream. Singapore had offered them a taste of serenity: slow mornings beneath swaying palms, laughter over glorious meals, long strolls along the marina as the city shimmered like a jewel in the dusk. Change had come knocking, unexpected and insistent.

Anthony, ever the steady thinker, took a month to fully absorb the news. Even while fulfilling his duties at Sentosa Online Ltd., his mind was consumed with the weight of what lay ahead. He had never been impulsive, and this decision would be no different. Every dollar was accounted for, every possibility played out. And it was during one of those late-night conversations with Carol, when the world outside was still and their son Philip slept soundly, that the path forward became clear.

They would trade in the glitz and rush of California, with its endless commutes and high-octane social life, for something quieter, slower, truer. It was a bold move, one rooted in love and the desire to give their son a life not of excess, but of meaning. They envisioned a return to simplicity, the kind of life they once dreamed up in their earliest days together, when love was young and hope was boundless.

And so, they chose Lincoln City, Carol's childhood home on the rugged Oregon coast. It wasn't just a sentimental choice; it was the fulfillment of a long-held dream. Their new house, where waves thundered and whispered in equal measure, sat perched on the cliff. The vast Pacific stretched out before them, a daily reminder of the beauty in stillness, in nature, in home.

They weren't giving up on the world, only redefining how they wanted to live in it. Winters would be spent in Singapore, reconnecting with Anthony's roots, giving Carol and Philip a deeper taste of the culture and vibrancy. It was a delicate balance between two worlds, stitched together with intention and love.

In the end, it wasn't just a move. It was a reclamation, a return to the life they had always promised each other. It was not one built on prestige or pace, but on purpose.

- 2 -

Life at Villaggio della Speranza on the island of Mallorca was, for Vittoria Picorini, the tender epilogue she had never dared to imagine. Nestled in the gentle rhythm of this serene village, her days were now graced by the comforting presence of her daughter Francesca, a bond once severed by time and circumstance, now mended with warmth, forgiveness, and laughter. For the two women, each day was a precious gift, a chance to reclaim the moments they had lost. They lunched beneath the olive trees in the courtyard, their laughter mingling with birdsong and the soft clinking of wine glasses. Evenings were filled with music that stirred their souls, sometimes jazz, sometimes the nostalgic hum of old Italian ballads, often ending with a spontaneous dance beneath the fairy lights that sparkled like stars strung between the cypresses.

But behind Vittoria's gentle smile lay a lifetime of burdens carried in silence, until now. Hers was a life marked by sacrifice and secrets, by choices made in the shadows. She had been more than a grandmother to Paolo, she had been his quiet protector, his guide, his hidden anchor in a storm he never fully understood. Now, with her daughter by her side and her beloved Paolo flourishing in his own life, she could finally exhale. Her heart, once heavy, was full. Her journey, complete.

At forty-five, Paolo stood at a threshold of his own. Still brimming with curiosity and the fierce love of art and history that had always defined him, he maintained his cherished position, albeit part-time, at the Contemporary Art Museum in Palma. Yet, with time and freedom now more abundant, he found himself yearning to explore life more deeply, to follow creative threads that had long been tucked away.

Spending more time with his Aunt Francesca opened unexpected doors, not just to her world, but to the close-knit circle of friends who surrounded her. Among them was Isabella, the youngest of the group, a woman whose soul spoke the language of art as fluently as his own. A gifted jewelry designer with over two decades of delicate craft behind her, Isabella carried herself with both elegance and fire. What began as shared conversations about design, culture, and aesthetic theory soon stretched into hours of connection that felt both familiar and electric. There was a spark there, one neither Paolo nor Isabella could fully name yet, but it lingered in every conversation, every shared silence, every glance held a moment too long.

And so, within the cobbled heart of a village steeped in hope, three lives wove themselves into something whole. In the autumn of one life, the spring of another quietly began.

- 3 -

Tom and his family had stayed in the shadows for months, deliberately distant from the media circus that followed his mother and former model, Gretchen. After the scandal of her bounced check, she somehow managed to turn public disgrace into yet another steppingstone. Not one to retreat from the spotlight, Gretchen wielded charm like a blade, sharp, deliberate, and dangerously effective. Her eyes, still bright with the seduction of her youth, enchanted anyone weak enough to linger. Soon enough, she'd found herself attached to a well-heeled philanthropist, the kind who collected beautiful women like rare art. For him, Gretchen was not just a lover, but an accessory, glimmering, poised, and entirely self-aware.

From afar, Tom and his wife Felicia watched the spectacle unfold. It wasn't voyeurism, it was inescapable. Her image was everywhere. Paparazzi snapped her poolside with champagne in hand; gossip sites speculated about wedding bells. For Tom, it was less painful than it was surreal. Felicia offered quiet support, her hand always finding his in moments where words would fail.

Then came the email.

The subject line was sterile, almost clinical: *"Urgent Legal Matter."*

The body, even more cryptic:

Mr. Schumer. Please call this number and ask for Mr. Johan Kruger. There is a legal matter of urgency we wish to settle at this time. All will be explained when you call.

There was no signature. No law firm. Just a name.

Tom raised an eyebrow. "Spam?" he asked, turning the screen toward Felicia.

She frowned. "Maybe. But it's... oddly specific."

Out of curiosity, and maybe boredom, they searched for Johan Kruger online. The name barely registered, just a few sparse mentions in passing as the son of Jürgen Kruger, the once, iconic actor who had faded into reclusion before passing away quietly weeks ago.

With little to lose, Tom dialed. "This is Tom Schumer. You asked me to call. You're on speaker phone. My wife is here as well."

Johan's voice was calm. "Mr. Schumer, thank you for calling. I know this must be strange for you. Please allow me to explain."

And then came the confirmation.

"You and I are brothers. Half-brothers," Johan said. "My father, Jürgen, was also yours."

A silence stretched between the three of them.

Tom blinked. "I...believe you are correct. I uncovered a story about the Portage Hotel baby while doing some research a few years back. I believe I am that baby."

Johan sighed. "Yes. My father and your mother. According to a private letter in his safe, they had an agreement to keep the pregnancy secret. He didn't want to jeopardize his rising career. She, perhaps, wanted to preserve her independence. Either way, they parted ways... but my father never forgot."

A tremor ran through Tom's hand. He looked to Felicia, who squeezed his arm.

"He watched you grow from afar," Johan continued. "He knew about you, and he carried the guilt of that decision for decades. He even tried to reach out once, but your mother denied him. Said you had a good life. Maybe she was right. Maybe she wasn't. Regardless, in his final will and testament, he made his intentions clear: you are to receive half his estate."

Tom leaned back, stunned. "Half of... what exactly?"

Johan let out a faint chuckle. "The Kruger estate includes real estate, film royalties, and a considerable art collection. Valued collectively... well into the tens of millions."

Felicia gasped. Tom's mouth went dry.

But it wasn't the money. Not really. It was the void. The missing puzzle piece of his past, dropped suddenly into place. A father he never knew. A legacy he hadn't asked for. A brother who, strangely, didn't seem bitter.

"I don't want a penny unless you're okay with this," Tom said after a long pause.

Johan replied gently, "You are his son. That alone entitles you. I'm not calling to argue. I'm calling to welcome you. We are family."

That night, Tom sat on the back porch, the stars glinting like the secrets still hidden in the folds of his life. Felicia sat beside him, silent, her head on his shoulder.

"Are you okay?" she whispered.

Tom nodded slowly. "For the first time in a long time... I think I might be."

- 4 -

Manuel had always dreamed of giving back to the community that raised him, and when fate handed him the means, he did not hesitate. After securing a generous nest egg for his family's future, he poured the remaining twenty million into the heart of Mendoza. Scholarships began flowing like spring rain, nourishing the dreams of young minds. Streets were repaved, parks revived, and a gleaming new music academy rose at the town's edge, complete with a state-of-the-art performing arts center. It stood as a temple of rhythm and hope, a sanctuary for those yearning to create.

One golden summer evening, the sun melted into the horizon, brushing the sky with hues of rose and amber. In the backyard, Manuel and his dear son-in-law Pedro strummed guitars beneath a whispering jacaranda tree. Their laughter mingled with the soft breeze, and soon, the yard blossomed with music and life. The children tumbled in like a chorus of joy, their voices as light and bright as windchimes. Neighbors wandered in, drawn by the familiar pull of song, clapping and swaying, their hearts lifted by the notes that danced through the air.

From the porch, Sandra watched with shining eyes. Her father, once a solitary man whose songs were echoes in an empty room, now played surrounded by love. The once, duo chords of "Él y Yo" had evolved, reshaped by tiny hands and youthful voices. The quadruplets, now old enough to cradle their own guitars, added their innocent harmonies, and the song was reborn: "Él y Nosotros" - Him and Us.

What began as a personal passion had grown into something far greater. The family band became the soul of Mendoza, lighting up festivals, birthdays, and quiet Sunday mornings. Their music stitched together generations, reminding all who listened that joy could be found in the simplest things, in unity, in melody, in shared breath and beat.

Life had surprised them with a crescendo of blessings, unexpected, beautiful, enduring. Four little miracles had joined their song, carrying its tune into the future with laughter and love. And so, in the rhythm of their days, as guitars gently wept and laughter floated through open windows, Pedro and Sandra knew their story had never been a duet.

It was, and always would be, a symphony.

- 5 -

For six months, Nozomi wandered across Japan with her camera, chasing whispers of tradition through the narrow alleyways of Kyoto, the mist-veiled forests of Nara, and the sun-drenched coasts of Shikoku. Her lens captured the soul of a nation, the delicate curve of a teapot mid-ceremony, the weathered wood of a centuries-old pagoda, a child's laughter behind a paper fan, the bright silence of cherry blossoms in full bloom.

What began as a quiet project to reconnect with her roots soon ignited the public imagination. Within days of sharing her photographs, Nozomi became a household name. The images, poetic and precise, spread like wildfire. They shimmered on billboards across the country, flickered across late-night television, and filled the glossy pages of high-end travel magazines. She had reminded Japan of itself, and the country fell in love all over again.

Yet behind the acclaim and applause, Nozomi's heart was rooted in something far more personal. Her fame opened doors, but it was the memory of her parents, once vibrant, now fading into the gray fog of dementia, that drove her forward. They still had good days, sometimes sparked by simple pleasures: the clink of a porcelain dish, the scent of simmered miso, a song from their youth playing faintly in a cafe.

Inspired by the fleeting clarity these moments brought, Nozomi threw herself into an idea born from hope and heartbreak: The Unpredictable Plate had evolved. It had started as a small experimental event, participating restaurants served nostalgic dishes designed to awaken dormant memories. The results were astonishing. Laughter returned. Eyes lit up. Perhaps the dish ordered was not the one served, but the smells seemed to awaken those with dementia, unlocking a past hidden within them.

Nozomi poured her earnings into expanding the experiment, opening full-time eateries in and around her hometown of Yokohama. Each was a living memory palace, walls adorned with traditional art, music drifting gently through the air, and menus that changed daily based on seasonal, regional, and deeply personal themes.

The restaurants became sanctuaries not only for those living with dementia but for families seeking connection, and for anyone longing to feel seen, known, and remembered. People traveled across prefectures just to sit at one of Nozomi's tables.

Her photographs had captured the beauty of Japan, but her greatest masterpiece was creating a space where people could rediscover the beauty within themselves.

And as she watched her parents smile over a bowl of rice just like the one they used to share in their youth, Nozomi understood; memory fades, but love, when nurtured with care, can last a lifetime.

– 6 –

In the sun-dappled hills of the Italian Alps, Alessandra found a quiet rhythm in her new chapter. Life slowed to the comforting cadence of mountain breezes and clinking wine glasses at twilight. Though she remained in her own home, just as she'd always wanted, she honored her playful promise to dine at Trattoria del Simone once a week, a promise she routinely broke, appearing two, sometimes three times more.

Luca, ever the charming host and now dear friend, welcomed her as if she were royalty. Her laughter became a fixture in the dining room; her stories passed from table to table like treasured heirlooms. One afternoon, with flour dusted on his apron and a glimmer in his eye, Luca leaned in and asked, "Alessandra, would you care to share a few of your secrets?"

She answered with a warm smile and a mischievous wink. In just weeks, the menu bore her name like a tribute: Tortellini di Alessandra, Pizza alla Alessandra, Insalata d'Alessandra, and others. Patrons began asking for "the Alessandra special," not realizing each dish came seasoned with her memories, her soul, her heart.

At the gentle urging of her son, Alessandra made modest but essential upgrades to her home, new shutters, modernized plumbing, better insulation for the winters. Yet she was careful not to disturb its rustic charm. The old wood beams stayed, the crooked stone steps remained. The house, like its owner, bore its age with grace and strength.

Meanwhile, across the ocean, Matteo and Tony embraced their own dream, one made of glass, steel, and an endless skyline of New York. Their Park Place condo soared above Manhattan like a private castle in the clouds. Art lined the walls, music floated through the halls, and love settled into every corner. It was a life of elegance and movement, where the clatter of subways echoed far below and ambition pulsed through the veins of the city.

Alessandra visited often. Her presence in New York was like a warm breeze in the middle of winter. Neighbors became friends over shared meals, and strangers became admirers at the first bite of her homemade lasagna. She stirred the pots and stirred the hearts of everyone she met.

But as much as she adored her time with her son and his beloved, the Alps called to her in a language only the heart could understand. Home was where the earth smelled of pine and wild rosemary, where the church bells chimed on Sundays, and where her past and future coexisted in quiet harmony.

Before she left, Alessandra handed Matteo a weathered recipe book, its pages splattered and worn with time.

"These are yours now," she said, pressing it into his hands. "Make them your own but never forget where they came from."

Matteo later gave a copy to Luca, who honored it not just by adding new dishes to the menu, but by telling her stories alongside them.

And so, in two very different corners of the world, one kissed by alpine mist, the other lit by city lights, Alessandra lived on. In the laughter around dinner tables, in the scent of rosemary and garlic, in the way love is always the main ingredient.

And in every bite of Pizza alla Alessandra, she was there, warm, unforgettable, eternal.

- 7 -

Aidan Harrington III, once the golden boy of Australian venture capital, heir to the sprawling Harrington estate, had stopped throwing money around like sand in a storm. He wasn't broke. Far from it. But the glint of excess had dulled in his eyes, replaced by something quieter, more dangerous: clarity.

The fall hadn't been sudden. It had been a slow, grinding collapse of the soul, beginning with the betrayal that cracked his perfect world in two. His wife, his partner in life, and his oldest friend had carved their affair into the soft flesh of his trust. What followed was a brutal, public divorce that left Aidan not broken, but hollowed out. Money could patch many things but not pride. Not love lost.

In the months that followed, he withdrew from the world of glitzy galas and backroom boardroom deals. His solace lay in the ancient, bronze statues whispering secrets of empires past, scrolls that smelled of dust and mystery. Antiquities had always offered him an escape, a reminder that everything, even heartbreak, was temporary.

Then came the accident.

Jason Young. The con-artist. The rival. A man who had tried to swindle him and his friends out of millions. Gone in a flash. One moment walking in a wealthy Melbourne suburb, the next, a smear of rubber and tragedy. The shock of it shattered something deep inside Aidan. He began to question everything. What did his billions mean? What legacy would *he* leave behind?

He started watching the people around him. His inner circle of twenty, the hand-picked titans of industry, art, and innovation. He studied how they spent their time, their fortunes. So many of them hollowed out like he had been. And Aidan Harrington, for all his wealth, didn't want to be just another forgotten name on a plaque in a soulless wing of a museum.

One night, over dinner on a moonlit deck in Sydney Harbour, Aidan confided in his longtime diving partner and fellow explorer, Oliver Bailey.

"We've wasted too much," Aidan said, swirling the last of his wine. "But we've seen things, Oliver. Touched pieces of forgotten worlds. Doesn't that mean we owe the future something?"

Oliver, a man with salt in his beard and stories in his bones, grinned. "Then let's give the past to the future."

And so, they did.

Together, they founded The Harrington-Bailey Foundation for Historical Discovery, a global initiative with a simple but profound mission: to awaken curiosity, preserve knowledge, and spark purpose in the hearts of the next generation.

They created scholarships for underprivileged students with an eye for archaeology, funded expeditions for young historians, and built digital libraries to protect fragile ancient texts from time's decay. They traveled, lectured, and were inspired. The wealth Aidan once used to numb his pain now breathed life into dreams across continents.

Years later, standing beneath the dusty pillars of a forgotten temple in Petra, Aidan smiled, not the brittle grin of a man pretending, but a quiet, full smile that came from deep within.

He had finally stopped running from the past.

He was building the future.

And that was a legacy worth leaving behind.

– 8 –

That weekend in Montreal changed everything for Leah, William, Sally and Henry.

It began with the unexpected, a weekend escape, nothing more, and ended with lives unspooling into something radiant and new. Leah and Sally returned home altered, not by some grand design, but by the quiet, unpredictable pulse of love and possibility.

Leah hadn't meant to fall in love. Neither had William. Love, as it often does, slipped in sideways, cloaked in serendipity. Leah, newly, bewilderingly rich, was a woman caught between two lives. A blank-check fortune had found her like a storybook twist: a multimillion-dollar windfall she hadn't yet grown comfortable enough to believe. And yet, in Montreal, she softened. She surrendered to wonder.

She chartered a boat one evening, just for the four of them, because she said the river "was calling." Dusk spilled violets and gold across the St. Lawrence as they drifted along, champagne flutes in hand, the city shimmering in the distance. She insisted they stop in a tucked away vintage boutique, where she bought several outlandish outfits, impractical and perfect declaring they looked "like people from a better story." She wanted that story. She was ready to live it.

William, who had spent too long in a world lit by screens and APP codes, stepped out of his own digital daze. Leah's presence cracked something open in him. She was real, achingly, vividly real, and made him remember that he too was real. In her, he found both invitation and challenge: to feel again, to dream again, to live untethered.

They sat in cafes until closing, mapping out dreams on napkins. In their fifties, they decided the time for waiting had passed. It was time to go. To see the world. To collect moments instead of things. Travis, Leah's grown son, cheered them on. For the first time in years, he saw his mother unburdened, her laughter not just soft, but free.

Sally and Henry watched the older couple with quiet awe. They too were in love, but theirs was young and urgent, the kind that wanted to plant roots *and* take flight. Standing beneath fairy lights strung across a hidden courtyard, Henry kissed the back of Sally's hand and whispered, "Let's not go back. Let's go forward."

So, they did.

Back in Plattsburgh, New York, they took on the slow, deliberate work of building a life. Uncle Frank's old house became their canvas. They sanded floors, painted walls, and hung twinkling lights along the porch. Sally, just eighteen, knew people would say she was too young. But she knew what was right. She felt it in her bones. Henry, at twenty-one, was steady as a rock finding work at the Strand Center for the Arts. His mind sparked with ideas; his heart rooted in purpose. Within months, the Center recognized his brilliance, his eye for beauty, his gift for connection.

None of them returned to who they had been before Montreal. That city, in the bright, blooming cusp of June, had rewritten them. They had tasted magic and weren't willing to let it go. They laughed louder. They said yes more.

Love had changed their coordinates. That weekend wasn't a chapter. It was a prologue. A beginning.

And from it, a new story bloomed.

– 9 –

Thanks to the bold vision and quiet determination of Aleena and Alexei, the semi-sleepy Russian village of Kozyrevsk awoke from its long slumber. What was once a quiet outpost nestled in the shadow of the volcanoes transformed almost overnight into a vibrant hive of purpose and pride.

Within just a few months, the cracked, dirt-worn roads that had for years mirrored the village's stagnation were paved smooth with fresh asphalt. The two main arteries of the town now shimmered black and new, breathing life into every corner they touched. Children roller-skated where potholes once ruled, and elderly neighbors strolled with newfound ease along freshly painted homes.

Aleena and Alexei had insisted that no one be left behind. Every household, whether a modest cabin or a crumbling concrete block on the village's edge, received a brand-new refrigerator and stove. The clatter of old pots and squeaky oven doors was replaced by the hum of efficient, modern machines. For the first time in years, kitchens filled with the scent of fresh bread, bubbling soups, and tea brewed with pride.

Then came the airstrip. The long-neglected landing strip, once buried beneath snow and silence, was cleared, and graded. A year later, when the first small plane touched down, bearing a group of eager volcano tourists, the entire village gathered to watch. Applause broke out as if welcoming a long-lost family. Kozyrevsk was no longer difficult to reach, it was alive, on the map, and humming with possibility.

But perhaps the most extraordinary change was the way work flowed through the town like warm spring meltwater. Aleena and Alexei ensured that improvements weren't imposed, they were shared. Labor was distributed fairly. Materials were sourced locally where possible. And for the first time in memory, people weren't just working, they were building something they believed in. Every nail driven, every coat of paint, every bolt tightened came with the sense that this future belonged to all of them.

With the arrival of snow and the shortening of days, the pace of work slowed, and Aleena and Alexei turned inward. They curled up by their woodstove, hot mugs in hand, planning their next steps. They had no desire to rush away from the home they'd helped reawaken. The winter was a time to dream.

That's when Ingrid and Owen, old friends and fellow wanderers, wrote to them from across the ocean with a spark of inspiration. "Come to Alaska," they said. "It's wild and beautiful, and just as raw and honest as the land you've just brought back to life."

The idea took hold.

By spring, as the volcanoes shed their icy cloaks and the village children chased melting snow down the streets, Aleena and Alexei packed their bags, not to escape, but to explore. They left Kozyrevsk in the hands of neighbors who had become stewards, guardians of a renewed place.

And as the couple boarded the same small plane that once brought strangers, now lifting them toward new adventures, they looked back at the village below, its smoke rising from chimneys, its roads gleaming in the sun, and its people waving them onward.

Kozyrevsk had been reborn. And so, too, were they.

– 10 –

Back in her hometown of Tivoli, with the ancient stones of Rome just beyond the horizon, Celeste made a quiet but resolute decision: she would not dig into the dark, tangled roots of her father's lineage. Instead, her gaze turned outward, toward a more ancient and expansive mystery: the stories etched into the very bones of the earth, a past carved into cliff faces, painted on cave walls, and etched across the continents by forgotten hands. Petroglyphs, pictographs, geoglyphs, these were the ghosts she longed to chase.

They stirred something in her, something older than memory. She knew then that this would be her life's work: to travel, to discover, to wonder. To become a seeker of meaning in the marks left behind by ancestors not just of blood, but of the human spirit.

Armed with notebooks, charcoal rubbings, and dreams as wild as the steppe winds of Patagonia, she would chart a new course. From the ochre pits and caves of Australia to the desert carvings of the American Southwest, she vowed to trace the story of humanity, not through bloodlines, but through stone. Her life would be spent listening to the earth's oldest stories, told in symbols and silence, in landscapes that were remembered long after people had forgotten.

Meanwhile, in the quiet Sicilian village of Castelbuono, Rodolpho stood at the edge of his former life. The hills that once seemed to protect him now felt like walls. He had never imagined leaving. But Celeste's courage had stirred something dormant in him, and as the autumn wind rustled the olive trees, he packed a small bag and took his first step into the unknown.

He followed Celeste to Rome, where their paths briefly intertwined before diverging again. She kissed him on the cheek at Termini Station, her smile bright with possibility. "Find what you're looking for," she whispered.

And he did. In the ancient city, he hired a discreet genealogist, whose quiet manner belied a relentless tenacity. Within weeks, Rodolpho stood on the deck of a ferry slicing through the azure waters between Naples and Capri, his hands trembling as he clutched the letter, her letter. His mother had responded. She had agreed to meet.

As the boat pulled into the island's harbor, framed by cliffs of white limestone and drenched in golden light, he saw her, an older woman with sea-gray hair and eyes rimmed with tears. She stood on the dock, her arms wide open, shaking slightly.

"Mio figlio," she whispered as he stepped off the boat.

He ran into her embrace.

They wept, not just for what had been lost, but for the time that remained. On the terrace of her little home overlooking the sapphire sea, they sat for hours, talking, crying, laughing, drinking coffee that turned into wine. She told him about the years she'd spent searching for him in dreams, and he told her about the hollow spaces that had always ached inside him.

In that moment, something shifted.

Not all wounds were healed, but the scar became a bridge, a passage, not a mark of pain. And under the Mediterranean sun, Rodolpho realized: sometimes, the past doesn't have to be buried. Sometimes, it can be rewritten with love.

After a lifetime chasing the dream he could barely name, Rodolpho finally found it, only to realize that wealth, true wealth, meant something far different than he had imagined. It was more than he could ever spend, more than he could ever want. And so, after a moment of quiet reflection, he decided to turn his fortune into a game, a whimsical experiment in generosity, just because he could.

He set aside enough to live comfortably with his mother on the sun-drenched Isle of Capri, where lemon trees perfumed the air and the sea sparkled like a secret. The rest? He began to give away, not to foundations or causes, but to strangers. Total strangers. But not just any strangers: only those who radiated kindness, joy, a rare and genuine warmth.

Each morning, he and his mother would walk hand in hand to the port, just as the ferries docked and the town filled with curious travelers. Over long lunches at sunlit cafés, they would strike up conversations, listening, laughing, savoring the simple beauty of connection. And then, once a day, they would choose someone. One unsuspecting soul, to whom they would gift forty-five thousand dollars to.

Their private game lasted more than three years. It brought delight not only to the lucky recipients, but to Rodolpho and his mother most of all. In giving freely, they discovered the kind of wealth that doesn't dwindle joy, wonder, and the exquisite art of surprising the world with kindness.

Meanwhile, across the ocean, in the deserts of Peru, Celeste stood before the Nazca Lines, the wind tossing her hair as she traced the great hummingbird with her eyes. She felt the earth pulse beneath her boots and smiled, knowing that somewhere across the sea, Rodolpho had found his own ancient truth, and like her, had chosen to walk forward, heart open, eyes wide.

The past, after all, is not always a weight. Sometimes, it could be a compass.

And their journeys were only just beginning. They were living a life, where dreams would never remain dreams.

- 11 -

Viktor and Katrín did not hesitate for even a heartbeat in pursuing the carefully hatched out plan they could now bring to fruition in their Icelandic homeland. No longer would they watch their neighbors slip into despair, their hopes fading like smoke. This was the moment. They would rise, not for themselves, but for the people around them, to lift them up, to remind them that even in the darkest hour, there is light, and it burns brighter when shared.

Once a bustling haven for fishermen and their families, the coastal village of Grindavík, tucked along the stormy southwest shores of Iceland, had been brought to its knees by the unforgiving hand of nature. For nearly a year, the village had endured the wrath of an unrelenting volcanic menace. Ash darkened the skies, molten rivers carved through the earth, and tremors unsettled the ground beneath their feet. What once was a close-knit community defined by hard work and ocean winds now lived in the shadow of destruction and uncertainty.

Fear lingered in the salt-laced air. With every rumble from deep below, hearts raced, and questions hung unanswered. Could they rebuild again? Would it be worth it? While many longed to escape, to find refuge far from the trembling earth, leaving wasn't simple. For generations, these families had drawn their livelihood from the sea, their identity rooted in Grindavík's soil. To walk away meant more than abandoning a home; it meant abandoning a legacy.

Viktor and Katrín watched helplessly as three of their closest friends lost most everything, homes eaten away and covered by the lava flows, memories turned to ash. Those friends, broken-hearted, made the painful decision to leave Grindavík behind for good.

Understanding that the town needed more than hope, it needed action, they devised a bold plan. They extended an extraordinary offer: financial assistance for any families who wished to rebuild or relocate.

One hundred families reached out.

With tears, gratitude, and renewed strength, these families either began to reconstruct what was lost or sought a safer future elsewhere.

And through it all, Viktor and Katrín stood at the heart of it, quietly, resolutely lifting their community in its darkest hour.

Their courage and generosity didn't go unnoticed. In the eyes of Grindavík's people, they were more than just helpers. They were beacons of resilience. Symbols of what it means to fight for home, even when the earth itself tries to take it away.

Viktor and Katrín hadn't just offered money. They had given Grindavík something far rarer in the face of disaster: a reason to believe.

Back in Reykjavik, Lilith basked in the triumph of her culinary creation, *Volcanic Glacial Cuisine,* though the real delight belonged to her ever-growing legion of patrons. Word had spread like wildfire, mouths watered, tables filled, and plates licked clean. Riding the molten wave of her success, she saw a chance not only to grow, but to give back. Several neighboring businesses, weathered by years of hard work and ready for rest, sold her their keys with bittersweet smiles. Lilith accepted with grace, transforming the adjoining spaces into a seamless extension of her restaurant.

Soon, the block pulsed with the energy of *The Modern Icelandic Alchemist,* a name that had become legend on social media. Tourists plotted pilgrimages around it; locals returned time after time, chasing the thrill of hot stone-seared lamb cooled with shards of arctic dill mist. Dining there wasn't just a meal, it was a performance of fire and frost, memory and myth.

But not everyone thrived in the shadow of the rising star.

Just down the street, Karl, her quiet, brooding rival, had opened *Eaten Mistakes* with high hopes and a menu full of obscure experiments. Yet his bold concept never found footing. Within months, his tables sat empty, his lights dimmed. When he closed his doors for good, it was as if he vanished into the fog of his own name. In the ever-buzzing streets of Reykjavik, Karl became little more than a ghost story whispered between bites of Lilith's enchanted fare.

– **12** –

Cosmo surprised Johanika in ways she never saw coming. Their connection had sparked like flint on stone, and though the fire was new, it burned with intensity. He longed to keep the adventure of their relationship alive but knew too well the danger of moving too fast, of overwhelming something precious. So, instead of flying back to New Zealand, Cosmo made a quiet, deliberate choice: he stayed.

He found an apartment tucked above the tidal edge of Kalk Bay, the very place where fate had brought them together. It was small, sun-soaked, and smelled faintly of salt and old wood, a perfect nest for reinvention. Cosmo had always nurtured a deep love for art, a passion left dormant in the shadow of obligation and practicality. Now, with Johanika gently in his orbit and his spirit stirred by the wild, untamed coastline, he gave himself permission to chase the dream.

Day and night, he poured his soul into his canvases, acrylics swirling with color and emotion, each wave a heartbeat, each cell created in the paint a secret. His style took shape: hypnotic abstracts of ocean waves, luminous and alive with movement. The sea outside his window mirrored the flow of his imagination, feeding the rhythm of his acrylic pours. Before long, the walls of his studio were alive with energy, and word began to spread.

Local shops displayed his work with pride. Commissions flooded in. His name, Cosmo, became whispered in art circles, spoken with curiosity, then admiration. But through it all, he remained grounded.

Johanika watched him grow, flourish, never pressured, never cornered. He gave her space, time, and unwavering support. And slowly, her fears melted away. Trust replaced hesitation. She became his fiercest advocate, his confidante, the calm center of his whirlwind.

By the end of the year, the future they once dared not speak of was suddenly real and within reach. They made plans over coffee and candlelight: Johanika would launch her own kayak adventure business, something uniquely hers. Cosmo would open a gallery and studio where he could teach others to feel what he had found in the waves. However, his biggest reward was providing many yearly scholarships, not only in South Africa but in New Zealand, where he and Johanika visited frequently.

Together, they were building something rare, not just love, but a life textured with courage, color, and the quiet certainty that they had chosen each other, and chosen well.

- **13** -

In India, Arav, code, named A1, had made his decision with the resolute swiftness of a man tethered by duty and blood. Despite the mounting pressure to leave Kodinhi, it was his twin brother's relentless mischief, always hovering on the edge of chaos, that rooted him there. More than that, it was the cave. The ancient, whispering cave hidden beneath the soil of his birthplace, calling to him like an echo from another age. He knew the authorities would soon descend with their bureaucracy and control, eager to claim what *they* had not unearthed. So, he stayed.

For two years, Arav worked in solitude, driven by obsession and reverence. He mapped every crevice, sketched every intricate carving, and cataloged every symbol like a devoted scribe preserving the language of forgotten gods. The cave had become his cathedral, and he its silent priest. When at last his work was complete, he stepped away, his spirit weary, his heart full. But it was no ordinary break.

One humid morning, seeking peace of mind, he wandered along a quiet trail in a sleepy village an hour's journey from Kodinhi. The forest loomed around him, thick, damp, and vividly green. That was when he saw it: a tree that did not belong. It stood like a sentinel, alien and ancient, amid the tropical evergreens. Intrigued, he hacked his way through the dense undergrowth. The vegetation resisted like a secret, but he pushed on, and what he found stunned him.

Beneath the tree's gnarled roots lay a stone, massive and weatherworn, its face covered in ancient reliefs that shimmered under the filtered sunlight like a forgotten language brought to life. Just beyond, the forest thickened, vines coiling upward over a large, rounded mound like nature's veil. Another hour of hacking, sweat pouring down his face, and Arav finally stood before it: a second cave, hidden by time and tangled foliage.

So much for rest.

Driven by the thrill of discovery and the weight of responsibility, Arav began again. For one month, he toiled alone securing the entrance, ensuring its secrecy. He knew what would come next. With his preliminary work done, he submitted his thesis to the Indian Institute of Science, detailing the astonishing complexity and historical significance of his first find. The reaction was swift. Authorities swarmed the site, sweeping in with scholars, scientists, and the heavy footfalls of bureaucracy.

But Arav was ready. He was rewarded handsomely, ceremoniously. A nod from the academic world, a quiet bow from the government. Then, with little fanfare, he left Kodinhi behind, bidding farewell to the village that had shaped his soul. He moved just an hour away, to the threshold of his next great secret. The second cave awaited. And Arav, patient, relentless, and now legendary, was ready to begin again.

– **14** –

Sofia and Edward had finally tasted the sweet relief of freedom from the heavy hand of bosses who never understood their passion. With renewed fire in their hearts, they moved quickly, wasting no time in laying the groundwork for their dream: their own trekking company in Cusco that would do more than just guide tourists. It would awaken people. They envisioned a space where every footstep held purpose, every ascent rekindled joy, and each journey breathed life into the soul.

Their vision was bold, their mission clear. With open arms and open hearts, they began forging a new trail, welcoming anyone who felt the same yearning for something greater. Word spread like wildfire through the Andes. The new company promised not only adventure and meaning but also fair wages, bonuses that honored the grit of the work, and a sense of community that had long been missing. It wasn't long before applications poured in, many from former colleagues at the Andean Trekking Company, eager for a fresh start under the inspired leadership of Sofia and Edward.

The mountain-climbing world buzzed with anticipation. Those who had followed Sofia's courageous recovery, her near-mythic return from the edge, now rallied behind her once more, eager to see her rise not just as a survivor, but as a leader.

And then came Pamela, a serendipitous blessing. What began as a chance acquaintance blossomed into a deep, fast friendship. Pamela's sharp mind, grounded presence, and heartfelt understanding of the business world made her invaluable. Sofia saw it instantly: this woman was no ordinary ally. Within months, Pamela stepped into the role of chief executive, commanding respect and steering operations with quiet strength.

With Pamela at the helm, Sofia and Edward found the rarest gift of all, time. Time to breathe, time to wander, and most importantly, time to simply be with their daughter, Marisol. They could now escape to Hawaii more often, their once, impossible fantasy finally real, the scent of plumeria and salt on the breeze reminding them daily of how far they'd come.

Back in the aging offices of the Andean Trekking Company, the air had turned stale. One morning, Peter walked into work and was met with an eerie silence. Desks stood abandoned. The phones rang endlessly, blinking with unanswered messages. Cancellations piled up. The machine he had built, once towering and unshakable, had crumbled.

Alone and livid, Peter stood in the ruins of his empire. Without a word, he turned on his heel and walked out. No goodbyes. Just the echo of his footsteps fading down a hallway that would never see him again. The city of Cusco had finally broken him. And from that day on, he vanished, gone from the trails, the offices, the stories. Forgotten by most. Missed by none.

- **15** -

In Kyrgyzstan, they watched in awe as a falcon sliced through the sky, wings stretched like whispers of history, guided by the centuries-old bond between hunter and bird. Stella's eyes sparkled, lost in the quiet strength of the moment. Max couldn't help but reach for her hand.

In Tajikistan, their breath caught at the sight of Iron Age petroglyphs etched into sun-bleached stone, humanity's need to leave a mark, to say they were here, written in every scratch. It mirrored his journey: the story of his voice that rose from the quiet corners of England to echo across continents.

Uzbekistan dazzled them with its colors, cobalt-tiled mosques, fragrant bazaars, silk-makers spinning gold threads between their fingers. Every alley seemed to hum with stories. Stella recorded fragments on her phone: a weaver's laughter, a child singing to a stray cat, the clang of coins as a vendor handed over spiced nuts.

But it was Turkmenistan that took their breath away.

There, in the vast emptiness of the Karakum Desert, they stood at the edge of the Darvaza gas crater. Flames leapt from the earth, licking at the night sky, painting their faces in flickering orange. It had burned for over thirty years, a symbol of something untamed and unending.

Max stared into the fire and felt something awaken. This wasn't just a trip. It was a calling. A story still unfolding.

And the world was watching and listening.

STAY TUNED FOR THE CONTINUATION OF

THIS STORY IN:

BLANK CHECKS
LOTTERY

www.ingramcontent.com/pod-product-compliance
Lightning Source LLC
Chambersburg PA
CBHW071147100726
47908CB00002B/283